D0455571

~ *Purcha___*
with interest income
from the
library's trust fund ~

Bloody Secrets

ALSO BY CAROLINA GARCIA-AGUILERA

BLOODY WATERS

BLOODY SHAME

Carolina Garcia-Aguilera

G. P. PUTNAM'S SONS

NEW YORK

Bloody Secrets

A LUPE SOLANO MYSTERY

G. P. PUTNAM'S SONS
Publishers Since 1838
a member of
Penguin Putnam Inc.
200 Madison Avenue
New York, NY 10016

Published simultaneously in Canada

Library of Congress Cataloging-in-Publication Data

Garcia-Aguilera, Carolina.
Bloody secrets : a Lupe Solano mystery /
Carolina Garcia-Aguilera.
p.   cm.
ISBN 0-399-14386-6 (acid-free paper)
1. Private investigators—Florida—Miami—Fiction.
2. Women detectives—Florida—Miami—Fiction.
3. Cuban Americans—Florida—Miami—Fiction.
4. Miami (Fla.)—Fiction.   I. Title.
PS3557.A71124B54   1998
813'.54—dc21   97-40842 CIP

Printed in the United States of America

1   2   3   4   5   6   7   8   9   10

This book is printed on acid-free paper. ♾

Book design by Gretchen Achilles

THIS BOOK IS DEDICATED TO MY THREE DAUGHTERS,

SARAH, ANTONIA, AND GABRIELLA,

THE LOVES AND PASSIONS OF MY LIFE,

AND TO CUBA.

MAY THE NIGHTMARE END SOON!

ACKNOWLEDGMENTS

Traditionally, in the acknowledgments page, the author thanks family, friends, agents, editors, and any other individuals who contributed in one way or another to the publication of the book. I will do that as well, later.

I would like to express publicly my profound gratitude to this country for allowing me the freedom to write my books and express my ideas freely without fear of persecution or threat of incarceration. In Cuba, the land of my birth, that is not possible. While it is not in my power to change that, I can, however, take limited action to alleviate my fellow writers' suffering there. Therefore, I intend to donate a percentage of the proceeds from this and any subsequent books I write to provide humanitarian assistance to dissident writers in Cuba who are persecuted for their ideas, and will continue to do so until Cuba is free. I feel it is the right thing to do.

I would like to thank my agent, Elizabeth Ziemska, of the Nicholas Ellison Inc. Agency, for all her hard work—she has accomplished so many mini-miracles in such a short amount of time. I am certain Christina Harcar, my foreign-rights agent, will not rest until Lupe is in every country in the world—for that she has my profuse thanks. I would like to thank my editor, Cindy Spiegel, for her superior skills in molding and forming the manuscript into a book and for being receptive to the complex world of Cuban society. As always, Quinton Skinner deserves special mention and thanks for his ability to decipher my words and render them readable.

My family, of course, deserves my heartfelt thanks: my husband, Robert K. Hamshaw, continually encourages me, always telling me I can do anything I set my mind to. My mother, Lourdes A. Garcia, should look into pursuing a career in publicity—she has done an outstanding job of shamelessly promoting the books wherever she goes—and I thank her for that. I wish to thank my sister, Sara O'Connell, and my brother, Carlos A. Garcia, for their support and for always being available when consulted; and my nephew, Richard O'Connell, for his obvious pride in me.

For Sarita, Antonia, and Gabby, words cannot properly express how blessed you make me feel. Thank you for asking "How's the book? How many pages today?" and then for answering your own questions with "You can do it, Mama. Keep plugging away." I will, *queridas,* I will.

Part One

One

At the exclusive Havana Country Club, the Sunday-evening tea dance was reaching its peak. Guests dined and danced on the enormous terrace under a brilliant moon so large and defined in the sky that the naked eye could discern its craters. The majestic royal palms behind the bar were lit from below, and the lamps also glittered on the polished brass buttons on the waiters' flawless jackets.

To the north end of the dance floor was an elevated platform. There the band played, led by a conductor who sweated profusely in the record heat. The sounds of gunfire were growing nearer, but the musicians were paid by the hour and they intended to work until the end of the party. The bandleader drove them on to play harder and louder, and they drowned out the shots with a deafening noise that only with imagination could be called music.

The guests were the reigning elite of Havana. They forced an air of ease and gaiety, pretending to hear only the mambo beat. In the dense swirl of human bodies glittered resplendent ladies in *haute couture* dresses accessorized by fortunes in jewelry, their hair perfectly coifed. They raised glasses with impeccably groomed men dressed in *guayaberas*—white cotton starched shirts, the Cuban equivalent of the serviceable navy-blue blazer.

Luis Delgado wiped his dripping neck with a linen handkerchief. "We can't go on this way," he said. "Just listen out there—Batista won't hold out much longer. They say Fidel is so close to Havana now that he can see the lights of the city at night."

A tall, thin man in his mid-thirties, Luis distinguished himself in this roomful of elegant men. Though his features were drawn from worry, he remained handsome and dignified. Seated to his right was his wife, Maria del Carmen. She avoided looking directly at her husband, opting instead to concentrate on the tablecloth.

Miguel de la Torre winked at Maria del Carmen with a reassuring half-smile. "Luisito, Luisito, *mi amigo*," he said. "Don't get all worked up. The country club has been searched for guns and bombs. We're perfectly safe here."

Miguel caught sight of a waiter and signaled for another Cuba Libre. His wife, Teresa, glared at him but kept quiet—with obvious difficulty.

Teresa was a striking woman who seemed to come almost from another age. Her thick, black hair fell nearly to her waist—in defiance of current fashion. She carried herself with an expectation of privilege, and she wasn't used to being ignored.

When it became obvious that Miguel intended to do just that, Teresa gathered up her evening bag, smoothed her red satin dress, and stalked off angrily to the ladies' room. She drew stares as she marched across the terrace. Miguel watched in blissful approval, but his libidinous reverie was shattered by a particularly loud explosion in the near distance. Even the music failed to drown it out.

"Miguel, listen to that," Luis said. "We may be safe here, but at the end of the night we have to go home. Fidel is going to win; Batista will be out. Then, *amigo*, you know what will happen? I'll tell you: pure hell for us!"

Miguel listened with an air of bemused tolerance. "Luisito, we have been friends our entire lives," he said calmly. "And business partners for eight years. What in the world could happen that we could not rise above together?"

Luis took a deep breath, his face pale and stark in the moonlight. "I want us to get our money out of Cuba," he said quickly, as though afraid of losing his nerve to speak. "I have thought about this constantly, Miguel. I'm convinced this might be our only opportunity."

"What do you mean?" Miguel said. His face flushed with astonishment and quick anger. "Surely you're not suggesting we sell everything?"

Slowly Luis nodded, pain evident in his eyes. Miguel looked to Maria del Carmen for support, but she sat quietly, merely observing the two men.

"I heard the Americans are going to back Fidel," Luis said. His voice quavered as though the rebels were in the club, their guns trained on the table. "There was an article in the *New York Times* that said as much."

"*Ay,* you always worry too much," Miguel said. "Suppose, just suppose you are right about this. We'll do with Fidel what we've done with others in the past—we'll pay him off. What do I care if we give payoffs to Fidel or Batista? In the end, it's the same."

A staccato volley of gunfire erupted from less than a mile away.

"This time it's different," Luis said. His eyes remained on Miguel's. "Fidel is different. All those priests in the hills with him are only for show. When he takes power, all the talk about democracy will be over."

Miguel glanced nervously across the floor, looking for Teresa. "Well, Havana has become a dangerous city," he allowed. "But soon things will be back to normal. Castro is a romantic figure, but he would not dare tamper with private property."

"We would be foolish to believe that," Luis said. "Listen to me, Miguel. Fidel has ties to Russia, and Che Guevara is a declared communist. Fidel's own brother studied behind the Iron Curtain. Do you think these people will hesitate to claim private wealth for the state?"

Miguel shrugged. He scanned the room with gleaming red eyes. It seemed he wanted to escape this conversation, as though it were becoming boring and irrelevant to him.

The band stopped playing. In that moment there was no gunfire, only a loaded silence punctuated by muted talk.

Luis leaned forward and lowered his voice to a whisper. "Why don't we consider selling part of our holdings—say, twenty-five percent? It's a conservative amount, when you think about it. Then we'll have some money to get out of here if things turn out for the worst."

Miguel feigned disinterest, his face half-turned away, but Luis could tell he was listening.

"Gonzales has been after us to sell him the property in Miramar," Luis said. "We'll accept his offer, then wire the money to someplace where it can gather interest. Like New York."

Luis knew Miguel heard him, but he also knew his argument wasn't a success. For Miguel, staying in Cuba would be a matter of manhood, of *cojones*. No true man would panic and sell. Luis looked again to Maria del Carmen, but she looked away, demurely wiping her forehead with a violet-scented handkerchief.

It was close to midnight, about time for the party to break up. The band was stowing their equipment in velvet-lined cases, and the conductor walked from player to player, distributing the pay for the evening. The terrace air was stifling, and for each person the silence was a void waiting to be filled by the far-off sound of shelling.

Miguel stood up when he spotted Teresa heading back to their table. He walked around to Luis and put his arm on his shoulder, pulling him close.

"You see, *viejo,* we'll be all right," he said. His face broke into a wide smile. "All this fretting, it will make you die young. Be like me, don't worry."

Luis started to interrupt, but Miguel put a finger across his lips. "If Fidel turns out to be as bad as you think," he said, "then the Americans will bail us out. They always have, and they always will."

Luis took his wife's hand as he watched Miguel and Teresa leave. "Well, that's that," Luis said. "At least he didn't say no. Not definitely, at least."

Maria del Carmen cooled herself with a silk fan. All around them was a crush of heat and bodies and the sound of low voices.

"Perhaps Teresa will have a talk with him," she said. "She has always been more practical than Miguel."

Luis nodded. "We will have to be more than practical in the times to come," he said. "We will also have to be very lucky."

They stayed together, waiting for the packed crowd near the exit to dwindle. The waiters passed all around them, clearing the tables. There was no sound of shots, as though the cacophony of music had brought the din of violence with it.

That night, Luis put Maria del Carmen to bed and poured himself a drink. He wandered the house in the dark, rubbing his neck with ice cubes, trying to envision a future that did not contain darkness.

Finally he reached his infant son's bedroom. Little Luisito slept soundly, unaware of the danger that had drawn so near. Luis watched him for more than an hour, praying for the child's future.

Two

HAVANA, AUGUST 11, 1994

In the oldest section of Havana, Luis Delgado lay under the oily chassis of a broken-down car. The garage was small and filthy, and the grime streaked even the lightbulbs suspended from the ceiling.

Just outside, Luis's friend Mario Echevarria appeared, poking his head over the cinder-block wall that ran along one side of the garage. "Hey, have you heard the news?" he called out.

Luis was so startled that he bumped his head on the car as he squirmed out from underneath. He wiped his hands on a dirty hand-kerchief, looked around, and stepped into the afternoon heat.

When Luis reached the wall, Mario reached over to grab at his friend's soiled work shirt. "Calm down, Mario," Luis said. "What news are you talking about?"

"Fidel is letting everyone go who wants to leave!" Mario said. His hands shook with excitement. "Hundreds of people are already getting together supplies to build rafts!"

Luis squinted in the sun. "This is happening openly?" he asked.

"*Sí!*" Mario said. "We have to meet tonight, to make a plan! This is our chance, I can taste it!"

Luis and Mario, along with three other men and two women, had formed over the past few months an unofficial dissident group to discuss the ever-deteriorating Cuban political situation. The group of seven came from disparate social backgrounds, but all shared the same yearning for freedom. They knew well that there was little they could do to improve their lives on the island, and therefore took comfort in their sessions of commiseration. Inevitably their talk would turn to the same fantasy: escaping to the United States.

"I didn't know," Luis said. He tried to keep his voice calm and level. "But if this is true, then you're right. We will meet tonight."

Luis glanced back into the gloomy garage, spotting his boss, a thuggish member of the Rapid Response Brigade, Castro's brutal enforcers of social order. The *chivato* didn't see Luis; he was busy with his usual pastime—cleaning his fingernails with a pocket knife. More than once, Luis had thought about grabbing the knife and plunging it into the man's heart.

The remainder of Luis's day crawled along in a haze of manual labor and suppressed excitement. Luis was so distracted he twice scorched himself on the soldering iron. Mario was prone to grandiose ideas, but Luis trusted that what he said was correct. Into the afternoon, Luis toyed with the idea of leaving within the next few days, the very notion like a secret treasure burning within him.

At nine o'clock that night, the group met in Mario's kitchen, the door closed to keep his mother from hearing. They sat together at a wooden table, all wearing expressions of mixed hope and fear. Now that escape was a real possibility, another reality presented itself: crossing the dangerous ninety miles of the Florida Straits.

Marta, a social science professor at the University of Havana, wore her long hair tied back in a simple braid. "We need to plan quickly," she began. "For all we know, Fidel might change his mind."

To her right was Ernesto, a bespectacled man in his early thirties. He was a civil engineer, working in commercial construction. He sat quietly, aware that he was the only person at the table qualified to design a raft.

"I'll steal as much food as I can," said Tomas Mesa. He worked as a pastry chef in a hotel that catered to foreign tourists, so he had access to food supplies denied to ordinary Cubans. Tomas kept his friends fed through hard times—and there had been many lately.

Amparo, a small-boned, serious young woman, was a nurse at Mazorro, Havana's psychiatric hospital. "I'll go through the supplies at work and see what I can take," she said. "The inventory is low right now, but I'll do what I can."

Though it was Mario's house, Luis Delgado sat at the head of the table. He had changed into clean slacks and a light-blue dress shirt, and his wavy hair was swept from his high forehead. He cleared his throat, and everyone turned to him.

"I'm in charge of tools," he said. "I'll coordinate with Ernesto. We need to be prepared if anything goes wrong at sea."

Pedro Aguilar, a tall man with a perpetually disheveled appearance, glumly rested his chin in his hands. A doctor, he was the head of a suburban medical clinic.

"I can't help much; we have no supplies whatsoever at the clinic," Pedro said. "We've been operating with supplies the patients' families send from Miami. Yesterday I did an appendectomy with almost no anesthesia."

Mario worked as an interpreter at the Hungarian embassy. He and Marta looked at each other sheepishly. "I'm sorry," Mario said. "I guess we have nothing to contribute."

"There will be plenty for everyone to do," Luis said. He smiled at Mario. "Right now, the important thing for all of us is to gather dollars. What we can't steal for the trip we'll have to buy. How much can we put together?"

Luis jotted down the numbers that each person recited to him, sums representing years of privation and saving. After everyone had spoke, the total hovered around three hundred dollars.

"I hear that oars are going for five dollars apiece," Mario offered.

A collective groan went around the table. Five dollars was almost an average worker's monthly wages. Their money would be stretched to its limits, possibly beyond.

"I'll stay up tonight," Ernesto said, fiddling with his glasses. "I'll design the sturdiest raft I can, with the least amount of materials. I'll go by a couple of construction sites on the way home."

"We can't waste time," Amparo said. "Everyone is going to be doing the same as us."

"We'll meet tomorrow night," Luis said. It had been long established, with no need for a vote, that Luis was their leader. "Bring all your money, and Ernesto will bring his plans. And I know it's very difficult, but you can't say a word about this to anyone—that includes your families, your friends, your colleagues."

"Luis is correct in advising us to be cautious," Amparo said. "I've already heard what happens to people who talk. One of the nurses I work with told people she was planning to leave, and people knew that meant she had money and supplies. A gang broke into her house and took everything."

"Disgusting," Ernesto spat. "Cubans stealing from Cubans. We're all in this hell together!"

"Luis is right," Mario said. "We can talk to no one." Everyone agreed, knowing how painful it would be to sever ties with their loved ones and friends.

They met the following evening to review their plans and further delegate responsibilities. It was decided that they would get together at noon the next day, build the raft together, and set off at dusk. By leaving at night they would avoid the scorching sun, at least until they had put many miles between themselves and Cuba.

Luis arrived early the next day and waited for the others. He was exhausted, having spent the night enduring terrifying dreams about the turbulent seas that lay ahead—twice he had awakened, dripping with sweat, feeling as though he were drowning. Luis hadn't told the others, but he could not swim. There in the cool morning air he questioned whether he should tell them—after all, he might need one of his comrades to pull him from the water. He decided against it; he was a leader, and they had to trust him without doubt.

Their designated spot was a beach called *el rincón de Guanabo,* a stretch of sand in eastern Havana frequented by foreign tourists. Luis was not alone. Dozens of small groups were building ragtag rafts there, and a growing sense of anxiety permeated the beach. Luis sat down under a royal palm and closed his eyes in the shade.

It was easier for him to leave than the others, in a sense, because he was alone. Luis had never known his father, who also had been named Luis. The elder Delgado had died in prison, a declared enemy of the revolution. Maria del Carmen had been left to raise Luisito, and she had sacrificed everything for him. Once a society lady, she had spent the later years of her life washing and cleaning like a commoner, all her energy spent to keep herself and Luisito alive.

Though he didn't dare, Luis wished now that he could open his shoe and look at the two diamonds hidden there. Once there had been four—his father having possessed the foresight to keep them for his family in case the Delgados' escape from Cuba failed. Luis's mother had told Luisito how his father had agonized in prison, in spite of his suffering, because he had kept the four diamonds without the de la Torres' knowledge. But his father had been right to do so—the four stones had allowed his family to survive.

Maria del Carmen had parted with one as a bribe to keep her son out of Castro's army, and Luis had quietly sold another for cash to help with the rafting expedition. Luis smiled in the shade as he thought of the stories his mother had told him about the jewels—she had made it seem like an adventure, the selling of their own and the de la Torres' real-estate holdings at fire-sale prices to acquire as much cash as possible to carry out their plans. Maria del Carmen vividly relayed to him how she had purchased the diamonds from foreign mistresses of Batista's henchmen so that their family holdings could be smuggled out of the country. He felt hot tears well up in his eyes when he thought about all that had happened to his family in thirty-five years under Castro.

The remaining diamonds were all that was left of the proud Delgados—for now. Luis had been prepared to sell off another diamond if it were absolutely necessary, but he had decided not to if the money for the escape could be raised without it. His one stone had contributed far more than his share for the expedition, and he didn't want to arouse suspicion by generating so much money on such short notice. Knowing they were hidden in his shoe gave him a measure of security. He wouldn't arrive in the United States with nothing.

If the sharks didn't eat him, Luis would claim his birthright from his father's friend and partner. He would demand that Miguel and Teresa de la Torre honor the agreement they had made with his father, the deal that led to his father's death: that one-half of the wealth produced from those diamonds which had been smuggled out of Cuba belonged to the Delgados. Although Luis and his parents had never been able to leave Cuba, they had listened to Miami radio from time to time. They had heard that Miguel and Teresa were successful and prominent. The idea filled Luis with optimism—he was nearer than ever to this dream, but there was still such a distance to travel.

"Hey, sleepyhead," a voice called out to him. "Do you want to doze all day and end up staying here?"

Luis opened his eyes and looked up at Mario, who stood silhouetted in the sun. Luis got to his feet and dusted the sand from his slacks. The entire group was gathered by the water, waiting for him.

Ernesto had designed a raft resembling a catamaran, with fifty-five-gallon tanks welded together, tied by ropes, and covered with planks of wood. The group worked quickly, not speaking except to ask for a tool or give advice on constructing the craft. All around them, others were doing the same. At one point Luis looked up in amazement; a few Canadian tourists, taking time off from sunbathing, were wandering among the rafters, taking pictures with their expensive video cameras.

By six o'clock the raft was finished. The group felt strange to be ready suddenly, to see their years of longing end there on the shore. Luis directed everyone to stand together in a circle, their hands joined, so they could pray. They all had heard what could happen to rafters in the Straits, and they had seen the corpses floating back into the harbor, bloated, decomposed, chewed by sharks, broken against the rocks and coral.

The seas were calm the first night. When the sun rose on the eastern horizon, Luis and his group were startled to see they were surrounded by hundreds of other small craft. Ebullient laughter filled the air. Everyone took turns rowing, and at one point they tied up with another raft, exchanging cigarettes and rum, giddy with their first taste of freedom.

Inevitably, some of the rafts weren't seaworthy and began to sink.

Panicked screams erupted across the blue waters. No one was left to die, and the occupants of these doomed rafts were pulled aboard others. The new exiles felt that nothing could stop them; surely at any minute they would be rescued by the United States.

By noon the sea became choppy, and the euphoria began to fade. The waves grew greater, with deepening swells separating the rafts. Luis's group lost sight of the others, and soon they stopped looking. A storm had come over them.

For the next twelve hours, into the night, the elements battered the makeshift boat. Luis handed out a rope, ordering everyone tied together so no one would fall overboard. Their compass fell into the sea, followed by the food that Tomas had stolen from the hotel. The ocean turned from blue to violet; the clouds rushed the night with blackness above.

The group spent the second day resting, recuperating from the punishing night. They attempted to repair the raft as well as they could, in anticipation of another storm. They did not see any other rafts, although they searched vigilantly, constantly. Mostly, however, they tried to ignore the burning sun, hunger, and thirst, which were draining them of their rapidly dwindling energies.

Luis stayed calm and confident, trying to keep his friends from losing all hope. At dawn on the third day, they saw their first corpse. They thought it had been a woman, but it was too bloated for them to tell for sure.

Then came the human parts, the arms and legs, then the shark fins moving through the waves. Luis silenced anyone who spoke of hunger, thirst, or fear.

The raft began to break apart. Rowing became impossible in the hard currents, and soon whenever an oar was lowered into the water, a shark would take notice and bump the craft. It seemed the merciless predators were teasing and taunting, ripping the corpses in the water as though announcing their primacy. Luis, his stomach empty and his throat dry, felt that he could accept death then—but not in the sharks' mouths or by drowning. He yelled at his companions stubbornly, keeping their spirits from falling into complete despair.

It felt as though these horrible seas were all they had ever known, or would know. Luis looked around at his group as the sun rose and set again, seeing their faces turn into expressionless masks of fear and hunger. Words were rarely spoken; individual personalities faded into catatonic nothingness. His own skin smarted from exposure as he watched the waves and fins, rapt. Only his diligence at keeping the wooden planks of the raft together gave him purpose.

On the morning of the fifth day they heard a small plane's engines flying overhead. They looked up, stunned. The pilot tipped his wings to them in acknowledgment, and they saw the Brothers to the Rescue logo emblazoned on the plane. This group was legendary, and when the pilot flew so close that they could see his face in the cockpit, they raised their hands to him. He dropped parcels to the raft—bags of processed food and liter bottles of water. Luis meted them out, waiting to serve himself last.

In the early afternoon the seas calmed, as though the pilot had somehow broken the angry storms. They could see around themselves now, and spotted other rafts in the same dire condition as their own. At four o'clock a Coast Guard vessel arrived, coursing through the water, and picked them up.

The cook on the boat must have been mistaken in his belief that Cubans liked their meals highly seasoned: The food was so spicy they could barely eat it, even in their semistarved state. Everyone in Luis's group, though sunburned and exhausted, was deemed healthy. They all were given blankets and ordered to stay on deck with the three hundred other *balseros* plucked from the water. Luis sat with his friends, unable to speak, watching the horizon and trying to stay out of the sun.

Later on they were transferred to a larger vessel called the *Carolina*. There rumors abounded that they might not be taken directly to the United States. For four days they stayed on the ship, circling and picking up more rafters. Now and then, Luis lost track of his group, but he always found them again, scattered among the hollow-eyed refugees. Soon there were more than thirty-five hundred miserable survivors exposed to the elements on the *Carolina*. Once a day the American sailors washed them down with a high-pressure hose, the only concession to hygiene in the August heat.

Luis tried to get information from the American interpreters, but they were uncooperative. One morning, after Luis had reassembled his group near the life rafts on the port deck, the rest of the refugees were awakened by a loudspeaker announcement.

The voice was dispassionate and female: "You have arrived at Guantanamo Naval Base," it said, "where you shall stay for an indefinite period of time. Because you will never step onto American soil."

Luis became more diligent about keeping his group together, knowing that their numbers might help them wherever they were going. They were led from the ship to their new home: canvas tents in an arid wasteland.

The tent that Luis's group shared with twenty-three other *balseros* was in the "Echo" camp. It had no electrical power and no running water, only an endless view of cacti. At times it seemed the iguanas and banana rats had more life than the dispirited refugees.

In spite of their best efforts to stay together until they reached the United States after all they had endured in Cuba and on the high seas, Luis's group gradually split up and lost contact with one another. It saddened Luis, but he recognized that the need for daily survival was eroding personal relationships all around him. He had been alone in Cuba after his mother had died, and he was alone again. With luck, he thought, he might one day find his friends again. But in his heart he doubted it.

More than thirty thousand rafters—men, women, and children—stayed in the eight Guantanamo camps for more than a year, pawns of the Cuban and American governments. It would be almost sixteen months before Luis Delgado, Jr., boarded the airplane that took him to his new life in Miami—and to the fortune that awaited him.

If anything, the time he spent in the camp—a year gone from his life—honed his hunger for retribution. Like a ghost from the past, he would emerge to claim what was his by birth.

And the hell with anyone who stood in his way.

Three

MIAMI, MARCH 1996

Luis Delgado sat hunched over, his arms crossed and his legs stretched out on a wooden bench along the walkway on the north embankment of the Miami River. He stared straight ahead, his eyes unfocused, listening to a freighter making its way out to sea in the predawn darkness. He was so engrossed in his thoughts that he didn't flinch when the boat emitted an ear-splitting foghorn to signal a bridge operator to open a gate for its passage.

It had been this way all week. The placed seemed surreal; the only light there came from the few cars that passed over the nearby bridge. In the dim illumination, Luis could faintly discern the men seated on the other benches. Some were overdressed for the warm weather; one even wore an overcoat. A few of them had shopping carts filled with their worldly possessions. Two mongrel dogs, surprisingly well-fed, poked their noses from a bundle of rags near a sleeping man.

After the third or fourth night, Luis found that some of his companions had begun to recognize him. A few had offered swigs of whatever they were drinking, an offer that was easy to decline.

Luis had been living out of a flophouse near the river for seven days and nights. He had made up his mind that this would be the last.

The homeless men by the river might look gentle and timid, but Luis knew that none of them would hesitate to slit his throat if they knew what he was carrying. Luis glanced around and swatted his neck. It felt as though the mosquitoes were eating him alive.

Then Luis noticed an unfamiliar man leaning against an electricity pole nearby. After a week of nights spent on the river, Luis knew the sort of men who slept there. This one was different: He stood straight and looked from person to person with definite purpose. Thirty-five years in Castro's Cuba had granted Luis a powerful instinct for sensing trouble.

Luis stood up and stretched, eyeing the man to see his reaction. As if on cue, the man stiffened. Luis braced for violence, then deliberately walked past the man. Luis couldn't smell alcohol on him, even though he was drinking from a paper bag. Luis was alarmed. This man had to be a professional.

Luis walked several yards before the man turned to follow him, then Luis saw the spot where he would make his stand—at the next turn, behind a pillar. There wasn't as much privacy there as Luis would have liked, but he doubted that any of the vagrants would cooperate with a police investigation in case he had to kill the man.

When the man turned the corner to follow, Luis was upon him with a knife at his throat. The man struggled and dropped his own blade.

"Who are you?" Luis asked.

Silence. Luis pressed the blade against the man's throat and repeated the question. Luis slid the knife against the man's skin. A light trickle of blood emerged from around the blade.

"My name is Pepe," the man said in a breathy voice. "Pepe Salazar."

Luis looked closer at him. Salazar was the sort of man little children would run away from. His eyes were darting and beady, his nose bulbous, his mouth like a lizard's. Luis noticed cigars bulging from Salazar's shirt pocket.

"Who sent you?" Luis asked, pressing the knife again into Salazar's throat. More blood flowed, and the knife felt slippery in Luis's hand.

"De la Torre," Pepe gurgled.

Luis wasn't surprised.

"What are your orders?" he asked. "What are you supposed to do?"

"Kill you," Salazar whimpered, staring at the hand that held the knife. "My orders are to kill you."

"How are you supposed to prove it to them? What evidence have they asked you to provide?"

"I'm supposed to bring back two diamonds," Pepe said. "I was told to check up your ass."

Pepe shuddered with fear; Luis paused to think, keeping his foot planted on the killer's knife.

"*Mira, comemierda,* this is what you are going to do," Luis said. "You call them and tell them you did what they asked. You will meet them and give them a diamond—tell them it's all you could find on me. They'll think you stole the other one, but that's your problem."

Pepe nodded, sweat mingling with the blood on his neck.

"Tell them you threw me in the water when a freighter went by, and that my body was torn apart by propellers. It was a clean job, everything went well. *Comprendes?* And start making plans to leave Miami permanently." Luis applied more pressure to the knife at Pepe's throat. The blood flowed more thickly.

"Now, turn around. Slowly. Look away from me and close your eyes," Luis ordered Pepe, roughly moving him into the position he wanted him in. Once the man's back was completely to him, Luis added, "You move, and I'll slit your throat."

In one quick motion, Luis bent down and felt around his shoe. As soon as he had located what he was looking for, he straightened up and took his former position with his knife at Pepe's throat. The maneuver had not taken more than ten seconds. Pepe had not moved a muscle.

Luis thrust a stone into Pepe's hand. "Take this and remember what I told you," he commanded. "You come back tomorrow night and tell me what happened. If you screw up, I'm going to find you and kill you. The same is true if I ever hear you're back in Miami."

Luis released the blade from Pepe's throat. The would-be assassin clutched his neck and staggered away. He shoved the stone into his pocket without even looking at it. Luis picked up the man's knife and threw it as far into the river as he could.

Luis walked slowly back to his rented room. He would have to move, because he knew that trusting Salazar would be foolish. He had to hope Salazar was scared, and willing to settle for the money Miguel and Teresa were paying him rather than run off with the diamond. Luis also had to rely on the de la Torres' believing he was dead. His life depended on this deception—otherwise there would be others of Salazar's kind hiding in every shadow.

Now only one stone remained—the best one, which he had saved for last.

The next night Pepe kept his appointment with Luis. He said that Teresa de la Torre had believed that Luis was dead, had accepted the single stone, and had given Pepe $25,000—which Salazar showed Luis as proof.

"You did well," Luis said. "Now remember what's waiting for you if you ever come back to this city."

Luis opened his jacket and casually showed Salazar his knife. Pepe backed off, muttering under his breath.

Luis was alone, without friends, in a strange country. His mind searched for the meaning of all that had happened to him. On impulse, he knelt down on the damp grass and took the last diamond from its hiding place in the heel of his shoe.

He gripped the stone and swore to his parents that he would avenge their memory. No matter what happened or how long it took.

Part Two

One

I was driving fast down Miami Highway, on my way to Solano Investigations. I took my first sip of steaming *café con leche* from my ceramic mug, turning it around so the Cuban flag faced toward me—I'm a stickler for those kinds of details. I was taking in the scenery speeding past, listening to the radio, daydreaming, when the ringing car phone brought me back to reality.

It was an annoying interruption. I reached for the receiver, blessing those sainted German engineers who designed their cars for people who wanted to do several things at once, in addition to driving—though I had sworn off applying mascara while steering with my knees. I grabbed the phone without spilling a drop of coffee.

"Lupe?" It was my cousin Leonardo.

"*Buenos días,* Leonardo," I said. "What's up?"

"Your nine o'clock is here." I glanced at the clock on my Mercedes dashboard. 8:45. How annoying. I was actually going to be on time for once, and I would feel like I was late.

"He's been here since eight-thirty," Leonardo added, sounding irritated. I knew the client must have interrupted my cousin's sacrosanct morning meditation. For some unknown reason his sessions absolutely had to take place at the same time every day. Lately Leonardo had been shopping for religions until he found one that suited him, but I couldn't see why he didn't opt for a twenty-four-hour god. It seemed that his current Main Spirit kept union hours.

"I'm passing the Playhouse right now. I'll be there in five minutes." The *café con leche* had cooled enough that I could gulp it. "Talk to me about the client. I don't really remember what you told me yesterday."

Leonardo sighed. He was really in a bad mood. "If you hadn't been in such a rush to leave last night, you *would* remember," he said.

"It'll never happen again," I promised. I punched the accelerator.

"You know, Lupe, you've been really distracted lately," he added. "You have to start paying attention to what I tell you."

Leonardo was my assistant, but he was also blood—the son of my mother's sister—so he could get away with talking to me that way. Though he was five years younger than I—twenty-three years to my twenty-eight—Leonardo could sound like an old lady when he had a gripe.

"Spare me the lecture," I said. I was minutes from the office. "Just give me the facts. The edited version."

"Well, I don't have much background on this one," Leonardo said. "He isn't a referral."

I knew Leonardo hated walk-in clients. As office manager, he felt personally affronted by the risk they could present. Most of the time these cases were genuine and there were no problems, but there's always a chance of getting burned. Whenever possible, we wanted cases referred by someone we knew.

"Don't worry about it, I'm pulling into the driveway right now." *Mierda.* I would have to talk to the client cold.

In the parking lot was a silver vintage Mercedes convertible, with the top down—a rarity in crime-ridden Miami. It was parked in the single guest slot next to the cottage. I pulled my own Mercedes, a navy-blue two-door SL, next to it. While I set my alarm I felt a trace of envy. The car was in impeccable condition; the paint sparkled in the morning sun.

After my alarm gave its usual reassuring beep, I paused before I began another day at the office. The typical terminally athletic Coconut Grove traffic of Rollerbladers, bikers, and joggers streamed by on the street. I could see them, but they couldn't see me unless they stopped and looked hard. Solano Investigations occupied a three-bedroom white cottage with deep-green window frames in the very center of the Grove, albeit hidden by thick foliage.

Leonardo and I had converted the place into our office seven years before, when we started the business. Five years ago, after ponying up monthly payments to a management company for two years, we took the leap and bought it. For one thing, we were tired of having to go through an approval process every time we wanted to change an aspect of the cottage's interior, and we looked forward to molding the place in our own image.

It was a sound business decision, but I also opened up a Pandora's box of new troubles. Leonardo quickly granted himself self-approved *carte blanche* to convert the spare spaces into a gym and, recently, a meditation area. He was loyal to me, and diligent in his work, so I didn't have the heart to say no to him. The end result was the sort of office in which new clients would look perplexed the first time they entered—they would inevitably see the workout machine and the floor-to-ceiling mirrors, hear the New Age music, and think they had entered anyplace in the world other than a private investigator's office.

Leonardo's appearance would never serve to dispel this confusion. An average day would find him at his desk dressed in his signature black spandex biker shorts with matching undershirt, sipping strange juice concoctions from a gallon-sized bottle. He also used silver barbells as paperweights. In the end I could live with it all—as long as we stayed successful and profitable.

I walked up to the cottage and opened the outer door. After half a second I knew the real reason Leonardo had sounded so pissy on the phone. Never mind the interrupted meditation or the walk-in client—the place reeked of cigarette smoke. In Leonardo's universe, smoking is an offense worthy of a war-crimes tribunal.

I groaned, my hand on the door. I knew that as soon as our new client left, Leonardo would go on the offensive with his cans of aerosol air freshener, spraying the hell out of the place. I was going to be breathing pine forest for the next few days. I inwardly resigned myself to Alpine Week.

There was a man waiting for me, standing in the middle of the reception area. He seemed familiar somehow, but I couldn't place him. He was tall, well over six feet, and thin to the point of gauntness. He was in his mid-thirties, maybe closer to forty, with a youngish face but graying hair. He wore a badly cut dark-brown suit with a chocolate-and-white-striped shirt, khaki tie, and thick scuffed worker's brown shoes. None of the brown hues came close to matching.

His modest clothes brought into relief an aristocratic demeanor. He turned when I came in and approached me with stiff formality, a cigarette in one hand and the other offered to me. I shifted the Cuba mug to my left hand and we shook. He had callused hands and a firm grip. I saw his intelligent dark eyes take in the flag on the cup—now facing him—and watched him blink.

"Miss Solano," he said in a low measured voice with a slight Spanish accent, "my name is Luis Delgado."

"*Buenos días,*" I said. I still couldn't remember where I had seen him, and it bothered me. "It's a pleasure. Let's go into my office."

Leonardo scowled silently at his desk as I escorted Luis to my open door. I winked at my cousin, trying to cheer him up. He huffed and pretended to be absorbed in a pile of invoices. I knew the tree-scent bombs were at his fingertips, seconds from detonation.

I pointed Luis to a chair and closed the door behind us. He sat down and gave me the once-over. I was glad I was wearing a skirt and blouse that morning, instead of a T-shirt and jeans. It always helps to have the psychological advantage of looking good.

Luis's gaze lingered on me, perhaps a little too long. I didn't mind; I'm used to the reaction. Most clients have a preconceived notion of what a P.I. should look like—like a currently practicing or semireformed alcoholic working to keep up alimony or palimony payments—a picture that I didn't fit. Men tended to want to look at me, besides, and I considered it a card I was dealt to play. Anyway, it gave me the chance to stare at him for a moment. Still I couldn't place him.

"Mr. Delgado, would you like some coffee?"

He shook his head dismissively. Apparently he was all business, without time for niceties. He folded his lean body deeper into the chair.

"I think I've seen you before," I added.

"You're very observant," he answered approvingly. "Most of the customers who come into the Mercedes dealership service area don't take notice of the employees."

I may be observant, but I still couldn't say I remembered him. But it explained how a man dressed as he was could afford to drive the Mercedes I saw outside. It may not have been a pretty question, but now I wanted to know: Could he afford Solano Investigations? We weren't a cut-rate operation.

Luis lit a cigarette. "I've only been in Miami for two years," he said. "I came in from Guantanamo. A *balsero.*"

I handed him a seldom-used ashtray from my desk and did some quick calculations. If he came to America then, from the camps at Guantanamo, he must have been part of the mass exodus from Cuba in August of 1994. Those Cubans had been stranded in the camps for more than a year while the Americans played politics.

Luis took a long drag from his cigarette, and I tried not to get paranoid about secondhand smoke. He seemed to want to take his time, staring out at the parrots sunning themselves in the avocado tree outside the window. It was fine with me. I charged by the hour.

Finally he looked away from the window. "I have a very serious situation," he said. "And it is very delicate."

This wasn't exactly news. No one sat in that chair as a client without a problem they considered serious. "Why don't you start by telling me about yourself?" I said. This always helped the client relax. "How did you find out about Solano Investigations?"

"I heard the men at the dealership talking about you one time when you brought your car in," Luis said with a faint smile. "They were joking around, you know, and they said that any man who would get involved with you had better be brave, because you were a private investigator and you carry a gun."

The man actually blushed as he spoke. I tried not to smile too much, because I knew he had probably edited out a lot of other things the mechanics had said about me.

Luis took a deep breath; he seemed to be trying to stay calm. It was a miracle he could breathe at all, considering how fast he puffed down a cigarette. "I think you came in for your air conditioner that time," he said. "Then I saw you all the time—when you were having those problems with your car's compressor. I admired the way you comport yourself—with dignity. I looked at the computer and found your office address and phone number. I've been thinking about you for over a year now, trying to decide if you are the kind of person I can come to with this information.

I replayed what he had just said. I didn't like this role reversal, with me being the subject of an amateur investigation. It was time to escort him out, I knew that. But curiosity was stronger than reason. Still, I followed one of the prime investigator's commandments: Show no reaction when you're told something weird or unexpected.

Behind my poker face I made a deal with myself. Hear him out, then tell him I can't take the case. And I wouldn't bill him for the time. This was, I knew, world-class rationalization, but I also knew it wasn't the first time curiosity had overpowered my common sense. Besides, Miami Mercedes was the only service provider for my car in Dade County—and I knew it wouldn't be prudent to alienate a mechanic who worked there. It would be a real pain to have to drive to Broward County every time my brakes started to squeak.

I took out a legal pad and wrote his name at the top of the page. I had him answer routine questions—full name, date of birth, address, social security number, education, and social background. He rattled off the information in Spanish so quickly I had trouble keeping up; my note-taking skills in my homeland's language were a bit rusty. I hoped I would be able to transcribe the mess into my report later—*if* I took the case. Finally I led him up to his real story, the reason he had come to see me—and why he had been thinking of me for so long before making the decision to come in.

Luis lit another cigarette, his eyes cold. "A terrible wrong was done to my parents by a man who is very well-known in Miami," he said. "This man and his wife took money that belonged to us. I want to hire you to reclaim this money."

He was smart, no doubt about it. He was portioning out the story in small dollops, telling me only enough to get me interested.

"It sounds like you should go to the State Attorney's office," I said. "Only they have the authority to press criminal charges. I'm an investigator. All I do is investigate."

"You don't understand." Luis remained dignified, but I could tell he was frustrated with me. I was again tempted to simply put an end to the conversation. "I have no proof of what happened," he said. "It started in Cuba thirty-eight years ago, and now these people are very prominent here in Miami. It would be my word against theirs, a *balsero* against a rich man. The government would never help me."

"What about going to an attorney and filing a civil suit?"

Luis, to my astonishment, lit another cigarette from the butt of the last. I was starting to wish for a gas mask and a turbo fan.

"I would still have the same problem," he said. "It would be my word against theirs."

I had to admit that there was something compelling about Luis. He reminded me of the circle of formerly well-off Cuban exiles my parents had known since we first came to Miami. They wore cheap clothes, their hands were rough, but they carried themselves with the bearing and dignity of their old lives. In spite of the social and financial gulfs that often separated them, my parents always welcomed old family friends from Cuba into our home. I always suspected that

Mami and Papi had helped them out in their time of need, but I had never seen it happen. Everyone acted as though our visitors were only temporarily down on their luck and that it would be just a matter of time before they were back on their feet.

It was at once heartening and a little sad. I coughed and looked away; I needed to keep my personal feelings out of this. Somewhat hesitantly, I asked him to go on.

"My father and mother were very close friends with another couple in Havana," he said. "The men were business partners, primarily in real estate. After the revolution they liquidated many of their assets and converted them into . . . transportable currency."

"What kind of transportable currency?"

Luis bent over and took off one of his shoes. With a grunt he unscrewed the heel and extracted a small, dingy gray sack from the hollow space inside. Carefully, almost ceremonially, he unwrapped the cloth and held it toward me.

On that soiled cloth lay a diamond. I was no jewel expert, but this one was a beauty, bigger than I had ever seen in person. I thanked the Virgin for all my past shopping trips with Papi, to Tiffany and Cartier in search of gifts for Mami. I had ended up with more than a passing acquaintance with precious stones.

Luis wrapped the diamond in the cloth and held it tightly in his hand. He knew he had my attention.

"My father and his friend were able to put together four million dollars in diamonds," Luis said. "It was only part of their wealth, but they were desperate. Bear in mind that we are talking about late-1950s dollars."

Luis had now completely dropped the immigrant-bumpkin act. I could see that he was shrewd, aware, and most of all ambitious. I was on the alert for danger signs, anything that would tell me he was a liar or a creep, but I saw nothing. I continued to take notes; Luis inexplicably switched from Spanish to English.

"My father's friend was able to leave Cuba with his wife. We couldn't all leave at the same time—it was too dangerous," Luis continued in almost accentless English. "The plan was for my parents and me to join them soon after. But my father was arrested and thrown in jail before we could escape."

"Why was he arrested?" I asked.

"As a counter-revolutionary," Luis said in a quiet voice. "Because he was wealthy."

"What happened to the diamonds?" I asked.

"My father's friend took them, except for four stones my father kept. I think he had a premonition that something was going to go wrong. They planned to go into business together here in Miami. Of course, that never happened."

"And what happened to your father?"

"He died after ten years in prison." Luis looked directly into my eyes. "He was in *Combinado del Este*. I know they tortured him, but I only found this out later."

"Why was that information kept from you?" I asked. I remained neutral in my tone, but inside I felt a chill of fear. Luis's story made me think of my own family. Papi, Mami, and my oldest sister, Fatima, had left while it was still possible—with nothing but the clothes they were wearing. If Papi hadn't left with the family when he did, the same fate might have befallen them.

"My mother wanted to protect me. She wouldn't let me visit him in jail," Luis continued. "She didn't want the police to notice me, or for anyone to know I was the son of a political prisoner. Just before she died three years ago, she finally told me everything."

So far I had jotted some words on my pad: "Guantanamo," "diamonds," "political prisoner," and "family agreement." Too much was still missing from the picture, but I realized that we were moving at Luis's pace.

"And why do you feel cheated by your father's friend?" I asked.

I saw a pulse of tension move up Luis's cheek, and I knew why. My wording suggested that he only *felt* cheated, not that his word was the truth. I could see he expected me to leap into his story without question. But if everyone who thought they were cheated by life got their due, the world would be a different place—and not necessarily a better one.

"The agreement was that the two families would divide the wealth when they reached Miami," Luis explained. "It was a pact designed to extend into the future. If my parents couldn't reach America in due time, the money would be held for them until they arrived and could claim it—or until their son did. Exactly half the sum the diamonds produced from investments would belong to the Delgados."

Now I understood what he was saying. If the story he was telling me in such a dispassionate, methodical manner were true—a big if, I reminded myself—then he stood to become a very wealthy man. "They must owe you a fortune. And I'll bet they don't want to give it to you."

Luis nodded patiently. "The money is my birthright, my inheritance. My father gave his life for it. I am not a man who cheats or—how do you say—swindles?"

He punctuated his question with a thick cloud of smoke. "That's the right word," I said. I wondered if this slip in his command of English was genuine or designed to ingratiate me to him. Previously he hadn't needed to use me as a thesaurus.

"Yes, then," he said. "I am not a swindler. I want only what is rightfully mine."

I had expected another routine day at the office. I certainly had been wrong. I rose to crank up the air conditioner another notch. Though the calendar said it was late spring, the day was turning out to be another scorcher. I also turned up the fan; at least the air would circulate, and I could breathe fresh smoke.

When I sat down again, Luis was watching me. He really was very good-looking, with a high forehead and refined features seemingly tightened by years of adversity. It was dangerous to think like this, and when our eyes met I looked down at my notes.

"There are things you're not telling me," I said bluntly.

Luis's eyes widened in what I took to be disbelief that I could even suggest that he hadn't been completely forthright.

"First: Who is this man in Miami you claim owes you money?" I began. "And second: Why are you completely sure he won't honor this agreement? Have you actually spoken to him?"

"The couple is Miguel and Teresa de la Torre," Luis said. My heart skipped in my chest. *Mierda.* "Miguel is my godfather. They sponsored my release from Guantanamo. Then they waited to see if I knew about their deal, and when they saw that I did, they threw me out of their home. They tried to have me killed."

"Killed?" I repeated.

"I don't know why they would have to resort to murder," Luis added, his voice tinged with sadness. "From what I saw, they have more than enough to pay me what they owe."

He was waiting to see how I would react. It went without saying that I knew who he was talking about. Miguel de la Torre was one of the richest men in a wealthy city. He was head of the First Miami Bank, and his wife was a noted philanthropist. Their names could have been listed in Webster's under "pillars of the community." They had one of the longest biographies in *la Guía Social*—the Cuban social register. More important, they surely had enough money to part with whatever Luis claimed was his—if they rightly owed it.

"I . . . I honestly find that hard to believe," I finally said. "I know them only by reputation, not personally. They're highly respected here. But you're suggesting that they cheated you and put a contract on your life. It doesn't make sense."

Luis's features sagged, a marionette with cut strings. "You see, this is why the police are no good to me. Even you do not believe me."

I thought for a moment. I had to admit that my attitude had changed since I had heard the de la Torres' name. It was as though I had just been informed that Mother Teresa was skimming money from the nuns' poor box or had been caught kiting checks. "I didn't say that I don't believe you. I said it didn't make sense—there's a difference." Anyway, the difference in my mind was slim. Even if his story were true, I didn't know what I could do for him. "Well, Mr. Delgado, you've obviously given it some thought. What do you want us to do for you?"

"I want you to investigate the de la Torres," he said. "I need you to find out everything about them, particularly their finances—"

"Wait a minute," I interrupted. "I don't know what you intend to do, but I won't be a part of some sort of blackmail scheme."

Luis ignored me. "At this moment, they think I'm dead."

I was angry with myself for not following up on the murder-attempt claim earlier. His story was too much. *He* was too much. I realized he was having an effect on me, and I didn't like it.

He continued: "I stayed with the de la Torres briefly after I arrived here, though they hadn't seen me since I was a baby. I think they wanted me close, to keep an eye on me," he said. Another cigarette emerged. "Or maybe to make sure I was who I claimed to be. When I brought up the arrangement they became angry and pretended there had never been an agreement. Then they accused my father of stealing—of keeping four diamonds out of the combined fortune of our two families."

"And you spoke with both Miguel and Teresa?"

"Both at the same time," Luis said. "I am glad my parents are not alive to see how they behaved."

All right, I thought. If he was a guest in their house, it would prove they knew him. The de la Torres weren't the types to take in a *balsero* stranger without good reasons.

"As soon as they knew I expected them to honor their agreement, they threw me out of their house." Luis frowned, and wrinkles appeared on the hollow slopes of his cheeks. "A few days later, they sent a man to kill me."

This was sounding more and more like fantasy. "And how did you know he was sent by the de la Torres? There's a lot of crime in Miami, Mr. Delgado."

"I have noticed that," Luis said wryly. "And, please, call me Luis. I know my claims are extreme, but let us not be overly formal."

I agreed, noting how he instinctively took command of a situation. He was the kind of man you would spot in a photo of a crowd: distinctive, intense, his eyes burning into you. I was surprised to find myself feeling uncomfortable.

"I know who sent him because I stopped him before he got me," Luis said. "It was by the Miami River, where I take a walk every night. Don't worry, I did not harm him."

"What were you doing down there?" I asked, trying not to react to what I had just heard.

"I have a room near downtown Miami," he replied. "It is an inexpensive neighborhood to live in."

That was an understatement. I knew the area; it was full of transients and people living on the margins of society and the law. It was not a neighborhood for the squeamish.

"I made the man tell me his name—Pepe Salazar. He said he was supposed to take from me the two diamonds that I had shown to the de la Torres. I made him agree to tell them he had killed me but that I was only carrying one diamond. I gave a jewel to him to take back. I'm sure he was very convincing."

It was a long time before I said anything. Luis was claiming to have subdued a hired killer. It was self-defense, but even so, that made him dangerous. I checked my gut feelings about this *balsero* and decided that I believed him. I wanted the case.

"You didn't think he would just keep the diamond?"

"I believed he would keep his word," Luis said. "I used persuasion."

Great. I didn't allow myself to speculate about what had happened; I suspected Luis hadn't simply talked the hired killer into doing what he wanted.

"You have to understand me," Luis said. "I once had four diamonds; now only one is left. I am not the sort of man to use a knife, but I am running out of options."

"You sent one diamond back to the de la Torres," I said, glossing over his comment about the knife. "What happened to the other two?"

"One was used by my mother as a bribe, when I was fifteen years old. She used it to pay off a doctor to declare me ineligible for the army," he answered. "I used another to get out of Cuba."

All right, I thought, for now his story was consistent. "You have to be careful," I said. "If they find out you're alive, we have to assume they'll hire someone else to kill you."

"I rented another room the next day," Luis said calmly. "It is an easy district in which to become invisible."

"What about the Mercedes dealership?" I asked. My mind kept returning to the knife he had mentioned: I glanced over him, looking for telltale bulges in his coat and pockets. There was none. "You're out in public every day when you're working."

"I got the job after I left the de la Torres," Luis said. "They drive Jaguars. There is no reason for them to come in. Anyway, I know how to survive and keep to myself." Luis reached down and patted his left calf, answering my unasked question. He shook his head with what seemed like regret. "I know I could have called the police after Salazar jumped me, but no one would ever believe my story. Then I would never get what is rightfully mine."

I wasn't thinking clearly; I should have told Luis to go to the police as soon as the story involved criminal activity. I had a professional duty to do so. It was as though my brain were lagging behind his.

"Maybe you're right," I admitted. "And you're probably safe in that area. I doubt the de la Torres ever venture down there."

I stood up and extended my hand. "I'll contact you in a day or so," I said, careful not to commit myself to anything. "In the meantime, be careful."

"Of course," he said. "I am nothing but careful."

When he was gone, nothing but a cloud of smoke remained. I was left at my desk, staring at the parrots outside.

It was an eerie feeling to know that a prospective client had checked me out so thoroughly that he knew more about me than I did about him. I wondered if he had observed me only at the Mercedes dealership. When he said he had learned about me through the dealership's computer, it seemed he wanted me to know he was a man of resources.

Had he ever been tempted to find out more about me? For all I knew, he could even have followed me home—and possibly not just once, but routinely. After all, this was obviously a matter of life and death to him, and he didn't seem to be a man who gave his trust freely.

I stared out into the trees, a part of me chiding myself for having gotten out of bed.

Two

I sat for so long after Luis left that the parrots nearly had enough time to construct a new nest for their ever-growing family. I heard a soft, barely audible knock at the door.

Leonardo didn't wait for an answer before coming in with my coffee mug. He had refilled it with fresh-brewed *café con leche,* and when he put it on my desk he made sure the Cuban flag faced me. He knew my quirks well and was enough of a sweetheart to indulge them.

Then he went into action. With a look of disgust, he opened my windows as far as they would go. He grabbed some brown file folders from my credenza and started fanning the room. In his frenzy he looked like a deranged giant butterfly, but he succeeded in sending some of the thick smoke out the window. Soon he had created a mini–jet stream, the cloud rushing out in a wide swathe.

He left the room, and I sipped my coffee. In a moment he returned with two aerosol cans. Like some Old West gunslinger he held one in each hand, pointing them upward and firing at will. I covered my coffee with my hand, attempting to spare myself chemical poisoning on top of lung cancer. Leonardo didn't stop until the cans were empty.

I don't know which was worse, the stale smoke or the pine-fresh scent, no doubt a holdover from Christmas. Finally he took mercy on me, tossed the cans in the garbage, and sat down.

He stared at me. My silence was obviously too much for him to bear. "Want to discuss it?" he asked.

I took a sip of coffee. "Leo," I said, "let me tell you a story. And pay attention. I want your opinion."

Leonardo could tell I was serious, so he set out to find a proper listening position. He moved from the chair to the sofa in the corner, then unsnapped his fanny pack and gingerly laid it on the table next to him. It wouldn't do to disturb the treasures within, all the vitamins and lecithin pills and garlic tablets he thought he couldn't live more than a few hours without. When this was accomplished, he arranged himself just so on the couch, pulling at his bicycle pants until the seams were aligned properly, fiddling with his tank top. Finally he clasped his hands across his chest and assumed a serious expression.

"Are you comfy now?" I asked.

"I am," he answered, without the slightest trace of self-consciousness. "Start."

"This client claims that Miguel and Teresa de la Torre stole money from his family in Cuba," I began.

Leonardo sat up. "*The* Miguel and Teresa de la Torre?"

"*Sí.*"

"They stole money?" Leonardo stammered. "How? Why? How much?"

"I don't know, but it's a hell of a lot. Luis Delgado claims they stole, at the very minimum, millions of dollars from his father and mother," I said.

Leonardo was so upset he reached for his fanny pack and started rummaging around for pills. "I'm listening. Start from the beginning."

I told him what Luis had said—omitting the part about Luis having observed me in the past. I knew how my cousin would react to that. Leonardo listened without interrupting once—a first for him.

"I can tell you want to take the case," he said glumly when I had finished.

"First I'm going to check up on Delgado as much as I can," I said. "I'll call Ted Rafferty right away. If the story checks out, you and I need to talk this through. We could be stepping into a real minefield. I don't like walk-in clients, either. You have to watch your back with them."

"Listen, Lupe," Leonardo said, "don't get attached to this case until you speak to Rafferty. You're talking about going against two of the most prominent people in Miami, on the word of a *balsero*."

"Please, don't sugarcoat it for me, speak your mind," I said sarcastically. "I can take it."

It was my call, but we both knew he wanted me to walk away from this one. I wasn't sure I disagreed, especially knowing what I did about the man, but I was intrigued by Luis and his story. The question I should have been able to answer was: Which did I find more fascinating, Luis or the case?

Leonardo watched me from the sofa with a wary frown. "Call Rafferty," he said. "He can get you some answers by the end of the day. How did you leave things with Delgado? You didn't promise him anything, did you?"

"Leonardo, I know better than that," I complained.

He gave me a stern look, but he let it pass. "You look really wound up," he said. "Why don't you let me make you some soothing extra-special tea, instead of that coffee? It'll make you relaxed and mellow."

"No, thanks, I don't want to be mellow right now." I went through my Rolodex until I found Rafferty's card. I started punching in the numbers while I drained the rest of my coffee. Leonardo gave me a look of total disgust and left the room.

"Rafferty here," a booming voice said. I smiled involuntarily; with Ted Rafferty, I never needed to use the speakerphone. Ted had been with the Miami police for thirty years, and nothing would surprise him. On a two-week trip to Ireland ten years past, he had managed to pick up an intermittent thick brogue and a slew of Irish colloquialisms. If you didn't know better, you'd think he'd just stepped off the boat.

"Ted, hello," I said. "It's Lupe."

"Lupe, my favorite Cuban lass!" Ted roared. I held the phone a little farther from my ear. "Top of the morning to you. What's on your mind?"

"How's the family?" I asked. We exchanged news for a while, but I cut him off before we went back too many generations. Believe me, when you're Cuban and Irish, a discussion about families can take quite some time. We'd talk about relatives five times removed as though they were siblings.

I had met Ted years before, when I was working undercover in a Miami Beach hotel that was being robbed regularly. Guests were returning to their rooms to find their money and valuables gone, and the management suspected someone on the staff. I was hired to pose as a waitress in room service. Ted was there working his second job as a security guard—his youngest daughter had been accepted by an Ivy League college and, joking that she had no athletic ability, he told me that he had to pay her full tuition. We became friends during the weeks I worked the case, and he had helped me monitor the service staff, where two men had been pulling off the robberies.

"I can tell you mean business today," Ted said. "What can I do for you?"

"A potential client came to my office this morning. He has quite a story, and I need to check it out. Do you still have friends at INS?" I injected some sugar into my voice. This was a big favor.

"Lass, if I didn't have INS friends in this town, I might as well retire," Ted bellowed, laughing at his own joke. I held the phone with my arm completely outstretched, my elbow locked. I wondered if my hearing could be damaged by talking on the phone. After all, cellular phones could cause cancer, so who knew? Anything was possible. I started thinking I might need one of Leonardo's teas—maybe one that was Valium-based, for medicinal purposes, of course.

"Uh, Ted," I said, pulling the phone to my face, prepared to live dangerously by jeopardizing my hearing again, "this guy came in through Guantanamo. He was a rafter picked up at sea."

"A rafter? You'd better be careful," Rafferty warned. "Don't go getting yourself in trouble. Those rafters are pretty tough."

I tried to keep my annoyance out of my voice. "His name is Luis Delgado," I said. "Hispanic male, obviously. Date of birth September 30, 1957. Spent just over fifteen months at Guantanamo. Admitted to the States December 7, 1995."

I heard Ted writing it all down. "Pearl Harbor Day—the day of infamy. I'll try to get something for you this afternoon," he said, his voice marginally quieter. "I'm not sure how the Gitmo records were kept, but I'll contact you if I run into a problem."

Ted hung up without saying good-bye, not a good sign. But even though he disapproved, I knew he would come through. I'd make it up to him somehow. I knew he had a weakness for Cuban restaurants.

I spent the rest of the morning writing up cases so Leonardo could bill out on them. I tried not to think about Luis Delgado.

At one o'clock there was a soft knock on my door. I knew Leonardo couldn't stay mad at me for long.

He had changed into a fresh set of clothes, which meant his morning workout in the spare room was over. "Want to go to lunch?" he asked.

"Is the Pope Catholic?"

I took my purse out of my desk. Whenever Leonardo and I went to lunch, the bill was mine to pay. I wasn't sure how this custom got started, but after seven years it hadn't changed. I guess being the older cousin, as well as the boss, put me in line for that honor.

"You'd better have a big lunch, Lupe. Remember, you have that domestic tonight." I must have looked blank. "You know, the accountant and the temp. You told the client you were going to do it tonight—the accountant claims he does the office audit on Tuesdays."

I had no idea what he was talking about. "Lupe, I'm worried about you," Leonardo said. "I'm going to have to start you on memory pills. I just read about a new kind—they're made from sea-horse spines."

The shocking idea of taking these pills jarred my memory a little. I vaguely remembered promising to work a domestic case. I hated domestics so much I tended to block them out of my mind.

I was cursing my luck when the phone rang. "Let the service pick it up," Leonardo said. He came around the desk and tried to hustle me out the door. "Let's go, I'm hungry."

I picked it up. Ted Rafferty announced himself and made my ears ring instantly. If I didn't recognize that voice straight away, I should have been stripped of my investigator's license. Leonardo stepped out with a disappointed look.

"I got the information you wanted." Ted must have been truly annoyed with me—first no good-bye, now no proper hello.

"I'm ready, Ted," I said politely. I grabbed a pad.

"Your guy was in Gitmo, all right, and the dates he gave you are correct. He was a model internee—no trouble, kept to himself, helpful, and cooperative. No record in Cuba, either, but that's no surprise. He never would have gotten into the States with a Cuban record."

I held my breath, torn between wanting to hear more and dreading it. "Anything else, Ted?"

"Well, one more thing," he said. His tone of voice was actually normal for once. "The name of his sponsors is a little surprising: Miguel and Teresa de la Torre. *The* Miguel and Teresa de la Torre. Interesting, isn't it?"

Mierda.

"Lass, are you still there?" Ted asked. "Listen, maybe it's not my place to ask, but are you sure you know what you're doing?"

Three

Timing things just right, I shot ahead of the patiently waiting couple and stole their parking space. Beneath their sun visors and Coppertone they both looked shocked, which meant they had to be tourists—only someone from out of town would have been surprised. Granted, in most civilized places the unwritten rules of society are respected. But this was Miami. There are no rules in Miami.

By the time the tourists pulled away, looking dazed, I was already changing clothes in the front seat of my Mercedes. This was the part of private investigative work they don't show you on TV. I got out of my shirt and blouse and into a black cotton dress with matching high-heeled pumps. I would look like all the other women at the bar, and the mark would never suspect I was investigating him.

I've learned over the years to stash several changes of clothes in a gym bag in the backseat of my car. On a surveillance I can change in less than a minute—modesty be damned—even quicker if I'm out of the car and not wrestling with the steering wheel.

I checked inside my purse: camera, beeper set at "vibrate" so it wouldn't go off and draw attention to me, tissues, pen, notebook, investigator's license, and, of course, my Beretta. I looked in the mirror, planted a simple expression on my face, and stepped out of the car.

I walked into the dim entryway and was instantly accosted by the bouncer, a sweaty barfly in a Key West T-shirt. He checked my driver's license just to be extra obnoxious—I looked young for twenty-eight, but not *that* young. He stepped aside to let me in, after shooting me a lecherous look that telegraphed more than I wanted to know about the state of his love life.

The bar was perfect for an illicit rendezvous. Even the sun wouldn't be caught hanging out in there; not so much as a sliver of early evening daylight penetrated the long narrow room. Waiting for my eyes to adjust, I walked to the bar, nearly tripping over a table. There was a floor-to-ceiling mirror running behind the bar— smudged, but clear enough. I was able to observe my mark without turning around.

He was sitting alone at a table at the far corner of the room, looking guilty. Just as his wife had predicted. He was balding, overweight, and his suit looked like he bought it when Kennedy was president and last dry-cleaned it when the Beatles were still together.

I sipped my tepid, iceless drink, feeling sorry for myself. The place was so cheap and low-class that my club soda came without bubbles—fizz would have cost extra. I couldn't wait to get this over with.

I hate domestic cases with a passion. Most investigators do, because they tend to cause nothing but pain and anguish all around. Florida is a no-fault divorce state, so adultery has no bearing on a court case, but still people want to hire investigators.

And Solano Investigations let itself be hired. We had to, really. It paid the bills. Whenever Leonardo felt insecure about our finances, or if he wanted a new piece of pricey equipment for his in-house gym, he would send me off on all kinds of lousy cases. Sometimes we farmed the work out to contract investigators, but I had promised to take this one personally. The client had heard of us from her cousin, who had hired us on a domestic a few years back. I agreed to do it, more to keep the peace than to keep in practice. I could tell from subtle clues that Leonardo felt sorry for the client and wanted the job done right, though he never would have admitted it to me.

I finished the club soda and thought about the client. She was a nice lady, a middle-aged housewife. She had sat in my office for almost an hour the week before, sobbing into a mess of wet Kleenexes. She was convinced her husband was fooling around with a temp at his accounting firm. After listening to her I decided that the husband probably wasn't worth the bother, but what did I know? I've never partaken in wedded bliss.

My thoughts drifted to Luis Delgado. So far his story had checked out. But I couldn't lose the feeling that even though Luis came to me for help, he was far from helpless. I wondered precisely what he thought I could do for him.

Before I could think it all through, a young woman who fit the temp's description walked into the bar. I had a chance to check her out while she stood uncertainly in the doorway. I sympathized with her, in a way—surely this bar wasn't her idea of a classy date.

By then the accountant was out of his chair, practically knocking over tables in his eagerness to get to her. All the other barflies pulled their faces out of their drinks, taking her in.

There was no way the wife could compete with this bimbo. The wife was pretty in her own way, but having three children in five years takes its toll. So does driving carpools in a Volvo station wagon, running the dog to the vet, and sitting through interminable PTA meetings. Glamour quickly fades from the picture.

The accountant gave the temp time to gulp down one lousy white wine before he started to work her out the door. I knew they were going to the motel behind the bar. It was all so predictable. The temp had finished her last sip when he threw some bills on the table. He pulled her to her feet as though the place were on fire and she were a bag of money. There wasn't even a pretense of courtship here—the purpose of their meeting was a foregone conclusion. I was no neophyte at these kinds of surveillances, but I still felt a stab of sadness at the tawdry, matter-of-factness of it all.

I paid cash for my club soda, got a receipt, and discreetly followed them out. Sure enough, they were headed for the motel. I pretended to look for keys in my purse while I watched the accountant fall all over himself getting into the motel office. The young temp waited nervously outside, probably thinking this wasn't such a great idea after all.

It took the guy less than a minute to register and get the room key. He wiped his forehead with a beefy palm and hustled the girl into the room, shutting the door loudly behind them.

By then I was ensconced in my car. I got busy as soon as I shut the door. I had to gather as much information as I could for my client, and it was impossible to know how long one would be able to stay in the same place. I pulled out my camera and long-distance lenses and started taking photos. The accountant's car. The temp's, parked next to his. The motel. Their license plates.

Later on I'd run the temp's tag, to give my client more background on her worst nightmare come true. If I had a sky's-the-limit budget I could have told the wife the brand and color of the temp's underwear, but she was just paying for the basics: name, address, age, employment history, driving record. More detail meant more heartache for the client, almost every time, but I always gave them what they asked for.

All that remained was to note the time the accountant left with the temp from the motel room. I also might get a picture of the two of them together. I always tried to get as compromising a photo as I could, but I didn't go in for peering through blinds. There was a time, six years before, when I *did* dress as a hotel maid to get into an occupied room, but I've been trying to forget about it ever since.

I checked my watch in the sickly glow of the fluorescent parking lights. It would probably be too late to go back to the office after the surveillance.

The overwhelming majority of surveillances are mind-numbingly dull. It's a real challenge to stay focused and alert hour after hour, especially at night. Good investigators have to learn how to stare out from wherever they are—houses, doorways, or cars—without interruption. Sitting in a parked car, not reading or even listening to music—because changing stations or CDs takes attention, and the sound is a distraction—is an exercise in discipline. Moving one's eyes away from the surveillance for even a moment can result in disaster; in that brief time, something crucial can happen, and you can't ask for an instant replay.

The hours passed more quickly if I could refrain from checking the time every few minutes. Years ago I had learned to use surveillances to my advantage. I tried to sharpen my mental skills by forcing myself to recall long-forgotten facts. Once I listed to myself the names of every schoolteacher I'd ever had. Another time I compiled every song Gloria Estefan had ever recorded, then hummed their choruses—even though humming tunes intended for conga lines wasn't easy. Tonight I concentrated on recalling my every summer vacation beginning with kindergarten and ending after my college graduation. I lingered on those summers that had involved a love interest. It turned out to be one of my more enjoyable intellectual exercises.

They stayed in the motel for close to three hours. My eyes popped when I looked at my watch and it read nine-thirty. I had pegged the accountant as a wham-bam-thank-you-ma'am kind of guy.

My back was killing me. I thought of a dozen jokes about checking her assets and going over her books, but I was losing my sense of humor. The wife had told me this was the first time he had cheated on her, but I didn't buy it. Adulterers tend to be like potato-chip junkies—they can't stop at just one.

Maybe the wife hadn't wanted to spend the money before to have him checked out. Maybe he had finally pushed her so far that she felt she didn't have a choice. If I questioned my clients' motives, I would go out of business in five minutes. I would be tempted to point out that they really did not need my services as an investigator. Their money would be better spent on psychological or psychiatric sessions. But then, my job was not to judge my clients—only to provide a service and charge accordingly. As long as I kept my investigations within the law, it was unproductive to speculate on the minutiae.

I started to entertain myself by counting the billable hours in my head. Leonardo quoted the wife a price of sixty dollars an hour, knocking ten bucks off the usual rate, with the usual ten-hour minimum. He must really have felt sorry for her. I figured that the accountant had to give out at any moment, and we would clear six hours for a four-hour job. Too bad they weren't all like that.

I didn't usually sit around and calculate bills on a surveillance. Leonardo takes care of our accounting. And then, all of a sudden, I realized what was going on. All these mental gymnastics were my way of not thinking about Luis Delgado.

What was it about the man that appealed to me? After all, I had known plenty of men, but I had never dated a Cuban before. I tended to go for tall, blond, American men. Part of my taste was rooted in self-protection: I was too independent for Cuban guys, even those who advertised themselves as progressive and liberated. Another aspect of the situation was that not one had ever asked me out. Ever.

So my thoughts about Luis surprised me. Maybe it was his aura of danger couched in civility. Or perhaps his lone-ranger, looking-for-justice quest. I worked in a profession that required toughness, but I was in many ways an idealist and a romantic. And, being Cuban, I understood Luis's need for retribution. I knew that his family's suffering burned inside him and had driven him to see me.

Luis was a complicated man with undoubtedly complicated motivations. None of that changed an essential fact—that, in 1997 Miami, we were far from equals in social or economic terms—but that wasn't enough to dim my fascination. Though I had grown up well-off, my life had been far from sheltered. My parents had brought up my sisters and me to judge people's characters before their social status. Besides, this was Miami, not Cuba. Here the classes mingled and a person's standing depended on his achievements rather than his family history.

My neck was on fire. I tried to soothe it by pushing back against the headrest. I had been thinking too much. I tried to focus on other subjects, but my mind soon returned to Luis. What was I so frightened of? He was good-looking, charismatic, attractive—so what? I had met attractive men before. The man and the case were starting to become one to me—an obvious sign that my objectivity was in jeopardy. I just had to keep things clear to myself, I thought. Surely I could maintain an uncluttered head.

I tried thinking about surveillances. I used to like them, when I was green and just setting out on my own, but the luster had fallen away long ago. Big-budget surveillances were interesting—there were people to talk to and consult and trade secrets with. But those kinds of jobs were scarce; only the government could afford them anymore.

Maybe if I honked my horn, I thought, that might get them out.

Finally room eighteen's door opened. The temp came out, looked around, then jogged to her car and drove away. The accountant waited a few minutes before venturing out, a postcoital cigarette glowing in his pudgy hand. I managed to grab photos of both of them, then I waited until he drove away.

I would hold off until morning to drop off the film. Bad news could always wait.

And, I thought, I had gone nearly half an hour without thinking about Luis Delgado. It was a start.

Four

I was ensconced on a slippery red plastic stool at the Cubanteria, the Cuban cafeteria across the parking lot from Eckerd's drugstore. There was an hour to kill before the film from last night's surveillance would be ready, so I savored a *café con leche* and pictured Luis Delgado in my mind. I saw his high forehead, dark eyes, and distinct cheekbones—and again wondered why. It wasn't as though I was an innocent—I had a good deal of experience with a variety of men, personally and professionally. Yet I might as well have been back in high school, smitten by a boy in algebra class.

My reverie was broken by a shrill, ear-piercing whistle coming from the kitchen. I looked up from my chipped white ceramic cup and smiled without much enthusiasm. "Hello, Gregorio," I said.

"Lupe, *amor!*" Gregorio boomed, his voice filling the entire room. "The most beautiful woman in Miami!"

I cringed as Gregorio maneuvered himself toward me from behind the counter. His opinion was certainly flattering—I just wished that men other than the octogenarian cook at the Cubanteria shared it. Gregorio was a Cuban Mahatma Gandhi in appearance, a totally bald, dark-skinned prune of a man. He was toothless because he'd had to relinquish his dentures to Cuban police when he left the country, in accordance with some obsure subsection of the island's emigration laws.

Gregorio leaned close. "Have another *café*," he said conspiratorially. "On me."

Gregorio wasn't much to look at, but his coffee was nearly legendary. I had almost finished my second cup, and I actually considered a third before I regained my sanity.

"*Ay*, don't tempt me," I said. "I've already had too much. I can feel my heart thumping."

To illustrate, I pointed at my T-shirt. Big mistake. His eyes fixed on my breasts and started to glaze over.

Time to change the subject. "Last night was a full moon, wasn't it?" I asked. "Did you do a reading?"

Gregorio was a member of some illegal, quasi-religious sect that sacrificed animals, barbecued them to a crisp, then took readings from the charred bones. If their priestess found strong omens—more specifically, if she could discern numbers—the sect would play them in the *bolita*, a lottery drawn in Puerto Rico. I wasn't even sure what the sect was called—as far as I was concerned, the less I knew, the better. I had asked Gregorio once if it was related to Santería, but Gregorio denied it vigorously, offended by my ignorance.

"It was a full moon, but we didn't do anything," Gregorio said, shaking his head sadly. "Our high priestess was on jury duty. Can you imagine? Locked in a room with eleven strangers on the night of a full moon, not being able to do anything about it?"

He slapped the counter over the unfairness of it all. I commiserated; all-night deliberations with a Miami jury was second-best to anything. I also remembered that the full moon the night before had been spectacular.

I didn't know all the details about Gregorio's sect; there were hundreds of sects in Miami. My older sister Fatima had shopped around for forms of alternative spirituality, and at one point had had some dealings with Gregorio's group. But it was consistent with her personality that she quickly moved on to another, one that better suited her needs that week. Some of her sects were more memorable than others, such as the one involving hermaphrodite piglets. Thank God her flirtation with that sect was short-lived—their ringleader was serving two to ten for breaking into the University of Miami School of Medicine's science lab.

Gregorio had wandered off to take a customer's order; when he returned, it was with another steaming mug of *café con leche*. I accepted it—I knew he wouldn't let me refuse—and the old man retired to the kitchen, satisfied with his own generosity.

I stared into the cup, wishing the coffee was a crystal ball that would divulge answers about Luis Delgado. Everything he had told me had checked out so far, which was in his favor. But I knew I was begging for turbulence. I was dangerously close to violating my cardinal rule: Never become personally involved with a client. I kept coming back to the indisputable fact that I was attracted to him, and that could make me lose my objectivity. I wasn't sure I had enough self-control to keep my distance, a fact that I hated but had to acknowledge. Luis might as well have been holding a sign flashing the word "trouble" in neon lights.

Professionally, I was tempting disaster. Miguel and Teresa de la Torre were, arguably, the most respected Cuban-American couple in Miami. I searched my memory for anything derogatory or negative that I ever might have heard about them, and came up with nothing. I would be careful investigating them, but I knew from experience that total discretion couldn't eliminate leaks. I had no idea what might happen to me—probably they'd use their influence to have me put out of business. If they found out that Luis was alive, it could cost him his life. They had tried to have him killed once, and they probably wouldn't hesitate to finish the job. That is, if what he told me was true. I realized that I had already assumed it was.

The Cubanteria was filling up; a young couple stood in the doorway, looking for a pair of open seats. It had been an hour since I had dropped off the film, so I finished the last sip of my third coffee and waved for them to take my seat and the vacant one next to it.

At the photo store, I looked over the pictures, waiting to pay while the manager took a phone call. They were perfect. I had several good shots of the two. Most of them were unflattering, which made things easier—there was no need to upset my client by showing her pictures of the temp looking attractive and young.

After I paid, I tucked the pictures and receipt into my purse. It took me a half-hour to get back to the office, a drive I spent in dread of calling the accountant's wife.

When I opened the front door of Solano Investigation's cottage, I was hit with a thick mist of Alpine Forever. As I inhaled the pungent, chemical-smelling air, I wondered if one could get high off aerosol room freshener. I couldn't decide which fate I preferred: death from secondhand smoke, or spending the rest of my days hallucinating about a pine forest in deepest Canada. It had been twenty-four hours since Luis's visit, but my cousin was still spraying the stuff. In matters pertaining to health, Leonardo invariably went for overkill.

"Your 'possible' client called," Leonardo shouted from the weight room. "The one with the death wish, smoking coffin nails."

I looked inside the door. Leonardo was heaving and sweating over the StairMaster. "Please show more respect for our clients," I said, annoyed by his sarcasm. "It's because of them that we have food and a roof over our heads—not to mention that extremely expensive torture device that you love so much."

"Sorry." Leonardo jumped off the machine and wiped the sweat off his face with a towel. "I forgot that domestics put you in such a shitty mood."

I ignored his comment. "What did Luis Delgado want?"

"Nothing, as far as I know," Leonardo said with a trace of disapproval. "He just left his name—at nine A.M. First caller of the day."

Leonardo walked over to the kitchen, avoiding making eye contact with me. He opened the refrigerator door and peered inside, studying its contents with the same intensity with which Marie Curie must have inspected the bacteria in her test tubes.

I shook my head and set out for my office. First I had to call the accountant's wife—not the best way to begin the day, but necessary. I knew that avoiding the call would take more energy than making it.

I sat at my desk and cleared away the mess of papers so I could write up my notes. Then I opened the file to the front page and stared at her phone number, avoiding looking at Luis Delgado's file to one side of the desktop. I dialed my client's number. She answered a second after the first ring.

"Lupe!" she said, eager and anxious. "Well? Did he meet her?"

I gave her all the gory details that she had paid for, then told her she could come by my office later for the report and the photographs. I could taste the three coffees rising up in my throat. I finally had to cut her off when she started to thank me profusely for my work. She was the kind of woman who, if she was facing a firing squad, would apologize for not being around to clean up the mess after they'd shot her.

I ran out of my office and nearly slammed into Leonardo, who was slurping from a gallon-sized jug filled with a repulsive, aqua-colored concoction. He nearly choked with surprise.

"Never again!" I shouted. I clutched the photos of the accountant and the temp, raising my fist to the ceiling in my best Scarlett

O'Hara impersonation. "As God is my witness, I swear by all that is sacred to me. I will never again take another domestic!"

Leonardo was unmoved; he delicately inserted a straw and took a sip. "Come on, Lupe," he finally said. "That's what you always say. Look at it this way: It's over, and we got paid cash in advance."

He left me there, making his way to the kitchen. I sulked as I heard water running in the sink. Leonardo was compulsive about washing dishes and cups the instant he was done with them. Whenever he got married, he was either going to make someone deliriously happy—or else he was going to turn them criminally psychotic. It could go either way.

He emerged from the kitchen and pointed at the pink message slip on his desk. "What are you going to do about this Delgado guy?" he asked. "You have to make a decision—the sooner the better. If you're not going to take his case, you need to cut him off right now."

"I need to check out a couple more things," I muttered. I headed back to my office, pointedly ignoring Leonardo's look of utter reproach. I closed the door behind me.

At least I had made a dramatic exit. Trouble was, I had no idea what to do next. For a few minutes I watched the parrots going about their business in the avocado tree. I wondered why they never gained any weight, even though they ate pounds of the stuff when it was in season. If I ate that much avocado I would balloon up, no question.

I shook my head to clear it of these weighty matters, then picked up the phone and pressed the second number on the speed dial.

"Tommy?" I said.

"*Hola, querida!*" he answered. "What's up?"

"I need to consult you about something," I said carefully. "It's a case. I'm not working it yet, but I might take it. There . . . there could be problems. Do you have any free time?"

"For you, all the time in the world," he said. "How about dinner tonight?"

"Sounds good," I said. "And thanks."

"Excellent," Tommy said. "We haven't gotten together in a while."

I heard papers rustling at his end. "So where are you staying these days?" he asked. "Still at the Cocoplum house?"

He was right to ask; my living accommodations confused everyone. I had an apartment on Brickell Avenue—not far from Tommy, but not as pricey as his place. The problem was, I rarely stayed at my own place anymore.

After I graduated from the University of Miami with a degree in advertising—a lot of good it did me—I signed a lease on a two-bedroom apartment, in the spirit of independence. It was the same place I was still renting, but at the time I had thought it was temporary until Solano Investigations made me rich and I could find a better address. At first it had been great to feel alone and grown-up—Cuban families can be a little smothering—but I quickly grew tired of the feeling. Seven years later I was still paying rent on the place, even though the oven was still covered with a plastic strip saying "Inspected by #27." I probably lived there most during the first six months after I "left home," until Mami became ill and I started coming back more and more to the Cocoplum house. I spent most of my time living out of my old room, while still maintaining the apartment.

I was Cuban enough to want to live with my family at age twenty-eight, while American enough to be embarrassed about it. The Brickell apartment was a perfect compromise. It gave me a convenient place to have some privacy, and yet I could leave it vacant for weeks at a time. Granted, it was sometimes difficult to explain to my American friends that I lived with my two older sisters, my teenage twin nieces, and Papi under the same roof—along with Aida and Osvaldo, the septuagenarian couple that had worked for my family since Cuba. My eldest sister, Fatima, is the mother of the twins, having returned home after her deadbeat husband, Julio, embezzled more than a hundred grand from Papi's contracting business. My other sister, Lourdes, is a nun with the Holy Order of the Rosary. She ostensibly lived in a small house in Little Havana with three other nuns, but came home so often that she took her mail at the Cocoplum house. What can I say? We Solano girls don't suffer deprivation well.

Papi had built a huge ten-bedroom house over Mami's objections. She had no aspirations of grandeur, but Papi prevailed. Maybe he had a suspicion that we would need all that room eventually. Since he was a contractor, it also probably seemed easy for him to build on a grand scale. The house was big enough to be in perfect proportion to the fifty-two-foot Hatteras docked in the back, fully stocked and gassed up for the day when Castro is finally overthrown or assassinated. Papi wanted to drive the first boat back into Havana Harbor and anchor it in front of the Malecon. His plan was meticulous—the boat contained three cabins for the family, as well as room for Osvaldo and Aida.

I told Tommy to pick me up at the Cocoplum house at seven. Just having him involved in some small way made me feel less anxious about Luis Delgado. Tommy McDonald was more than just the top criminal-defense attorney in Dade County—he was my friend and sometimes lover, and I knew I could trust him with my life.

I was contemplating what to wear to dinner—Tommy always took me to the best places in town—when I heard a tentative knock at the door.

"Luis Delgado on the line for you," Leonardo said, poking his head in. I knew he could have simply announced the call on the intercom and put it through, but he wanted to watch my reaction.

"*Gracias*," I said. I put my hand on the receiver but waited until Leonardo had closed the door before speaking.

"*Buenos días,* Luis," I said, trying to keep my voice even. My hand shook slightly. "What can I do for you?"

"*Buenos días,* Lupe," Luis answered formally. "I wondered if you need any additional information about my situation to help you reach a decision about taking my case."

I thought for a moment. "Actually, I'm happy you called," I said. "There's a question I need to ask. Would you be willing to take the diamond you showed me to an appraiser, to determine its value?"

"Of course," he said. He sounded pleased. "Whenever you like. I always carry it on my person, so please schedule this meeting at your convenience."

"That's good, Luis. But you do understand that I haven't agreed to take your case, don't you?" I warned.

He paused. "You have made that very clear."

"I'll call you as soon as I've decided what to do," I said, and hung up. It wasn't one of my better public-relations moments, but it seemed vital that I get off that line. I couldn't decide precisely what I wanted to do, or why, and it frightened me. I was buying time for myself—I understood this very well.

I called on the intercom for Leonardo; at least I knew it was time to mend some fences on the home front. "Want to go out for lunch?" I asked.

"Now?" he paused. "It's only ten-thirty!"

"Brunch then, Miss Manners," I said. "Since when did you turn into a stickler for correctness?"

Ten seconds later he opened my office door, his tank top neatly tucked into the waistband of his bicycle shorts. Taking his cue, I tucked my T-shirt into my jeans. Maybe we should get a dress code, I mused as I turned off the lights. Every day was dress-down Friday in our office.

Our brunch consisted of fruit salads and coffee at a little deli around the corner. I wouldn't have minded steak and eggs, but Leonardo knew I was trying to bribe him into being nice and so he insisted on health food. After forty-five minutes of listening to him talk about massage therapy and essential oils, I figured my debt was paid.

I spent the rest of the afternoon catching up on writing reports for old cases. At around four I realized that I was in a holding pattern, trying to avoid a decision regarding Delgado. At that point it was time to go home. I stuck my head into the gym, where Leonardo was doing squats with a barbell. Each time his knees bent he released such a yell that I was amazed the windows hadn't shattered. Maybe the neighbors thought I was running an obstetrics clinic as a sideline—and not giving the mothers any painkillers. I left him to his labor and headed home.

When I pulled into the driveway of the Cocoplum house, I saw my sister Lourdes's car parked on the grass, perilously close to Osvaldo's impatiens. I made a mental note to make her move it before she was caught—although she would probably get off with a reprimand, since she was Osvaldo's favorite. Actually, Lourdes was everyone's favorite. After all, how many nuns does the average Catholic have around the house? Catholics tend to be practical people—Cuban Catholics, in particular—and on some level they believe that having a religious person in the family means that some holiness is going to rub off. I, for one, count on my association with Lourdes to facilitate an easier entrance to Heaven—at the very least, a little rule-bending on the entrance examination.

I waved at the security camera, which recorded everyone who approached the front door, then bounded into the cavernous living room. Through the open glass doors to the patio, I heard a shout: "Marco Polo!"

I shuddered at the words. I had always hated that game, but my nieces never tired of it. When I reached the terrace I saw that Lourdes was in the pool as well. She was playing with so much enthusiasm that she could have been as young as the twelve-year-old twins. You'd think they all would have outgrown the game.

"Put on your suit, Lupe!" she called out, spitting water.

"Give me a minute," I said. I put my purse on a table and sat down. "Anyway, it looks like you're doing fine in there without me."

Lourdes stared at me for a moment, then turned to our nieces. "I'm getting out now," she said to them. "I want to visit with Tia Lupe for a while. Okay? You two play nice."

With that she heaved herself onto the deck with a single graceful motion. I stood up, and she hugged me tight, apparently oblivious to the fact that she was dripping water all over me. It had been only two or three days since we had seen each other, but Lourdes embraced me as though it had been months.

When Lourdes reached for a towel, I had a moment to marvel at her. She had turned thirty the month before, but she was so youthful in looks and spirit that she could have passed for a teenager. I knew she took pride in her appearance; just because she was a nun didn't mean she let herself go. She was tall and slim in her black one-piece bathing suit, her short black hair shiny with water, her light-brown eyes sparkling. I willed myself not to think it was a waste that the nun in the family got the height and the great figure—maybe it was a reward for pursuing her calling.

My sister was devout and dedicated to her vows, but she wasn't a stereotypical nun. For instance, Lourdes had a standing appointment every Saturday afternoon with a Hialeah beautician who plucked her eyebrows into an impeccable arch. A story had gone around that several years before, Lourdes had gone to the woman's house hours before Hurricane Andrew hit south Florida. Lourdes had wanted to look her best in the days to follow, when Miami would be without electricity and water. In all fairness to Lourdes, she had vindicated herself by helping the beautician put up storm shutters—after the critical tweezing. I never asked my sister whether the story was true, but she certainly looked better than the rest of us during the storm, when the city seemed like a war zone.

"What's up, *chica?*" Lourdes asked. She was giving me a look I knew well; it was impossible to hide anything from her.

"There's a case at work I might take. I'm not sure I will." I started to give her some vague idea what Luis's case was about, when Fatima walked in with a sour expression. Well, that was nothing new.

"I'm glad to see that you're both here," Fatima said. "I've been waiting to talk to you together."

Fatima was dressed in the kind of severe outfit that Lourdes was probably expected to wear: a no-nonsense brown shirtwaist dress that came down to her knees, and flat straw sandals that made her look short and stocky. Like me, Fatima had lost the genetic height lottery. Her beautiful wavy brown hair was pulled back into an unflattering ponytail. Her caramel-colored eyes were devoid of make-up.

I could recall when Fatima had been pretty and carefree—it hadn't been that long ago. Though Fatima was only thirty-two— Mami gave birth to the three of us in precise two-year intervals—she had aged in the past few years. Fatima had taken over the house after Mami died, and she took her responsibilities very seriously. Aida and Osvaldo did the cooking and cleaning, and the gardening, respectively. Mostly, Fatima's job was to worry about everyone.

Fatima put her hands on her hips. I knew what this meant: Lourdes and I were expected to fret over what was bothering her.

"What's the problem, Fatima?" Lourdes asked in a sweet tone, ever charitable. "What can we help you with?"

"I'm very concerned about Papi's state of mind. Yesterday, I caught him moving Mami's ashes from their bedroom out to the Hatteras." Fatima wrung her hands as she relayed this gruesome information. "I asked him what he was doing. He said he wanted to be ready at a moment's notice when Fidel got overthrown."

Lourdes and I glanced at each other; I considered crying, then laughing. "Why does he think anything's changed recently in Cuba?" I wondered. "I haven't heard of anything new going on."

"I don't know of anything, either." Lourdes shook her head, sending droplets of water in every direction.

"All I know is that he's acting strange," Fatima said. "I talked him into taking Mami back inside the house. I reminded him that she never liked sleeping on boats—not even the Hatteras."

Fatima seemed rather pleased with her solution. I smiled, because it felt like that was what she expected me to do. There didn't seem to be much else to say.

The twins emerged from the pool, chattering and dripping. Fatima scolded them for spreading water everywhere, even though they were dripping onto only the deck. After they were suitably dry, she took them into the house for a snack. Lourdes and I sat, our eyes closed in the afternoon sun. The air smelled of sea salt and pool chlorine.

"What do you think about what Fatima said?" I asked Lourdes, shifting on my cushion to get more comfortable.

"It's strange." When I glanced over, Lourdes was so relaxed that only her mouth moved. "But not too strange. She's making too big a deal of it. Papi's probably just been listening to those Cuban radio stations again. If you believed everything they say, you'd be sleeping in your clothes with your bags by the door, ready to leave at any minute."

Lourdes definitely sounded unconvinced; I was, too. "I guess you're right."

"Now what about this case you were starting to tell me about?" she asked. "I know you. You're confused about it and you don't know what to do. Why don't you tell me more?"

"It's nothing," I said. "I'm making too big a deal about it. I guess it runs in the family."

When I opened my eyes again, Lourdes was staring at me. She didn't believe a word I had said. "Whatever, little sister," she said. "I'm sure I'll hear all about it eventually."

I turned away. The worst part was, she was probably right. I had a vague premonition that a lot of people were going to find out about the case—maybe everyone in Miami. So why, I asked myself, hadn't I dropped it and run?

For one reason, of course. For Luis Delgado.

Five

"So, Lupe, what about this case you wanted to talk about with me? Not that I mind seeing you on short notice, of course."

Tommy was speaking to me for the first time since we left the house in Cocoplum. He had startled me—I had been preoccupied with what Fatima had told me about Papi.

"You've just got me curious is all," he said. "You almost never ask me for advice. Usually you just order me around."

We were driving over the Julia Tuttle Causeway, on our way to South Beach for dinner. I loved nights like this, cruising in Tommy's Rolls, the top down, and the soft Miami breeze caressing my fore-head, a Gloria Estefan ballad playing softly. I reluctantly dragged my thoughts back to Luis Delgado's plight. The two *mojitos* I had drunk at home hadn't done much to help my powers of concentration—double shots of rum rarely do.

"There's a man who wants me to take his case, a Cuban *balsero*," I began. "He came in through Guantanamo. The case could be really hot—and I don't mean that in a good way."

"You've never worried about difficult cases before," Tommy said. He steered with one hand, the other relaxed on the headrest of my seat. "What's so different about this one?"

"If what this *balsero* says is true—and so far, his story checks out—the bad guys in this case are Miguel and Teresa de la Torre."

Tommy whistled softly. "I see your problem."

We both fell silent. As always, driving over this particular stretch of road made me think of my mother. She had died seven years before, but a day never passed without my thinking of her. I was re-membering how much my mother loved the ocean, as Tommy drove us past the cruise ships anchored in the port of Miami awaiting their cargo of tourists. Sometimes she would wait after school for me and my sisters and then take us to Miami Beach to play in the surf. We were raised on stories about the waters around Cuba, and told how seawater flowed in our veins.

Mami also firmly believed in the healing powers of the sea. Her trips to the beach had become more and more frequent as her cancer progressed. After her death, Papi and I would go together to her favorite spot on Miami Beach, where we would look out over the breaking waves. Her every moment had been filled with thoughts of her native country, and I imagined that looking out over these waters—which also caressed the Cuban coast—had brought her homeland closer to her. I was very attuned to my mother's way of thinking, since I shared her love for our home and the waters that surrounded it.

"Still awake?" Tommy asked.

I snapped out of it. "Of course," I said.

"Well, I didn't book a table anywhere in particular, because I didn't know what time we'd be leaving your house," he said. "Is it all right with you if we just drive up Washington Avenue and see what looks good?"

We had gone through this routine countless times before. Tommy rarely booked a table anywhere; he didn't need to. "No problem," I said. "I knew it would be impossible to drag you out of the house once you got started on Aida's conch fritters and Osvaldo's *mojitos*."

In the six years that I had known Tommy, he had managed to wrangle as many invitations to my house as possible. I didn't flatter myself by thinking the main attraction was me; rather, it was Aida and Osvaldo's creations that kept him returning. The old couple often commented that Tommy must have been Cuban in a previous life or, after they had drunk a few *mojitos* themselves, that Tommy's mother must have taken a secret Cuban lover. For them, this was the highest of compliments.

"I always have too much!" Tommy exclaimed, stopping for a red light. He grabbed his stomach. "I must have had three dozen fritters!"

"And, of course, the fritters made you thirsty," I said, mocking him. "Your mouth was like the Sahara, so you had to down a few *mojitos*."

Tommy hung his head in shame as the light turned green. "Ah, Lupe, I can't hide anything from you."

Tommy and I had a lot in common: warped senses of humor; pride in our work; and the fact that, as a private investigator and a defense attorney, our paths tended to cross. Our attraction for each other didn't hurt, either. Tommy was tall, blond, blue-eyed, with an athletic build. I was small, dark, curvaceous: the typical Latina. Miami should have incorporated us into one of their advertising campaigns for cultural diversity.

We arrived at the intersection of Fifth Street and Washington Avenue, where Tommy switched on his blinker to turn left. While we waited for the parade of oncoming traffic to thin out, I thought about how much Miami Beach had changed since the early '80s. It was once a sleepy little district, home to elderly Jews, and Cubans who came over in the Mariel boat lift. Since then it had become relentlessly trendy, forcing out a lot of its original residents. Traffic had become a nightmare, parking was nonexistent, rents were exorbitant, and drugs were everywhere. The new Miami was trendy and hip. Nevertheless, we both were prepared—which was why Tommy was carrying a .357 Magnum in his glove compartment, and I had a loaded Beretta in my purse.

Tommy cruised slowly down Washington Avenue, looking for inspiration. I didn't really care where we ate; I was still quite full, not that that had ever stopped me from eating more. We drove until we reached the end of restaurant row. Nothing had seemed all that appealing. Tommy navigated a U-turn and headed back the way we had come.

"I know," he said, accelerating. "Let's try China Grill."

"Without a reservation?" I asked. "Boy, you're living on the edge tonight." It was impossible to get inside China Grill without having made a reservation weeks in advance. The place was perpetually mobbed, and deservedly so. It may have been terminally chic, but the food was delicious and the service was good.

I should have remembered: Tommy was born lucky and he rarely suffered the indignities the rest of us have to bear. The hostess didn't even flinch when we walked in off the street and requested a nice table for two. A minute later we were seated by the window in the main dining room. We had eaten there often, so we didn't even ask for menus. As usual, we ordered too much: lamb, duck, scallops, fried spinach, and a delicious California Merlot.

Tommy waited until we were on our second glasses of wine before talking about the case. "Miguel and Teresa de la Torre," he said in a reflective voice. "I thought they were so good and pure that God was only loaning them to us until He called them back to His right hand."

"I know they walk on water as far as Dade County is concerned," I said. I was drinking the wine too fast, but Tommy never cared. He would just order another bottle when I wasn't looking. "But that's not what my client tells me."

"Your 'client,' huh?" Tommy asked. "I thought you weren't sure whether to take the case."

"And that's what I wanted to discuss with you." I took a dollar out of my purse and handed it to him.

Tommy laughed and put it in his jacket pocket. "All right, now I work for you," he said. "We've covered our asses. So talk."

As Tommy had said, we had protected ourselves. If I was working with an attorney, I was allowed to exchange privileged information with him as part of the client-attorney relationship. Money had to change hands as a formal retainer, but the sum was of no consequence.

I started to pour out Luis's story, keeping my voice low so that no one at the nearby tables could eavesdrop. Halfway through my recital, dinner arrived; the food looked so good I had to stop talking. When we slowed down a bit, I continued my story. Tommy didn't interrupt once.

"So what's your next step?" he asked when I had finished. He pushed aside an empty plate of lamb and picked at the remains of the duck.

"I want to get the diamond appraised," I said. "In my mind, it represents the last question mark in terms of his credibility."

"That makes sense," Tommy said. He poured us fresh glasses of wine. "Let's project into the future. Let's assume this guy Delgado checks out—then what? You can't take these people lightly."

"Which is why we have to maintain secrecy," I replied. "We can't afford any mistakes, or else they'll probably come after both Luis and me. I plan to start out with their financial information, through public-records searches. None of that can be traced. Then I'll go on from there."

I could tell I sounded hopelessly naive. Tommy swirled the wine in his glass and stared at me.

"I guess there's no pressure on you at all," he said sarcastically. "What can happen? If you screw up, you get the pants sued off you. No more custom Chanel bags made to fit your Beretta. And your client, what's he got to lose? Breathing?"

At the mention of my leather bag, I protectively reached for it on the chair next to me. I had ordered it made after its predecessor met with an unfortunate fate.

Tommy was still chuckling at his own joke. "Just make sure you do your homework," he added. "Don't get taken for a ride by this guy. It sounds like he's done a snow job on you."

He pushed his tortoiseshell glasses high on his nose and shook his head. "Dessert?" he asked.

"Why not?" His realism was making me depressed. "Anything chocolate. Pimple food—and lots of it."

"Why are you so intent on this case, anyway?" Tommy asked. He looked at me suspiciously. "It's not like you need the work. Speaking as your lawyer, not your friend, it looks like a real loser."

"I know, Tommy, I've thought about it carefully. I really have." What was I going to tell him? That I was fascinated by the client? Tommy would have blasted me. "I simply don't appreciate the fact that so-called pillars of the community can take advantage of their position to back out on a deal. It offends my sense of decency and fair play."

"When did you turn into Mother Teresa? I thought that was Lourdes's domain." Tommy took a sip of wine. "You know the saying—follow the money. This guy's a *balsero*. He works as a mechanic. Do you honestly think justice for his family is his primary motivation?"

Dessert arrived and we silently slurped our impressively elaborate creation consisting of ice cream and chocolate sauce. Tommy knew I was bullshitting him. I was probably bullshitting myself.

"Maybe you're right," I hedged. "Maybe there are other reasons."

"Suit yourself," Tommy said, licking the spoon. "I don't have to know your reasons, I just have to bail you out if you get in trouble. But if you do take this guy, I demand you let me draw up a tight contract with him. If the whole thing blows up in your face, you need to be protected as much as you can. Solano is still a Subchapter S, isn't it? You need to limit your liability."

"Sounds great. And you can be Luis Delgado's lawyer as well, can't you?" I asked. I batted my eyelashes shamelessly. "You've already been paid, after all. I assume you're still holding that dollar."

Tommy felt his breast pocket and roared with laughter. "That's why I love you!" he said. "You're as devious as I am."

"Almost," I said. "Don't sell yourself short."

Tommy considered this for a moment; very briefly, his good

humor disappeared. "No, no," he said. "After what went on here tonight, I officially put you in the same league as me."

I stared at him, unable to tell whether he meant it as a compliment.

Six

For the trip out to Key Biscayne to see the jeweler, Luis had mercifully traded in the fecal-colored brown suit he had previously sported for khaki pants, a pink cotton polo shirt, and blindingly white canvas tennis shoes. I had cautioned him to dress casually because I wanted him to blend in with other visitors to the Key. I was pleasantly surprised to see that he had followed my instructions—even though he looked as if he had studied the Brooks Brothers' catalogue as a basis from which to take his cue. In his casual clothes he seemed younger, more carefree, even healthier. His natural elegance shone with these clothes, whereas the brown suit had made him look shabby and worn-down.

Even Leonardo seemed impressed with Luis's new look. When I came out of my office, after making a last-minute phone call, Leonardo was actually offering Luis one of his fruit shakes. Luis politely declined; he hadn't lit a cigarette in the twenty minutes he had been in my office, but apparently he hadn't transformed into a health freak either. I suppressed a smile.

When I had my purse ready, I pulled Luis aside and whispered to him, "You have the stone, right?" He wasn't wearing the brown lace-up shoes with the hollow heel.

Luis took a pack of Marlboros from his pocket and extracted a chamois bag from it. His body turned to block out Leonardo as he showed me the diamond.

I was astonished anew by the stone's beauty. Luis put it back in the pack and stuffed it into his pants pocket. That explained why he wasn't smoking: The diamond took precedence over cigarettes.

There was one last thing. I asked Luis to excuse me, then went into my office and closed the door. I stood on top of the sofa, touching the wall for balance. I took down the hanging painting—a Cuban landscape—and lay it down carefully on the couch. Before me now was my secret safe. I dialed the combination and pulled on the door, retreating a little to keep from being knocked over by the door's powerful spring. From inside I pulled out a box that held extra magazines for the Beretta, as well as the holster.

Before closing the door, I groped around until I found a second, identical box—the one that contained my back-up gun. This was Miami, after all. A second gun wasn't obsessive or paranoid. It was prudent.

After I replaced the painting and hopped down off the couch, I put the gun into my Chanel bag. The holster distorted the leather's shape, so I did without it. I took one last look around and stopped to straighten the painting—I had hung it crooked, so the palm trees looked like towers of Pisa in the countryside.

Outside I told Luis we were ready. "Leonardo, we're going to Key Biscayne," I said. "We'll be back in a couple of hours."

Leonardo pretended not to care, but I knew he was burning with curiosity. He would have been infuriated to know that I had set a deadline on our trip only because I was worried about getting caught up and spending the entire afternoon with Luis.

We walked to my Mercedes in silence. Luis escorted me to the driver's side, waited until I had deactivated the alarm, then opened the door for me. I noticed that he had lost the haunted look I had seen the first time we met. I sensed that he was a man of action—as long as something was happening, he would feel relaxed. His long period of waiting and inactivity had preyed upon him.

It was an unusually pleasant morning; for once, Miami's oppressive heat and humidity hadn't descended early. I drove west on Twenty-seventh Avenue and headed north on U.S.-1.

We drove a few miles in silence before Luis spoke. "Who are we going to see in Key Biscayne, if you don't mind my asking?"

"We're going to see a man named Tony Fuentes," I said. I understood the need to reassure Luis because of the importance of his diamond. "He's a jeweler who specializes in appraisals. And he's the best in the business."

"Very good," Luis replied with satisfaction.

I took a deep breath. "You should also know that Tony lost his professional certification about a year ago," I added, to deflect any embarrassing questions Luis might ask later.

Luis waited for more until his curiosity won out. "And why did this happen?"

I drove on to the next traffic light before answering. "He was caught dealing in stolen property. Diamonds, actually."

I turned right just past the Museum of Science, leaving U.S.-1 and heading east toward the ocean. Soon we reached the tollbooth marking the entrance to the Key. I glanced over and saw Luis staring at the life-size sculpture of a gray shark revolving on a pedestal advertising the Miami Seaquarium. One time some pranksters had strategically placed a pair of pants in the shark's mouth, suggesting that the monster had eaten a hapless tourist. As if our visitors didn't have enough to worry about.

At the booth I gave the unsmiling attendant a five-dollar bill. As I waited for change, I turned to Luis; he looked like he needed reassurance.

"It was a first offense," I said equanimously. "Tony cut a deal and got off with five hundred hours of community service. He's still the best in the business. He can give us a realistic appraisal and, if necessary, broker the sale of the diamond. And he's good at keeping a secret."

The tollbooth barrier lifted, and I stepped on the pedal, careful not to accelerate over the forty-five-mile-per-hour limit. Key Biscayne police were notorious for handing out speeding tickets. I knew this to be a fact—I had received a few myself, sometimes for going just a few miles over the limit.

As we drove on the high bridge separating the mainland from the Key, I sensed a change come over Luis. He became quieter, and his carefree air seemed to be replaced by some sort of deep sadness.

"I've been here before," he said quietly, gesturing out the window. "When I first arrived from Guantanamo, Teresa de la Torre sent me here with their housekeeper. It wasn't just so that I could enjoy the beauty of South Florida. They used the time while I was gone to search my room. I was under so much pressure then that I wasn't able to concentrate on how beautiful this place is."

My heart gave a lurch. "You never mentioned that before."

"Oh, how could I have forgotten?" Luis slapped the side of his head with an open palm. "This is something that you would want to know, am I correct?"

Seething inside, I said nothing and tried to concentrate on my driving. To either side of the causeway were pristine white beaches with pelicans swooping down low over the waves, trying to outwit the tiny minnows in the water. I tried to excuse Luis's omission by telling myself that I couldn't possibly have expected him to remember every single detail of his time spent with the de la Torres. Every client forgets certain facts or—even worse and after repeated warnings not to do so—neglects to give me information because he or she decides it won't be important. Then there is the third reason clients withhold facts: out of shame or a feeling that certain episodes might discredit them in my eyes.

I had a strong suspicion that Luis was purposefully doling out the facts to me piecemeal, as he saw fit. I didn't appreciate it. He wasn't ashamed of anything, I knew. He was manipulating the situation, controlling the flow of the case out of arrogance and planning every move in advance. He was an old-world Cuban man in more ways than one.

Luis sensed my disapproval; he looked over at me and smiled apologetically. He tapped the side of his head again and looked chagrined. I smiled back at him. He was no ordinary client, not with all he had suffered. Lies and deceit were necessary parts of life in Castro's Cuba, especially for the son of a deceased patriarch. I willed myself not to judge Luis too harshly—after all, I never had to endure what he had gone through. But I reminded myself to keep my eyes open. I wasn't sure how I was going to maintain this balance.

"They searched my room after sending me away. I suspected they would try something like that," Luis said, staring at the sea. "While I was at Guantanamo I had heard that the exiles in Miami were suspicious of the Cuban rafters. They thought Castro was sending spies, just as he had done during the Mariel boatlift. In a way I understood their fears. Maybe I wasn't even the real Luis Delgado; I could have been an impostor who had heard of the agreement between my father and Miguel. Cuba had made me accustomed to suspicion and paranoia, and I knew Miguel and Teresa would not simply welcome me with open arms. So they did a little investigation of their own.

"I'd have done the same. And that's how they discovered the diamond. I left one there on purpose—to see what they would do and how they would react if they found it after they realized that I knew about their treachery. They confronted me at dinner that evening and asked me about my intentions. After I told them that I expected the agreement between our families to be honored, they asked me to leave their home."

"Where did they find it?" I asked.

Luis kept his eyes focused on the sea. "They searched thoroughly. I had hidden it at the bottom of a shampoo bottle—it was somewhat visible, but not too conspicuous. I had almost no possessions, so searching my things was easy. The shampoo bottle was light yellow, and I knew you could see the stone if you held it up to a light."

"That's a new one on me," I said.

"I had seen the trick in a spy film. They probably did, too. I had placed small strips of dental floss in certain places in the room, so I could see if anyone had disturbed my possessions. An old strategy, but effective."

I tapped the steering wheel, trying not to ponder what other tricks Luis might be capable of to ensure his survival. "Luis, an investigation hinges on tiny details," I said. "If you remember anything else, be sure to share it with me. It only hurts your case when you hold back."

"Of course, Lupe," he said with a smile that didn't quite convince me. "I will try to be a good client."

"I'm running this investigation, not you," I added. "You came to me because I'm a professional. And professionals don't play games."

"Of course," he responded, quieter than before.

We passed the Seaquarium and approached the University of Miami Marine Lab. Windsurfers dappled the water, their vivid sails contrasting with the blue horizon; the riders perched gracefully, even acrobatically, against the seeming infinity of water and sky. On the beach, families were lounging around smoky portable barbecues or wading in waist-deep water, their dogs romping in the shallow surf.

Luis gave a low whistle of appreciation. "This is such a striking place," he said. "Those things there—what are they called?"

"Windsurfers," I answered. The tension between us had dissipated. "You should try it some time. It's fun."

"Amazing," he said. "When this is over, maybe I will. We can go out there together."

I didn't reply; I would have thought he had spent enough time on the water escaping from Cuba. His idle dream seemed so touching somehow that I didn't want to take it from him. I also knew he was trying to get back on my good side—he must have sensed he had crossed a line with me and that he would have to earn my trust anew.

On the last stretch before entering Key Biscayne, the beaches were replaced by a forest of eucalyptus trees along either side of the road, remnants of a long-vanished, undeveloped south Florida. It was only seven miles between the tollbooth in Miami to the Key, but it was a stretch that evoked a world of distance and isolation. I signaled a left off Crandon Boulevard into Key Colony—an exotic-looking, sprawling apartment complex occupying all the land between the road and the ocean.

Key Colony was impressive, even to a jaded native like myself; its towering units were fashioned into the stark forms of Aztec pyramids. Each apartment came with a balcony fecund with tumbling vines like floral waterfalls. The guard at the gate checked my name to make sure we were expected, then lifted the formidable wooden bar blocking the road.

Tony Fuentes's apartment was in the last building from the entrance, closest to the ocean. As I cruised through the Colony slowly, past the tennis courts and shade trees, we saw groups of maids and nannies with baby carriages and strollers. They chatted, relaxed and easygoing.

Luis was spellbound. "All of these women, none of them Anglos."

"No, they're all Hispanics." I slowed down to let an energetic black Labrador retriever jaunt across the road. "The easiest way for a female illegal alien to find work is as a maid or a nanny," I said. "They work for cash and usually send a lot of their income back home."

"A city of refugees and exiles," Luis mused, studying a small child bouncing a rubber ball on a concrete sidewalk. "You know why those women look so happy? Because of the children."

"But those aren't their children," I explained patiently, searching for a parking space in the packed lot.

"Of course not," Luis said. "But they remind them of their own children—and how much they look forward to seeing them again. The family, having children—that is how life gains meaning."

I was only half-listening to this family-values speech; I had finally found a parking space, squeezed in between a vintage Porsche and a beat-up Volkswagen convertible. I put on the dashboard the temporary parking permit that the security guard at the gate had issued me, and turned off the engine. My ears rang with the sudden silence.

"You don't have any children, do you?" Luis asked.

I reached for the door handle. "No, I don't." I got out of the car before he could say anything else. The last thing I wanted was to open myself up to a personal conversation. Maybe I didn't really want to know Luis's views on women—I suspected he was very old-fashioned, thinking that women have to become mothers to find fulfillment.

We took the elevator to the top floor in silence. I stared straight ahead, trying to get my thoughts together for meeting Tony.

A few seconds after I rang the bell, a beautiful young woman opened the door. When I walked past her I realized that she was *really* young; I wondered if Tony was aware that there were laws against that sort of thing. She was a Latin Lolita, braless in a revealing sundress, all slim legs and suntanned shoulders.

"Lupe, *mi amor!*"

Tony Fuentes burst into the room, his arms outstretched with outrageous theatricality. Luis took a step back as Tony crushed me with a bear hug, giving me sloppy kisses on my cheeks and forehead.

"*Querida,* it's been too long! And you, you're even more beautiful than I remember!" He smiled at Luis and received a stony stare in return.

Luis had probably been expecting a conservative jeweler-type, which Tony certainly wasn't. He was short and fat, with a cherubic face and curly black hair. He wore three diamond studs piercing each ear to complement the pavé diamond-and-gold choker around his neck, the latter sporting a gold likeness of the Cuban Virgin.

All that was the conservative stuff, relatively speaking. Shiny gold bracelets, with audacious diamonds and precious stones, hung from Tony's beefy wrists. As for his clothes, Tony had confided to me in an unguarded moment, years before, that his mother had once told him he would look slimmer if he wore matching shirts and trousers. Subsequently, he had adapted the monochromatic look as his fashion rule. Today he wore form-fitting cream trousers and a matching silk shirt unbuttoned to the waist, enabling anyone interested to count the rolls of fat between his chin and belly. Inside all that flesh he was still a little boy, clinging to his mother's advice. She should have added that he should stick to dark colors. Foncé hides a multitude of shortcomings.

Tony's hug was entering an asphyxiating phase when Luis cleared his throat behind us. Tony released me and fixed his gaze on Luis. I knew Tony wouldn't like him; he felt threatened by thin men. Tony remembered his manners, though, even if he greeted Luis with far less enthusiasm than he had me.

"Tony Fuentes," he said, extending his hand. "You must be Luis. Please, be welcome. Here, let me get you something to drink."

Tony stepped toward the enormous white leather sofa that ran along one entire wall, and snapped his fingers at the young girl. She stared at him as though he were crazy.

With a shrug, Tony walked over to the bar and started fixing Cuba Libres—Coke with Bacardi. After handing us the drinks, he led us into his study. Before he closed the door behind us, I saw him shoot a look of embarrassment and entreaty at the girl, a look that said too much. I shuddered to imagine what went on in Tony's private life.

The living room had been sunny and open, but in the study the windows were covered with heavy wine-colored drapes. Only a single lamp afforded light, creating shadows about the dark reds and mahogany of Tony's private sanctum.

He took a seat behind his desk, producing coasters from a drawer for our untouched drinks. A sort of metamorphosis had come over his face and movements: The jovial host had been replaced by the somber professional. He stared gravely at Luis.

"Lupe tells me you have a stone to show me," he said. "She said you want an appraisal, and perhaps a sale. Can I see it?"

I was used to Tony's business demeanor, but I could see that Luis felt off-balance. He slowly reached into his pocket for the pack of Marlboros, then reverently unwrapped the chamois cloth.

Tony grasped the diamond with a steel instrument, examined it, then put it down on his desk blotter. From a set of drawers set flush into the study wall, he took out a velvet bag containing an eyepiece, which he screwed into his eyesocket. He switched on a more powerful light and murmured with appreciation at the stone.

"Very nice," he purred. "Let's see what it weighs."

Out came an old-fashioned jeweler's scale. With a delicate touch that belied his sausagelike fingers, Tony gently placed the diamond on the scale's steel tray.

"Almost six carats, just a tad short," he said. "We'll call it six and not quibble about it. What a remarkable stone. Definitely D flawless. It's nearly perfect, Luis, with good color. It'll bring top dollar."

Luis edged back a step from the desk. Tony had started to wheeze, which I knew meant he was excited. "You want to know what it's worth?" Tony asked, pulling a calculator from his shirt pocket. "Six carats at twenty thousand dollars a carat for a stone in such good condition. Right now, the wholesale price for a diamond such as this would be between fifteen thousand and sixteen thousand dollars per carat. The price per carat increases with the weight, so a round stone like this would bring around twenty thousand dollars per carat. So, that comes to a hundred twenty thousand dollars. That's a number I'll stand behind."

I took a deep breath and pondered whether to drink the Cuba Libre. Luis nodded, looking as though he were hypnotized.

"Unfortunately," Tony began, some of his glee worn off, "That's nowhere near what you'll get for it. Lupe told me you want this done quietly. Is that still the case?"

"Yes," Luis whispered. He continued to stare at the diamond.

"Well, you're going to take a real beating for that," Tony said. "If I went to Cartier's with this stone, questions would be asked."

"The diamond isn't stolen," Luis said.

"Fine, fine. Whatever." Tony waved his hand. "Lupe brought you here, and I trust her. But you have to understand what happens when you try to sell a precious stone. The buyer has to fill out papers for the government. They want social security numbers, fingerprints, taxes. We want to avoid all that, if I'm not mistaken."

Luis listened like a schoolboy. "That's right," he said.

"So we sell it on the street, where they ask no questions." Tony sighed, as though saddened by the injustice of the world. "But the street is a place where buyers expect discounts. That's simply how it is."

"My God," I said. "I had no idea it was so valuable." I felt slightly shaken to be in the same room with something so precious.

"It's obviously been well cared for," Tony said laconically. "You're sure it's not stolen," he said to Luis, more a statement than a question. "Not that I care so much, but it affects my sales strategy."

"You have my word," Luis said sharply.

A smile played at the corners of Tony's mouth. "That's good," he said. "I can get more money for it that way. I'll put out some feelers, with no commitment to sell. Any figure I give you is minus my fifteen-percent commission."

"What do you think it will bring?" I asked. I hadn't been sure Luis wanted to sell the diamond, but he hadn't stepped in.

"I'd guess between eighty thousand and a hundred thousand, taking into account that it's a fast sale without documentation. Let's average it out and call it ninety thousand minus my fifteen-percent commission. That would net you seventy-six thousand, five hundred dollars—probably less," Tony said.

"If it's all right with Luis, we'll leave the diamond with you." I said. Luis gestured his assent. "Give me a call when you have some idea of a definite price."

"I'll start working it this afternoon." Tony looked at Luis and pounded on his bearish chest. "Never fear, Tony Fuentes is here."

I was still in shock from learning that Tony thought of himself as a superhero when he crouched down in front of his filing cabinet and pressed a recessed button on one of its side panels. An entire book-filled shelf swung out from the wall, revealing a small cast-iron shelf with a combination lock. With a flourish, Tony opened the safe and put the diamond inside.

Tony locked up and turned to us. "You see how much I trust you both," he said. "I have let you see my greatest secret—my baby safe."

He put his beefy arms around Luis and me, surrounding us with his fireplug body as he led us out to the front door. Lolita was still in the living room, now wearing a flashy diamond choker. She stared ahead blankly as she closed the door behind us; we heard the clattering of several locks clicking into place.

"I'm glad he uses such good security," Luis said numbly as we stepped out of the elevator.

Glancing up at Tony's apartment, I spotted the young girl watching us through parted curtains. "Tony may not have the most admirable lifestyle," I said, unlocking the Mercedes, "but he's an honest businessman."

Luis rubbed his eyes and groaned softly as I started the car. I could see he was feeling out of control, and who could blame him? This new life had to be radically different from anything he'd ever encountered in Cuba. As we drove back, his dark mood persisted.

"Luis, remember, you haven't promised to sell the diamond," I reminded him. "And if you do decide to sell it, remember that your mother wanted you to have it. I know it's your last link to your family, but they saved it so that you'd have something to fall back on."

Luis reclined in his seat, closed his eyes, and allowed the sun to caress his face. I glanced over at him and let my eyes linger on his chiseled nose and high, dignified forehead. Keep your eyes on the road, I reminded myself.

"I was just thinking about all you've done for me," Luis said. "And I wondered how I could possibly repay you."

With this, Luis turned and stared into my eyes. His look sent a cascade of gooseflesh down my spine. I hoped he didn't notice that I shuddered, just for an instant.

Ay, Dios.

Seven

After Luis had left my office, I remained at my desk for a while. I returned the Beretta to the safe, superstitiously patting it farewell. I'd had to use it only once in all the years I'd been working as a P.I. Lethal weapons weren't my favorite possessions, but this one had saved my life.

I made sure the royal-palm painting over the sofa was hanging straight—I knew it would drive me crazy every time I sat at my desk unless it was perfect—then lay back with a yellow legal pad in my lap. I wrote my notes in a flurry: the entire story, from Luis's demeanor during our initial interview, all the way to the trip to Tony's apartment. It sat there so stark and cold on the page; none of it explained why I was certain that I would see the case through to the end.

I had always had a strong sense of self-preservation, though, and now I realized it was time to start counting on it. Maybe it had been procrastination, but I still hadn't officially committed to taking the case. Never mind that I had, for all practical purposes, been working on it for several days now. I still had enough leeway to explore the case without digging a hole I couldn't climb out of.

I wondered if, on some level, my ego was driving me to try to become a David to the de la Torres' Goliath. I remembered seeing them once when I was a young girl, at a charity function my mother had been involved with. The room had been packed, but when the de la Torres entered, the crowd had parted like the masses making way for royalty. The picture that Luis painted of their true natures seemed almost unbelievable—but I had learned long ago not to trust appearances.

Of everything that Luis had told me, perhaps only the de la Torres themselves could confirm or deny his story. Asking them for help was obviously out of the question, so this left one other participant: Pepe Salazar. I opened up my address book and dialed the first of four numbers listed for perhaps the only person who could help me on short notice. I needed to find Sweet Suzanne.

It was never easy to find her—it seemed as though the four numbers I kept for her merely scratched the surface of her maze of voice mail and answering services. I left a message with her, though, and she called back within the hour. We agreed to meet at six, at one of the outdoor tables at Monty Trainer's in Coconut Grove. This was standard protocol—we often went there together after our aerobics class at the Superdance studio. We had met there after we noticed that we were the only two women there who weren't jiggling half-naked for the benefit of the oversexed male teacher. In addition, we suspected that we were the only women there who still had all our original body parts.

When I reached the restaurant I saw Suzanne waving to me from a far table, and I felt the gaze of every man in the place as I walked across the patio. It was flattering to think they were staring at me on my own merits, but part of it was because I was joining Suzanne. She was tall, statuesque, with a Botticelli face and very blond hair. In Miami, she had absolutely no trouble attracting attention.

Suzanne had grown up in Minneapolis, surrounded, I assumed, by tall, blue-eyed people—until a Cuban family moved in at the end of the block during the late '60s. They were refugees from the Castro regime who had moved to Minnesota as a part of a Catholic Church relocation program. The two parents, four children, two grandmothers, a cousin, and a puppy had left the tropics for the frozen north. Suzanne had been assigned to help the family's youngest son during elementary-school orientation, and she soon became a good friend of the lively Perez family. It had been the first time she had experienced openness and warmth in a family setting, a contrast to her caring-but-repressed Nordic parents.

In college, Suzanne majored in Spanish Studies—and had her first affair with a Latin man, a professor who convinced Suzanne that he was trapped in a sexless marriage that had mysteriously produced seven children. And the wife wasn't even Catholic. Two years later, Suzanne had a community-college degree and few opportunities. It was then that Miami beckoned.

Her parents had been aghast; they considered Miami one small step up from Gomorrah. Her amorous professor had come through with some job contacts, but Suzanne wasn't suited for the nine-to-five life. On the way out the door from her third job in as many weeks, the owner of the company suggested that she was wasting her looks. He offered to set her up with an apartment—and within six months she was one of the most sought-after call girls in Miami.

She was thirty-one but looked barely out of her teens. She shied away from the sun—it was bad business to turn dark and lose her distinctive market niche—so her skin stayed porcelain and perfect, her hair wavy and platinum. She had always thought about getting a tattoo, so in a moment of craziness she had a Cuban flag permanently painted on her right buttock. The next morning she had been devastated at her rashness, but soon she discovered a side effect of countless hours spent on the StairMaster: She was able to contract her muscles and make the flag wave. She worked on it until she was able to make it wave in two different directions. It was just like Suzanne to make an advantage out of a mistake. Her Cuban clients loved it; for the others, especially Colombians, she covered it with stage makeup. She had learned long before that there was no love lost between Cubans and other Hispanics.

"You're looking good," I said as we exchanged a hug.

"So are you, sweetheart," Suzanne said. "Have a seat and let's get down to business."

Suzanne and I were close friends, although we didn't get together as often as we'd have liked. In addition to sharing gossip and chitchat, we also met to exchange information—facts were money in both our professions. I ordered a wine spritzer and gave Suzanne a drastically abridged account of Luis's story, mentioning no names except for one.

"Pepe Salazar!" Suzanne blurted. She recovered herself and leaned toward me, talking close to my ear so I could hear her over the band playing Bob Marley cover songs across the patio.

"Sure I know him, Lupe," Suzanne said. "He's a son-of-a-bitch. He likes it rough—real rough. I had to cover up the bruises for a week. If he didn't pay so well—double my usual fee—I wouldn't have anything to do with him."

I winced. She could have been talking about a stubbed toe or a chipped nail. Sometimes I wondered about Suzanne—surely her business was doing well enough for her to pass up even a client who paid double.

"I don't need to know his sexual preferences," I said. "What else do you know about him—for instance, what does he do for a living?"

"I think he does hits." Suzanne took a sip of her planter's punch. "But I'm pretty sure he's an independent, not with the mob or anything. As far as I know, he's not into drugs. He's just an enforcer."

It was chilling to think about this professional killer-for-hire going after Luis, who had just arrived in Miami and was suffering from extreme culture shock. But before I started feeling sorry for Luis, I reminded myself about out interview in my office. Though he hadn't gone into detail, it was clear that he had handled Salazar with dispatch. From what I was hearing, Pepe was one of the real scary types roaming around Miami. It wasn't comforting to think about Suzanne being with him.

"What's the matter, sweetie?" Suzanne studied me for a moment, then lit up a slim cigarette. Any man there would have felt lucky to breathe her secondhand smoke. "You're working a case connected to Pepe, aren't you? Please, Lupe, be careful. That guy is bad news."

I wanted to know more, but I didn't want Suzanne involved. "Do you think you might ever run into him again?" I asked delicately.

"I don't know. I heard he left town." Suzanne blew a single perfect smoke ring. "After the last time, I don't care if I ever see him again. I've decided I don't need to do rough trade to make money."

I changed the subject; we talked about frivolous subjects for a while—mostly clothes, movies, and restaurants. I paid the bill, since it was my turn.

As I left, I turned to watch Suzanne making a call on her cell phone. She was strong and she was beautiful—but she wasn't as invulnerable as she thought. No one was. I hoped she kept to her resolution about Salazar, and I promised myself to remember her in my prayers, whether she wanted me to or not.

Eight

That afternoon, Lourdes, Fatima, the twins, and I were lying on the couches in the den of the Cocoplum house, watching Martina Hingis ready herself to serve the second-set tiebreaker in her French Open match against some young upstart from Switzerland. Papi came into the room with a grim expression and placed himself in front of the TV.

"Have you heard the news?" he asked us, blocking most of the wide-screen picture.

All five of us shifted around in all directions, trying to see the tennis match. Papi just stood there, not moving, waiting for a reaction.

"What news?" I finally said.

"My friend, Hector Ramos, he died this morning." Papi rubbed his eyes. "Are you sure it wasn't on the news?"

I didn't have the heart to inform him that it was highly unlikely that ESPN would interrupt its ladies' French Open coverage to announce the death of a septuagenarian Cuban exile. Papi's face registered his shock; I recalled that Hector had been very important to him.

Lourdes sighed and reached for the remote control. Martina would have to wait—there was no point in trying to watch the match with Papi so distraught. Anyway, we all knew the match would be replayed at midnight.

"You told us so many times how much we owe Hector," Lourdes said to Papi in a kind voice. "He was the man who helped you, Mami, and Fatima escape Cuba, wasn't he?"

Papi sniffed. "If it wasn't for Hector, we might all be living under Fidel's communism."

When I was a girl, Papi had often mentioned Hector's bravery in the fight against Castro, from Hector's counter-revolutionary actions in Cuba to his postexile leadership in the disastrous Bay of Pigs invasion to his volunteering to fly—at age seventy—as a spotter for *Hermanos al Rescate* (Brothers to the Rescue), the pilots who risked their lives searching for rafters in the Florida Straits and the group that had rescued Luis. Hector had spent nearly his entire adult life fighting against Castro.

"Papi, please, sit down." Lourdes patted the empty seat next to her. "Tell us what happened."

Papi moved with slow, hesitant steps, then lowered his body laboriously. I exchanged looks of alarm with my sisters; Papi was so grief-stricken that he was moving like a zombie.

Aida appeared in the doorway with a silver tray, on which were several bottles of Coca-Cola, a bucket of ice, glasses, and a small dish with slices of lime. She knew about Hector and seemed worried about Papi—Coke was served in our home only as treatment for sickness. As is true of most Cubans, Mami had believed the drink had medicinal properties—it was called "Cuban penicillin."

Aida set the tray down on the coffee table and poured a glass for Papi. After she handed it over, she stood watching, not moving until she had seen him take a few healthy swallows.

"I got a call from Paula," Papi said sadly. "Apparently it was a heart attack. He just fell over while he was reading the newspaper. Poof! Just like that."

"At least it was fast, Papi, and he didn't suffer." Lourdes always knows what to say in moments of crisis. I didn't remember her being so sympathetic to others' feelings when we were little girls—as a matter of fact, she had been quite mean to her little sister, namely me. Perhaps it was a trait she acquired when she took her vows.

"Such a patriot!" Papi whispered between swigs of Coke. "Such a loss to the exile community. He will be missed."

Satisfied that her patient was no longer in danger of collapse, Aida retreated to the kitchen. The twins leapt from the sofa and started pouring Cokes, and after a dirty look from Fatima, they offered glasses to their aunts before downing their own. Lourdes and I declined. Papi missed all this intrigue, engrossed in thoughts of his old friend.

"What are the arrangements, Papi?" I asked. "Did Paula tell you?"

"Huh?" Papi tried to focus on what I had just said. "Oh, the arrangements. Yes, Paula said the viewing is starting tonight at eight at Caballero's on Douglas Avenue. Mass is tomorrow at St. Raymond's, then burial at Woodlawn."

Paula, Hector's wife, had planned a carbon copy of most upperclass Cuban-exile funerals, including Mami's. I dreaded it already. There was no question that we would accompany Papi. Fatima, Lourdes, and I glanced at one another. So much for the midnight replay of the French Open. We would have to remember to tape it. I didn't mind so much, because I knew our family owed a debt to Hector. I also knew Papi needed our support; at his age, it was difficult to see one friend after another passing away.

"Papi, Caballero's is going to be a madhouse," Fatima fretted. Leave it to her to point out the obvious. "It's going to be impossible to find a parking space. What time do you want to go? Early or late?"

"It doesn't matter. Of course the place is going to be packed," Papi replied impatiently. "The man was a hero."

"We'll have dinner here, and then we'll go," Lourdes said with authority. "I'll go tell Aida our plans."

With that, she left the room. Contemplating the scene of the memorial, I suddenly had an idea. "Papi, I understand what kind of hero Hector was—I mean is," I quickly corrected myself. "What kind of people will be there to show respect?"

"All kinds, Lupe, from the lowest to the highest. He was known to all." Papi drained the last of his Coke. "*Niñas,* I'd better shower and put on a dark suit for tonight." He looked at us—Fatima in a shapeless housedress, me in cutoffs and a T-shirt. "I suggest you do the same."

Shrugging, Fatima rose from the couch. "What are you going to wear, Lupe?"

"Let's see." I waited until Papi had left the room. "My tight red tube dress, black fishnet stockings, my fuck-me pumps." I couldn't resist. "You know, standard funeral wear."

Fatima frowned in disgust. I didn't really blame her. Sometimes I'm out of line, but teasing her is just too much fun. I always thought that Fatima should have been the nun instead of Lourdes—she wouldn't have necessarily been a better one, but she surely would have better fit the stereotype.

Dinner was rushed that night, with little conversation. Aida had put special effort into making *palomilla* and *arroz con fríjoles*— Cuban flank steak with black beans and rice—but Papi barely ate, a rarity for him. I knew that Aida had prepared such a traditional meal in honor of Hector, and I did the deceased Hector justice by putting away two helpings.

While I ate I contemplated the odds that Miguel and Teresa de la Torre might be at the service that night. From the sound of it, a wide spectrum of the exile population would be present. I hoped to have the chance to see them close-up, although I also felt anxious. I hoped it would be the perfect setting—crowded, so I could observe them without being noticed.

After dinner was finished and we all had thanked Aida, we piled into Papi's Mercedes, which Osvaldo had brought around from the garage. I thought somehow that we looked as though we were setting out on a sea voyage, with Papi in his black suit, Lourdes in her midnight habit, Fatima in her indigo shirtwaist—a nun wannabe— and me in the dark-teal two-piece linen Armani I wore on solemn occasions.

On the way, Papi told us how he had met Hector. He had

told us the story before, but he obviously wanted to talk about his friend.

"It was in Havana, in 1959," Papi recollected, driving slowly. "Hector was a tenth-grade teacher in a poor school, and he came to me to ask for funds for his organization. It was a group that helped young men—students at his school—who were in danger of being taken from their families and drafted into the Cuban armed forces. Hector used the money he collected for bribing officials at foreign consulates, and he used foreign visas to buy documents that allowed the boys to leave Cuba. Hector must have gotten my name from a list of donors to his school. Your mami had helped support the school for years."

My sisters and I listened in respectful silence. Papi kept his eyes on the road, his voice calm.

"I was very impressed with Hector," Papi continued, "and I gave him several thousand pesos. Little did I know that I would need his services in six months. One of my employees at the construction firm had a son who worked at the Ministry of Housing. This young man found out that Castro's government had its eye on our family home in Miramar, and that it was scheduled for confiscation."

"What did you do, Papi?" I asked, although we all knew the answer. He looked at me in the mirror, deciding whether to take my request seriously. We all were familiar with the story, so much so that we could prompt him when he forgot a fact. But I knew that Papi loved to tell of his escape from Cuba and that, though the story often made him sad, it also soothed him.

"Well, until then, your mami and I had hoped to survive by going unnoticed," he said. "We believed it would be a matter of time before the Americans stepped in and got rid of Fidel. But now that we were going to lose our home, we knew we had to act."

"What about bringing money out?" Fatima asked, sitting in the front seat next to Papi.

"It never occurred to us," Papi answered dismissively. "We were young and strong. We knew we could start over in Miami. Besides, if we were caught exporting funds we would have been jailed. So I contacted Hector and gave him some cash I had saved for emergencies. He got us passage to the United States via Prague, under the pretense that we were Czechs going home. After three days we reached Miami."

"Wow," I said, "Prague."

"That's right." In the mirror I saw Papi crack a small, sad smile. "I guess that makes you girls honorary Czechs."

When we neared the Caballero Funeral Home on Douglas Avenue, it became obvious that we weren't the only family planning to pay homage to Hector: The line of cars was three blocks long. All around us, cars were being parked haphazardly, taking up any open spaces on the side streets.

We were discussing our dwindling options when Lourdes remembered that four sisters of her order lived in a small house about a block away. She reached under her habit and pulled out her cellular phone, along with a black leather address book. She flipped on the dome light on the car's ceiling, looked up a number, and dialed. A couple of minutes later we were parked in a driveway right behind Caballero's—a perfect parking place supplied by the Virgin via the Sisters of the Holy Rosary.

Like many other Cuban exiles, the Caballero family operated the same sort of business that they had in Cuba: Cubans that had entrusted their loved ones to the Caballeros in Cuba did the same now in Miami. Most exile burials were routine, though some people— like Mami—refused to be buried outside their beloved homeland, preferring instead to be cremated and stored somewhere until the day they could rest in peace in Cuba. Others with the same wish but who didn't care for cremation chose to be buried temporarily in Miami with the understanding that they would be disinterred when Castro fell. Whatever the individual wanted, Caballero's would deal with it.

Papi, Fatima, Lourdes, and I pushed and shoved our way toward the entrance, through the throng of smokers outside. Papi had been right—the place was packed with mourners from all walks of life. My heart fell when I saw how many people were there. I didn't see how I would be able to observe Miguel and Teresa, or if I would even be able to tell if they were there.

Inside, hundreds of people milled about. I tried to shrug off the upsetting memories of Mami's funeral, and sensed Lourdes next to me doing the same. Papi steered us toward the room where Paula was receiving mourners. Smells mingled: perfume, hairspray, *agua de violeta* cologne, and *gomina,* the oil that Cuban men use to slick back their hair until it is gleaming and immobile. I felt like Proust with the madeleines—the odors took me back seven years, to when Mami died.

Just before joining the line to see Paula, Lourdes motioned us to an open book on the table just outside the room. I had once thought that signing a guest list at funerals was a pretty stupid custom, but when Mami died we had been too tired and distraught to know exactly who had come to pay respects until we looked at the book. I waited for Papi and my sisters to sign in, then added my name to the list. Seeing that no one was watching, I flipped the pages and scanned for Miguel and Teresa's names. Bingo. They had signed on the page before ours, which meant they were probably still here.

I rejoined Papi, Fatima, and Lourdes, and we waited as the line crawled toward the rows of chairs placed on either side of the open coffin, where the family received friends and relatives. Several dozen wreaths and baskets of flowers surrounded the casket. Many were in the colors of the Cuban flag, and one arrangement of carnations approximated the shape of the island. I was searching visually for the wreath Lourdes had ordered on behalf of our family when I saw a man grab Papi's arm, patting him kindly on the back.

The light wasn't good, and it was very crowded, but I recognized Miguel de la Torre's face bending close to Papi's. I held my breath. I had imagined that I would spot him first, that I could study him at my leisure. But instead Papi was turning around, proudly introducing his three daughters. I politely acknowledged the introduction, avoiding eye contact. A woman appeared at Miguel's side—Teresa. Introductions all around. People kept crowding our small group, pushing us close. I bumped into Teresa and apologized, turning my face away.

Mercifully, the crowd prevented meaningful conversation among us. I was able to take a half-step back and watch. Miguel was wearing a beautifully cut dark suit with a white shirt and burgundy tie—basically the same outfit as Papi. Teresa wore a stylish pearl-gray suit with a cream silk shirt underneath. Her face was smooth. It was too dim for me to see if she had gone under the knife, but it seemed that her skin was too taut and seamless for her age. Her chin-length black hair was pulled back and held in place by a velvet headband—

the same style I had seen in the society-page pictures of her. It was a style that worked for her and that she obviously felt comfortable wearing.

The de la Torres had a commanding presence. They had been ahead of us in line to greet Paula, but they graciously allowed others to cut in front of them so they could stay with Papi. I could hear only snatches of their conversation, but they were talking about Hector. Several contemporaries of Papi and Miguel's came up to them and whispered into their ears, almost conspiratorially. I couldn't hear what they were saying, but it seemed to have something to do with Hector and with Cuba.

Well, what else was new. Cuba was practically all Papi ever talked about. As we moved forward in line, I was able to see why the de la Torres were so well-regarded in Miami. Their social skills and manners were impeccable; they greeted everyone who came to them with the same affection and good grace, even those who were clearly beneath their station.

We reached the front. As soon as Paula spotted our group, she rose to her feet, kissing us all and dabbing at her eyes with a sodden handkerchief. Her grief was powerful and painful to watch. Papi's eyes glistened.

"Promise us that you will call us if you need anything," Papi said, standing next to Miguel. They each held one of her hands.

People were pressing us from behind, so we all kissed her again and moved on. All six of us—my family, plus the de la Torres—left together. It was a relief to breathe fresh air again, even if it was another hot, humid Miami night. Inside the building I had felt as though I were suffocating.

I hung back from the group, trying not to attract Miguel and Teresa's scrutiny. It worked; Miguel and Papi conferred in low voices, while Teresa walked slowly a step behind her husband.

We split up in the parking lot. I looked around for the Jaguar that Luis had told me about, but couldn't find it. Miguel, his face tight with emotion, waved good-bye instead of kissing each of us. Relieved, I moved behind Lourdes. She seemed not to notice.

No one spoke on the way home, save once, when Papi said, to himself, "What will happen to us when we have lost all our heroes?"

None of his daughters had a reply for him.

Nine

The next afternoon, Luis and I were ushered into Tommy's office, without the customary thirty-minute wait to which his clients were typically subjected. I loved Tommy, but his lack of respect for punctuality was something I could live without. And coming from a Cuban, that was truly strong criticism.

Luis was dressed in a black suit with a white shirt and a black-and-white tie decorated with indistinguishable geometric designs. He looked like an apprentice undertaker. I noticed that he was wearing the same run-down shoes he had worn the first time I met him. Today, however, there was no diamond hidden inside a hollow heel—the diamond was in Tony Fuentes's safe in Key Biscayne. I was also dressed for business, in a dark-red dress with a wide, tight brown belt. I wore my hair loose but held off my face by a pair of antique tortoiseshell combs I had inherited from my mother.

The night before I had done some serious thinking. After meeting with Sweet Suzanne and seeing the de la Torres with my own eyes, I decided that I had been stalling long enough over taking Luis's case. It was time to fish or cut bait. Luis's story had consistently checked out, and I instinctively trusted him, for all his quirks. I told myself that I could drop the case if things turned strange. Besides, Leonardo had tried to convince me that morning to take a new domestic. I was willing to try anything to avoid another descent into someone else's heartbreaking personal life—not that Luis's case might not turn out that way as well, but it would unquestionably be more interesting on all accounts.

I watched Luis out of the corner of my eye as we moved down the maze of corridors; our guide was Sonia, Tommy's twenty-something drop-dead-gorgeous secretary. It was speculated among the Miami legal community that Tommy had been sleeping with her for years, but they were mistaken. Sonia was a Cuban born-again Christian who lived with her tight-knit extended family in Hialeah. This didn't keep her from having an angel's face and the kind of body teenage boys fantasize about, though. Luis was sticking to her like a tourist to his flag-waving tour guide.

Tommy's firm occupied the top two floors of the tallest office building in downtown Miami. It was always abuzz with activity. There were only four partners in the firm, but they kept more than fifty employees busy nearly around the clock with a staggering caseload. Law students would cut off their right arms to land positions as summer interns there. My favorite aspect of the place was the carpet, the inches-thick deep-green wool—the color of money, which clients found themselves parting with as soon as they stepped through the door.

The back of Tommy's chair was turned to us when Luis and I came into his office. I had been there countless times, but I was always struck by the view: The room faced southeast, and the walls were glass, so it seemed we were floating forty-two stories above the waters of Biscayne Bay. I couldn't understand how Tommy was able to concentrate on his work.

Luis paused in the doorway, his mouth open. Tommy whirled around in his chair and flashed a smile at me. As usual, he looked like he could have been a model. In addition to his pinstriped suit and gleaming white shirt, he was wearing two gifts that I had given him: a Ferragamo wine-red silk tie with a monkey design, and Cartier gold cufflinks.

Tommy crossed the room in three strides and kissed me on the cheek. "So nice to see you, Lupe," he said. He extended his hand to Luis. "And you must be Mr. Delgado. Please, sit down. Can I offer either of you anything to drink?"

"Have the coffee, Luis," I said. "It's delicious here." That was no lie. After an hour in Tommy's office, I could have flown home unassisted from all the caffeine in my system.

Tommy asked Sonia to bring coffee for three, then graciously gestured to the seats facing his desk as he wheeled his chair around to sit with us. It was all so proper and polite, I expected the queen of England to appear with cucumber sandwiches.

"Luis, Lupe has told me about your unusual situation," Tommy said, relaxed and conversational. "She thinks it would be best if you retain counsel to represent you in this matter."

Sonia knocked softly at the door, then came in bearing a silver tray with cups of steaming coffee. I nearly swooned at the smell. Being the lady there, I handed the men their coffee—so much for women's lib.

"She and I have discussed this," Luis said. "And that is why we are here. She thinks very highly of you."

Tommy beamed. "It's mutual. Lupe's the best in the business."

Tommy tilted his head toward me, and for some reason I found myself unconsciously shifting away from him. "Luis, why don't you tell Tommy your story?" I said. "It would help him to hear it from you. He'll have questions for you when you're done."

Luis ran through his story in a poised, self-assured manner. I could see that the opulent setting of Tommy's office hadn't fazed him—what I had taken for amazement had merely been interest. The man certainly showed his background and breeding, despite his upbringing in a Communist, supposedly egalitarian society.

I could tell Tommy was concentrating intently, because his eyebrow would climb up his forehead a bit whenever the story became hard to believe. When Luis was finished, Tommy opened up a wooden box on his desk and reached for a Montecristo Number One. The embargo never much affected Tommy.

"What do you plan to do with any information you receive regarding the de la Torre family?" Tommy asked. He struck a match to the end of the cigar, and I caught a whiff of the smoke. I love cigars with the same passion that I hate cigarettes. When I was growing up, all the men in my family smoked cigars—Papi, my uncles, my grandfathers. Not even the trauma of leaving Cuba in the early sixties and coming into exile had interrupted this lifelong habit. In Cuban circles, debate rages on as to whether cigars produced now in Cuba are as good as they were in pre-Castro days, given that the best "rollers"—the men and women who hand roll them—left the island and are working in other cigar factories abroad. But the best tobacco leaf is still grown there. So, the question becomes, which is more important, the rollers or the leaf?

"It's a matter of honor that I get my family's money back," Luis said. "My father and Miguel de la Torre made a deal—and when I appeared to collect, he tried to have me killed."

He hadn't directly answered Tommy's question. From the expression on Tommy's face, I saw that he'd noticed the same fact.

"I've told Luis that I might not be able to obtain much information," I said. "Their public records are one thing, but their personal assets are more problematic. I can find out about real estate, cars, boats, airplanes—all of that is recorded and readily available. One obstacle, though, is that they might protect their assets under corporations. If that's the case, then discretion becomes essential."

"I want you to go ahead anyway," Luis said.

Tommy frowned. "If we file a lawsuit—and I'm not saying I think we should—then we could get information through legal discovery."

"No, I don't want a lawsuit," Luis said. He slapped his thigh with sudden agitation. "I want them to think I'm still dead. A lawsuit would expose me to them."

"Well, it's going to be very difficult for Lupe to begin an investigation in total secrecy," Tommy said. "It's going to tie her hands a great deal."

"It can't be helped," Luis said with a shrug. "Anyway, I have faith in Lupe."

Tommy puffed away on his Montecristo, his eyes narrowing. "So, do you want me to represent you?" he asked.

"Certainly. I like you," Luis said. "You seem to be the kind of person who understands honor."

I reached for my coffee and took a sip, trying not to burst out laughing. I had heard Tommy called plenty of things—but honorable had never been among them.

"Thank you," Tommy said, turning red. "Now, since you've officially retained me, any information Lupe discovers will be confidential. It'll be protected under attorney work product."

"We've already evaluated the diamond for a possible sale," I said to Tommy. "I'm expecting a call in the next day or so regarding a price. Luis plans to use the money to finance investigative and legal fees."

Tommy nodded soberly. We both knew this investigation would be expensive and that the de la Torres had practically inexhaustible funds.

"I will spend whatever I have to, as long as justice and honor are restored to my family," Luis said. "I will not stop until I have achieved my goal. I know you will be fair with your fees."

Tommy, the quintessential WASP, seemed embarrassed by Luis's display, not to mention his accepting the case's costs without hearing any details. "It's all settled then," he said. "I can see this means a lot to you. We'll do what we can."

When Tommy extended his hand, Luis stood up from the chair so quickly that it seemed as though he had springs in his knees. After they shook, Tommy gave me a chaste kiss on the cheek. I smelled his neck, his natural scent combined with cigar smoke.

Tommy mouthed the word "Dinner?" as Luis turned his back. I nodded my agreement. As we left, I couldn't help but notice that Tommy gave Luis an odd look, which I interpreted as a mix of regret and trepidation. I sensed that Tommy thought he shouldn't have agreed to take the case but that he also believed it was too late. I could have been wrong, but in my years of working with him I had learned to guess what was on his mind. And I understood that he was less than fully convinced by his new client.

I pulled out of Tommy's parking garage to head back to my office, where Luis had met me that morning. Luis leaned back in the passenger seat, his eyes obscured by a pair of cheap, oversized plastic wraparounds with mirrored lenses.

"Where'd you get those?" I asked, motioning toward the sunglasses.

"A street vendor in South Beach," Luis replied. "Do you like them?"

No surprise there. "I've seen nicer-looking ones," I said, stopping for a red light. I'm usually more diplomatic to my clients, but his sunglasses were truly frightful. "While we're on the road, Luis, I want you to tell me more about your life in Cuba."

"My life in Cuba," he repeated. "Will it help you with the case?"

"Yes, and it'll also help me understand you a bit better."

Traffic lurched forward, and I kept my eyes on the road. In my peripheral vision I saw Luis looking at me.

"I was the son of enemies of the revolution," he began. "I was branded a pariah almost from birth. When she was alive, my mother tried to shield me as much as possible while instilling in me a sense of where I came from, of our family's background. We kept to ourselves, remained quiet. We avoided trouble, because we knew the regime would imprison us if we stepped out of line. Our situation was tenuous; it could have changed at any time."

"I understand," I said, signaling a left, trying to keep Luis talking.

"Since I was not a member of the Communist Party, I wasn't even considered for a university," Luis said, his voice flat and cold. "A good career was reserved for supporters of the revolution—one more incentive by Castro to make sure the population stayed loyal to him. My mother and I were also denied ration cards, so we had to resort to the black market for food and provisions."

"How did you get by?" I asked.

"Barter. Cuba's underground economy is strong. I traded my services as an auto mechanic. My mother took in sewing—all the nuns in Cuba used to teach the little girls how to sew as part of their education. Clothes started to become scarce under Castro, so Mother's abilities came in handy."

The afternoon traffic had thickened. I glanced at Luis, but his gaze was focused straight ahead, out the windshield. He spoke slowly and clearly, as though making sure I understood.

"We lived in two rooms in an old house that had been converted into apartments," he said.

"In what part of Havana?"

"The Vedado district," Luis answered. "The house was crowded but bearable. Some of the neighbors kept livestock in their apartments. The family who shared the third floor raised pigs for sale—and so the place turned into a disgusting pigsty for about two years. The worst part came when the sow gave birth to piglets, which were kept inside until they were slaughtered or sold. My mother and I were city people, but we learned every intimate detail about pigs. It was information we weren't exactly excited to learn."

I glanced over at Luis. Beneath his hideous sunglasses his mouth was curled into a tiny smile.

"Our other neighbor was a *jinetera*—"

"An 'equestrienne,'" I translated. "A—"

"A prostitute, in Cuban slang," Luis said. "She slept with tourists, mostly. But her great occupation was getting married."

I searched my memory. "Castro's government gave something to married couples, didn't it?" I asked. "Some kind of gift?"

"The newlyweds received three cases of beer, a cake, and a bottle of rum," Luis said with a laugh. "They were meant for the wedding party, but more often than not they ended up being sold on the black market. Anyway, I became friendly with the *jinetera*—just friends, mind you, but my mother didn't like it."

"I'm sure she didn't," I said.

"Well, she was a very proper woman," Luis answered. "But at last count, my friend had been married and divorced almost three dozen times—most of them using false papers. But the reason I tell you about this woman is because my mother used to do some sewing for her. In exchange, she would give us a beer or two and a slice of cake. It's a special memory I have: my mother and I, sitting together in candlelight, eating the cake, talking about our day. It was like a ceremony for us."

As I drove I pictured Luis and Maria del Carmen, with their pauper's celebration. "Your mother sounds like a very strong woman," I said to Luis.

We lived under hardship," Luis announced, his voice hard again. "But she kept an atmosphere of culture and civility in our home. She taught me to speak English and French for the day when I would escape. She always told me she would never leave the island, but that I would one day. She made me promise to leave when I had a chance, even if that meant leaving her behind."

I pulled off the highway into the Grove, listening silently. I sympathized with Luis but I couldn't help thinking of myself—his was the kind of life I might have lived if it hadn't been for Hector Ramos.

Luis smiled, this time with more good humor. "It wasn't all bad," he said. "You should understand that. My mother and I laughed together, she told me stories. We were friends. But at the end of the day—"

Luis searched for words to finish his sentence. I hung a left; we were about a block from my office. "I understand," I told him.

He grabbed my hand on the steering wheel; I pulled hard to keep us going straight.

"At night, just before I turned off the light to go to sleep," he said, leaning toward me, "my mother used to make me promise her that I would find Miguel and Teresa de la Torre. She said all that kept her alive was to stay with me until I was grown, until I was old enough to find them and make them give our family what they had promised."

I was able to push Luis's hand away in time to turn into my office's parking lot; I had thought for an instant that Luis was going to make us crash. He sat back quickly in his seat, seeming to realize that he had momentarily lost control.

After we said good-bye and Luis drove away in a borrowed car from the dealership, I stood outside. I pictured Havana at night, hot, the streets only partly lit by the cash-strapped regime. I pictured Luis and Maria del Carmen, talking together of lost glories and future retribution. Did she know that the de la Torres, her old friends, wouldn't honor their agreement? Could she have sensed what would happen to her son when he fought back against them?

If she had, I was jealous. I couldn't even predict what was going to happen for the rest of that day, let alone what the outcome might be between Luis Delgado and Teresa and Miguel de la Torre.

Ten

"Nestor? It's Lupe." I switched hands with the receiver so I could grab the gallon-sized mango-guava–passion fruit concoction Leonardo had made for me. When I arrived in the office late that morning, he had said I looked like I needed a lift. It had been a late night with Tommy.

"*Mierda,* Lupe," Nestor groaned. "I just got to sleep after a three-day surveillance. What do you want?"

It must have been a hell of a three days. Nestor Gomez was my favorite contract investigator, and he was usually sweet-natured, despite his chronic sleep deprivation.

"I have a job for you," I said. "That is, if you're not too tired."

"A job?" Alertness popped into Nestor's voice. "What kind of job?"

"Background checks, surveillance. The usual."

"Yeah, sure, great, thanks," Nestor said. "When do I start?"

"Now." I hung up and started writing down information for him. Nestor never turned down a job—he was gradually and methodically bringing his siblings from the Dominican Republic to Miami. At last count he had relocated nine, with three more to go. I secretly hoped he would then start with his cousins. He was a crack investigator—smart, hard-working, resourceful, and dependable.

I pushed the fifth button on my speed dial and listened to the phone ring. It was answered just as the machine was coming on.

"Marisol?" I asked. "Are you busy?"

"Oh, hello, Lupe," Marisol said, sounding weary. "I'm just writing up a case from a month ago. I'm so behind, it's terrible."

Marisol Velez also was one of the best; her specialty was photography and video. Born in Valencia, Venezuela, she had married a Venezuelan diplomat while still a teenager. After three years of marriage, her husband had been posted to Miami as a commercial attaché at the consulate. A year later he was called back home—and he returned without Marisol. There had been no contest between Valencia and Miami.

She had taken photography courses during her marriage, which enabled her to start supporting herself as a freelance photographer. I had met her at an insurance appraiser's office after she had taken pictures for an arson case I had been working—which wasn't unusual, since individuals with special skills were often brought into cases. I encouraged her to apply for an investigator's license, which she did, thanking me ever since for the advice. She was smart and savvy. Her brains combined with her looks—tall, bottle-blonde (in Miami, beauty is rarely natural), blue-eyed, with long legs and a sexy body—catapulted her to the top of our profession.

"I have a case I want you to work," I said to her. "What's your schedule like for the next couple of weeks?"

"I have some more reports to finish, then a domestic that'll take a couple of days," she said. "After that I'm yours. A couple of weeks sounds great. I need the money—I've got my eye on a baby-blue BMW convertible."

No shocker, that. Marisol used a nondescript blue Buick for her work, but she was flamboyantly passionate about cars. She changed them as often as she switched boyfriends—in other words, frequently.

"Call me the second you're free," I said. "I just called Nestor—he's working the case, too."

"Oh, good, I love that guy!" Marisol said brightly. "If he ever got some sleep he might be good-looking."

"I never thought about it, but you're probably right."

"Maybe I'll give him a jar of concealer for his eyes," she added. "And if I ever have liposuction, he could use my fat to plump up his frown lines."

"You're a maniac," I said. "Call me if you can start any earlier."

The phone rang about five seconds after I had hung up.

"Lupe, it's me. Do you recognize my voice?" It was Tony Fuentes, completely paranoid as usual. From the static hiss on the line I knew he was calling from a pay phone somewhere.

He took my silence as an affirmative. "Listen," he said, "I have some news about that item you wanted me to check out."

"Good news?"

"I have a buyer and a favorable price," he replied. "I think you'll be pleased."

I could understand Tony's caution; he was petrified that he might break the terms of his parole and receive another thousand hours of community service. I suspected Tony would have preferred hours inside prison than life on the outside involving community service—the concept of helping others without the prospect of personal gain was foreign to him. He had spent some time in jail once on lesser charges, and had confessed that it wasn't all bad—it had required him to stick to his diet and he had lost eight pounds.

"I'll need more details," I told him. "Where can I reach you in a couple of hours?"

"Don't call me—I'll reach you. It's for the best." He hung up abruptly. Calls from Tony seldom lasted longer than a few minutes. He was convinced short calls were impossible to trace, which was absolutely wrong. Anything could be traced with the proper equipment, no matter what they show on television.

I looked up Luis's work number at Miami Mercedes and requested the service department. I could hear him being paged over the intercom system.

"Luis, it's Lupe," I said when he picked up. "Sorry to bother you at work, but I just heard from Tony Fuentes. He says he has a buyer on the phone, and it's a good price."

"Lupe, please don't apologize for interrupting me," Luis said. His soft voice was as courtly as ever; in the background, I could hear the clatter of machines. "It's always a pleasure to speak with you."

"All right," I said, keeping my voice neutral.

"Thank you again for your help," he added. "Tell Tony Fuentes to sell the diamond."

I swallowed hard. "Don't you even want to know how much money he can get for it?"

"That's not necessary. You introduced me to him, so I know he can be trusted. I need the money for expenses and fees, and the sooner we start, the better."

I heard Luis inhale on a cigarette. Apparently he was back on the Marlboros—and disregarding the "No Smoking" signs prominently displayed in the service department of the dealership.

"I'll tell Tony to go ahead with the sale and to take his commission," I said. "I'll get in touch when he has the money for you."

"Excellent," Luis said. "At that point we will discuss your fee. I wish to give appropriate retainers to you and Mr. McDonald."

I told Luis about the two extra investigators I had hired, and he gave the go-ahead to hire as many more as I needed. After saying good-bye, we hung up.

I took another swig of Leonardo's juice and grimaced. I must have looked bad that morning, because he had made it so thick that it had the consistency of a cement milk shake. Not only that, but the drink tasted like it was strong enough to walk out of the room on its own power.

An hour later, I was writing up information for Nestor and Marisol when Tony Fuentes called back. I told him to sell the stone—in coded language, of course, for his benefit—and that I would drive to Key Biscayne to pick up the money.

I was bone tired, so I picked up the phone and dialed Nestor, telling him I wanted to go home early. He didn't mind the change in plans. Actually, he sounded relieved that our meeting was postponed. I hoped he would use the extra time to get some sleep.

Before I left, I sat alone in my office and listened to the sounds that had become so common to me—the parrots outside, the breeze blowing through the screens, the sound of metal being dropped to the floor in Leonardo's weight room.

I was in deep. I had helped broker the sale of Luis's diamond, the last remnant of his heritage—unless I could help him regain his family's honor.

Honor. I rolled the word around in my mind. I believed in it, and so did Luis, I thought. That was why I had taken the case—not because of Luis's handsome face or the cultivated manners that took me back to my lost childhood. But did the word have the same meaning for both of us?

In Miami, honor was a concept that had been virtually discarded, left by the wayside like an aging beauty no longer worthy of attention. It was an old-fashioned concept, antiquated, outdated in a city with no real past.

Honor in Miami was almost exclusively discussed by older people who recalled where they came from. My contemporaries—second-generation Cubans—rarely mentioned it. They were too busy with the present and the future to contemplate the past. The past was something that had happened to someone else—to people with gray hair who still paid with cash instead of credit and who went to Mass.

My sisters and I had been brought up differently. Mami and Papi always spoke to us of the past, of the histories of our families and of Cuba. Lourdes, Fatima, and I had heard much about betrayal and treachery—and their opposites, honor and trust.

Our prime example of betrayal was Fidel Castro's penchant for lying to the people who trusted and believed in him. Cuban prisons are filled with individuals who made that mistake.

Our example of treachery was the U.S. government's actions in the Bay of Pigs invasion of 1961. The U.S. had promised air cover to the Cuban exile force if they were to launch an invasion of Cuba aimed at toppling Castro. The exiles invaded, but the U.S. government failed to provide the critical air coverage. The exiles went to their deaths. Papi always told us that the Bay of Pigs was aptly named, because the exiles were slaughtered like pigs.

The Cuban exile invasion force, however, was a group of men of honor. They sought to free their island from Castro's dictatorship. They were willing to sacrifice their lives for Cuba. My sisters and I had been thoroughly indoctrinated with the concept of honor. It was instilled in us that an individual's greatest achievement was to be considered a person of honor.

Honor. Now was my chance to do something right, to win a fight for the underdog. I repeated the word again to myself, until I reached the point at which I believed what I was saying.

Eleven

I was the new-and-improved Lupe when I awoke the next morning. There's nothing like the rejuvenative powers of fourteen hours' sleep. I was actually waiting in the kitchen when Aida came in—she was so surprised to see someone there, she clutched her heart. As soon as she put on the coffee, she sat down next to me and said she needed to confide in me about something.

"Of course," I said. "What is it?"

"I'm worried about your father," she said in a quiet voice. "You haven't been home much, so you wouldn't notice, but he's become obsessed with going back to Cuba. He's been seeing some strange men and talking nonsense with them."

"What kind of nonsense?" I asked. "And which men?"

Aida made a mysterious hand gesture that told me nothing. "Osvaldo and I are both worried," she said. "We don't want to tell Fatima. You know how she gets."

Aida then got up and started banging some pans around. I don't know how anyone slept through it, though after a few decades we'd become immune to the racket.

"You're right not to worry Fatima," I said, thinking back to our recent poolside conversation. To say Fatima would overreact was an incredible understatement. We were still trying to live down the episode last summer, when she called 911 after her daughter Magdalena had a sneezing fit after coming out of the swimming pool.

I sidled up to Aida. "You said Papi and some men were talking. What sorts of things were they discussing?"

"They go down to the boat and study charts of the waters around Cuba," Aida said, glancing at the doorway to make sure we were alone. "And your papi has Osvaldo start the Hatteras's engines every day—he even asked Osvaldo to stock extra gasoline in the shed. Osvaldo refused, of course. It's against the law to do that."

"Papi's been talking about going to Cuba as long as I can remember," I said. "Don't worry."

I wanted to sound reassuring—I wasn't going to tell her about Mami's ashes' recent travels. Mostly, I was interested in a hit of *café con leche* before setting out for the office. It was going to be a busy day.

"I have a bad feeling about this," Aida said. "And so does Osvaldo." She continued to mutter to herself as she attacked the counter with a rag. I made a mental note to speak with Lourdes, as I always did when I needed a realistic, levelheaded opinion. I was hearing too much lately about Papi's preoccupation with Cuba. As every Cuban exile knows, it's impossible for us to think rationally about Castro and his eventual demise—but even by those standards, it sounded as though Papi was becoming extreme.

Gulping down breakfast, I skimmed the *Miami Herald*. I found a story about Miguel and Teresa de la Torre and how they had sponsored a charity function for children with AIDS. I cut out the article and accompanying photo and stuffed them into my purse.

"Your Papi is going to be angry when he sees you tore up the paper," Aida warned me. "Even if the *Herald* hates Cubans, he likes to read the whole thing—not just parts of it."

I retreated with an apology. Aida was convinced that the liberal views of our local American newspaper editors were attributable to their positions as secret pro-Castro Communist agents. Even in the face of this scandalous fact, though, she remained loyal to Papi's wishes.

Osvaldo was just finishing rinsing off my Mercedes when I stepped outside into the morning light. "You have to stop parking under that tree where you work," he scolded in his hoarse voice. "It's destroying the paint on this car. Look—just look."

He motioned me closer so I could examine some microscopic imperfection on the hood. For a man in his seventies, he was sharp and fastidious about every aspect of his life. His remonstrations about my car had become a routine for both of us. I leaned so close to the hood that my breath fogged the finish; Osvaldo intervened with a chamois cloth, wiping it clean.

"I'm sorry, Osvaldo, I promise to be more careful. And thanks for cleaning the car. It looks beautiful." And it did—the navy blue sparkled in the sun.

I had opened the door and gotten in when the old man leaned

close through the open window. "Your father, Lupe," he whispered. "Aida and I are worried. We don't like the people he's been seeing."

"I know, Aida told me," I said. "I'll see what I can do." Now I knew I had to investigate—Osvaldo was no alarmist.

"You're a detective, Lupe," he said. "Find out what he's up to. Your mami told Aida and me to look after your father. We promised your sainted mother." Osvaldo crossed himself and straightened up.

"I'll look into it," I told him. I hated it when Osvaldo and Aida played dirty, bringing my mother into the conversation. They always knew which buttons to push. But I would keep my eyes open. My father had always wanted the honor of being the first exile to enter Havana harbor after Castro's ouster, but I doubted he was crazy enough to launch the revolution on his own from Cocoplum.

It was still early, and the traffic on Main Highway was light. I reached the office in fifteen minutes, parked the Mercedes as far as I could from the frangipani tree that was maiming my car, and went inside.

Leonardo hadn't arrived yet. Since Nestor was coming soon, I finished writing up his fact sheet for Luis's case. I divided all the work into three areas of responsibility—Nestor's, Marisol's, and mine. I also put in calls to three junior investigators, setting up a round-the-clock surveillance on the de la Torres' home in Coral Gables. It was going to be expensive, but I knew I had Luis's authorization.

Leonardo finally showed up. He frowned when he saw the steaming mug of *café con leche* on my desk and left the room without a word, returning minutes later with a fresh fruit shake. I thanked him, but I thought he was definitely carrying his obsession too far. He was Cuban, after all, and no amount of nuts and berries was going to change that. If he doubted his ancestry, all he had to do was check out his rear end in a full-length mirror. We can't escape our origins, no matter how hard we try.

Leonardo was definitely fighting an uphill battle. No green vegetable ever willingly crossed a Cuban's lips. The traditional Cuban diet is based on meats and starches, and a Cuban thinks he's eating organically if the mountain of French-fried potatoes in front of him was fried in olive oil instead of pure lard. In an average Cuban restaurant, there usually is no place on the menu listing vegetables as a side dish, except for the occasional in-season avocado. Instead there is a galaxy of starch options: rice, potatoes, yams, yucca, malanga, and plantains, all soaked in *mojo,* an incredibly delicious Cuban sauce consisting of hot oil and garlic. No wonder there are so many liposuction specialists and cardiologists in Miami.

Half an hour later, Nestor poked his head in the door. He looked quite human that morning, which meant he must have caught an hour or two of sleep.

"Hola, querida." He gave me an affectionate peck on the cheek. He had definitely gotten some sleep—he had never been that warm with me before.

"Good morning, Nestor. Not you, too?" I groaned. Nestor was holding one of Leonardo's juice shakes.

"Vitamins," he said with a shrug. He stretched out on the sofa, his favorite position. He had told me once that sitting upright reminded him of his endless surveillances. "So, what's the case?"

I relayed to Nestor all the pertinent facts, noticing the glimmer of interest in his eyes when I told him Marisol was working with us. "I've divided the work," I continued. "You're responsible for tracing the origins of their money, from their arrival in 1959 to the present. I know it's going to be hard, but I have faith in you. Remember that secrecy is vital. Our client's life might depend on it."

"And maybe ours." Nestor swung his legs over the side of the sofa and stood up. He was a real professional—a few words from me, and he was on his way. He blew me a kiss, still slurping his drink.

That left Marisol, whose talents were best for following Miguel de la Torre. I wanted to know everything he did—where he went, whom he met. She could get me pictures and videos of everyone he came into contact with. I had assigned myself the most difficult task of all—trying to assess the de la Torres' current net worth.

As soon as Nestor was gone, the phone started to ring. The three junior investigators called one after the other, all asking for assignments. And they all had the same reaction when I told them their job was surveillance in Coral Gables: They cursed, colorfully.

Surveillance in Coral Gables was the worst. There were few places to conceal a car in the area's winding streets, big houses, and wide-open avenues. Hurricane Andrew had blown away most of the ancient oak trees, with their wonderfully thick branches and leaves that had blocked lines of sight. And even after a precautionary call to police to announce their presences, investigators often found themselves the focus of attention from neighbors or overeager cops. Investigators often were reduced to a "rolling surveillance"—driving around aimlessly, checking on the target when they could. Even that tactic could catch the attention of vigilant, wealthy, and paranoid residents.

I explained to the juniors that, for now, I needed only tag numbers, pictures of visitors, and the comings and goings of the residents. I assigned shifts: Joe Ryan, with his flaming red hair and freckles, took the morning shift; Lucy Mahoney, a petite laid-off special-ed teacher, wanted the night shift because her husband could watch their children when he came home from work; Mike Moore, a process server, was indifferent to the hours he worked, and so he got the afternoon slot. I wished them all luck; after all, it was Coral Gables.

When all this was sorted out, I was startled to see that it was almost noon. I knew that Tony Fuentes should be calling soon about the sale of the diamond—at least, I hoped he would. The meter was running, and I was hiring enough people to staff a hamburger stand.

The phone rang. I expected it to be Tony, but instead I heard Sweet Suzanne's cheerful greeting. I knew it was important; she never got up before the afternoon.

"What's going on?" I asked.

"Remember a couple of days ago, how you asked me about that scumbag Pepe Salazar?" Her light tone darkened. "Well, I had a date with him last night. Want to hear about it?"

"Are you kidding?" Of course she wasn't. "Listen, I'm starving. Want to have lunch?"

We agreed to meet at a Cuban place on Twenty-seventh Avenue. I raced out of the office before another call kept me chained to my desk.

Islas Canarias was a one-room cafeteria that, like so many others, served excessive amounts of delicious food at minimal prices. Credit cards were not accepted, which was rarely a problem because a meal there never cost more than walking-around money. Its specialty was *papas a la española,* a serving of delectable golden-fried "inflated" or "balloon" potatoes that were full of fat and calories.

The first thing I noticed was the bruise on Suzanne's neck; she had tried to disguise it with a lot of skillfully applied makeup, but I spotted it anyway. I allowed her to chat about the weather until she was ready to talk business.

"So, last night, Pepe Salazar left a message on my machine saying he was back in town and wanted a date," she said. "Normally I'd have said no, but I was curious because of our conversation."

I shook my head. Beneath her veneer, I knew, was still a Midwestern girl out of her league with thugs like Salazar. I had helped her once, on a time-consuming case involving an ex-boyfriend who not only had stolen money from her but had stalked her as well, but I had made it clear that she owed me nothing. The fact that she had put herself in danger on my account was enough to drive me crazy, but I also knew it fit perfectly with her character.

Suzanne gave me a withering look; she knew what I was thinking, and she didn't want to hear a lecture. "He was staying at the Hyatt downtown," she said. "I got there a little early, by coincidence."

"Coincidence?"

She winked so fast that I almost missed it. "Pepe wasn't alone. I could see right away that he had gotten his hands on some extra money, because he was renting a whole suite instead of just a room. As soon as he opened the door he pushed me into the bedroom to get me out of the way. But I saw who he was with: Ramon Hidalgo. Noted ambulance chaser."

"Ramon Hidalgo?" I was turning into a real parrot, but I couldn't help myself. Suzanne was incredible.

She scrunched her nose and smiled. "I thought something might be going on that could help you, so I opened the door a crack to listen," she said. "Anyway, Pepe is so obnoxious that he was practically screaming the whole time—and the lawyer was yelling right back at him."

"Suzanne, you have to be careful." I winced at the thought of her eavesdropping on a killer and a notorious underworld lawyer. "You could get hurt—or worse."

She shrugged, ignoring my comment. "You want to know what I heard?"

I sighed. "You know I do."

"Hidalgo bailed Pepe out of the Dade County Jail the night before. Pepe was busted for selling coke."

"That's not so implausible," I pointed out.

"I didn't think he was into drugs, but I was wrong," Suzanne said. "Pepe walked right into a sting. Five guys got busted, and Pepe was the only one who could make bond. I got the impression this wasn't the first time Hidalgo has represented him."

It made sense. Hidalgo's client list included a variety of lowlifes, but drug dealers were his specialty. Everyone in town knew it.

"Then things got really interesting," Suzanne said. "Hidalgo said that Pepe was going to do hard time because of all his priors. But Pepe shut him right up. He said he had some really hot information to bargain with."

The food arrived, and the waitress stared at Suzanne as she unloaded her tray. Not too many natural blondes came into Islas Canarias.

"What kind of information?" I asked.

"Some woman named Teresa hired Pepe to knock off this Cuban rafter a few months ago. Hidalgo got really pissed off, yelling at Pepe not to waste his time with stupid stories. But—get this—Pepe played him a tape recording."

I bumped the table with my knee; my drink nearly spilled.

"The tape was real fuzzy, but Pepe cranked it up loud," Suzanne said. "It was all there—this Teresa ordering the hit, everything. Then there was another part, with Pepe reporting back to her that he had done the job and killed the guy."

The noise of the restaurant receded. The tables and diners around me vanished. I was left with the ramifications of what I had just heard.

Suzanne studied me. "Eat your food," she said, pointing to my untouched plate. I tried to chew a bite. "You know some of this already, don't you? Is this about the case you're working on?"

"It is, yes." I put down my fork. "I knew about the hit. But I didn't know Pepe had made a tape. I'm trying to figure out what it means."

Suzanne put away a huge forkload of potatoes. I had no idea how she kept her figure. As she chewed, I noticed again the bruise on her face.

"God, Suzanne, I'm so sorry you got hurt finding all this out," I said weakly. "If I'd known you were meeting Pepe Salazar, I wouldn't have let you go. That's why you didn't tell me in advance, isn't it?"

"Maybe. Don't ask so many questions."

A burst of uproarious laughter erupted from the table next to ours, where five guys sat in jackets and ties. A few of them glanced over at us, checking to see if we had noticed them. I looked away.

"Anyway, Hidalgo told Pepe to put the tape in a safe place," Suzanne added. "He told Pepe it implicated him for murder, but then Pepe said that he never actually killed the guy. He just lied about it so he'd get paid. Does that sound true?"

"It's true," I said.

"Well, Hidalgo said that he'd better be able to deliver the guy alive and well, if he didn't want to get sent away on a murder-for-hire. Then they talked about the coke case and how they might use the tape. Hidalgo said that an Assistant State Attorney hadn't been assigned yet, but when one was, they could plan a strategy."

"Have you ever thought about being a reporter, Suzanne?"

"There's no money in it. Anyway, the point is that if an ambitious prosecutor gets assigned to Pepe's coke case, someone who really wants to make a mark, then they might be able to make a deal. Is this Teresa someone important?"

"I can't answer that."

Suzanne held up her water glass to a passing waiter for a refill. "Hidalgo told Pepe to stay out of trouble, then he whispered something and they both laughed. It probably had to do with me."

The thought chilled me, but I didn't say anything. Suzanne picked up on my mood and gave me a frosty look in return.

I think Suzanne thought that I disapproved of her life more than I actually did. She assumed that the good little Cuban girl inside me was condemning her morality. But more than anything, I was just worried about her. I cared for her deeply, and I wanted her to stay safe. She had once talked about modeling or starting an agency, and I wished she would do it. I knew, though, that she was simply making too much money in *la vida* to give it up and take on the mundane work of running a business.

"Men," Suzanne muttered bitterly. "They're so arrogant. It never occurred to them that I could understand Spanish."

"After what you heard, don't let on that you do," I warned.

"Yes, Mother."

Suzanne finished her lunch while I pushed mine around on the plate. It struck me as odd that Teresa de la Torre had personally arranged the hit. It might have meant that Miguel knew nothing about it, because no self-respecting Cuban man would let his wife negotiate with a creep like Pepe. But I reminded myself not to jump to conclusions about his sense of propriety and honor; after all, I knew how he had dealt with Luis, so traditional rules about honor didn't necessarily apply to him.

The waitress brought our check. I ordered a double Cuban coffee and drank it in one gulp. Big mistake. In addition to feeling stressed and worried, I was now also completely wired.

Suzanne watched me shiver and sweat. "I still have enough Midwestern blood in me to stay away from that stuff," she said.

I had to agree there was a certain wisdom in that. When we stood up to leave, I gave Suzanne a big hug. She felt slight and thin in my arms, and I couldn't help feeling protective.

"I did a good job, didn't I?" she asked, her hands on her hips. The lunch-time boys were getting an eyeful.

"Of course you did, and I appreciate it," I said. "Just don't put yourself in that kind of position—"

"I'd probably be a pretty good investigator, right?" she interrupted, tossing back her platinum hair with girlish satisfaction. "You go on without me, I'm going to have dessert. I'll see you in aerobics class—after this lunch, I'm going to need a double Butt Blaster."

On the way back to my office, my mind was racing faster than my car—which was saying something, because I was breaking just about every traffic law on the books.

I was trying to figure out how I could use the information Suzanne had just handed me when it occurred to me that the tapes might not even be real. Pepe could have hired a woman to read Teresa's lines. Suzanne had said the voices weren't very clear.

Pepe was surely enough of a lowlife with sharp survival skills to know the value of a tape containing the voice of a society woman ordering a hit. He would also be able to figure out, though, that Teresa would have access to the best attorneys in town. If the tape was a fake, then it was only a temporary insurance policy.

Just work the facts, I reminded myself. There was no percentage in speculation. The case would lead me to the answers.

I had to assume that Luis had told me the truth about Pepe Salazar and what had happened that night by the Miami River. I had been worried about lawsuits and damage to my business. But now Pepe was back in Miami. And he was the kind of man who would take a life as easily as he would tie his shoes.

Twelve

Tony Fuentes called as soon as I got back from lunch; he had sold the diamond, and I could pick up the cash anytime. I immediately hopped into the Mercedes and headed north for Key Biscayne. Because I was going out alone, I checked the Beretta to make sure it was loaded and working. I had decided not to bring Luis—I suspected that the transaction would make him nervous, and I didn't need any more anxiety than I already felt. On the way out of the office I asked Leonardo to call Luis and have him meet me as soon as the garage closed.

Tony's apartment was basically unchanged from a few days before, except that there was a different girl lingering about. She was younger than the other and even more spaced-out—if that were possible—and she was sporting an impressive emerald and diamond bracelet.

Tony brushed her aside after he opened the door, granting me the full effect of that day's outfit. He looked like he was heading out for the Kenyan bush as soon as we completed our business. In compliance with his mother's edict about matching shirts and pants, Tony had chosen a two-piece safari suit. It was skin-tight, of course, with a belt cinched tightly at his waist, and khaki socks peeking out from the tops of his desert boots. His interpretation of the great-white-hunter look included wraparound glasses dangling from a cord, and an orange bandanna around his neck. I looked him over, half-expecting to find a canteen, compass, and pith helmet.

Tony, of course, behaved as though nothing were out of the ordinary. He led me into his dark office and, once the door was closed and locked from the inside, ambled over to his wall safe.

"Here it is," he said, handing me a big manila envelope. "We did all right. Not fabulous, but all right. I took the liberty of collecting my commission for the transaction."

He sat down behind his desk and, with considerable effort and a lot of grunting, lifted his feet onto its polished surface.

"When you first showed me the stone I quoted you a price of approximately ninety thousand dollars," he said gravely. "Well, you have to keep in mind that was at the wholesale level. And since you wanted it sold in a hurry—"

"Tony, please, how much did you get for it?" I remained standing, feeling the wad of bills in the envelope. I didn't have the sense that he was setting me up for bad news; rather, he was merely savoring every nuance and detail of the deal.

"The best I could do was eighty thousand. Minus my fee of fifteen percent, or twelve thousand, that leaves sixty-eight thousand dollars." He shook his head with regret, sending a couple of his chins jiggling. "If the circumstances had been more favorable, then we could have done better."

"Tony, we did fine—and I know you did your best." His expression brightened. "That's why I came to you." I had hoped the diamond would have brought in more cash, but I was realistic enough to accept whatever Tony said he could come up with. Since Tony's fee was tied directly to the sale price, I knew this was truly the highest sum he could get.

"It's always a pleasure to help out a fellow Cuban," he said.

I opened up the envelope and took out the packets of cash. There were seven bundles, each containing about ten thousand dollars in hundred-dollar bills. While Tony looked on with mellow curiosity, I took my money belt from my purse and carefully arranged the cash inside. I spaced it evenly, so I wouldn't look too obvious once I tied it around my waist.

When I put it on I looked a little thick around the middle, so I rearranged it. I still looked as though I was either in the early stages of pregnancy or else dangerously constipated. I knew the belt would get hot and uncomfortable in the car, but I only had to drive to the office before I could get rid of it. It was the best measure I could take—in Miami, I knew I could get held up just for the car I drove. I owed it to Luis to make an effort to protect his money.

Tony walked me to my car, oblivious to my anxiety as he babbled about a new find in a South African mine. I reminded myself that I would be alone and exposed with the cash for only a short time. Surely I could handle it. I was just being paranoid.

Half an hour later I pulled into my space at Solano Investigations. We were in a secure part of the Grove, but I knew my chances of being robbed didn't disappear until I was inside and the cash was in the safe. Leonardo's black Jeep was parked in its usual spot, so I honked the horn, hoping he would come out and escort me into the building. I leaned on the horn as long as I dared—I didn't want to draw attention to myself. Nothing. I picked up my car phone, ready to call inside.

All of a sudden I felt very silly. There was no one around. I switched off the safety on the Beretta and got out of the car. I switched on the car alarm and started walking. I had covered about ten yards with quick steps when I head someone moving fast behind me. Before I had time to turn around, a pair of hands grabbed me firmly around my shoulders.

This is what I thought about: Someone was going to rob me of Luis's money, and I would end up paying him myself; Tony had tipped off someone about the cash, because he was the only person who knew I had it; and that I didn't have time to pull out the Beretta and, even if I did, I really wasn't in the mood to shoot anyone. I settled for whirling around and raising my hands in self-defense. I wasn't willing to die for the money, but I would fight for it. I prayed my attacker wasn't carrying a weapon or, if he was, that he didn't know how to use it.

"Lupe, it's only me! I'm sorry, did I frighten you?"

I went through about five stages of shock before I became thoroughly pissed off. "Luis!" I shouted. "Are you crazy? Why the hell did you sneak up on me like that? I could have shot you!"

Luis raised his hands in the air. "Don't shoot! Don't shoot!" He began to laugh.

I saw that he had changed from his work clothes to his cruddy brown suit. "I'm not playing around, Luis, you could have gotten hurt." I noticed that I was breathing too fast. "What were you thinking, hiding from me like that?"

"Do you really carry a gun?" he asked, seemingly amazed. "A lady shouldn't carry a weapon. It's dangerous. You could get hurt."

"Don't start with me." I turned around and started walking toward the office. I couldn't believe what a sexist, chauvinistic remark I had just heard from him. He knew what I did for a living—I sure as hell wasn't an assistant buyer at Bloomingdales. The gun wasn't a prop, it was a necessity. He caught up with me quickly.

"Don't be angry," he said dolefully. "Leonardo told me you

would be here soon, so I waited outside. When I saw you pulling into the lot, I decided to hide and give you a surprise."

"You surprised me, all right," I said. "You surprised me by being a total jackass." In spite of my annoyance, part of me wondered if Luis's actions had been calculated to see how I would react to danger. If that were the case, I didn't appreciate it.

Luis held the door open for me, and we walked inside together. Leonardo watched us from his desk with a mixture of curiosity and disapproval.

"You're right, I am a jackass," Luis said. He gestured grandly over the sloppy reception area. "I'm just so happy to have such good friends and skilled professionals helping me. Perhaps my spirits ran a little too high."

I couldn't help but laugh as I felt the adrenaline in my system begin to flag. "I'm going to try to stay mad at you for a little while," I said. "Even though it's obvious you can't help acting like a lunatic."

Leonardo wore an expression of profound unamusement; he gave a little cough and turned back to his computer keyboard. I didn't know what had gotten into him. Maybe his workout had been unsuccessful or his protein shake had curdled or something. I knew that he didn't like Luis, but there was no reason to be surly.

I ushered Luis into my office, closed the door behind us, and directed him to an empty chair facing my desk.

"Well, Luis, we're on our way," I said, turning serious. "As of this afternoon, we'll have the de la Torres' house under constant watch. In a couple more days we'll start following Miguel."

"Excellent." He brushed a stray lock of hair off his forehead. I tried not to look into his eyes. Without realizing it, I had become more informal with Luis since our near shoot-out in the parking lot. I was trying not to think about Luis as a person or, more specifically, as a man. It wasn't the time or the place.

"Tell me," he said, "about this surveillance. I'm not sure I understand. Where are the investigators going to work? How do they watch Miguel and Teresa?"

"I'm sorry, I thought I had explained this already. To put it simply, they watch the house and what goes on there from the outside. I don't know where the investigators will station themselves. It's up to each one individually to find the best place and to assess the situation as they see fit."

"Of course," Luis said. "I hope you don't think I'm asking because I question how you do your job," he added anxiously. "I've just been thinking about the investigation for so long. It makes me more comfortable to know all the details."

I stood up and untucked my blouse from my skirt; Luis's eyes widened. "I just got back from seeing Tony Fuentes," I said. "I picked up your cash from the sale of the diamond."

Luis slapped his forehead. "I'm so sorry. That's why you were nervous. Why didn't you call me? You shouldn't be carrying so much cash by yourself."

"It's really all right," I said, unsnapping the belt. I noticed that he hadn't asked how much money Tony had gotten for the stone. Luis's reaction perplexed me—in some respects he was a stickler for details; in others he seemed totally unconcerned. "To tell you the truth, it's nice to see you in such a good mood. A lot of my clients let their cases take over their lives."

"Perhaps I was so happy because I knew I was going to spend time with you." Luis smiled.

I ignored the implications of what he had just said and rubbed my eyes with the back of my hand. "Luis . . ." I began. I tossed the belt on my desk. "Do you want your money now?"

He held up his hand. "No, I want you to keep it here for me, where it'll be safe. You can take money for the case as you need it, and I'll collect the remainder when we're finished. Where I live, I could be killed for having so much cash."

Luis laughed, and his eyes narrowed. I got the sense that he was embarrassed to mention that he lived in one of the rougher parts of the city. It was as if the aristocrat inside him still couldn't accept his day-to-day reality. Or perhaps he didn't want to call attention to the differences between us. There was quite a gulf between Cocoplum and the Miami River, and not just in terms of geography.

"I think I should mention your other option," I said, taking a deep breath. "You could take the cash and move elsewhere. You have enough here to live wherever you want if you're frugal."

"Absolutely not," Luis said quickly. "That money will buy justice for me and my family."

I wondered precisely what he meant by "justice" and reminded myself about his past. "It just seemed the moment to remind you that you have choices. You don't have to start down the long and difficult road we're about to take."

"Thank you for your consideration," Luis said.

Silence hung over the room. For an unaccountable reason, I felt both pleased and disappointed. Maybe I had expected Luis to take the money and leave forever. But given what I knew about him, I understood that he wouldn't.

"I'll write you a receipt," I said. I marked down a record of Luis's cash on a piece of company stationery and held it for a moment. "I'll write down withdrawals for expenses as I make them—with your approval, of course."

"I approve of everything you do," Luis said with a thin grin, "in your handling of my case."

Ignoring his comment, I said, "You should know that Tony didn't get as much money as he thought for the diamond."

I handed him the receipt. Luis's feature stiffened, but when he noticed I was watching him he relaxed again. He rubbed his lips absently and stared at the sheet of paper.

"That is less than the price he quoted," Luis said, his eyes narrowing a bit.

"Tony did everything he could, under the circumstances," I said. I felt a flash of guilt for having suspected that Tony had betrayed me when Luis grabbed me in the parking lot.

"Of course he did," Luis replied. "He seemed like a good man."

"I know you're just being polite. Tony doesn't always make the greatest impression." Luis looked amused. "You know, Luis, I was thinking that you might want to take a small portion of this money to buy yourself a thing or two. Maybe a new suit—or shoes without holes in the heels."

Luis pressed self-consciously on the worn crease of his trousers.

"It's not that you're dressed poorly," I lied. "It's just that I think you could afford a few small items."

"Maybe you could help me select some new clothes," he said bashfully. "I must admit, I don't know of any stores in Miami that would sell a quality suit."

I didn't want to encourage Luis to start spending too much of his money, because if the case didn't work out the remainder of his cash would have to last him. Mostly, though, I didn't want to go shopping with a client. It felt as though, at every turn, Luis was trying to pull me closer into a personal relationship. Clients had tried it in the past, but I had always kept things professional. I wondered for an instant how good a job I was doing this time. So I changed the subject.

"There's something else you need to know," I said, opening my briefcase. "Pepe Salazar is back in town."

"He came back?" Luis's eyes widened; he unconsciously clenched his fists. "He might try to kill me again—if I don't find him first."

"I heard this from a reliable source," I said, ignoring his macho display, even though the same thought had occurred to me as well. "From what I've heard, he's going to be here for a while."

"*Mierda.*" Luis pawed at his jacket pocket. "Can I smoke?"

"Sure," I said. What the hell. The smoke from his prior visits had nearly cleared out. I cranked up the air conditioner fan another notch. Luis lit a Marlboro and blew out a huge cloud of smoke.

"I don't really have any advice for you, Luis," I said. "I know that Salazar is in trouble with the police and that he might use his connection to Teresa to get out of trouble. I have no idea what might happen—it's possible that you could be named as a witness if Salazar's case gets messy. In the meantime, be extra careful. I'd recommend renting a different room, making yourself harder to find."

"I know Salazar told Teresa he killed you," I said to Luis, who averted his eyes. "I think it's time you tell me everything that happened by the river that night."

"It's as I told you. He attacked me, but he was unsuccessful." Luis leaned his head back, speaking with his eyes closed.

"I know all that," I said. "What else happened?"

"I told him to leave town and that I would kill him if I ever found out he had returned to Miami." Luis took another drag on his cigarette and looked at me through squinted eyes.

"Is that what you intend to do, Luis?" I asked. "Because I have to warn you right now—"

"Of course I didn't mean it, Lupe. I had to act like an animal because I was being threatened by one."

"I've heard that kind of thinking before," I said. "If I find out—

and I will, trust me—that you're involved in any kind of violence or stupid revenge, then you're on your own."

Luis smiled and shook his head as if I were overreacting. "I've been forthright about what happened. I ordered him to lie to Teresa and leave the city. I told him that I would kill him for the sake of . . . what is the word . . . intimidation?"

"Intimidation." I stared at my pad. "How is it that you were able to fight off a hired killer like Salazar?"

"Havana is a violent place, especially where my mother and I were forced to live." He paused, watching my reaction. "So I took up boxing."

"And that defeated a gun?"

"Salazar tried to cut my throat." Luis put out his cigarette in my ornamental Jamaica ashtray—a yellow, gold, and red-striped atrocity that Lourdes had passed on to me after her convent's Jamaican gardener presented it to her for her birthday.

"It also occurred to me that Salazar might have come back to finish the job," I said. Luis was now officially on notice about Salazar.

"Yes. He's a professional, and he was paid for work he didn't complete. That sort of thing is bad for one's reputation. He might also feel the need to find me as a matter of personal pride."

I sensed the cold, analytic track of Luis's thinking; he was so detached that he could have been talking about slicing bread. It clearly demonstrated to me the aspect of his personality that had enabled him to survive, in Cuba as well as in Miami.

"If that happens," he added, "I will have to defend myself. I hope you understand that."

"Just don't go looking for him," I said.

"All right. I won't." Luis fidgeted with his jacket button. I couldn't say if he was telling me the truth.

"I know that Teresa hired Salazar, but I don't know if she was acting alone," I said. "We have no reason to think either Teresa or Miguel knows you're alive. For now we should sit tight and see what happens."

"Just as long as we don't involve the police," Luis said. "They would complicate my case too much."

Of course he was right, although I hadn't considered it. I realized I wasn't thinking clearly.

"We're hoping Salazar doesn't implicate Teresa," I thought aloud. "Because . . . because then you might never get your money."

"Exactly."

Luis left after signing a document authorizing me to use his money for the investigation. I saw him to the door, and when I walked back inside I found Leonardo fuming at his desk.

"I know, the smoke," I said, cutting him off. "Just do me a favor and make sure Nestor and Marisol are keeping time sheets. Neither one is any good at paperwork."

Leonardo opened his desk and found a can of Pine Away. "I hope you know what you're doing," he said, starting to spray. "I think that guy is bad news. If you ask me—"

"I didn't," I said. I went into my office and closed the door behind me. It was the first time I had ever dismissed Leonardo so rudely in the seven years we had worked together.

Thirteen

I circled around the Metro Justice Building parking lot for a third time, looking for a spot reasonably close to the street. The whole place had a nasty feel to it; every pedestrian looked like a just-released prisoner or someone on parole. You took your life in your hands if you went to the area after dark.

I dreaded having to come to that part of Northwest Twelfth Street, but for an investigator it was one-stop shopping. Wedged together in a three-block circle were the vital statistics building, the county jail, the courthouse (linked to the jail by an elevated walkway), and three hospitals—Jackson Memorial, the Veteran's Administration Hospital, and Cedars Medical Center. It was a chaotic mess of criminals, attorneys, and the sick.

The weather was turning lousy. Though it was early afternoon, the sky was so dark I had to switch on my headlights. Black ominous clouds threatened to open up at any moment, and I had nothing in the way of rainwear. I didn't relish the thought of conducting research in a freezing-cold building while wearing wet clothes. I finally gave up and settled for a space so far away that I might as well have been in the next county.

I sprinted across the lot and maneuvered the obstacle-course sidewalk in front of the Metro Justice Building—hot-dog carts, the accused conferring with their lawyers on the street, weeping families, cops drinking coffee and sneaking cigarettes. I reached shelter just as huge drops of rain started to fall.

I took the elevator up to the seventh floor—the escalators stopped at the sixth—and made a left turn toward the Felonies Division. I could have checked Pepe Salazar's record using a computer data information search from the comfort of my office, but I would have to come to Metro Justice to request the official court files anyway. For many years investigators had had to look through alphabetically arranged log books, which looked like New York telephone directories but contained the names of people you would never want to call. A few years ago, though, the information was transferred to computers. Now an investigator can sit at an individual terminal and punch in requests, just like at the public library.

I didn't have much data on Salazar—no date of birth, no social security number. I was reduced to reading through all the listings for men named José Salazar, Pepe being the diminutive for José. Out of two dozen José Salazars in the book of felons, two dozen fit the profile: a Hispanic man between the ages of thirty and forty.

I called up the files to see which one was my man. One guy had six drunk and disorderlies, dismissed. Another had a few petty breaking and entering charges and had done time twice. The third was still in prison for a series of armed home invasions. Charming. But the fourth José had the most impressive record.

I gave a whistle of appreciation. This Pepe Salazar's documented life of crime began when he was eighteen, but surely had started earlier—under Florida law, juvenile records are expunged when the offender comes of age. Pepe had wasted no time afterward, inaugurating his career as a documented criminal just three months after his eighteenth birthday. He'd started small, as a lookout in a series of convenience-store robberies, then gotten involved in three burglaries. He served short stretches for the B&E's, then moved into drugs: possession, then dealing. He was sentenced to serve two years on the first charge but actually served three months. He received four years on the second charge and served one.

For seven years after that, Pepe hadn't been caught doing anything. Then he started up again: two convictions for aiding and abetting in the commission of a crime. In other words, pimping. He'd only pulled probation for that one.

Ramon Hidalgo must have come into the picture about that time. In spite of all his priors, Pepe started to receive light sentences. By the time Pepe turned thirty-six, he was regularly receiving good deals in court. The last entry in the log had been two years earlier, for extortion. The case had been dismissed.

The latest charge—selling drugs to an undercover officer, the crime Suzanne overheard Pepe arguing about with Ramon Hidalgo—wasn't there. I jotted down the case numbers for the last few entries and went to the directory that contained the most recent records. Sure enough, there was Pepe's drug bust. I noted the case number and went to the clerk's office next door to request the files.

The clerk was a bored, heavyset African-American woman. She took the slip of paper without a word of greeting, pointed at an empty chair, and said, "Wait."

I was about to say something about my being a taxpayer who supplied her salary when I checked myself and sat down. Experience had taught me that sarcasm and antagonism never made things happen faster in the city bureaucracy. She had control of the files, and I needed them.

The file room itself seemed to have been decorated specifically to depress people. Too small, too little fresh air, and in dire need of paint. At one end was a row of windows through which people like me shoved requests at overworked and probably underpaid clerks. There was also a long, chipped wooden table pushed against the wall, where the public could sit to pore over case files. The same clerks who handled file requests also handled demands for copies, which was invariably time-consuming. I suspected the whole system was devised to discourage requests; it had certainly worked on me before.

Realizing what a depressing place it was to work in, I smiled at the clerk and thanked her sincerely when she returned with the Salazar files. She surprised me with a warm, sweet grin.

I settled down into an uncomfortable plastic chair and started to read. My hunch had been right. Ramon Hidalgo had been the attorney of record for Salazar's most recent charges. Pepe had the same home address on all of his arrest forms, which was actually quite unusual. I wrote down the name of his probation officer, thinking it might come in handy.

I had to give credit to Hidalgo. He was a sleazebag and an ambulance chaser, but he had done a hell of a job and had made outstanding deals for his client. I hoped Pepe was sending him a case of liquor every Christmas, or, at the very least, a box of contraband Montecristos. The final file, for the drug bust, contained only the A Form—an arrest record listing the time and the place of the arrest; the reason for the arrest; witnesses, if any; and the arresting officer. Again Pepe claimed the same home address, and again Hidalgo was the attorney of record.

When I was finished leafing through the inches-thick folder, I made my request for copies, which effectively terminated my clerk's goodwill toward me. I prepared myself for a long wait, and sure enough, it was almost closing time when my name was called. Instead of heading back to the office, I decided to go home to Cocoplum.

Once off the elevator downstairs, I began fishing for my car keys in my purse. Passing through the metal detectors at the security checkpoint, I looked up and saw a familiar face: Assistant State Attorney Charlie Miliken. He also was leaving the building, and I watched him without him noticing me for a few moments. I marveled at the ease with which he bobbed and weaved through the crowd milling around the entrance—I recalled that he had played football in college and high school. He shifted and dodged like an old quarterback, greeting some people and deftly avoiding others.

Charlie Miliken was a good-looking man, no doubt. He possessed all the physical attributes I found most attractive in men—he was tall, with blond hair and blue eyes. He was the quintessential Anglo in a town of small, dark men, and it was easy to spot him in a crowd. I was surprised to feel a pang of regret as I watched him work through the mob. If I had married him when he proposed to me, we would be about to celebrate our fifth anniversary—assuming we were still married.

"Lupe!"

Charlie had spotted me. I knew he eventually would. His antenna was usually on target as far as I was concerned. He edged through the throng, pushing several people aside to get to me.

"What the hell are you doing here?" Charlie asked. Oblivious to the stares of those around us, Charlie hugged me and kissed me lightly on the lips.

"Just looking up some records." He smelled the same as always—a whiff of cigarettes mixed with a trace of last night's Jack Daniel's.

He took my arm and escorted me outside. "Well, come over and visit with me," he said. "I'm almost done for the day. We can catch up."

I suspected Charlie had other motives for inviting me to his office besides catching up on current events, but I went with him anyway. I hadn't seen him in a couple of months, and being around him always cheered me up.

When the rain had passed, we crossed the street where his office was formerly housed, in the Graham Building, to the Metro Justice Building, where it had been relocated. We stepped out of the elevator on the third floor. A receptionist behind a bulletproof glass partition waved us through.

I followed Charlie down a snaking corridor, turning at right angles every few dozen feet past countless offices until we reached Charlie's. Everyone in the State Attorney's office looked exhausted—prosecutors returning from court, clerks clutching stacks of files to their chests, secretaries fielding calls amid paper-strewn desks.

Time seemed to stand still there; there was a perpetual sameness in the sterile reception areas, the bland corridors, the employees looking overworked, underpaid, unappreciated. The one certainty that kept the lawyers going was the knowledge that the State Attorney's office was a training ground for trial work. Fresh-out-of-law-school attorneys paid their dues for a few years, working impossible hours at insulting wages, until they could go into private practice. When they did, they would be hot commodities, because it was common knowledge that prosecuting in Dade County was the best courtroom training available. The cycle repeated itself endlessly. The prosecutors knew that in a few years they would be opposing their successors in the same courtrooms—but for dramatically better money.

Charlie was the exception. At age thirty-one, he was an old veteran in the office. He could have been division chief by then if he'd played the game better, but he hated office politics. He was incapable of kissing the asses of those he didn't respect, and he paid the price accordingly. He was an idealist who thrived on putting bad guys in jail—even if it was the same bad guys over and over again, sentences being what they were. His lack of ambition to do anything else had been a sticking point in our relationship.

Charlie opened his office door, which he never kept locked. I think he figured the place was such a mess that anyone courageous enough to want to steal anything was welcome to it. I could vouch for that; every time I went in there, I prayed my immune system was strong enough to handle all the germs and microbes I knew were lurking in the air.

He closed the door behind me, removed a perilously leaning stack of files from a chair, and motioned with a flourish for me to sit. I lowered myself into the wooden seat, glad that I had worn a dark skirt and T-shirt. At least that way the grime wouldn't show.

"What records were you looking up?" Charlie asked as he opened the file cabinet. He pulled a bottle of Jack Daniel's and two plastic cups from the bottom drawer.

"Some scumbag," I said. "The usual."

"Did you find what you were looking for?" He poured what looked like a minimum of three inches of bourbon into each cup. "Anyone I know?"

After handing me my cup. Charlie walked around behind me and started rubbing my knotted shoulders.

"Could be," I replied. It was a given that Charlie knew Pepe Salazar; he had been the prosecutor on one of Pepe's B&E's a few years before. I knew Charlie never, ever forgot anyone he sent away—even for a misdemeanor.

I sipped my drink as Charlie worked on my neck muscles. I was tempted to confide in Charlie and ask him about Salazar, but I decided to wait. I would save Charlie for when I needed concrete information. He always came through for me, in spite of all his protestations.

I looked out the window and saw that the storm had passed, leaving the sky full of delicate shades of pink and purple. I drained the last of the bourbon and stood up. Charlie's massage was starting to feel a little too good.

"Leaving?" Charlie asked. He obviously had other plans.

"Sorry, I have work to do. Thanks for the drink." I stood on my toes and kissed him, breathing in the welcoming scent of his neck.

"Come back any time, Lupe," Charlie said, already fishing through a haphazard mound of files on his desk. "My door's always open for you, you know that."

I was relieved to see that the Mercedes was still where I had left it and, miraculously, it was in the same condition as I had last seen it. It was actually pleasant to walk through the lot, because the storm had freshened the air and washed away some of the heat.

The traffic was light, so I made it home in half an hour. There was plenty of time for a swim in the pool before cocktails and dinner on the terrace with Papi, Fatima, and the girls. Lourdes was at the convent, which relieved me. It had been a confusing day for me, which she would have known instantly.

I went up to my bed early and cringed at the ungodly hour of five to which I set my alarm clock. I was going on garbage detail before the sun came up, and there's nothing like knowing you have to get up before dawn to send you off to sleep with a less-than-rosy outlook.

Fourteen

"*Mierda!* Nothing in this one, either!"

I threw my hands in the air in frustration, in the process sending a fragment of unidentifiable, mustard-colored kitchen waste splattering onto my office baseboard. I was down on the floor and in no mood to contemplate the extent of the mess I was making.

For a couple who ate almost every meal out of the house, the de la Torres produced enormous amounts of garbage. According to the investigator's logs, Miguel and Teresa ate only breakfast at home. The one person who regularly ate in was the housekeeper, who was very petite but apparently had a hell of a metabolism.

I peeled off my plastic gloves and had a look around. It had taken me two hours to sort through three days' accumulation of the de la Torres' garbage—two hours' worth of coffee grounds, soggy toast, junk mail, and rotting vegetables. Only a clear plastic drop cloth had saved my office from total ruin. The place stank, and I was exhausted. It wasn't the first time I had played archaeologist, sifting through the ruins, but continued experience didn't make the job any more pleasant.

I had awakened before dawn to make the garbage switch. Privacy laws pertaining to trash varied from area to area, and the first step was to determine whether the jurisdiction's trash pickup was done through the county or had been contracted out to a private company. The latter case is no problem, because few private sanitation employees will resist a crisp fifty-dollar bill for putting someone's garbage into the trunk of your car rather than in their company's truck.

As for the former, it's illegal to bribe a county employee—which doesn't necessarily mean an individual won't take the bribe, just that an investigator would find herself without a license if she were caught. The placement of garbage outside a home is also crucial. Under Florida law, it's illegal to enter private property for the purpose of taking someone's garbage. If the cans or bags are left out on an easement, however, then the trash is public property—and all the old tuna cans and cigar butts are up for grabs.

Miguel and Teresa lived in Coral Gables, in the expensive zone of Dade County consisting of canals, big homes, and winding streets. The city takes care of trash collection there, so bribery was out of the question. My junior investigator Lucy had reported that the de la Torres' garbage was picked up on Tuesdays and Fridays, at around 7:30 in the morning. A plan had started to form in my mind as soon as I heard this news.

The de la Torre household rubbish was packed into four huge green plastic bags, which were then left by the side of the house—on public property. I had arrived an hour before the noisy city truck would arrive for the scheduled pickup. It would have been easy for me to load the bags into my car and simply drive off. But I couldn't risk someone noticing that the trash was missing, or have one of the sanitation men knock on the door, thinking that the maid had forgotten to leave it out—and, believe me, in Coral Gables that might happen. So after loading up all four bags of de la Torre trash, I replaced them with substitutes full of old crumpled-up newspapers.

Unfortunately, after returning to my office with my newfound treasure, I discovered that the de la Torres had discarded absolutely nothing of any importance. This meant that I would have to repeat the entire process again, maybe several times. That didn't disturb me as much as I would have thought; I was happy to be immersed in the investigation and working toward a goal.

At this stage of the case, as in the beginning of many investigations, I wasn't even sure what I was looking for. I hoped to find a pattern of behavior, some sense of something unusual. I had organized the "keeper" garbage by category: credit card records, discarded mail, phone bills. The last item was important, because it would allow me to track any international phone calls made from the residence. It was possible that Miguel or Teresa was involved in international dealings, whether financial or otherwise. Phone records were my best hope for finding data that would otherwise be completely inaccessible to me.

I started to gather my things, ready to go home for a steamy shower and to throw my pungent jeans and T-shirt in the washing machine. Before I could finish, there was a gentle knock on my door. Nestor let himself in, wearing an expression of amusement.

I was pleased to see that he was looking more relaxed than usual. Maybe he had doubled his normal two-hour nightly sleep allotment. Though he was in his early thirties, lately he appeared to be in his forties instead of his fifties—a real improvement.

"Lupe, Lupe, didn't your mother ever tell you not to play with the garbage?" he said. He skirted the edge of the drop cloth to make his way to his favorite place—the sofa—twirling his sunglasses in his hand. "Lucy warned me you were going on a garbage run. Did you enjoy it?"

"Thanks for the sympathy, Nestor," I said. "It really makes it all worthwhile. Help me get this cloth rolled up. I'll have to hose it off outside."

"Lupe the garbologist. Oh, sorry, the environmental engineer," he corrected himself. "I'll never forget your teaching me about stealing household trash. It was very educational."

"I'm glad you enjoyed it. Now take that end."

"I'm far too important for that," he said. He stretched out on the sofa, enjoying himself. "A man in my position shouldn't get his hands dirty."

I was ready to throw him out of my office, but I stopped myself. Nestor was this sassy only when he was on top of his game—which meant he had information to share with me. And he hated to be rushed. He twisted into a semisitting position and halfheartedly folded an edge of the tarp toward its center.

"Did you find anything?" he asked.

I shook my head. "Nothing yet. Why do I always think I'll crack the case on the first garbage run, Nestor? Why do I torture myself like that?"

He laughed. "I'd call it hope over experience," he said. "We're all guilty of it. We don't like peeking into other people's things, even their trash, so we hope we'll get it all over with quickly."

He rolled back onto the sofa and wiped his palms on his handkerchief. Peering at the trash mound with distaste, he added, "This case is very unusual, after all. We all wonder where it's going to lead us."

"You can say that again," I replied with a little too much vehemence.

Nestor cocked his head, staring at me as though trying to read my thoughts. We both turned uncomfortably quiet, absorbed in the trash as if it were a map of our futures. It was impossible to ignore—the smell was overpowering. Nestor then became immersed in his sunglasses, holding them up to the light and rubbing them with a chamois cloth he pulled from his shirt pocket. He loved those glasses; he had told me a dozen times that they were better than anything he could afford in the Dominican Republic.

"By the way, I have some good news on this case of ours," he said laconically. "I got it at a church dinner that I went to last night."

If Nestor noticed my look of total surprise that he would exploit his religious convictions to gather information, he chose to ignore it. Although I always teased him by pretending to be amazed that he was religious, I knew that for Nestor his congregation was a sort of surrogate family. Whenever he had spare time—that is, rarely—he was usually there.

"One of the members is named Veronica Pelaez. It just so happens that she works in the mail room at First Miami." Nestor rubbed his glasses. "She's been there for five years, and just last year she was put in charge of the entire department."

"Very nice," I said. We both knew this was potentially huge as a source of inside information.

"I asked her a few questions about her work. I found out that she's in a position to see what mail comes addressed to Miguel de la Torre. But there's a problem."

Nestor actually sat up on the sofa, a sure indication that this was important. "Veronica, she . . . *appreciated* my paying attention to her. Frankly, I don't think that any man had ever asked her so much about herself. I couldn't very well say that I only wanted information for a case. When I went to the bathroom, she told my sister Bernadette that she thought I was interested in her—and that I was too shy to do anything about it."

I covered my mouth, trying not to laugh too hard. "Is she pretty?"

"Lupe, how could you ask me that?" Nestor said. "This is strictly business."

"I'm just curious." I shrugged. "Some people can't help being irresistible to the opposite sex, you know. It's a burden you'll just have to bear."

If it were possible, Nestor would have blushed. He was too dark-skinned, though. "I hate this part of the job, Lupe," he moaned. "I hate using nice people to get information. Veronica should know that I can't think about getting serious with a girl until my whole family is here. It could be years. But it doesn't seem to make any difference to her."

"I'm sure you could cultivate an innocent friendship with her, without being unfaithful to your brothers and sisters," I suggested.

"I know, I know," Nestor said. "And I will."

"But be careful," I added. "Some women find hardworking men *extremely* attractive."

Nestor walked out of my office, mumbling something about the unpredictability of women. After he was gone I realized he had never helped me with the tarp. I was in no mood to deal with it, so I sprayed it with Alpine Forever and left it heaped in the corner for the time being. I considered throwing it in the Dumpster and buying a new one for next time, but I didn't want to get in the habit of wasting the company's funds.

I sat at my desk for a while. I wanted to leave, but I was too chicken to face Leonardo's accusing stare. Instead I opened up a file that Leonardo had left on my desk. It contained a week's accumulation of press clippings concerning the de la Torres.

I idly flipped through the newsprint. Leonardo had been thorough, clipping articles from both Spanish- and English-language papers. I took out a magnifying glass and looked closer. The pictures spanned back several years, but the couple seemed not to have changed much. They looked just as they had at Hector's funeral. The photos and accompanying articles all were from the social pages, and from the sheer volume in the file it seemed as though the de la Torres never spent a night at home. It was a fact I had already confirmed through the first of the junior investigators' surveillance logs.

Here was photo after photo of them dressed in formal wear at banquets and charity dances. Even in black and white they reeked of prestige and social power, and they shared the same beneficent expression I had seen at Caballero's. I looked closer at a photo of Miguel leading Teresa out onto a dance floor, graceful and confident, his free hand waving at the photographer. These people had been close friends with Luis's parents. They were lifelong aristocrats, first in Cuba and now in America. Although there was a smile on her lips, Teresa's eyes were fixed firmly ahead, as if she were sizing up an opponent. When I imagined I saw a killer's icy coldness in her face, I knew it was time to go home.

I put all the clippings back in the file and started cranking shut the windows. The phone rang, and I considered not answering it.

"Oh, what the hell," I said aloud, and picked it up. "Hello?"

"Feel like getting dressed up?" It was Tommy. "Want to go to a ball? You know, Cinderella and the magic pumpkin?"

"Are you serious?" I said curtly. "I hate those things." I was smelly and sweaty. It would take about a dozen washings to get the trash smell out of my hair. The last thing I wanted to contemplate was attending a fancy dress ball.

"I hope it's not tonight. I already committed to a thing with Leonardo. And you know how much I *detest*—"

"This one is different," Tommy purred. "I think you'll be very interested."

"All right, I give up," I said. "What ball are you talking about? Is it a fund-raiser for criminal-defense attorneys who make less than a million a year after taxes?"

"I am going to rise above your sarcasm." Tommy sniffed. "But this will appeal to your sense of the absurd. The ball in question is the

First Annual Cuban-American Friendship Ball, to be held at the Intercontinental Hotel."

"So what?" I answered. "It's nice that Cubans and Americans want to get along with each other. *Mierda,* after forty years of living together, it's about time."

I truly couldn't stand myself anymore. I dug around in my purse for some perfume and sprayed it all over my body. Now I smelled like more-expensive garbage—coffee grounds and chicken bones mixed with Chanel No. 5 and Alpine Forever air freshener.

"If you would just be quiet and let me finish—" Tommy paused. "You would find out that we're seated at a table with great pillars of the community. Including, Lupe, Miguel and Teresa de la Torre."

"Wow." This was certainly an unexpected opportunity. I wondered if they would remember me from the wake.

"I thought I'd have your attention after that. It's not often you get to break bread with the bad guys, is it?" Tommy couldn't hide the pleasure in his voice. "You'll have a better chance at getting close to them than at Caballero's."

"Why do we have an invitation?" I asked.

"One of my partners, Marcel, bought a table for twelve and invited me along," Tommy explained. "His wife is a friend of Teresa de la Torre's. They sit on a couple of charity boards together, so in the spirit of the theme of the ball, she persuaded Marcel to invite Cuban friends. I just happened to have a close one."

This was no surprise; it was a classic case of intermingling. The movers and shakers of Miami all sat on one another's boards and committees. It was almost incestuous.

"When is the dance?" I asked. I focused my thoughts on the sad, neglected state of my wardrobe. A quick mental run-through of my closet revealed that I had nothing appropriate to wear.

I heard paper rustling. "Saturday, June seventh," Tommy said. "Less than a week from now. Is it a date?"

"Of course. Wouldn't miss it for the world. There's no legal problem with us going, is there? After all, our client is paying us to dish up dirt on these people."

"Lupe, there's no conflict of interest, and no law against meeting someone you're investigating." Tommy chuckled. "If we had to stay away from people we were checking out—hell, we'd have no social life at all."

"And you don't have any moral or ethical problems with this situation?" I knew I was sounding naive, but it was important to be careful.

"None whatsoever," Tommy said seriously. "It simply gives us an advantage. We get to study our marks up close in their preferred social setting, where their guards will be down. Lupe, *querida*, you sound like you're going soft on me."

"You know better than that. I was just trying to figure out how this could backfire on us."

My thoughts wandered. Part of me was dying to see the couple up close and to interact with them. But I also had reservations. What if I liked them? What if I didn't? What if I lost what was left of my objectivity?

"You're on, Tommy," I said. "Dust off the cufflinks."

Life isn't fair. A man can keep the same tuxedo he wore to his high-school prom—assuming he could still button it—and be ready for a formal occasion on a moment's notice. For women, dressing up is like planning a war, from finding the right undergarments to choosing the shoes with just the right heel length. I would have to start from scratch to prepare for the ball, like Cinderella—though I had no fairy godmother at my disposal just at that time. It looked like my entire life was turning into a scavenger hunt—first through a mountain of trash, and now in search of a decent outfit.

Fifteen

As soon as I got home I stood in the shower for at least twenty minutes. I cranked the steamy water as strong as it would go and scrubbed myself until my skin was almost raw. I used about half a bottle of shampoo, all the while cursing my chosen profession. Finally I had scrubbed away the last traces of the de la Torres' garbage.

My closet was in even worse shape than I had remembered. Wrapped only in a thick white bath towel, with my hair up in a turban, I flipped through the rack. I was primarily looking for a dress to wear to a dinner Leonardo had invited me to that night, but I also needed something for the Cuban-American Friendship Ball.

It was all too much. I lay down on the bed, thinking I would close my eyes for a few minutes. The next thing I knew, Aida was standing over me, shaking me awake.

"Leonardo's on the phone for you," she said apologetically. "I told him you were sleeping, but he insisted."

I knew Aida hated to wake anyone up. Sleep was sacred to her, which I understood perfectly. I felt the same way.

It took a major effort to extricate an arm from under the covers to pick up the phone. I mumbled a hello into the mouthpiece.

"You didn't forget, did you?" Leonardo, typically, dispensed with the formalities.

"Of course not. I'm almost ready," I lied. I opened my eyes to look at the bedside clock and nearly jumped out of bed. Seven o'clock. I had slept for five hours.

"Lupe, come on. You're not ready at all," Leonardo said. "Aida said you've been asleep since this afternoon! Stop bullshitting me and get dressed. You want me to pick you up?"

I knew his offer was entirely intended to make sure I would appear at the dinner on time. Sometimes my cousin was like an old lady—and a very crotchety one.

"I'm getting out of bed right now," I said. "I already took a shower, so all I have to do is get dressed. I'll be there in, I don't know, twenty minutes at the most. I'll speed all the way there."

"That's not saying anything. You always speed." I could visualize Leonardo; right about then, he would be nervously looking at his watch. "It's seven-ten. I expect to see your car pulling up to the building at seven-thirty."

"Come on, give me a break," I whined. "I'll only be a half-hour late. They expect that—we're Cuban, aren't we?"

I hung up thinking that only Americans would start a dinner party at the appalling hour of seven P.M. To Cubans, that was a late lunch.

Leonardo had talked me into this dinner a few days ago; it was to be given by a couple of friends of his, Elliot Barnes and Clive Houseman. I knew I would enjoy myself once I got there, but I was preoccupied with the Delgado case. It was obviously too late for a dignified refusal.

Elliot and Clive lived in the penthouse apartment of Leonardo's building in the Grove. I had met them six years before, when Leonardo had left the safety and comfort of his parents' house for his first apartment. Elliot and Clive had introduced themselves to us the first day and helped carry the boxes and furniture upstairs. They also showed Leonardo the ropes, including sharing hilarious gossip about all the other tenants. They were antique dealers and, as you would expect, their own apartment was exquisite. It was a duplex, with high ceilings, carved moldings, and lots of windows and natural light. I always thought of it as a tree house, since it was level with the treetops surrounding the building.

I was pleased to be one of their few straight friends. Although Elliot and Clive were very social, they tended to stay within the gay community. I was also grateful for how much they helped Leonardo, taking him under their wing and always looking out for him.

When they issued the dinner invitations, Elliot and Clive had said it would be an informal party. I knew better—casual to them meant not wearing a black tie. Cutoffs and jeans wouldn't make it. I also knew that some of their friends' idea of dressing up entailed elegant drag that they pulled off quite nicely. The thought of this party was beginning to stir up my natural sense of competition.

I tore through the closet again, as if the clothes in there had miraculously bred chic offspring while I had been napping. My stomach started to growl. I didn't feel like going out, but the food would be lavish and delicious. The music would be perfect for the occasion, and the company would be original, if not scandalous.

I had just wasted a good five minutes daydreaming in front of my closet. I picked out a slightly trashy tight, short, red dress. I was about to opt for a pair of black high-heeled sandals when I spotted a pair of red stiletto heels under some old pumps. Holding them up against the dress, I saw they weren't a perfect match. But they'd do. I had bought them in Dadeland Mall a few years before; I had been working undercover looking for a professional shoplifter, a job that allowed me to shop at a discount. I had gotten carried away with being thrifty and bought way too much. Most of the merchandise was still in the original boxes, untouched by human hands.

I quickly put on makeup and bathed myself in perfume to rid any trace of garbage lurking on me. A mere seven minutes later I pulled into the parking lot of Leonardo's building. As I locked up the Mercedes I noticed him standing outside, checking his watch every few seconds. I heard the bing-bong of a Coconut Grove church announce the half-hour the instant I pecked my cousin on the cheek with a sweet smile. I really am insufferable sometimes.

A small group had already gathered upstairs; most guests were familiar to me from previous parties. Clive spotted us as we walked in and slapped margaritas in our hands before we could close the door.

"Guadalupe!" he shouted, loud enough for the entire room to hear. "You are divine! Red is your color! Swear to me this instant that you'll always wear it!"

I could see that Clive had already sampled a few margaritas of his own. He squeezed Leonardo's shoulder. "*Chico*, may I add that your attire is tasteful, with just the proper hint of flash." Leonardo glanced down at his relatively boring off-white linen suit, which he had spiced up with a lime-green silk shirt.

"Thanks, Clive," he said. "Your suit is pretty great, too."

Clive did indeed look elegant in his superbly tailored silk suit. "Let me see," Clive said, turning serious. "I think you know everyone here. Oh, except for Sergio."

He pointed toward a man sitting alone on a sofa, looking dismal. "Be kind to him," Clive added in a low voice. "His lover just died. Come on, I'll take you over and introduce you. Leonardo, you don't mind taking a shift as bartender, do you?"

"Of course not." Leonardo took off his jacket and started rolling up his sleeves. "How drunk do you want your guests?"

"A man after my own heart," Clive said. "Mix them strong."

"And not worry about all those brain cells that will never regenerate?" Leonardo asked with a twinkle. "Well, I'll put a little extra lime in each one for the vitamin C. There has to be something therapeutic to counter the alcohol."

Clive clutched his heart melodramatically. "If it will help you sleep better tonight, Leonardo."

"Your cousin is such a dear," Clive said as he led me by the elbow across the room. When we reached the sofa, he said to Sergio in a cheery voice, "Sergio, meet Guadalupe Solano. I'm sure she'll let you call her Lupe. This is Sergio Santiago, a countryman of yours. And now, I'll go see if anyone needs anything."

"*Hola,*" I said, settling down on the leather sofa. I could see why Sergio was alone; he looked like a man who didn't want to be bothered. "Nice to meet you. How do you know Clive?"

"We work out at the same gym," Sergio said. "He told me about you and your cousin before you got here. He's very fond of you both."

Sergio was soft-spoken, with deep eyes whose gentleness and vulnerability reminded me of a doe's. He and I chatted about nothing much until Clive announced that dinner was ready.

The entire party, which numbered ten people, all trooped together into the Art Deco–inspired fantasy that served as a dining room. The decor was dominated by a set of Erté figurines and smoky glass that covered the walls and gave the room a sense of limitless space. The room contained no electric light fixtures and was brightened only by tall tapers along the walls. Red velvet curtains with gold tassels sealed the room from natural light, creating a whorehouse-parlor effect. When people ate in the room for the first time—on the gold-rimmed glass dining table perched atop thigh-high Corinthian columns—they often lost their appetites while trying to adjust to the surreal environment.

I assumed, since I was the only genetic woman there, that I would be placed next to Clive—the place of honor. Sure enough, when dinner was announced I was escorted to the chair at Clive's right. To his left was Sergio. Dinner was spectacular: medallions of veal in mushroom sauce, potatoes au gratin, and a medley of vegetables carved in shapes that I had seen only in magazines. It was all washed down with an expert wine selection, and for dessert, mountains of sherbet were served with hot fudge and strawberry sauce.

I was basking in my contentment, checking from time to time to see how Leonardo was faring farther down the table, when I heard the words "First Miami," followed by Miguel de la Torre's name. I snapped out of my daydream, trying not to look overinterested in what Clive and Sergio were talking about.

"I remember perfectly well telling him that I was gay when he hired me," Sergio said to Clive. "First Miami is a conservative place, and I didn't want any hassles down the road. De la Torre seemed surprised—not because I was gay, I think, but because I was being so direct about it. He said that as long as I didn't flaunt it, and as long as it didn't interfere with my work, there wouldn't be any problem. He told me that this was the nineties, that no one really cares anymore."

Clive nodded sympathetically and gave me a small smile when he noticed that I was listening.

"And that's the way it was—until Mario got sick," Sergio continued. "I had worked for Miguel for six years. I thought we had a pretty good relationship. I couldn't believe he'd turn out to be such a bastard."

Clive seemed stuck for a response, so I broke in. "Excuse me, Sergio," I said, "did you just mention Miguel de la Torre?"

"Yes, that's right. The bastard." Sergio was more than a little drunk, and his voice was now loud enough that other conversations at the table halted abruptly. "I've been working as his personal assistant for six years. We got along great—until now."

Sergio's eyes were red. He clenched his wineglass so tightly in his hand that I was afraid it might break at the stem.

Clive spoke to me in a tone that I knew was meant to calm Sergio. "The problem, Lupe, is that Sergio's lover, Mario Garcia, got sick. When the AIDS progressed, he was breaking out with sores and was in a lot of pain. He went downhill fast, you know how it goes. The doctors said that Mario had only a few more months to live, at the most, and Sergio was the only person left to take care of him."

"What about his family?" I asked. "Couldn't they help?"

"Come on, Lupe, they're Cuban. You know what that means." Sergio laughed bitterly.

"When Mario came out and told them he was moving in with Sergio," Clive added, "they told him he wasn't their son anymore."

"Okay, he was an only son," Sergio said. "But it's not like the name was going to die out—there are plenty of Garcias in the world."

"When things got bad, Mario wanted to die at home," Clive said. "I remember. It was the only thing he cared about."

"I was grateful when the hospital let me take him," Sergio said in a hollow voice. "I couldn't cure him, but I would be able to see that he died in peace, and with dignity."

There was nothing I could say. I had known others—more and

more, it seemed—who had lived the nightmare of AIDS. Sympathetic silence seemed the only appropriate response.

"So, you know, I had some accumulated sick leave and vacation time," Sergio said. He stared at the tablecloth. "I was going to ask Mr. de la Torre for an additional six weeks to take care of Mario. He was going so fast. I knew it was my only chance."

"What happened?" I asked.

Sergio's eyes turned cold. "Miguel knew about Mario when he hired me. I didn't want it to become an issue, so I made no secret about it." Sergio glanced at Clive for confirmation, and Clive nodded. "But when I asked for special leave he wouldn't even discuss it with me. I explained everything, thinking he would understand. And the damned employees' manual says the bank can authorize compassionate leave in special circumstances—but only with the boss's permission. He turned me down flat."

"What happened?" I asked. "Did you quit?"

"I couldn't," Sergio said. "Mario and I were living on my salary by then. His insurance had been canceled, and there were bills stacked up to the ceiling. All those drugs were so expensive. Poor Mario . . . thank God, at least he's at rest now."

I was quiet for a moment. Then, without thinking, I said, "So you're still working for Miguel de la Torre? I thought you would have left after your lover died."

Sergio grimaced with hatred. "I thought of going to another bank, but I didn't want to start over someplace else. I tried to transfer to another department, but he wouldn't let me. He said he's put too much time and energy into training me. I knew he was thinking I'd get over it, that Mario's death had made me irrational."

"Sergio's boss is the big boss at the bank," Clive explained, though I already knew. "So there was no one to complain to."

"Anyway, I need the job," Sergio said, taking another long gulp of wine. "Mario left me with a lot of debts. But I tell you, someday I'll get back at him for this. If it hadn't been for de la Torre, Mario would have died in my arms instead of dying while I was at work. He would have died with dignity instead of full of worry, in the arms of strangers. He would have had peace."

My mouth had just opened with a question when Clive explained, "Mario died at Jackson Memorial."

"Indigent. A damned charity case," Sergio said. "I think de la Torre has a guilty conscience, because he gave me a token raise a month after Mario died. That bastard, thinking he could buy me like that."

The room was uncomfortably quiet until Elliot stood up and asked Clive to help him get the coffee ready. Talk for the rest of the evening was considerably lighter, including a hilarious description of a Caribbean vacation taken by Pete and Julio, a couple I'd met at a barbecue a few months before.

I knew instinctively that I'd stumbled onto a gold mine, but it was best to wait. I didn't want to seem uncaring, and I really sympathized with the poor man. He had suffered more than anyone should have to. After coffee was served, Sergio said his good-byes and headed home, sad and alone. It was heartbreaking.

The dinner party turned into an excuse for everyone to dance and drink. I was dancing with Leonardo when a guy named Bernard tried to cut in on us. Leonardo and I looked at each other, not sure which of us he wanted to dance with. I decided that it wasn't the night to see my cousin in the embrace of another man, so I waltzed into Bernard's arms. He was definitely my type—it was too bad that he was gay.

It was after midnight when Leonardo walked me to the parking lot. I was feeling blissfully full of good food and wine, but my mind kept returning to Sergio. I was sorry that I couldn't simply feel bad for the man but, professionally, I had to figure out how to exploit the situation to my client's advantage. This sort of detachment was vital to being a successful investigator—and was also one of the less palatable aspects of the job. I couldn't allow my feelings to stand in the way. It was always a great break to find someone with inside access to the subject of an investigation. Now I potentially had two, including Nestor's Veronica.

As I drove home I wondered if Lourdes had asked for divine intervention in my work—because these coincidences struck me as miraculous. Sometimes when I was this fortunate I wondered if the Virgin were repaying Lourdes's service to the Church through me. Maybe the Virgin felt that Luis had special merit and was putting in overtime on his behalf. Or it could have been just wishful thinking and I was imagining that we had her protection.

It was late when I got home, and I was tired, but I was also wound up and wanted to share my good news with Tommy. I knew he would be awake when I called—he was an incurable insomniac, the kind of man who starts off his evening with David Letterman. On my way up to my room I stopped in the kitchen and grabbed a split of Veuve Cliquot champagne from the refrigerator. I popped the cork on the way up the stairs and, dispensing with the flute glasses Aida kept chilled for such situations, drank straight from the bottle. I paused for a second to pay tribute to the genius of the French.

In my room I peeled the tight red dress off my body and kicked the stiletto shoes from my feet. I lay in bed naked and dialed Tommy. As I expected, he answered on the first ring, sounding alert and wide awake.

"What's up, Lupe?" he asked. "Can't sleep, or maybe you can't stop thinking about me?" He sounded genuinely hopeful.

"Remember when I told you about Leonardo's neighbors, Elliot and Clive? You know—the antique dealers?" Silence on the other end. Tommy wasn't always the best listener, especially about subjects other than work and romance. I took another sip of champagne. "Well, I went to a dinner party at their apartment tonight."

"Lupe, I assume that there's a point to this story." Tommy sounded out of sorts—not his usual response when I called late at night. I must have been interrupting something important on TV.

"Yes, there is a point," I said, a bit of annoyance creeping into my voice. "I met a young man there named Sergio Santiago."

"I'm listening."

"He's Miguel de la Torre's personal assistant at First Miami."

"I see," Tommy said. "And you persuaded him to help you with your investigation into his boss's activities—which could get him fired as well as guarantee he never gets another banking job again, ever, for the rest of his life. Not to mention the fact that he could be prosecuted for divulging bank secrets."

"I didn't ask him anything," I said, a little angry with Tommy for bursting my bubble. "I just met the man tonight."

"Then don't get so carried away. You know better than that." Tommy must have sensed my change in mood, because his voice softened. "Lupe, *querida,* it's great that you found this guy. Just keep him in the back of your mind as a possible source. He could be more trouble than he's worth."

"The thing is, Sergio despises Miguel." I told Tommy the whole story, adding, "We might be able to use this resentment. It sounds like Sergio is his right-hand man. He probably knows where all the bones are buried."

"What bones? You're assuming there *are* bones. Lupe, listen to me." Tommy sighed. "It's one thing for this guy to let off some steam at a dinner party after God knows how many glasses of wine. It's another for him to jeopardize his career to help you."

"I tell you, Sergio hates Miguel de la Torre," I said. "I saw it in his eyes."

I wasn't naive enough to think that Miguel's lack of sympathy for Sergio's plight necessarily meant that Miguel had an evil character. After all, Miguel was a heterosexual, married, middle-aged Cuban man—not the most liberal type—so his attitude wasn't a total surprise. And Sergio's anger and frustration at losing his lover to AIDS might have found a convenient outlet in his boss.

Maybe Tommy was right and I was jumping to conclusions, finding evidence of the de la Torres' shady character everywhere. Obviously, having someone on the inside who bore a grudge was definitely an asset to the case.

"All right, there are still plenty of unknowns," I conceded. "It's early in the investigation. It is possible that Miguel and Teresa are the fine, upstanding citizens they present themselves as. I'll maintain my skepticism, but I tell you, I have a feeling about this one."

"Well, I trust your instincts," Tommy allowed. "That's why you're the best investigator in town. Just remember: Talking is one thing; doing is another."

While I had him on the line, I brought Tommy up to date about selling Luis's diamond, Nestor's break with Veronica, the junior investigators who were monitoring the de la Torre house, and my garbage run. I promise to send him over a written report in the morning.

A glance at the bedside clock told me it was after two in the morning. In a few more hours I would have been awake a full twenty-four hours—excluding my lengthy afternoon nap. I said good night to Tommy and shut off the lights. I think I was asleep before the room got dark.

Sixteen

"Papi, how well do you know Miguel de la Torre?"

My father and I were outside on the terrace, drinking *café con leche* and awaiting the feast Aida was preparing in the kitchen. It had been a long time since just the two of us had had breakfast together—too long, I thought.

"I've known him for a long time." Papi looked at me strangely. "Every Cuban of my generation in Miami knows him as well. Why do you ask?"

"No reason. His name came up in conversation the other day." I hated lying to my father, but I couldn't involve him in the case. "Some American client asked me if I knew him. I said I recently met him and that I knew him by reputation. What's his story, anyway? They came over in the first wave, didn't they?"

My father knew precisely what I was referring to. The "first wave" of Cubans to arrive in Miami did so in the first years following the revolution, around 1959 to 1963. They were generally considered to be the moneyed, educated aristocracy of Cuba. Many had foreseen what the future held for them under Fidel Castro and had managed to take their money with them. The majority of them had previous investments in the United States, as well as connections that enabled them to live comfortably in exile until a political change took place on the island. They were the fortunate ones. They had lost their homeland and had to live below the lifestyle they were used to, but their new lives were generally without hardship.

"They did," Papi replied. "Miguel and his wife, Teresa, have done very well here. They had vision. They didn't waste time feeling sorry for themselves over leaving Cuba. They put their money right to work."

I was a little surprised at the vehemence of Papi's tone. It was clear that he admired the de la Torres.

"I suspect they did even better here than they would have if they had stayed in Havana," he added. "But that's just my opinion."

Papi refilled his coffee cup; a faraway look was in his eyes. He shuddered a little when he took a sip—the coffee was very strong, the way he liked it. He stared off across the bay, toward Key Biscayne, no doubt thinking of his own early days in America. Our family was also considered part of the first wave. Mami and Papi had come over as a young couple with a baby girl—my sister Fatima. We were one of the more fortunate ones—not only were my parents and grandparents on both sides able to leave Cuba within six months of each other, but so were other members of our extended family—cousins, uncles, aunts. There was no one from our family left in Cuba now.

Prior to the Cubans' arrival in the sixties, Miami had been a sleepy southern town. The Cubans take full credit for revitalizing it into a world-class city. There are skeptics, though, who claim that the invention of air conditioning put Miami on the map—before this development, it was impossible to live in Miami year-round. Whatever the reason, Miami became a bustling city, with diverse ethnic groups giving it an unprecedented vitality.

Inevitably, the Cubans had started to affect the Dade County ruling structure—not only in politics, but in business as well. Americans who had been in control for decades suddenly noticed that the balance of power was shifting, and they didn't like it. It became a different game, with new players who conducted meetings in Spanish, wore *guayaberas,* drank unbelievably strong coffee, and had plenty of money. Time passed and a sort of uneasy truce was declared, based on the realization that the Cubans were going to stay. It was apparent that everyone had to try to get along—if not by becoming friends, then at least by coexisting peacefully.

"You know, Lupe, your mother knew Teresa de la Torre quite well," Papi announced. "They sat on several charity boards together."

I perked up. "Really? What did Mami think of Teresa?"

Papi sighed. "You know your mother—she never said a bad thing about anyone. She was a saint."

Papi actually peered up at the sky, as though he could see his wife's face there. I wondered why my mother might have had a bad opinion of Teresa—the implication was there in Papi's words. Before I was able to ask for clarification, a voice interrupted us.

"Saint?" Lourdes said, walking toward us. "Did someone call for me?"

Lourdes was dressed in her typical missionary style—in an olive-green Banana Republic outfit, looking as though she were about to leave for deepest Africa to convert the indigenous peoples to Catholicism.

"So, who's the saint?" she asked, taking a seat. "I think this is my department."

"Papi was just talking about Mami," I answered. Lourdes nodded. It had been seven years since Mami's death, but we all still ached for her presence.

Osvaldo emerged, tottering beneath the weight of a heavy silver tray. The three of us dug in, starting with the scrambled eggs and bacon and then moving on to the exquisitely ripe mangoes. My favorite part of breakfast was dipping the buttery Cuban bread, which was toasted to a perfect golden color, into the *café con leche* and then gobbling it up. We were a nutritionist's nightmare.

After breakfast, Papi leaned back in his chair and lit up what I hoped was his first cigar of the day. He puffed for a while, then stood up, ready to head inside.

"You should eat here more often," he said. "We miss you around here."

"Thanks, Papi," Lourdes and I said.

"Well, I'm going to the office." He stretched. "You girls stay out of trouble today."

Lourdes and I watched Papi leave. "You know, every time I'm here, he asks me to move back," Lourdes said. "It's tempting, but it wouldn't look good. I mean, I'm a nun. I took a vow of poverty. How can I live in a ten-bedroom house in Cocoplum?"

I thought for a moment. "Well, you could take the back bedroom—you know, the one facing the street, without a view of the bay. The worst bedroom in the whole house."

"I don't think it would work," Lourdes said with a sigh, tearing a piece of bread. "But imagine, Aida's cooking three times a day. I'd be in Heaven ahead of schedule."

I watched her continue to eat. It was beyond me how she stayed so thin. "By the way," I said, "Aida mentioned to me that Papi's been mixed up with some strange men who are dedicated to going back to Cuba. Do you know anything about that?"

"Nothing more than usual," Lourdes said. "Papi's always planning what to do after Fidel, isn't he? What's new about that?"

"Well, that's what *I* said."

Lourdes looked worried. "He hasn't moved Mami around again, has he? You know she hates sleeping in the Hatteras."

I laughed. "Not that I know of. But Aida and Osvaldo are both worried. They think it's different this time, and they don't like these men."

"Aida doesn't like anyone. You know that," Lourdes said, completely uninterested. "So, what were you and Papi talking about when I came outside?"

I tried to think for a moment how to answer her question without being evasive; in the end, however, I decided to be direct. It was rarely worth it to hide anything from Lourdes.

"I asked him how well he knows Miguel de la Torre. We saw them at Hector's funeral, remember?"

"Oh?" Lourdes asked. "Mami knew Teresa de la Torre. I remember Mami coming home one day after a charity meeting and telling me about her."

I tried not to appear overly interested. "What did she say?"

"Well, it wasn't so much about Teresa specifically as Cuban exile society in general," Lourdes said. "You know, Mami didn't really like Miami Cuban society much. Mami said she was on all those boards because she had compassion for the people they helped, not just to get her name in the paper."

"Who did she mean? Teresa?" I couldn't resist the dig, even though I knew Lourdes would never openly admit to our mother's having strong negative feelings about anyone. I, however, could admit that Mami was human. She had failings, too—not many, but some.

"Maybe," Lourdes conceded. "Mami didn't like to speak ill of anyone, but she did mention once that Teresa got herself placed on all those charity boards mostly as a vehicle for her social aspirations. Mami must have really questioned Teresa's motivations, to say even as much as she did."

"What else did Mami say about Cuban society? She never really talked to me about it."

My curiosity was awakened. My instincts told me that to get to the core of the relationship between the de la Torres and the Delgados, I had to understand the world they moved in in Cuba. And I was curious as well to learn about my own family's life in Cuba.

"Mami had very definite views on Cuban society—both in Cuba and in exile," Lourdes said. She poured herself a fresh cup of coffee and sat back, ready to educate her baby sister. "And Mami could be a very critical observer of Cubans, so take what I tell you with a grain of salt."

"Sounds juicy," I said.

And it was.

Mami had told Lourdes that Cuban snobbery was unparalleled anywhere—which galled Mami, who was very egalitarian. She told Lourdes that even having money in Cuba didn't necessarily guarantee acceptance into society. It was only when that money became third- or fourth-generation, and then made only in a legitimate fashion, that acceptance became a realistic achievement. It was only then that "new" money became "old" money.

Those who had been considered nobodies in Cuba found a different situation in America. They quickly learned that in the United States, who you were and where you came from weren't as crucial as in Cuba. People learned that they could gain acceptance on their own merits and that financial success was applauded, no matter how new the money was or how it was made. It was possible to become pillars of the community without the benefit of a foot-long pedigree.

This newfound social freedom also claimed some victims. In America, divorce didn't carry the same stigma as it had back home. In Cuba, many marriages had been held together only by the fabric of societal pressure. But because divorce was taboo, many men found satisfaction with mistresses while their wives focused on their children. Since upper-class couples were able to lead completely separate lives, marriages endured that might otherwise have been doomed. Of course a few women did have affairs of their own, but given the societal constraints on women and the high price they would pay if discovered, they were exceptions. The classic double standard was definitely strong in upper-class Cuban society.

After coming to America, these couples—many of whom had been married twenty years or more—faced the daunting reality that for the first time, they were going to have to live in each other's company on a daily basis. In the beginning these marriages lasted for financial reasons. After all, if a husband was having a hard time paying for one household, he couldn't support two. The wives also were trapped, by their overall lack of marketable skills. But once they had been in America for a few years and their financial situations had improved, then the divorce rate climbed. Nothing was as it had been in Cuba.

Cuban society ladies also had prodigious memories. They knew exactly whose grandmother had been the daughter of a slave, and whose great-grandfather had been the result of an illicit union between the son of a sugar-mill owner and the daughter of the mill's manager. There were no secrets—and not much was forgiven or forgotten.

It was well known that certain men with means had had two families in Cuba—one legitimate wife and children, and a mistress with illegitimate children. Some of these men had paid to have both families brought across the Florida Straits, which caused financial and social problems for themselves. The difference in the status of the second family dropped precipitously on American soil, and informal understandings started to vanish. Though divorce was accepted here, other social mores weren't as permissible and understood in America as they had been in Cuba. And whereas in Cuba people had known their stations and their places, Americans didn't understand such concepts. The old guard wondered if there were still any rules at all.

I was completely mesmerized by everything that Lourdes was telling me. I hadn't been aware of any of this. And to top it all off, I couldn't remember Lourdes ever having spoken so much at one time.

"So . . . Comments? Reactions?" she asked.

"That's how it all worked?" I asked.

"That's what Mami explained to me," Lourdes said simply. "That was how she saw it."

It was getting close to ten o'clock, time to go to the office.

"I like things better the way they are now," I said. "It sounds like women could become second-class citizens pretty easily. And I know I wouldn't have been able to keep my opinions to myself."

"You're telling me," Lourdes said. "We have our share of hypocrites, but at least some of them pay for it."

I told Lourdes I had to leave, stood up, and kissed her cheek. I walked quicker, pretending not to hear when Lourdes called out, "Hey, why did you want to know about Teresa de la Torre, anyway?" "Lupe?"

But by then I was gone.

Seventeen

Driving to Coconut Grove, I found myself entirely preoccupied with what Lourdes had told me about pre- and post-exile Cuban society. I tried to reconcile this information with the de la Torres and their rise to prominence in Miami. All I had known about them was a pair of diametrically opposed viewpoints: Luis's, as well as Mami's and Sergio's, version of them as evil and greedy, and their near-deification by the public-at-large. Miguel and Teresa de la Torre had been abstractions to me—vague stick figures instead of flesh-and-blood people. I needed some hard facts.

As soon as I got to the office, I placed a call to Nestor.

"How are you doing on the de la Torres' financials?" I asked him.

"I haven't really gotten that far yet," he replied sheepishly. "I just started on the public records searches, and I was waiting to see what comes back. Today I was planning to go to the library to check out newspaper accounts."

I wasn't going to give Nestor trouble for starting late. He had earned my respect and I knew he'd come through for me.

"I'm glad I caught you," I said. "In addition to the financial background, get me some more information on personal stuff as well. You know, newspaper-feature stuff. Tours of the house, soft-news articles—especially on Teresa."

"God, I'll be there for days," Nestor groaned. "I'll bet those two have had thousands of articles written about them."

"Well, you'd better get started," I said. "And keep track of your billable hours."

Leonardo knocked on the door and announced in an agitated voice, "Joe Ryan's on the phone. He says he has to talk to you right away."

I told Nestor I had to go, then punched the other line.

"Lupe, I'm calling across the street from the target's house," Joe said. He was a pro and knew not to use his target's name on a cell phone. "I'm here to relieve Mike, but he's not here. Did you pull him off the job or something?"

"No, I didn't. Hey, wait," I said, puzzled, "don't you have the afternoon shift?"

"Usually, but we switched schedules for today. Lucy's kid is sick, so Mike and I split her shift. He took midnight to noon, and I took noon to midnight."

This was nothing out of the ordinary; the three junior investigators had worked together before, and they always had been willing to help one another out.

What *was* unusual was for Mike not to be at his post. We all knew it was vital to keep someone on surveillance without interruption. I felt a little pang of anxiety in my stomach. "Did you try to call him?" I asked.

"Yeah," Joe said. "I called his beeper, his cell phone, his house. Nothing. He's not answering."

I heard a slight buzzing in my ears. Something was wrong. "Meet me at Cocoplum Circle," I said. "I'm leaving right now."

I grabbed my purse and shot out of my office, stopping at Leonardo's desk. "Mike's missing," I said. "He's not at his surveillance post."

"That's not like him—" Leonardo began.

"I know. I'm going to check it out. If he calls, contact me immediately."

I jogged to my car, fired the ignition, and hit the street without looking. I knew I could make it in minutes if I ran all the yellow lights and a few of the red ones.

When I was almost there I opened my cell phone and dialed the office. Leonardo answered. "Tell me Mike called," I said.

"He didn't," Leonardo said. He sounded even more worried than I.

Joe was waiting for me where we'd agreed. I pulled over and he hopped into the Mercedes, his face grim.

"I looked around a little more after I called you," he said. "I found his car, but I didn't see him anywhere."

"Did you check out the car?" I asked.

"I would have, but I had to meet you."

The de la Torres' house was just a few blocks away. My hands were sweating so much that I had to grip the wheel hard to control the car.

"Where is he parked?" I asked.

"On an embankment off a bridge. This way." Joe directed me to turn right. "It's weird, because Mike told me he hardly ever parks. Mostly he just drives around. Believe it or not, he said two days ago that he'd stationed himself up a tree. This surveillance is a real bitch. You should have heard Lucy complaining. She's a mother of two, but she can cuss like a sailor."

Joe was babbling; I tuned him out and slowed the car as we made our first pass in front of the de la Torres' house. It was a stately place, two stories in salmon-tinged pink with white shutters around oversized windows, and a sweeping circular driveway. I could see why the juniors hated this job—there was almost no camouflage from which to watch the house.

No sign of anything happening. By then my heart was pounding in my ears. I sneaked a look at Joe, who was nervously rubbing his cheeks. We both knew Mike, and it was hard to believe that he would leave his post and his car.

"I'm parking," I said. "We'll walk from here."

I slowed down and pulled off onto the grass several houses away from the de la Torres'. Joe and I got out of the car, and he directed me to the bridge. I had to hope we would get lucky and that no one would drive by and notice us.

We knew from our sweep that Mike's car wasn't visible from the street. Joe pointed it out, along one of the stone bridges that crisscrossed the Coral Gables waterways. There was only one house between the bridge and the de la Torres'.

I looked down the embankment, and my heart thumped in my chest. There was no sign of life down there. I took a step and almost lost my balance, which would have sent me falling into the canal. Joe saw me wobbling and grabbed my shoulder. We both could see Mike's gray Honda parked close to the edge of the water. Apparently this time he hadn't been conducting a rolling surveillance.

We both stood there, neither of us relishing a further investigation. But then the far-off noise of a lawn mower jarred us back to reality. I looked up and down the street: No one. Coral Gables was so insular and heavily patrolled that someone would inevitably spot us and think we were behaving suspiciously.

Joe and I scrambled down the embankment and approached the Honda. It was unlocked. The air was deathly quiet; even the lawn mower had stopped. I heard the low buzz of bees.

I was sweating so much—from the heat and anxiety—that I felt rivulets of water moving down my back. It was then that I heard the faint beep a pager makes when it's received an unacknowledged message.

I motioned for Joe to stay where he was, then took a deep breath and opened the car door.

"The keys are gone," I told Joe.

Inside the Honda was a vintage investigator's mess—fast-food wrappers, empty coffee cups, tollbooth receipts, and old pens that looked like they didn't work. I leaned in and felt around the seat. The unmistakable shape of a legal pad met my touch, so I pulled it out.

Joe was ignoring my instructions, joining me and opening the passenger side. "Is that the surveillance log?" he asked.

"Yeah." I looked at it closely. Mike had, in his usual scrawl, written shorthand notations to the effect that nothing had happened during the first four hours of his shift other than the uneventful arrival home of the de la Torres themselves.

"It ends at four in the morning," I said.

"Let me see that." Joe stared at it for a minute, then looked at me. His eyes were wide. "Why does the log stop eight hours before his shift was supposed to end?"

I couldn't answer him. Still I could hear the faint sound of a beeper, but I couldn't find one. I searched the car further and found nothing interesting. There were no strange objects, no spills or messes, and—encouragingly at this point—no blood.

"I think we're going to have to call the police," I said.

Joe glanced around nervously but said nothing. We both were thinking the same thing: that someone might have discovered Mike hiding near the de la Torres' house. But I had an even more specific fear, of which Joe was unaware: The de la Torres were known to associate with at least one felon—Pepe Salazar—and they recently had faced a multimillion-dollar demand from Luis. If it was they who had discovered Mike, they weren't likely to be in a forgiving mood.

"The trunk," Joe said suddenly. "That beeping noise. I think it's coming from the trunk."

I felt under the dash until I found the lever that tripped the trunk's locking mechanism. Joe stepped back and stuck his hands deep in his pockets. Apparently this was my show now.

I looked around to make sure no one was watching, then walked to the back of the car. The trunk was open about an inch; I grabbed the lid and threw it completely open.

My surroundings melted away from me, and my ears filled with a roar like that of the sea. I had to brace myself on the bumper to keep from fainting.

Mike looked like he was merely sleeping. He had been stuffed diagonally into the trunk of his own car, his long body folded at the waist, his head wedged near his feet. An angry red line was traced across his throat, and his face was frozen into an expression of surprise.

He was dressed, as usual, in blue jeans and a light-blue work shirt, with scuffed sneakers over his sockless feet. His beeper was still clipped to his belt, and it gave a weak whine. Feeling my eyes starting to fill with tears, I looked over at Joe. Though none of us had been close friends, we had known one another for years. Mike and Joe had worked a number of cases together for me.

Joe brought his fist down hard on the roof of the Honda. "Fuck!" he yelled out. The trunk lid swung up and down on its hinge.

"We have to call it in," I said. I looked up at the overcast sky, blinking away tears as I felt in my purse for the cellular phone. Before I could find it, I pulled my hand out and held it away from my body, as I was not going to need to use it.

"We've got company," I said.

The police car had pulled up next to the bridge, and two officers stepped out, their hands on their holsters. They stood on the embankment for a moment, not saying anything, just watching.

"*Mierda,*" I muttered under my breath. Joe and I stood completely still. "It's funny they came so fast. I certainly didn't call them."

"Lupe, wake up," Joe whispered back. "They don't know about Mike. It's us they want."

The shorter of the two officers, a Latino with a neat mustache, moved first. He shuffled down the embankment, calling out, "Is this your car?"

"No, officer," I replied.

"Then what are you doing here?" He kept his gaze moving from Joe to me.

"My name is Guadalupe Solano," I said. "This is Joe Ryan." I kept my voice as polite as I could, knowing this was going to turn ugly in a minute or two.

"You didn't answer my question," the cop said. "What are you doing down there?"

The officer's hand moved toward his holster. In the corner of my eye I saw that his partner on the bridge had already pulled his weapon. Sweat dripped into my eyes; I heard Joe next to me, breathing in short jagged breaths. We didn't look good, that was for sure. Wait until they open the trunk, I thought.

"Officer, we're private investigators working a case in this neighborhood," I said. Of course I had to tell the truth, but relating this fact to a cop was tantamount to waving a red flag in front of a bull. Animosity between cops and investigators runs deep—both resent what they perceive as the others' meddling in their work.

"Move away from the car and put your hands up," the officer commanded. He yelled up to his partner, "Call for backup!"

Joe and I did as we were ordered. As I reached for the sky, I said, "There's a body in the trunk of this car." I figured I might as well take the offensive, since we were in trouble anyway. When they dusted Mike's car for prints, they would find ours everywhere.

The officer studied my face, trying to tell if I was serious. He pulled his gun out and kept it trained on us as he lifted the trunk's lid.

He covered his mouth with his free hand and yelled up to his partner again, "We got a body down here!"

An instant later, four police cars roared up, their lights flashing. Cops clambered out of the cruisers. It was going to be a long day.

I took a chance with the Latino cop. "Can I make a call?" I asked in a sugary voice. "I have a phone right here in my purse."

He thought for a moment. "All right, take it out," he said. I complied, the officer watching my every move. Once I had it out, he reholstered his gun. This was fun for him, I realized. It wasn't every day a cop found a body next to the Coral Gables waterways.

Joe dropped his hands and crouched on the ground. I dialed Tommy's direct line and reached him immediately. "No time to chat," I said. "We have a problem." Speaking low so I wouldn't be overheard, I gave Tommy the facts quick and dirty, ending with our location.

The Latino officer—I noticed his name tag, which read "Guerrero"—called for Homicide in an excited voice. I knew the Homicide unit would also call the Medical Examiner's office. Guerrero then radioed everyone else needed for the crime scene: the lab technicians, the photographer. His duty was to preserve the scene and to make sure none of the witnesses got away—which meant Joe and me. No one was allowed to touch the body, so Mike's beeper continued to let out a little whine every now and then. Its batteries were almost dead.

Within minutes the news trucks started to arrive, having learned about the body by listening to police-scanner frequencies. The reporters weren't allowed to come down the embankment, but they started to fill the bridge, tripping over one another for the best camera angle. I turned my back; the last thing I needed was Papi seeing me on TV, on the off chance that he watched the local news that night.

Finally I sat down on the grass next to Joe. The cops were keeping an eye on us, but for more than a half-hour, no one stepped forward to take our statements. Finally a nice-looking, sandy-haired man with an athletic build approached us. He had just finished introducing himself as Detective Anderson from Homicide when Tommy sprang down the embankment to join us. Anderson looked up and down at Tommy's impressive suit, probably knowing his day was now ruined.

"Tommy McDonald." Tommy extended his hand. Anderson looked at it as though it were a smelly fish, then reluctantly shook it. "I see you've met my investigators, Guadalupe Solano and Joe Ryan," Tommy added with a disarming smile.

I could tell that Anderson knew Tommy, at least by reputation. And hearing that Tommy was the attorney of record on a case sent fear and loathing into the hearts of Miami cops. Tommy was known as a fierce dealer on behalf of his clients, and a lawyer who was heartless in the courtroom. Whoever opposed him knew they had to be prepared for a real bloodletting on the witness stand.

Tommy's navy-blue pinstriped suit was that day complemented by a light-pink shirt with the gold Cartier cufflinks I had given him for Christmas years before. When the wind shifted I could smell his expensive cologne.

"Is there anything I can help you with, officer?" Tommy asked.

"No," Detective Anderson said. He took the cap off his pen and flipped open his notebook. "I'm going to take statements from Ms. Solano and Mr. Ryan."

Tommy clucked with regret. "Actually, Ms. Solano and Mr. Ryan are working a case for me, which makes them my employees," he said. "Therefore anything they know is privileged information."

The policeman knew that in spite of Tommy's friendly, affable manner, he was outmatched. Still, to his credit, he kept trying.

"Look, either I talk to them here or I take them to the Coral Gables Police Department for questioning," Anderson said.

Tommy was unfazed. "I understand they've told the police all they know about this situation," Tommy said. "They found the body and they don't know how it got here."

"I want to hear it for myself." Anderson shifted around on his feet, getting agitated.

Joe looked at Tommy; Tommy shrugged.

"Well, I was coming to relieve Mike and couldn't find him," Joe said. "I called Lupe, then I saw Mike's car. Lupe came, and we went down to the car. We popped the trunk and found Mike stuffed in there. That's when the police showed up."

Joe was talking in a flat monotone. He had been quiet and withdrawn since we found Mike. I knew that Mike's death hadn't hit him yet, nor had it shaken me the way I knew it would.

Detective Anderson flipped his notebook closed. "All right," he said. "But you still have to come downtown for more questioning."

"You just heard what they saw and found," Tommy interjected. "They saw the car, they found the body. That's obviously all there is to know."

Anderson smirked, trying to look amused by Tommy's pressure tactics. "Why were you in the neighborhood in the first place?" he asked, turning to Joe and me.

"I've already told you, whatever else Ms. Solano and Mr. Ryan have to say is privileged," Tommy said. "They really don't have to answer your questions. I'm sure you're aware of that."

Anderson sighed, and I felt a pang of sympathy for him. "Well, if they won't answer my questions," he said, "then I'm just going to have to arrest them."

Tommy countered with a laugh. "Nice try," he said. "You know you can't do that without a court order." He took a step away and motioned for Joe and me to follow. "If there's nothing further, we're leaving."

We walked carefully up the hill and onto the road. I expected that at any moment the cops would follow me up and clamp handcuffs on me. We walked in uncomfortable silence to Tommy's Rolls, which was parked a block away. I hadn't seen the extent of the crowd from below, but the whole area had filled with official vehicles, as well as news trucks with towering antennas. A couple of reporters approached us, but Tommy waved them away.

I waited until we were completely out of earshot before asking Tommy, "We didn't really get away that easily, did we?"

"All I did there was buy us all some time." Tommy pulled his keys out of his pocket and unlocked the Rolls.

"Give me the worst-case scenario," I said.

"Well, Detective Anderson might go and find some overeager prosecutor who'll want to haul you in front of a grand jury," Tommy said. "Then I'm pretty sure you'll have to talk."

"A grand jury," I repeated. That was serious business. There was no way I could withhold information about the Delgado case in that situation.

Tommy rubbed his chin; I could almost hear the wheels spinning in his head. "I'll get one of my interns working on that point," he said, seemingly to himself. "You might get offered immunity to talk, but then you'd have to tell everything about the case anyway. Don't worry about it right now, either of you. I'll protect you as much as I can."

Joe was barely listening. "I'll call you tomorrow, Lupe," he said. He walked toward his car, his head drooping. After he'd gotten about ten feet away, he stopped, turned, and waved to Tommy.

Tommy shook his head. "Damn. Lupe, this is ugly."

"Thanks for your help, Tommy." I hugged him, not caring that we were in public. "I knew I could count on you."

Tommy smiled, seemingly rejuvenated by our bodily contact. "What are you going to do now?" he asked.

"I'm going back to the office. I have to look in my Rolodex for the contact person Mike gave when he registered to work for me. If I remember right, it was his sister. I know for sure that he was single. I think his family would rather hear it from me than the cops."

"Just call me if you need anything," Tommy said, giving my hand a squeeze. People thought he was a cold, unfeeling bastard, but I knew better. It just paid to stay on his good side.

Eighteen

The next morning Nestor and I met in my office. I sat behind my desk, and he lay back on the sofa, quietly digesting what I had just told him about discovering Mike. I had yet to feel the emotional toll of discovering dead a man I had known for a few years. I probably would allow myself that luxury only when the case was over and, I hoped, Mike's killer was found and punished.

"Choked to death," Nestor said, a look of disbelief on his face. "Choked to death with a wire across his throat."

"His camera is missing," I said, trying not to relive the memory.

Nestor picked up on my cue, transforming himself back into an investigator. "Anything else?" he asked.

"Not that I know of. The police got his beeper, his wallet with nothing missing, the gun he kept in his glove compartment, his keys, and his investigator's log."

"But no camera," Nestor said. "What does that tell you?"

"You know what I'm thinking: That camera is missing for a reason. There's no way Mike would go on surveillance without it. That camera was almost surgically attached to him," I said. "I think Mike might have had time to take a picture of the person who killed him."

It was a wild guess, but then I knew that Mike always took a surplus of pictures during a surveillance—much more than other investigators. He had claimed it helped ward off boredom, but I had always chalked it up to a mildly obsessive personality.

Nestor looked skeptical. "All right, Lupe, tell me your theory," he said. "I know you have one."

"Picture this: Mike was out of his car, hiding somewhere on the side of the road, when he heard or saw something suspicious. He followed whoever it was, then took a picture of him."

"And Mike blew his cover then," Nestor said.

"Exactly. The murderer saw Mike and followed him back to the car. He killed Mike because Mike had seen him, then stole the camera because he knew Mike had taken his picture."

"Mike was a big guy," Nestor mused.

"Which means the killer surprised him," I said. "Because there weren't signs of a struggle at the scene. The killer had to be strong enough to strangle Mike, then stuff him in the trunk of the car."

"Maybe so," Nestor said. He looked away from me. "So what have you learned from the cops?"

"Not a damned thing. Ever since Tommy stonewalled them with attorney-client privilege, they don't want to divulge anything to help us out." I let my mind drift back to the crime scene. "We gave them some minimal information, of course, just enough to get them off our backs. But we didn't say a thing about the case."

"No wonder the cops hate Tommy so much," Nestor said. "He protects his clients, and the hell with what the police need."

Nestor spoke with a combination of admiration and admonishment. But then, Nestor had the sort of mind that saw all sides of every story.

"What's next?" he asked me.

"As far as Mike's murder is concerned, we have to be really careful," I replied. "Tommy didn't win any popularity contests yesterday, and neither did Solano Investigations. We can't interfere with the ongoing police investigation in any way, or we'll end up in jail."

Nestor leaned back on the sofa with a sigh and closed his eyes. Sometimes I could swear I saw him aging right in front of me.

He pointed to a brown accordion file next to his feet. "This is what I've got so far on the case. It's all pretty straightforward. Shake me when you need me."

With that, he started to drift off. It was a gift he had, falling asleep at will. By the time I had retrieved the file and opened it on my desk, I could hear him begin to snore gently.

I started reading the credit report on the de la Torres. I saw they each carried two credit cards, with zero balances. I was suddenly jealous and wished I had as much financial discipline as they did—or money. It is almost unheard of in present-day America to be so debt free! It's un-American!

The file section on the de la Torres' real-estate holdings was extensive. According to Nestor's research, Miguel and Teresa owned their Coral Gables house outright. Its assessed value was recorded at $2.5 million. I had seen that house, and this estimate was low. Based on land value, a lot that size and in that location was worth a million alone. The home itself contained eight thousand square feet of space and was on the Grenada waterways, with no bridges between them and the bay. The numbers didn't add up. Either the City of Coral Gables hadn't assessed the property in decades, or someone at City Hall was doing them a favor and minimizing their tax bill in the process.

Then I found the warranty deed, along with the history of the property. The de la Torres had bought it in May of 1960, six months after they had arrived in Miami. They had paid cash, and records put the purchase price at $125,000. Nestor had inserted a note to himself saying that this purchase might have been part of a larger deal. Since no mortgage company was listed, the terms and conditions of the sale weren't divulged. The buyers and seller had agreed what to report to the county, which wasn't unusual. Nestor had included a couple of photos of the impressive house, taken from different angles.

The next item in the file regarded the condo the de la Torres owned at the Ocean Reef Club in the Keys. I knew the place well; my parents had been members for years, though Papi had given up his membership after Mami died. A lot of Miamians were members, especially those who were fishing enthusiasts. Miguel and Teresa had bought the condo in 1975, when it was assessed at almost a million dollars. Ocean Reef was a private club, so I knew it would be hard to get a true property value. There was no mortgage on this property, either. The de la Torres had paid cash and owned it free and clear.

As I delved deeper into their property records it became apparent that the de la Torres didn't believe in having unnecessary debt. Which was sensible enough. But it also meant they wouldn't get credit-related tax deductions, and they were definitely in the highest tax bracket. There were two possible reasons why they did this: First was refugee mentality, a state of mind in which they could sleep at night only knowing they wouldn't lose their possessions through debt; and second, they didn't want to leave a paper trail of their investments, other than the minimal records technically required by law. It was interesting. Bankers, by the very nature of their profession, knew the financial advantages of debt. Miguel, it seemed, was the exception.

Miguel and Teresa didn't deny themselves toys. They had his and her Jaguars—surprise, owned outright—as well as a blue Chevy station wagon that was used probably by the housekeeper. They had a fifty-two-foot Hatteras, the same as Papi's, docked in the canal behind their house. It was their fifth boat to date. I saw from marine records that they had started with a Mako 22 in 1963 and had gradually worked their way up. Nestor had somehow managed to include a picture of the Hatteras—the *Teresa V*—docked behind their house on a sunny afternoon.

Last were the aircraft records. Miguel had owned a Gulfstream and employed a full-time pilot as well, but had sold the plane five years ago. Poor Miguel and Teresa, I thought meanly, having to fly commercial.

Nestor suddenly opened his eyes and sat up. "How'd I do?" he asked. He looked younger after his twenty-minute nap, I realized with a bit of envy. "What do you think of the visuals? Pretty good, huh?"

"Great job. I just finished looking through the property, vehicle, and aircraft records. They certainly live well." I flipped through the files. "What else do you have in here?'

"Not much. I started on the corporation check, but I couldn't finish it." Nestor wore a pained expression. "Because I heard about Mike."

I put down the file. "Look, I spoke to Tommy about some concerns I've developed about this case, especially since we found Mike dead. We don't know who was responsible for Mike's death, but I'm dismissing the possibility that it was a random murder."

"I'm with you," Nestor said.

"It has to do with the investigation," I said. "These people have been known to associate with hit men. They're dangerous."

"I know what you're saying," Nestor replied. "Killing Mike is a way of sending us a message: 'Fuck off, or this is going to happen to you, too.'"

"I don't know who did it," I said. "It could have been Salazar. Maybe they've hired him full-time for protection."

"It doesn't really matter who it was," Nestor pointed out.

"Exactly. So if you want off the case, I understand and I have no problem with it." I stood up from my desk. This conversation was making me nervous. "I'm going to call Marisol to tell her what's going on. She'll have to decide whether she still wants to work the case, and the same goes for the junior investigators. I know Joe was pretty shaken up." I sighed. "At least Mike was working as a contract investigator," I added. "As of this moment, there's been no public connection made between him and us. Hopefully it'll remain that way."

Nestor stretched; I heard his back crack. "What are you going to do?" he asked.

"I'm going to work the case," I said. "I'm going to keep going."

"I knew that. I just wanted to hear you say it." Nestor stood up and retucked his shirt. "Count me in. I make it a point never to walk away from a case. Call it macho pride, if you want."

"Maybe," I said. "Or else professionalism."

"Or insanity," he countered.

Nestor winked and headed for the door. I shook my head. He never backed off from trouble or refused work—no wonder he looked like a walking train wreck half the time.

"By the way, I forgot to tell you," he said, "I'm having drinks with Veronica tonight."

I must have looked blank. "Veronica Pelaez, the mail lady at First Miami."

He gave me a knowing look and walked out, closing the door behind him. Nestor always had a flair for the dramatic.

I sat down at my desk again and opened my Rolodex. Leonardo was out in the kitchen, the blender at top gear. A small pile of unopened mail lay in my in-box. A typical morning.

Except that I couldn't keep from my mind the red line that ran across Mike Moore's neck.

Nineteen

"Suzanne?"

"Lupe?" Her voice was thick with sleep. "What time is it?"

I checked my watch. "Two-thirty."

"Afternoon or night?" she asked. "It's pitch black in here. I have the curtains closed." She sounded slightly more alert; I wondered what it would feel like not to know the difference between day and night.

"Afternoon," I informed her. "And it's a lovely day outside."

"Hold on." I heard her put the phone down on the table, and the sound of blinds being pulled up. A moment later she was back on the line. "You're right. It is a beautiful day. So what's up?"

"Do you want to go shopping with me?" I asked. "I need to buy a dress for a ball."

"You?" Suzanne laughed, a high-pitched cackle that cut through my ear directly into my brain. "Shopping for a dress for a ball?"

I wasn't in the mood for editorial comment. "Do you want to come with me or not?" I asked. It wasn't easy to ask someone to come shopping with me—for some reason, it seemed as though I were swallowing my pride. But I felt depressed and figured some company would help. Otherwise I might be prone to pick out something floor-length and black.

After some negotiating about place and time, we agreed to meet later that day, then drive out to Bal Harbour. This plan was created to accommodate the several hours Suzanne needed to wake properly.

Earlier that morning I had arranged to have Luis come to my office for a meeting. Though I hadn't gotten in touch with him for a few days, to his credit he hadn't called or stopped by.

He showed up early for our three-o'clock meeting. He looked better than I had ever seen him, dressed in perfectly pressed tan cotton pants with a lizard belt, and a light-blue short-sleeved shirt. He wore new loafers without socks, and a silver Swiss Army watch on his wrist. He must have felt free to spend more of his paycheck on clothes, knowing that he had a considerable nest egg in my wall safe.

He called out my name from my office doorway, seeming positively ebullient. He headed toward me with energetic strides; because I had the feeling he was going to kiss my cheek by way of greeting, I stuck out my hand for him to shake. For a fleeting second I saw him register displeasure, but he regained his composure by lighting up a cigarette after we had shaken.

I motioned toward the client's chair, and he sat. "How is the investigation going?" He asked.

"Actually, quite a bit has happened."

I wanted to ease him into the ugly reality of Mike's murder. We hadn't learned anything additional about what had happened—only that he had been strangled with a wire, or something similar. The Medical Examiner had estimated the time of death at sometime between two and six in the morning, but because Mike's last entry had been at four, it had to be closer to the end of that range. I had found out this much from Ted Rafferty after Nestor had left. Nothing much more was forthcoming, at least through police channels.

"We started the financial investigation, first of all," I said. Luis puffed on his cigarette as I told him about the de la Torres' property.

"What else do they have?" Luis asked. "What about stocks, bonds, money in the bank? What's their equity position in First Miami?"

"We're getting to that," I said, feeling pressed. "We'll know later this week, or early next week. It takes time to compile that kind of information, especially since we're working in secrecy."

"And what else have you found?" Luis was smiling easily, dragging on his cigarette. A loose curl of his dark hair wound its way down his high forehead.

"We've come up with two people employed at First Miami who might be in positions to give us information," I said. Luis straightened. "Don't get excited yet. It's good news, and we were lucky, but it's too early to know if we can count on them."

"I understand," Luis said. He stared at the burning end of his cigarette.

"The junior investigators I hired have been watching the house 'round the clock, noting all license-plate numbers of vehicles going in and out of the residence. They've also been photographing visitors. We'll compile all the tag numbers at the end of the week and run them through Motor Vehicles. Maybe we'll find something that way."

Luis nodded, apparently satisfied. "You've been getting some sun," he said out of the blue. "You look very good."

I took a deep breath. "Never mind that, Luis. There's been an unfortunate situation you need to know about."

I hated to refer to Mike's murder in such a way, but it was the best I could do. Luis stared at me expectantly. "One of the junior investigators, a man named Mike Moore, was killed while watching the de la Torres' house two days ago."

"K-Killed?" Luis stuttered. His mouth dropped. "How?"

"We don't have much information yet," I said. "We don't know positively whether it was a random attack or if it was related to your case."

"*Dios mio,*" Luis whispered. "Tell me everything. I feel responsible. I have to know what happened."

I told him everything, from Joe's phone call to Tommy's confrontation with Detective Anderson.

Luis looked horrified. "This is a tragedy," he said in a pained voice. "A man is dead because of Miguel and Teresa de la Torre. I know they had your investigator killed. It's the only answer."

I agreed, but I didn't want to upset Luis further. "You can't say that for sure," I said. "The police are still investigating."

"You know as well as I do that he was killed because of my case," Luis insisted.

"You might be right," I said weakly.

"I haven't lived in Miami for a long time," Luis said, angry now. "But I know that people don't get killed and stuffed into car trunks very often in Coral Gables. I'm not a child, Lupe, you don't have to hide the truth from me."

"I'm not—" I began.

"I'll call soon, or you can contact me," Luis said. He stood up. "I'm sorry this happened. Please promise me you will be careful."

"Of course I will," I said. "The same goes for you."

"Don't worry about me," he said, putting out his cigarette. "Those damned people. You see—you see how they are!"

I started to talk, but Luis interrupted: "We have to find a way to—" he began. He stared into my eyes. "You are doing a good job, and I thank you. But I'm so angry now, I have to leave. I have to be alone."

Luis stormed out of my office, leaving only a cloud of Marlboro smoke. I chided myself when I realized that my first instinct was to chase after him.

Great.

Five o'clock finally rolled around, and I was more than ready to leave to meet Suzanne. I found Leonardo in the kitchen, spooning a mess of refrigerated goo into a big plastic cup. I knew better than to ask what it was, probably some algae grown off a Bornean atoll. Calling out from the doorway—I didn't want to get too close to his experiment and end up miraculously pregnant or something—I told him I was leaving for the day.

I had driven for about five minutes when I realized that I had left my credit cards in the office safe. I wasn't a shopping addict, so I kept my cards there in case my wallet was stolen. Cursing, I made a U-turn and headed back to the office.

I stepped into the cottage and looked around for Leonardo to tell him that I'd returned, not wanting to startle him.

Strange, I thought. His Jeep was still in its parking space, and the front door had been unlocked, so he couldn't have gone far. I called out his name and received no reply. I looked in all the rooms, even in the closets, but couldn't find him.

Checking my watch, I saw that I was going to be late if I didn't leave right away. I got my credit cards out of the locked safe, where I kept them, then grabbed a pad of paper to write Leonardo a note asking him to call me on the cellular phone to tell me where he had been. I was feeling more than a little paranoid since Mike had been killed.

I had just scribbled a few lines when I heard a loud squawking and shrieking outside my office window. I looked out in time to see a dozen or so parrot-family members fly out of the avocado tree, riled up about something. I hoped it wasn't a cat or a raccoon trying to eat them.

I walked over to the window and peered out. It hadn't been an animal at all; Leonardo emerged from the hedge behind the tree, holding a rake and a hoe in his hand. He wasn't the Martha Stewart type, so I watched him, wondering what he might be up to. He put the gardening implements in the small shed outside and locked it up.

"Leonardo!" I yelled out. "What are you doing?"

He jumped about a yard off the ground. "Lupe!" he cried out in a high voice. "What are you doing here? I thought you had left!"

"I forgot my credit cards. I had to come back to get them," I said. Now I was curious. I had seen guilt on my cousin's face plenty of times before, but never like this.

"Well, I guess you'll have to be leaving now, right?" he said nervously. "Otherwise you're going to be late to meet Suzanne."

Leonardo had taken a few steps toward the window; I could see perspiration on his cheeks. From exertion, or from fear?

"That's right," I said brightly. "I'm leaving right now. I'll see you tomorrow."

I left, knowing that I had to check out what was going on by the avocado tree. I hate when it's personal.

I drove north toward Brickell Avenue, where Suzanne lived. I dreaded having to pick her up, because security at her building was so tight it seemed as though they actively discouraged visitors. The place was fortified with guardhouses, security officers, and surveillance cameras. The atmosphere made me feel as if I had done something wrong every time I walked up to the front door.

I telephoned Suzanne from the car and asked her to come down to the lobby, a tactic that at least enabled me to bypass two checkpoints. She was waiting for me when I came in. She looked like a cheerleader: blond, happy, smooth-skinned, oozing health. I could visualize a milk mustache on her, and a straw tucked behind her ears, not to mention a 4-H Club T-shirt on her curvaceous body. She must have driven them insane in the Upper Midwest.

We took the expressway to Bal Harbour and got off at the 125th Street exit. I parked the Mercedes in a prime spot in the covered lot, just next to the stairs that led to the mall. All the shops at Bal Harbour were upscale: a long block anchored by Neiman Marcus at the north and Saks Fifth Avenue at the south end. For those who needed a quick jewelry fix, there was Cartier's, Tiffany's, Bulgari, and a couple of others. I was lazy about shopping, so I liked going to the Bal Harbour shops best—I could almost always find what I was looking for, with a minimum of hassle.

Suzanne dragged me to Saks first, thinking this was my best bet. In the second-floor designer section I found what I wanted to get away from but never could quite manage—a Vera Wang dress in long, black, sheer chiffon. I knew how good I looked in black. The cost was outlandish, but it would be worth every penny among the inevitable snobs and social climbers at the ball.

Suzanne loved the dress and wouldn't allow me to protest about the cost. We went downstairs to find some nice matching black satin

Chanel shoes. The last stop was buying proper stockings to complete the outfit. I was pleased to see that I had pulled off the whole operation in less than an hour.

"It's still early," I said as we walked to the parking lot. Suzanne was in a good mood; she was the kind of girl who loved spending money, and who loved watching other people spend it almost as much. "Want to stop off for a drink on South Beach before we go home?"

"Sure," she said. "I have a date, but not until after nine."

We went south on Alton Road to Ocean Drive, talking the whole way about the clothes we had seen. It struck me how much I enjoyed the company of women and how seldom I got together with my few woman friends. I used to have lots of friends, but ever since my best friend, Margarita, died in a car accident, I had withdrawn more and more from my other friends. My work had incrementally taken more and more of my time, and I had lost touch with most of them. It was a shame.

"News Café all right with you?" I asked Suzanne.

"Sure, but that place gives me a complex," Suzanne answered.

I knew exactly what she meant. The customers there were uniformly young, attractive, and toned. Anyone older than twenty-five was practically considered eligible for a senior-citizen's discount. You had to have thick skin to go there, but what the hell—we were on a roll.

We sat down at one of the minuscule tables on the terrace and ordered Coronas with lime. We looked around as we waited. It was the usual crowd of models, photographers, stylists, and hangers-on. They ranged from Latinos to African-Americans to foreign tourists to non-Hispanic whites (as they're referred to in Miami demographics). There were also nonhumans—a smattering of designer dogs. Pooches on South Beach seemed to come in two varieties: two-pound ankle-biters carted around in Louis Vuitton bags, or two-hundred-pound Great Danes with bandanas tied around their necks. At other times I had seen pythons, parrots, even iguanas on leashes. No one gave anyone a second look; "normal" was a very relative concept on South Beach.

Our waiter took a good twenty minutes before returning with our drinks. No doubt he was on the phone with his agent.

"Lupe, are you still working that case?" Suzanne asked after the beers finally arrived. "The one with Pepe Salazar?"

"*Sí*, that's what the dress is for." Suzanne looked puzzled. "The reason I have to go to this ball is because some people will be there whom I'm investigating. It gives me a chance to check them out."

"Great! Then you can write off the dress, the shoes, and the stockings!" Suzanne said with delight. "My accountant says all the clothes you wear for work can be written off."

"I don't know if I can get away with that," I said.

"Well, you can bill the client for the stuff," she suggested.

I laughed. "I don't think so. I might try to write it off my taxes, but I can't see an IRS auditor allowing it. I mean, I didn't have to buy a dress priced in the mid-four figures. Not to mention the Chanel shoes."

"I guess not," Suzanne said. She sipped her beer. "So, is Pepe Salazar going to jail?"

"I certainly hope so," I said. I couldn't tell her what I suspected—that he was responsible for murdering one of my investigators.

I saw that Suzanne had finished her drink. I polished mine off as well. Neither of us wanted another, so I signaled for the bill.

"If you need any help putting him away," Suzanne added, "just let me know. I'll be happy to do whatever I can. He's a pig. I'd be delighted to help bring him down."

"I'll remember that," I said.

"I mean it." She tapped the table lightly. "He's a son-of-a-bitch. You remember to call me."

Given the company she kept, that was a real condemnation.

"Do you promise?" she said.

"Oh, all right, I promise," I said, not meaning it. After all, how in the world could Sweet Suzanne help me with Salazar, the de la Torres, any of it?

"Don't forget," she said. "I have a good feeling about this. You'll be needing me. Just wait and see."

I had no idea what she meant.

Twenty

"So what else do you have?" I asked Nestor, feeling a bit impatient. Nestor was giving me the next stage of his financial report on Miguel and Teresa de la Torre. As usual, he was installed in his favorite position—stretched out on my sofa. One of these days I was going to buy him one just like it, so he could attain such comfort in the privacy of his home.

"This case is a bitch, Lupe, as you well know." He ran his fingers through his hair. He looked about fifty again. "Just about all their financial investments are protected under corporations. It's a pain in the ass for me."

"It's been hard for all of us," I snapped. "Give me a break. Stop complaining and get on with it."

Nestor had to crane his neck to give me a dirty look. "When he arrived in America in late 1959, Miguel invested under his own name. That didn't last long." Nestor settled back into the sofa. "After two years most ownership—at least as much as he could—was set up under corporations. It seems that Señor de la Torre isn't fond of the tax man. Every deal he makes, as far as I can tell, he structures with taxes in mind."

I looked at the printed file Nestor had deposited on my desk; it was at least an inch thick. "Maybe it makes him feel macho to outwit the IRS," I speculated. "Lots of smart businessmen do that, Nestor. The more money they make, the more they hate to pay taxes on it."

"Fine, but it also makes it hard to trace the money," Nestor said. It's going to be impossible to find out precisely how much money they have. I got the names of hundreds of corporations, but the majority of them are privately held. Public corporations have to make disclosures about their investors and assets, but private companies can keep all the information secret."

"We're going to have to try a different approach," I said.

"Well, let me give you some good news," Nestor said. "Remember Veronica? We had drinks two nights ago."

Nestor smiled mysteriously, and I knew he was going to make me pay for my bad mood earlier by dragging out his story. Nestor was a good person and a great investigator, but he was also a *prima donna*.

"Tell me, Nestor," I demanded. "What happened?"

"I was right about her job," Nestor began. "She runs the First Miami mail room."

"With access to Miguel's mail?"

"*Sí*, but I couldn't pry too much without making her suspicious. Next time I see her, we'll find out more." Nestor reached into his canvas bag and produced another file. "News clippings on the de la Torres. I edited them for importance. It wasn't easy—both of them have been in the *Herald* several hundred times."

"Thanks, Nestor, I know you're trying." I decided it was time to cheer him up. "You know, Marisol starts work this morning. I told her about Mike, but she still wants to work the case. I think she cares more about a new BMW than about her own safety."

"Marisol?" Nestor sat up a little. "She's following Miguel, right?"

"That's her assignment, following him and taking pictures." I looked at my assignment sheet. "I hired Raul to replace Mike. He wasn't scared; I think he needs the money too badly. The juniors have compiled dozens of tags and photos of movement in and out of the house. Nothing jumps out at me right now."

"And what's next for you?" Nestor asked.

"The more I think about it, the more I see that we're not going to get far using conventional investigative techniques," I said slowly, thinking as I went. "Miguel and Teresa are very public people, but they're also intensely private about their dealings. I have another garbage run planned for tomorrow morning."

"You love your garbage, don't you?" Nestor laughed.

"I could throw up thinking about it," I said. "But I'm also going to work on Sergio Santiago, Miguel's assistant. Clive told Leonardo that Sergio enjoyed meeting me and that he was embarrassed for getting drunk and talking too much. He also mentioned that Sergio is probably HIV-positive and maybe even has AIDS, though he refuses to talk about it. I don't know how all of this fits. It's not much, but it's a start."

"Try it. What can you lose?" Nestor asked. "Hey, Lupe, I know how much you hate garbage runs. You want me to take this one for you?"

I was touched; Nestor rarely played Sir Galahad. "You're a *mensch*, Nestor," I said, blowing him a kiss. "But no. Doing that kind of work keeps me grounded."

"Atoning for your sins?" Nestor asked.

"Something like that."

Nestor heaved his lanky body off the sofa. "I'll call you when I have something," he said. "Why don't you send me on surveillance with Marisol? I hear she needs backup."

"You wish," I replied. "Good-bye, Nestor."

After he left I started flipping through the news clippings, looking for anything out of the ordinary. The first thing that struck me was the extent of their community work; I don't think a charity existed in Miami that they weren't in some way affiliated with. Then I found an interview that Teresa had given to *Tropic* magazine.

It was dated July 14, 1974. *Tropic* was a Sunday magazine, filled with personality puff pieces and home and gardening tips. The article was entitled "Teresa de la Torre: A Courageous Life."

On the first page was a photo of Teresa, poised and smiling on the patio of her home in Coral Gables. The house looked sprawling, with twin columns centering two wall wings painted pastel salmon. Teresa looked considerably younger than she did in more recent pictures. I moved on to the text.

The reporter was obviously in awe of her subject. She began by writing about the "restrained elegance" of the house and the "charming candor" with which Teresa spoke. The first few paragraphs focused on the Children's Wish Society, a group Teresa led that gave gifts to needy children. They were still around—in fact, I had sent them a check for fifty bucks last Christmas.

Then it got interesting. The article discussed Teresa's life in Havana and her adjustment to the United States. I think Teresa had been flattered to be the subject of such a lengthy magazine profile, because here she talked more than in any other article I had seen.

> "In Havana, Miguel and I were part of what you would call high society," Teresa said with a self-deprecating smile. "But it is never as simple as one would like. In Havana, people had long memories, and many people thought it was unlikely that Miguel and I would ever wed."

It sounded to me as though Teresa were talking in code. Had people thought that Miguel had married below his station?

"Miami was a fresh start for Miguel and me, especially after what we had been through. My first priority was to find a suitable home. Miguel's primary business in Cuba had been real estate, and he was able to make several deals in Miami which led us to this house in Coral Gables."

More pictures of their humble abode.

"It took careful effort and patience to make this home resemble the one we had owned in Havana—so that we would feel comfortable in it. We duplicated our old furnishings and many other details. Many of our friends have commented that our decor reminds them of old Havana. Of course, this makes us very pleased."

I had to read between the lines again. Teresa said that nostalgia had led her to duplicate traditional Cuba in her house, but I suspected otherwise. From what I knew about old-line Cubans, and with my amateur psychologist's skills, I thought her actions had been designed to demonstrate that she and Miguel had been people of stature in pre-Castro Havana.

The article went on to discuss a dinner-dance that Teresa had thrown back in 1961, a little less than two years after their arrival in Miami. It had been an affair intended to entertain the cream of the Cuban exile community. Teresa talked about how nervous throwing the party had made her, and I thought I understood—the gesture had probably been meant to imply that the de la Torres were old money and not *arrivistes*. Whatever she had done, it had worked; soon the de la Torres were considered the epitome of established society.

As Teresa remembered those early days in Miami, so different from the world of today, she put her hand on my knee and asked, "My dear, would you like to hear the story of how Miguel and I escaped from Cuba?"

This was the stuff I really wanted to hear. As I read, I saw that Teresa's version confirmed nearly everything Luis had told me—and this was as good a source as I was going to find for confirming this aspect of his story, other than from Miguel or Teresa in person. She discussed Castro's rise and Batista's fall in the late fifties, and how she and Miguel had liquidated their assets into diamonds—with the understanding that they would soon have to flee the country. But nowhere did she mention Luis's mother or father.

"We had to get the jewels out of the country, but we knew we would be arrested with them at the airport," Teresa said. "So we had to find a way to hide them. That's when we thought of *arroz con pollo*."

I tried to picture the reporter's expression as she tried to think of how to respond. Chicken with rice? What did that have to do with smuggling diamonds out of Cuba?

"Miguel and I sat up all night with a bag of chicken parts. Miguel would find a good-sized piece, then slide the diamond inside a hollowed-out pocket we created within the bird. We had a friend who was also there that night. He stitched up the chicken so that the naked eye couldn't detect that the food had been tampered with. Our friend was very fastidious, so we felt confident leaving that task to him."

Luis's father, I thought. If he had been anything like his son, he would have been the sort of man you would trust with the most delicate part of the operation. But why would the de la Torres trust someone to do this, unless that person was closely involved? Teresa had edited the Delgados out of her story with surgical precision, but she had slipped with this mention.

"We boiled the rice with saffron, then we added the chicken," Teresa continued. "We started to worry, because we hadn't thought about the smell. We never cooked for ourselves, and we thought one of the servants might wake up. The way things were then, one of them might have been willing to report us to the police.

"To escape, we dressed as peasants. Miguel shaved his beautiful mustache, and we put on dirty clothes. Our friend drove us to Rancho Boyeros Airport early in the morning. We had two economy-class, round-trip tickets to Miami, with faked passports and letters postmarked from Miami— we told the police we were visiting relatives for two weeks, and the food was for my daughter in Florida. It was really a grand adventure, but I didn't think so then. I was far too frightened!"

I could hardly finish the article. I was both repulsed and awe-struck by this woman. Teresa ended her story by pointing to her diamond choker, which Miguel had made for her after they arrived. It contained some of the original diamonds—the combined fortune of the de la Torre and Delgado families. It was beautiful and elegant, and only a few people knew how much it had really cost.

The reporter summed things up:

During an afternoon spent in the gracious company of Teresa de la Torre, I was nearly moved to tears several times by her dignity and bearing while recounting her escape from certain imprisonment and possible death. She has maintained her sense of humor, and put her wealth to the best use possible: helping unfortunate children and supporting many other worthy causes. Teresa truly is a remarkable and courageous woman, an exemplar of integrity, strength, and honor.

Boy, what a snow job Teresa had put over on that reporter. After reading this article, most people would be ready to canonize Teresa. What I saw was merely evidence of Teresa's power to charm, perhaps mixed with a strong dose of survivor's guilt—that particular feeling on the part of Cuban exiles who live well while their brethren suffer in Cuba.

I thought about showing the article to Luis, thinking that he might like to see his story corroborated in print, but I figured it would be too much for him. His entire family heritage had been reduced to one veiled allusion in a silly puff piece. I had heard that the winners and survivors wrote history, making themselves into the heroes. Never before had it seemed so true.

Twenty-one

I had requested an upstairs corner table, away from customer traffic, so I could watch everyone coming in and going out. It was also a bit out of the way, intended to make Sergio feel at ease.

The East Coast Fisheries was an old restaurant on the banks of the Miami River, popular mostly with locals. Few tourists had the desire or the nerve to venture into the decaying neighborhoods near downtown, where the homeless had set up encampments under the freeway overpasses. Which was too bad, because the East Coast sent out its own boat every day and served only fresh catch. The complimentary fish pâté portions served as soon as a diner was seated were out of a seafood dream. More than once I had filled up on fish pâté and saltine sandwiches before the main course arrived.

The decor there was pure unintentional kitsch. Fluorescent lights dangled dangerously from the ceiling, barely supporting the moth-eaten fishing nets draped across them. Big conch shells were stuck haphazardly along the walls, alternating with stuffed fish caught and mounted decades before. Boaters came to eat in bathing suits, businessmen in jackets and ties. Young ladies usually came in overdressed, having thought that their dates were taking them to a regular restaurant and not a famous local dive. There was a common theme among the diverse patrons: All seemed to carry beepers and cellular phones, which would go off at varying pitches during the meal. Sometimes it sounded like a jungleful of electronic animals.

I downed the two mineral waters the nautically clad waitress had brought me, and checked my watch: a quarter after four. I worried for a moment that Sergio wasn't going to show up, then I reminded myself that he was Cuban. Five minutes on the clock equated to one Cuban minute—by that reckoning, he was only three minutes late.

I stepped over to the window overlooking the river, where pleasure boats and fishing boats bobbed in the current. I counted the hulking rusted freighters preparing to set sail for Port au Prince, overloaded with cargo. I instinctively checked out the bicycles on the deck of the boat nearest my window, in the forlorn hope that I might spot my Schwinn, which had been stolen the year before. This was the spot near where Luis had been attacked by Pepe Salazar. It looked lonely and seedy enough during the day; I really didn't want to contemplate its ambience by night.

When Sergio finally ambled in a few minutes before five, he looked a wreck. It seemed likely that Clive was right about his being ill. I hadn't told Sergio why I wished us to meet, but it was obvious he knew I wanted something. It was too bad, really, because Sergio would have made a good lunch or dinner companion—if I hadn't found Mike Moore stuffed in the trunk of his own car, and if I hadn't suspected that Sergio's boss had something to do with it.

I convinced Sergio to order a margarita, remembering that he was more talkative when he drank. He relented when I said that I was paying. When he got his drink, he took a few sips and looked at me with open suspicion.

"Sergio, what I'm about to tell you is confidential," I began. "I'm trusting you with information that, should it become public knowledge, could hurt a lot of people."

Sergio looked a little flattered. "All right, go on."

"When we met at Elliot and Clive's dinner party, you told me that you had been Miguel de la Torre's personal assistant for six years."

Sergio nodded, now looking less flattered.

"You also said that you were angry with him, because of how he treated you when your lover got sick. Do you still feel that way?"

"More than ever," Sergio said cautiously. "Time doesn't heal my wounds, you know. They just fester." He took a sip of his margarita. "Sometimes I imagine that Mario might still be alive if I had been able to take care of him the way I wanted to. He was at peace with me, but he couldn't stand strangers seeing him so weak and sickly. I should have been able to be with him. He needed me so much."

Sergio looked down so I couldn't see him gently weeping. I waited a moment for him to compose himself. Callous as it may have been, I was pleased with what I heard. It was the answer I had hoped for. "I have a client who came to me for help," I said. "Miguel de la Torre took money from my client's family and abandoned them in

Havana. Thirty-eight years have gone by, and this man has finally made it to America. And now Miguel has refused to honor an agreement to repay this man money that rightfully belongs to him."

Sergio's eyes narrowed. "Then why doesn't this guy take Miguel to court, prove that he swindled his family, and collect his money?"

I didn't want this conversation to wander too far from the moral aspects of Luis's situation; Sergio was filled with righteous anger toward Miguel, and I was counting on that feeling.

"Because there's nothing in writing," I said. "It was all based on Miguel's word. It was an agreement of honor between friends. Without divulging too much, I can tell you that Miguel and my client's father were childhood friends."

It was important that Sergio see the parallels between his own situation and Luis's. Both were underdogs fighting against a powerful and wealthy man. They both had been wronged by Miguel, who wielded what amounted to life-and-death power over their lives. It was classic David and Goliath, with the force of moral right on their side.

"You see, Sergio, my client assumed that Miguel would be a gentleman and behave in an honorable fashion," I said. "But he was deceived. Miguel was cold and unreceptive to him, even though he was only asking for what was rightfully his."

"Where do I fit into all of this?" Sergio asked, pushing his chair away from the table a couple of feet.

I didn't want to appear threatening or pushy, so I gave him a relaxed smile. "I want you to help us find information about Miguel's dealings," I said. "You're in a unique position after working for him for so many years. He must trust you."

If Sergio wasn't going to help me, this was his cue to stand up and leave. He didn't. I gave him some time to drink more of his margarita.

"I need you to find out what sorts of business he's involved in, inside and outside of the bank," I continued, as casually as I could. "I need to know as much as possible about his financial situation—his assets, his net worth, even anything vaguely suspicious that he might be involved in."

I had thrown in the last part to see how Sergio would react. He looked as though he couldn't believe what he was hearing. "Do you know what you're asking me to do?" he said. "You're asking me to spy on my boss. I may hate the man, but he pays me very well. If I got caught, the best thing that could happen is that I'd be fired. I'd probably never work in a bank again, and I might even face criminal charges. Why on earth would I take that kind of chance? What in the hell would I get out of it?"

I was ready for this. "Revenge," I said. "Payback for Mario. I saw it in your eyes at the party, how you felt about what had been done to you and your lover. And because this concerns honor, Sergio. I know that means something to you."

I was gambling that Sergio would understand and believe in the concept of honor—after all, he had considered it a point of honor to care for his dying lover. I knew it was a reach, but I had to try.

"Are you trying to tell me that I wouldn't be betraying Miguel because I would be avenging Mario's death?" Sergio pushed his drink away, shaking his head. "Lupe, please. I can see that you need me, but don't be insulting about it."

"I'm not trying to insult you, Sergio," I said.

Sergio became sullen and quiet, rudely waving the waitress away when she came to take our additional orders.

"I have a proposal to make to you," I said. "Before you say no, at least meet with my client. I want you to hear the story from him personally."

Sergio glanced at the staircase leading out; I could sense his body was about to follow his gaze. "He's only going to give me some sob story," Sergio said. "Look, Lupe, I'm sorry. I like you, and I can see you're trying to do good. But you're wasting your time."

As he stood up, I resisted the urge to grab his sleeve and pull him back down into his chair.

"Don't worry, I won't tell Miguel about this," Sergio said in a confidential tone. "I'm not that loyal to him. I just need the money he pays me."

"Sergio, wait," I said. I had badly miscalculated. I suddenly wasn't sure that I could trust him not to talk to Miguel. "Please, just meet with my client. You owe Mario that much. I believed you that night, when you were talking about honor and right and wrong. I really did."

It was vital that I calm Sergio down, to make him see things as I did, but from the look on his face I could see that I hadn't been successful.

"You know what, I'm not so sure I like you anymore," Sergio said. "That was a cheap shot. Stop pushing my damned button by bringing up Mario."

"I know," I said. "I'm sorry." And I was.

Sergio paused, placated somewhat by my apology. "All right. Apparently this means so much to you that you're willing to use my own predicament against me. But I'm warning you, I have to work two jobs now to pay off my debts. Set up this meeting for early in the morning, before I go to the bank, or later at night, after I get home from my job at the gym."

"Sergio, I really am sorry about all that's happened to you," I said sincerely. "It's so unfair, I know. It's all unfair."

He looked at me oddly. "Who said life was fair?" he asked. "Some idiot who never had to live it. And just so you know—I consider this a favor to Clive and Elliot, because I know they care about you. This has nothing to do with Mario."

He left me sitting there at the table.

I went to a pay phone in the bar, called Luis, and gave him a quick report on what had happened. Luis took down Sergio's phone number. Now all I could do was wait and pray—and try not to feel too dirty about what I had just done.

Twenty-two

"*Oye,* Lupe, I don't mean to pry or anything, but is business going all right for you?" Marisol asked. She was perched on my office windowsill, her binoculars zeroed in on the cottage's backyard.

"What?" I asked. I had barely heard her, I was so immersed in the report she had just submitted. It detailed Miguel de la Torre's activities over the last two days.

"Forget I said anything," Marisol replied. She unfocused the glasses and put them on her lap. "It's none of my business."

I put down the report. "Marisol, what the hell are you talking about?"

She picked up the binoculars again and looked outside. "Well, Miss Sunshine," she said nonchalantly, "unless I'm mistaken, you've got quite a marijuana garden out back, right behind the avocado tree."

"Gimme those." I almost strangled her with the cord as I wrested the binoculars away from her.

I adjusted the dual lenses so I could see clearly. Marisol was right—I could make out a row of wispy green shoots that definitely weren't baby tomato plants. At twenty-eight, I was long past the point of getting high. Well, not exactly—but growing and harvesting were activities that I never would undertake. Still, I wasn't too old not to recognize marijuana when I saw it. There was only one answer.

"Lupe, you surprise me. I didn't now you had a single drop of farmer's blood in you," Marisol said, rubbing her neck. "I know you're not into that stuff, so what's the deal? Medicinal purposes? Or a little cash on the side? Because I have to tell you—"

"Leonardo!" I yelled at the top of my lungs. Marisol recoiled; now, in addition to rubbing her neck, she was unclogging her ears. Working for me was turning out to be physically dangerous. Marisol was so mercenary and calculating, I knew, that eventually she would have to wonder if her injuries were eligible for worker's compensation. She was probably imagining that her dream of owning a BMW might come true sooner than she had thought.

My cousin poked his head in the door a few seconds later. Dread and fear were written all over his face. "Yes, Lupe?" he whispered.

"What the *hell* have you been growing in the backyard?" I pointed out the window to the avocado tree, my voice cracking with anger.

"Oh, that." Leonardo had started into the room, but now he backed away. "You mean the marijuana."

"Yes, Leonardo, I mean the marijuana." I enunciated each word slowly and carefully.

"You see, it has to do with this new drink that I'm working on. It's a total cure for anxiety. I blend some grass with some fruit juice—well, I don't have the proportions right, and there are some things I have to do first to the—"

I clenched my fists. I could feel blood flowing into my cheeks.

"It makes you really mellow," Leonardo added warily. "Actually, Lupe, you look like you could use some right now. You seem tense. That's just what I'm trying to . . . you see, all this stress isn't good for—"

Marisol looked at her cuticles. I could see that she was trying desperately not to laugh.

"You will go out there and dig up each plant." Leonardo flinched as I stabbed my finger at his chest. "You will destroy them all, without leaving a trace. And you will not get caught doing this!"

"Destroy them?" Leonardo asked. "But I'm finally getting somewhere with the formula."

"I know where you're going with the formula." I felt perilously close to losing control. "Excuse me, I know where *we're* going with the formula. We're going to be guests of Uncle Sam—and for a very long time. Do I need to remind you that neither of us looks very good in stripes?"

"Lupe, trust me," Leonardo begged. "It's all hidden away. And if you just have one glass of my formula, you'll feel much better. Once you're relaxed I know you'll reconsider."

This was my fault, I told myself. I had been trying to drum up ambition in my cousin for years. I had encouraged him to get imaginative and to try new things. I never dreamed he would actually follow my advice.

"Actually, could I try a glass?" Marisol asked.

"I give up!" I threw my hands in the air. "I'm surrounded by children! We're going to jail for drug possession. You wait! You'll all see!"

I returned to the reports on my desk as Leonardo and Marisol left the room together.

I started flipping through the license-tag printouts Leonardo had run, based on photographs Marisol had taken of a gathering at Casa Juancho, a Spanish restaurant on Eighth Street. She had followed Miguel de la Torre there on one of his many lunch dates.

There was also a series of pictures featuring Miguel walking out of the restaurant with the men he had met there. I took out the magnifying glass I kept in my desk drawer and peered intently at one particular photo. There was a man there who looked vaguely familiar, but he was too far in the background for me to clearly make out his features.

I had just started reading all the tag-number search results, hoping to spot a familiar name that might help me identify the man in the picture, when Marisol entered with a funny look on her face.

"How was the magic potion?" I asked. "Worth spending fifteen years in federal prison over?"

"Thirty," she said. She lay down on my sofa, crossed her arms over her chest, and fell into a slumber.

I sat there and stared at her, sorely tempted to follow suit.

Saturday night came too quickly for me. I found myself rushing to get ready, not wanting to keep Tommy waiting when he picked me up for the Cuban-American Friendship Ball. I knew it would make me late, but I couldn't resist taking a bubble bath. However, Tommy wouldn't suffer too much—a couple of Osvaldo's *mojitos* would take care of that. As for me, a soak was a necessity and not a luxury. I agreed completely with W. Somerset Maugham that "There are very few ills in the world that a hot bath and a bottle of Gevrey-Chambertin cannot cure." I couldn't possibly say it better.

The "ill" I needed cured was my dread. Tonight I would come face-to-face with Miguel and Teresa de la Torre and would have to interact socially with them. I wondered if they would remember me from Caballero's. I knew I was ready—there was nothing like a drop-dead dress for bolstering confidence—but I stayed too long in the tub anyway. By the time I got out, the bathroom was awash in steam, the mirrors impossible to see into.

I put on my makeup, arranged my hair into a French twist, clipped to my ears the uninsured diamond earrings that Mami had left me (the premiums were too expensive), wiggled into my long dress, pulled on my stockings, and hunted in my closet for the new Chanel shoes. I opened the small evening bag I had bought to match the shoes, and filled it up with tissues, a lipstick, and a small perfume atomizer. There was no way the Beretta was going to fit into the minuscule purse, so I slipped some mace in as a second-best option.

Tommy was waiting for me at the kitchen table, just starting on a fresh *mojito* that Aida had passed him. He looked terrific. I waited in the doorway, hoping to make a grand entrance, but he and Aida were too engrossed in conversation to notice me.

Finally I cleared my throat. I must have passed inspection, because Tommy choked on his drink. Either that, or the *mojito* was too strong.

"Ready?" I asked. "We're going to be late."

"You look great," Tommy said. He kissed me on both cheeks—I'm not sure where he picked that up, since Cubans kiss on only one side. But he looked so good that I didn't object.

Aida rubbed her eyes. "You look so much like your mother, standing there like that."

I was taken aback; Aida had never said I looked anything like Mami. I knew she was trying to be nice, complimenting me like that, but I also felt as though I'd been punched in the stomach. Just then Osvaldo came in; he gasped when he saw me. It was easy to see that the same thought had crossed his mind that his wife had just expressed.

Tommy was sensitive enough to see how emotional the moment was making us; he opened the cabinet where the glasses were kept, took out three fresh ones, and poured just-made *mojitos*. He handed out the glasses and raised his in a toast.

"To Mami," he said gravely, his eyes raised Heavenward. Although it may have seemed theatrical, it was sweet of him to honor my mother. We repeated the toast and drained our glasses.

Tommy and I walked out to the Rolls in silence. Again I thought of Tommy's reputation as a ruthless, heartless bastard. I knew he had a great big bleeding heart inside that chest. Sometimes it was hard to find, but it was there, buried beneath layers and layers of toughness and billable hours.

As we pulled out of the Cocoplum security gate, Tommy began to speak. "Lupe, I have some news you're not going to enjoy hearing."

I steeled myself. Typically, when Tommy said news was going to be bad, it was nothing short of catastrophic.

"Remember after Mike Moore was killed, when Detective Anderson was throwing his weight around, trying to get you and Joe to talk?"

"Yes," I said. A knot in my stomach tightened.

"Well, we talked after that about what could happen." He slowed the car and stopped for a red light. "The worst-case scenario has come to pass."

I knew it. "Let me guess," I said. "The worst-case . . . my enemy, Aurora Santangelo, has taken a personal interest in my case. I'm going to have to testify in front of a grand jury."

"You guessed it," Tommy replied.

He couldn't even look at me; he knew what a crushing blow this was. Aurora Santangelo was my mortal foe at the State Attorney's office. We had had a run-in a few years before, and I had come out on top. Ever since, the prosecutor had been after me—she blamed me for everything from blown cases to her menstrual cramps. I had managed to avoid her wrath so far—barely—but I knew it was just a question of when she was going to come after me again. And she played dirty. I was sure I was going to have to speak to Charlie about this; I needed inside information about what was going on at the State Attorney's office.

"When does it start?" I asked.

"Soon. Maybe next week. I'll see what I can do to stall it—but you know that a grand jury subpoena is a very serious matter."

I couldn't say that I was completely surprised. It would have been foolish to think that the persistent Detective Anderson and his questions were going to disappear. Especially if he was able to find a zealous and enthusiastic ally—which described Aurora perfectly.

Tommy and I drove on in silence. Soon after he pulled off the interstate at the Biscayne Boulevard exit and headed east, we saw the long line of cars waiting to go up the ramp to the hotel entrance. We joined the queue and patiently awaited our turn for one of the athletic valets to arrive to park the Rolls.

To distract myself from Tommy's grim information, I asked, "Do you think the de la Torres will remember that they've met me before?"

Tommy took my hand in his, raised it to his lips, kissed it, and said, "Lupe, *querida*, what kind of a question is that? Don't you know you're unforgettable?"

What a prince! Of course, we were on the same side of the case.

"I was just wondering," I said. "At Caballero's, I was with my father and my sisters. It was dark and somber, and there were a lot of people around. They couldn't have gotten a very good look at me."

I realized I was rationalizing as much for my own benefit as Tommy's, so I willed myself to stop thinking about it.

"Any news on how the police investigation into Mike's death is proceeding?" Tommy asked. He cranked down the window a half inch.

"Nothing new," I said. I had asked Ted Rafferty for more information, but he'd come up empty, promising to call after the autopsy was performed.

Just then a valet opened the car door for me, and I stepped out into the humid night. Almost all of the guests arriving were Cuban, showing up the requisite forty-five minutes late. The American guests would have arrived more or less punctually at the hour printed on the invitation. After nearly forty years together, neither culture had gained much understanding of the other's concept of time. In some cases—at mixed weddings, for example—two sets of invitations, with different starting times, were printed for the same event. It was the only sure way of getting everyone to show up at the same time.

Tommy and I followed the crowd upstairs to the main ballroom, where we were stopped by a hostess. It would have been impossible to crash such an event, where tickets were inspected like passports at a customs station. Once inside, we were ushered over to a huge hand-drawn poster showing the ballroom layout. With a flourish, our young hostess pointed out the location of our table. A solicitous waiter held out a tray of champagne glasses while we puzzled over where to go.

I felt Tommy's hand at the small of my back as we made our way into the impeccably dressed throng. Soon we were greeted by a few of Tommy's law-firm partners, as well as other high-caliber Miami attorneys. I made a mental note to tell Suzanne that the dress had been a perfect choice. I certainly received more than my share of looks. I still hadn't spotted the de la Torres when dinner was announced fifteen minutes later.

As we filtered through the other guests toward our ten-place table, I wondered which of the beautiful people would be sitting with us. Tommy walked to the far side of the table and motioned for me to join him; with as much discretion as I could feign, I checked out the place cards as I made my way over.

I wasn't fated to be seated next to Miguel de la Torre. Whoever decided these matters had placed me between two of Tommy's colleagues from the firm: Marcel Parrish, whom I knew because he'd once hired me for a case; and Peter Wright, whom I knew by reputation. Before I had the chance to ask Tommy for the inside dirt on my dinner companions, the table began to fill. After a few minutes we all were seated—with the conspicuous exception of the de la Torres.

I started to panic, not wanting to consider the horrific thought that they might have canceled at the last minute. I hated to think I had lost the chance to check them out up close, but another part of me was relieved to have put off the encounter.

Both feelings disappeared when I saw Miguel de la Torre approaching our table, shaking hands as he neared. Teresa followed a few feet behind him—apparently some old traditions were hard to break. She was even more regal and striking than at the funeral. She had the look of a woman who had access to the best hairdressers, makeup artists, personal trainers, and clothing designers—not to mention dermatologists handy with collagen shots to crucial spots.

Miguel circled the table, shaking the men's hands and kissing the women. I held out my hand for Miguel to shake, which seemed to throw him for a second; he obviously expected me to sit still and show him my cheek—no doubt, as an older male Cuban, he expected to be the one making the choice of greeting. Teresa followed behind him with a Mona Lisa smile, nodding as each person was introduced. When the de la Torres greeted me, neither acknowledged that we had met before, but then their greetings to all the guests at the table had been the same. When the formalities were concluded, we were finally served dinner: mushroom soup, followed by filet mignon with béarnaise sauce.

I had no appetite. I ate mechanically, stealing frequent glances at the de la Torres. The woman next to Miguel, an attorney's wife, laughed hard, showing perfect little white teeth every time the banker leaned close to tell her a story. It appeared that whether it was funny or not, when Miguel de la Torre told a story in Miami, the listener would act as if it were riotous.

Teresa was listening intently to the man seated to her right. I knew from hearing Mami talk that Cuban women of her generation were taught to listen with rapt attention to men, even if they were dying inside from boredom. Teresa was facing away from me, so I allowed my gaze to linger. She was wearing the diamond choker, and the jewels were large and shimmering against her tanned neck. If those stones could have spoken, I would have solved the case then and there. Once, when she glanced over at me, I noticed her checking out the earrings Mami had left me. It made me glad to have worn them.

Marcel Parrish and Peter Wright looked mystified; the main course had been served, and I had deflected all their attempts at making conversation. I knew I had to talk to them, so I brought up a notorious case their office had been involved with the year before. That got them talking, and I felt I had covered my social bases. It wouldn't do Tommy or me any good for me to appear rude and uninterested.

Between the main course and the dessert, Peter Wright asked me to dance. I exchanged pleasantries with him on the dance floor while asking him about his wife, Ellen—whose name I miraculously remembered.

Soon Marcel Parrish also invited me to dance. As I accepted, it dawned on me that at some point I would end up dancing with Miguel. We were apparently following traditional social protocol, which dictated that each man and woman dance together at least once during the evening. It was an old custom designed to ensure that no woman would end up a wallflower.

I had just finished my coffee when Miguel de la Torre appeared by my side, bent over slightly at the waist with his hand outstretched. He wore a pleasant smile, but his eyes were devoid of emotion. He resembled an exquisitely programmed social automaton.

"May I have the pleasure?" he asked in a deep voice.

My heart leapt into my throat when I saw that Tommy was leaning over Teresa, asking the very same question.

"Of course," I said with a smile.

Miguel led me out to the dance floor and slid his arm around my waist. He looked into my eyes and gave me a more personal, focused smile. His thick mustache bristled.

"Please accept my apologies, *señorita*," he said, glancing at my ringless hand. "I didn't quite catch your full name. I find in my old age that I don't hear the things that matter, especially in a crowded room."

"Guadalupe Solano," I answered. I felt his hand tighten around me.

Miguel examined me closely. "I think we've met before. Are you Ignacio Solano's daughter?"

My heart started to pound. "Yes, his youngest." Miguel's hand tightened still more; he was positively pinching my waist. I feared I would have bruises in the morning. For all his affability, the man was wound as tight as a drum.

"Do you know my father well?" I asked. I couldn't resist.

"Yes, quite well. I've known him for years," Miguel said. "Your father is a true patriot and an old-fashioned man of honor."

We twirled around the dance floor. *Honor.* That word again—this time in connection to my father. What a strange thing to say, I thought—even stranger than Papi not admitting he knew Miguel as well as he apparently did when I had asked him at breakfast several days before.

"Your father has been very successful," Miguel continued. "But he's never forgotten his *patria.* He should serve as a great example to the younger generation of Cubans."

Before I had the chance to digest what Miguel had said, the band suddenly leapt into a Latinized version of "New York, New York." I tried not to laugh as the American guests improvised by shaking their hips frenetically from side to side. They looked like Waring blenders gone haywire, but at least they were trying to get into the spirit of the evening. Mercifully, the band didn't play the macarena—if they had, I might not have been able to keep my dinner down.

Miguel and I kept dancing. All through the song, people walked by and gave him discreet, deferential greetings, as if he were the God-father. I didn't mind, though—our conversation had started to make me nervous, and the constant interruptions kept Miguel from talking.

Just before we finished dancing, however, Miguel turned his full attention to me gain. "Do you remember Cuba at all?" he asked.

That was a complicated question; I had been to Cuba, in the last couple of years, but it was a secret. Anyway, I had been to a small fishing village only and had never seen Havana.

"I was born here," I replied.

Miguel seemed taken aback for an instant; perhaps he had momentarily forgotten that an entire generation of exiles who had never seen their homeland had been born in America.

"Your generation is the hope of Cuba's future, you know," he said. "The young people like you will be responsible for rebuilding our nation after Castro is overthrown."

"Yes," I agreed, trying to keep things light.

Miguel took a deep breath, his black eyes flashing. "And the ones who say they aren't going back—they're traitors. Traitors! They don't realize that America is not their country! There are traitors everywhere!"

Miguel was nearly showering me with a spray of spittle as he spoke. I was too shocked to react. Obviously I had hit a nerve, and I had to wonder what elicited this inappropriate reaction toward me, a stranger.

"There are the traitors among us," he continued, "the spies that Fidel Castro sets on us. The ones who infiltrate our organizations—they're the ones we have to watch out for!"

"I—I see," I mumbled.

"The ones who seem the most anti-Castro, the ones who swam, the ones who braved the Florida Straits—what do you think of them?"

"I think they were courageous in seeking their freedom," I offered.

Miguel shook his head bitterly. "Spies! All of them!" he spat out. "We have to be on our guard and not believe their stories about how harsh their lives were in Cuba, how much they suffered. We have to be always vigilant!"

We were no longer dancing. I didn't know what to say; it seemed that Miguel had launched into his monologue without considering his audience. His anger and resentment were palpable. Then, without warning, he started moving again, leading me in a dance.

He smiled, more composed now. "All Cubans here have a duty to work for *la lucha*," he said. "The struggle to overthrow that assassin Fidel belongs to every single one of us!"

Miguel's voice had risen so much that people had begun to look at us, but they seemed to lose interest now that he was calm again. I was startled by this change in him. Only moments before, we had been sharing a typically inane dinner-dance conversation. It seemed that my innocent remark about never seeing Cuba had set off some kind of storm in this man; the calm, self-assured aristocrat had turned into a seething political ranter. Here was a man who refused to honor an agreement between best friends and their families—how could he reconcile that with his speech about nationalistic obligations and honor?

The music thundered to a close. A saxophonist took center stage to wail out the final notes of the outrageous congalike rendition of "New York, New York." Gloria Estefan would have run for shelter.

Miguel took my arm and gently pulled me closer to him, even though the other dance partners were beginning to break up.

"Cuba after Castro will be a place where our people can regain their freedom and heritage," he explained. "We will have a strong, proud country—not a little island that survived for thirty years off the Russians' charity. That indignity made us the whorehouse of the world. Any Cuban who doesn't work toward rebuilding Cuba has betrayed the heritage of our nation and our people."

I suddenly felt irritated. It was difficult not to ask him how he could feel this way and steal from one of his countrymen at the same time. Then, as quickly as he had been set off, Miguel again regained his composure.

"I'm sorry," he said, smiling. "I have visited my personal grievances upon you. Sometimes I fear that I am becoming a bore in my advanced age."

"Of course not," I said. "Thank you for the dance, and for sharing your opinions with me."

With a courtly gesture, Miguel led me back to our table. Somehow I sensed that he was unsatisfied with my response. Miguel's imperious behavior and tempestuous moods reminded me so much of Luis that they could have been father and son. Once I was alone, I grabbed a fresh glass of wine and caught my breath.

Tommy took the empty chair next to me. "You look upset, *querida*," he said. "Do you want to go home?"

"Could we?" I asked. "I've had all the fun I can take."

Tommy scanned the room; though I hated affairs such as this one, they truly were Tommy's natural element.

"I don't see why not," he said. "The dance is breaking up, anyway. No one will think we're being rude."

Before we could escape, though, a man I recognized as a Dade County judge yelled out Tommy's name from a nearby table. Tommy turned to me apologetically.

"I know you have to schmooze with him," I said. "Just hurry back."

"It's a promise."

Out on the dance floor, Miguel was dancing with Peter Wright's wife—whom I hadn't even noticed was in attendance that night. Peter must have thought it odd when I asked about her health while we were dancing.

Oh, well. I was busy with my impressions of what had just happened, when Teresa de la Torre slid into the empty seat next to me. She was smiling vacantly and sipping a glass of champagne. I reminded myself that I had an advantage: I knew plenty about her, and she knew nothing about me. Still, I didn't have the courage to initiate a conversation.

"I saw you dancing with my husband. I only now remember meeting you at Hector Ramos's funeral at Caballero's. Please forgive me for not remembering until now. It was a very emotional evening, to lose such an asset to the Cuban community." I looked at Teresa. She was as placid as Miguel had been dynamic, looking down at me from on high with a sense of haughty cool even as she apologized.

"You dance well," she said with a smile. "That's rare in younger girls."

"Thank you," I said, grinning like an idiot. She was charming, all right, if a bit condescending. Even with all I knew about her, I wanted her to like me.

"I overheard you talking during dinner," she added. She sipped her drink and cast her gaze over the room. "What did you say you were—a private investigator? I think that's interesting. But it's a strange profession for a woman, especially with your background."

I was so lost in examining her immaculate features, and her raven hair pulled back into a perfect bun, that it took me a second to realize she was expecting a response. I ignored the implications of what she had just said. "It's not as interesting as people think," I offered. I knew what she really meant—as the daughter of Ignacio Solano, I had no business working in such a sleazy profession.

Teresa hadn't seemed to hear me. "So you spend your days looking for wrongdoing, is that right?" she asked. "Finding out when people have committed crimes?"

Our eyes met, and I felt a chill. "Sometimes. In a way," I stammered. I had the sense that she was used to making people feel nervous. "More often than not, it's really boring. You know, checking up on adulterers, or gathering evidence when people commit fraud on their insurance claims."

When I mentioned adultery, Teresa glanced at her husband, almost imperceptibly. The band had stopped playing. Miguel returned to our table at the same time as Tommy, and they exchanged handshakes.

Miguel noticed that his wife was speaking with me. "Dear, do you know who this is?" he asked, gesturing at me.

Teresa smiled. "A lovely young lady with a very interesting profession."

"Oh? And what profession is that?" Miguel asked, temporarily sidetracked.

"She's a detective," Teresa told him. "A private investigator."

"A seeker of secrets. Is that right, Miss Solano?" Miguel asked. He noticed his wife react to my name, and added, "This is Guadalupe Solano, *querida*—Ignacio and Concepcion's daughter."

"I know, dear. We met at Hector's wake," Teresa said. She took my hands in hers and squeezed them tight. "Your dear mother and I sat on several charity boards together. Oh, your mother was a true saint. It was such a loss when she passed away."

Mierda. It was all I needed for my parents to be canonized like this by the de la Torres—my father for being a patriot and an inspiration to all exiles, and my mother for her charitable good works. Tommy sensed my discomfort and put his arm around my shoulder.

"Thank you," I said to Teresa. It was all I could manage.

Tommy made a show of looking at his watch. "Well, we really must be going."

"So soon?" Miguel asked, though he didn't really seem to care.

"Yes, well," Tommy's voice trailed off. I knew it would be politically beneficial for Tommy to stay longer. "But the evening was a great success," he added.

Teresa, Miguel and I mumbled that it certainly had been. Tommy and I shook hands and kissed our way around the table, then we were finally able to leave. As we turned to go, Teresa and Miguel repeated that I should give their regards to Papi.

Tommy and I walked together down the long corridor out of the ballroom. At the hotel entrance, Tommy presented his ticket stub to the valet. I knew the Rolls wouldn't be parked very far away; most parking lot attendants liked to keep such exquisite cars where they could see them.

When we had settled into the car and were heading down the ramp, Tommy turned to me. "Well, what do you think?"

"I liked them, in spite of trying not to," I replied miserably. "So help me, God, I really liked them."

We drove on for a while. "So who are the real Miguel and Teresa de la Torre?" I finally asked. "Interesting, charming socialites—or murderers and swindlers?"

Tommy accelerated onto the highway, taking his time before answering. As he merged into the fast lane, he said, "Both. But you suspected as much, didn't you?"

Tommy responded to my question as though the answer were inevitable.

Twenty-three

Two mornings later, ball gowns and refined manners were distant memories. I was going through a bag of garbage pilfered from the de la Torres—a theft that had made me very anxious, now that they had seen my face and knew who I was.

But all the trash-sifting was definitely worth it, because I had finally found something unusual. Miguel de la Torre had received a letter from Uruguay, from a hotel in Montevideo. Although the letter had been torn up, I was able to put together enough pieces to learn that Miguel had stayed at the Victoria Plaza Hotel the previous March and that he had been overcharged for his room. The error had been discovered only after Miguel's departure, which was why repayment was being tendered through international mail. The letter went on to apologize for the misunderstanding and to say that the hotel's management sincerely hoped that Miguel continued to choose them when he traveled to Montevideo in the future. In conclusion, the letter said that it had "always been a pleasure to welcome Señor de la Torre to the Victoria Plaza during his visits to our country."

It seemed quite clear that Miguel traveled often to Uruguay—but why? The nation certainly was off the beaten track. He was Cuban, and I didn't think he had relatives there. That left business—either the bank's or his own. But if it had been the bank's, wouldn't the bills and correspondence have gone to his office rather than his home? He could have a girlfriend there, but I dismissed the possibility. It was too impractical, and Cuban men of his generation weren't shy about having their mistresses in the same towns as their wives.

I still hadn't found any phone bills—Southern Bell's monthly statements were coming out in a few days. I figured Miguel and Teresa were the type to pay their bills right away, but if the bills didn't show up in the trash soon, I'd have to shell out some of Luis's money to my contact at the phone company to get duplicates. I wondered if any other connections to Uruguay might show up in Miguel's credit card records, but I found nothing in that day's two bags.

I looked again at the soggy letter fragments. The hotel had chosen to send their refund with a check, according to the letter. It could have been insignificant, but maybe not. If Miguel had paid for his room with a credit card, then the hotel would have issued a credit to the card company and not to the client. It seemed that Miguel had paid in cash—and that smelled almost as weird as the trash strewn around my office. No one pays cash for hotel rooms anymore. There was only one reason for a man of Miguel's resources and status to pay cash when he traveled: to avoid leaving a paper trail.

In the credit card statement I had found that morning, there were only household and personal expenses—restaurants, department stores, and supermarkets. That meant Miguel's business expenses were on another account. If I couldn't find any record of that account, I would have to call my contact at American Express. For more of Luis's money than I would have liked to spend, my contact could give me complete statements on a specific customer dating back through the previous three months.

I sat at my desk, staring at the letter for the Victoria Plaza Hotel, as if by looking at it hard and long enough, answers would leap out at me. It didn't work, but I kept staring. I was so lost in reverie that I nearly jumped when the phone rang.

"Lupe, this is Luis. I just left Sergio Santiago."

"How did it go?" I asked eagerly.

"I can't tell." I heard a car horn honk in the background; Luis was calling from a street phone. "He didn't say much. I told him some things about myself."

"What kinds of things?" I asked.

"About my mother bribing a doctor with one of our remaining diamonds," Luis said. "So that the doctor would proclaim me unfit for military service. At the time, Castro was sending young men to Angola and Ethiopia."

"How did the doctor get you out of service?"

"By labeling me a homosexual," Luis explained.

That somewhat accounted for how Luis had been able to fight off a professional like Pepe Salazar. In Cuba, a young man who had been branded gay would face more than his share of fights and bigoted attackers.

"Is that true?" I asked.

"No!" Luis's voice rattled the receiver. "I am certainly not a homosexual. I only told Sergio about it in order to gain his sympathy."

"No, no, Luis. I meant about your mother bribing the doctor."

He paused before saying, "It's all true. My mother was taking a very big risk. The doctor could have turned us both in as counter-revolutionaries."

I wondered why I had questioned his story. It was almost as if I were laying traps for him, waiting to see if he could extricate himself. It seemed that I wanted something from Luis that was perilously close to reassurance—for taking the case, for endangering my friends, for not telling the police what I knew about who may have killed Mike. I knew I was asking too much of him.

"I'm sorry, Luis," I said. "I'm very tired. How did you leave things with Sergio?"

"We met for coffee and talked for nearly an hour," Luis said. "I told him my story and he left—that's all that happened. But I think the fact that he heard me out is a good sign, don't you?"

"I hope so," I said neutrally. "Anyway, we tried."

"I suppose you're right." Luis paused. "So, do you have any new information pertaining to my case?"

"Just a few leads I need to follow up," I said. I didn't want to share my Uruguay musings with Luis; there was no need to have him riding the same up-and-down pattern I had to endure as an investigator. My new lead could turn out to be nothing. "But don't worry. Even if Sergio doesn't come through, we still have other options available to us." What those options were, I really couldn't imagine. I didn't want to tell Luis that Sergio was our best bet at the moment.

"I suggested you move again after we found out about Pepe Salazar," I reminded him. "Have you thought about it?"

"Yes, I've already moved," Luis said. "I took another efficiency apartment in Little Havana. Not too far from my other place, but I think it's far enough."

"Good," I said. "It seems like the prudent thing to do, given recent circumstances."

He knew what I was implying. "I know I've said it before, but I'm very sorry about your investigator," Luis said. "I know I'm placing you and your people in danger. Maybe . . . maybe you would like to talk about stopping work on the case."

I could hear the strain in his voice even through the rough phone connection. I imagined him standing on the street, slim and tall, smoking, staring straight ahead with his uncanny intensity. It made me want to see him. It would have been easy to ask him to come to the office. But I held back.

"Is that what you want, Luis?" I asked. "After all, this case could mean as much—if not more—trouble for you."

"It's not what I want," he said quickly. "I just don't want you to feel trapped."

"You have to realize by now that this case is important to me," I said. "It's given me a chance to do something beneficial for one of my own people. Also, if I gave up now, it would be like betraying Mike's memory."

Silence. Then, "Yes. I've always been aware that you are a woman of honor."

That word again; Luis had a knack for bringing it up at crucial moments.

We listened to each other breathe for a moment. My eyes alit on the gutted trash bags lying on my office floor. A mess. Just like the emotional mess Luis was capable of creating within me.

"I have to go, Luis," I said. "We'll talk soon when something new develops. Take care of yourself, and be careful."

I hung up, then sat at my desk for a long time with my head in my hands. Where had my objectivity gone? I felt as though I were already in Purgatory and all I had done was allow myself to think about the man. Luis obviously knew I was attracted to him, or fascinated by him—whatever you wanted to call it—and he seemed to be relying on my feelings to keep me on the case, taking risks on his behalf. What kind of penance—spiritual or professional—would I have to endure if I let these feelings go any further? That was Lourdes's area of expertise, not mine. A sigh escaped from me that was so deep it shook my rib cage.

I had decided to clean up the trash, when I heard a loud knock at the door. I told whoever it was to come in.

Nestor poked his head in my office, took a whiff, and screwed up his face in distaste. He pulled a handkerchief from his pocket and held it under his nose like some medieval damsel.

"I'm almost done," I said. "I'm about to take it outside."

Nestor plopped himself down on the sofa. He mumbled through his handkerchief, "Wait until you hear what I have to tell you. I think you'll be very proud of me."

"I'll be even more proud if you take that thing off your face so I can hear you," I responded, almost too fatigued to be curious.

Nestor lowered the cloth, frowning. "I talked Veronica into helping us, and I didn't even have to compromise myself. I just told her that I was working on a huge, top-secret case."

I was about to berate Nestor for betraying confidentiality, but he held up a hand to stop me. "I mean it," he said. "I mentioned nothing specific about who the client was. I led her to believe that there was funny business going on at First Miami and that I had been called in to investigate."

"You know, if she talks to anyone, we're going to be found out." I shook my head angrily; as far as I was concerned, Nestor was walking a fine line in terms of the case's confidentiality.

"No, no, that's the beauty of it. I'm such a genius!" Nestor slapped his head with glee. Modesty had never been one of his stronger traits. "I told her I was going to be sending letters to various bank officers and that they should be tracked to make sure everything is in order. No one was exempt from this, I said, not even Miguel de la Torre himself. I said that some individual claimed he had passed on crucial information to a particular bank officer and that the officer hadn't acted on it. So it was my job now to prove that the first guy was lying. In order to do that, it's vital to verify that mail always gets delivered to the correct recipient."

I thought about this for a moment. Despite myself, I was impressed. "You made up that bullshit story and she believed you?"

Nestor shrugged. "Hey, she likes me," he said. "She wants to believe me. Remember, too, we met at a church group. It's total bullshit, but I talked it for a long time. I got her so confused, she said it made perfect sense. Hell, I was even starting to confuse myself."

I ran through it again in my mind. "You know, it doesn't really make sense. If you wanted to—"

"Hey," Nestor interrupted, "she believed it."

"Well, what did you ask her to do?"

"She's going to copy all the senders' addresses from personal envelopes sent to top bank officers, before the mail goes into internal distribution. It sounds like a lot, but there are only eight senior officers, and I told her to deal only with the personal mail. She was afraid she might be breaking the law, but I told her it was a federal offense only if she actually tampered with the mail."

"That's *good*," I said. "And you didn't even have to sleep with her?"

"No!" Nestor said, genuinely appalled. Maybe Veronica wasn't as attractive as I'd been led to believe. I hoped Nestor wasn't positioning himself for combat pay.

Nestor got up from the sofa. "Anyway, I have to go," he said. "Give me a call when you fumigate this place."

Before he left, I told him about the possible Uruguay connection and asked him to work it into his story with Veronica. Any mail to Miguel from that country would reinforce my suspicion that I had found a gem amid the rotten fruit peels and used tea bags. It looked and felt like a solid lead to me, and I had been running on instinct all week.

When Nestor was gone, I realized that he hadn't offered to help me take out the mound of trash. As usual, his hands remained clean.

The Uruguayan Consulate was housed in a modest two-story Moorish-style structure just off Alhambra Circle in Coral Gables. I wore a faded Miami Hurricanes baseball cap, out of fear that Miguel or Teresa might spot me so close to their neighborhood. I probably looked ridiculous, but I felt inconspicuous. The de la Torres might not have recognized me right away at the dinner dance, but now we had seen each other twice. I doubted they would miss me on the third go-around.

I explained to the woman at the counter that I was a grad student at the University of Miami and that I was working on a study of banking practices in Latin America.

"Someone told me I should research the way banking is conducted in Uruguay," I said, trying to look wholesome and curious. "They said it was interesting."

It didn't really matter how I looked; even though closing time was only thirty minutes away, the consular officer seemed eager to get involved in any sort of activity. She even made me a cup of hot English tea while she rummaged around in a carton of pamphlets extolling the advantages of Uruguayan banking.

I could see why she was so eager to help me. The phone didn't ring the whole time I was there, and there were no other visitors. A sign at the front desk had said that the consulate was closed two hours daily for lunch, which left the place with four operational hours per day. The consular officer, a bit plump and wearing lots of make-up, tapped the stack of pamphlets with obvious pride when she had rounded them all up. If nothing else, I had provided her with some job satisfaction for the day.

"This is literature printed by the Uruguayan Council of Commerce," she said in a syrupy voice. "It explains all the benefits of Uruguay as an international banking center. Also, here's a map of Montevideo—complete with transportation schedules and a list of hospitals."

She put it all into a frilly envelope and handed it to me with ceremony. "And, finally, an invitation to our monthly tea social," she said. "I genuinely hope you can make it here this Friday afternoon."

It was hard to imagine that the tea social would be much more exciting, or more extensively attended, than the consulate had been while she had searched for the literature. But I shook her hand anyway and said I would have to consult my schedule.

Back at the office I read through the pamphlets and was soon amazed by what I found. One section touted the fact that of the approximately ten billion dollars deposited at any one time in Uruguayan banks, more than one-third is from foreign money-market sources. I had dabbled in financial investigations and I knew that banks usually underreport dollar figures to be prudent. The real amount of foreign-investment cash was probably much higher.

Also, I had worked a case a few years before that had required me to gain a passing knowledge of banking regulations in Panama and the Cayman Islands. My client had been heading for a divorce, and she knew that her husband had been stashing money in both countries. Both countries had secretive and secure banking laws. From what I could see, Uruguayan laws were similar; if anything, even stricter secrecy laws were in place. The pamphlets did everything but scream aloud: "Foreigners! Forget Switzerland and the Caymans! Forget Liechtenstein! Deposit your money in Uruguay and *nobody* will ever find out about it!"

I decided to have Tommy review the pamphlets and give his professional opinion. Knowing him, I suspected that after helping me he'd start having dreams about hiding his own money down there.

I took out the street map of Montevideo—I always loved maps, no matter what they depicted—and located the Victoria Plaza Hotel on the Calle Colonial, right on the corner of the Plaza Independencia. Then I cross-checked this location with the list of major banks in Montevideo. Most, if not all, were within a few blocks of the hotel.

When I stepped out of my office I found Leonardo on the phone, nearly hidden by a huge stack of books on nutrition and health.

"Leonardo, can I ask you something, *querido?*" I said.

He was holding the phone, not talking, with his eyes glazed over. On hold again.

"Lupe, darling, of course," he said. His mood had certainly improved compared to the previous week. I hoped it was a new vitamin regime and not that he was disposing of the backyard marijuana patch by making use of it himself.

"Take this literature over to Tommy's office and ask him if he can look it over. Tell him I specifically need his input on foreigners having accounts in the Uruguayan banking system."

"Sure, no problem," Leonardo replied.

I looked at him closely, trying to determine the cause of his sud-

den good-naturedness. Usually he hated leaving Coconut Grove because that meant "dressing up"—changing out of his bicycle shorts
and muscle shirt into regular clothes.

"You don't mind going downtown?"

"Of course not." He hung up the phone and dug his car keys out
of his desk. He went to the closet and procured a blue button-down
shirt and a pair of khaki pants, his uniform for dealing with the outside world. I gave him a kiss on the cheek and told him to take his
time. I knew that for him, wearing those clothes represented a small
compromise of his principles.

"Don't worry, I won't be long," he said. I was about to comment
on his dedication when he added, "I have to get back by three. That's
when I'm due for my spirulina infusion."

I didn't even want to know what he meant—something about his
alimentary canal and large intestine, I guessed. After he was gone, I
put the phone on voice mail and took advantage of the peace and
quiet to brainstorm.

First I reviewed some notes I had made after meeting Miguel and
Teresa at the Cuban-American Friendship Ball. The largest section
concerned Miguel's diatribe about Cuba and its future. At the time I
thought that he was merely caught up in his own fervor about patri-
otism among the exiles. But I had soon realized that this was only one
aspect of his beliefs—he had also been quite specific about being part
of Cuba after Fidel. I placed these notes into a file next to my impression of Miguel and Teresa at Hector Ramos's funeral. The connection to Cuban exile activists was growing more pronounced.

Then I took out Joe Ryan's reports on the de la Torres' activities.
Poor Joe. After finding Mike, he had gone into virtual seclusion save
for continuing his surveillance work. He used to fancy himself a Sam
Spade tough guy, a façade that was now completely gone. Not that I
blamed him.

I opened up Marisol's packet on Miguel. He had attended three
different functions sponsored by Cuban exiles in the past five days. I
hadn't thought much of this initially, but now I noticed something
that had escaped me before. I recognized the names of two of these
groups: *Associación de Alcaldes de las Provincias de Cuba,* an association of former mayors of Cuban provinces; and *Grupo 20 de Mayo,* a
paramilitary group, named after the date of Cuba's independence

from Spain, which trained in the Everglades for a projected forceful takeover of the island.

The third group—*Los Presos Sin Razón,* or Prisoners Without Reason—rang a bell. It sounded like it was composed of former Cuban political prisoners, but I wasn't absolutely sure. Miguel also had met with other Cuban groups since. He was devoting a lot of time to some of these groups, including multiple meetings within a single week, which seemed odd. It wasn't unusual for an exile to donate money or time to such a group, but this seemed excessive. What purpose could all this activity have served? Miguel wasn't a politician, and it wasn't likely that any of these groups were large investors at First Miami.

I waited patiently for my brain to process this information and bestow the gift of an answer. Before it did, my phone rang. It was Sergio.

"I imagine you know by now that I met with Luis Delgado earlier today," he said. I started to speak, but he raised his voice and continued: "Listen, I like him a lot. But I simply can't help you. I can't spy on Miguel, there's too much risk for me. I only called to wish you luck and to make sure you knew I had followed up on what I said I was going to do."

"It's all right, I understand," I said. I was completely crushed; I had counted on him, despite his initial refusal. "I have to respect your feelings and your judgment. I appreciate your time, Sergio, and I hope we can meet again under better circumstances."

There was silence on the line. I heard a static pulse and some distant voices as the connection faded out and back in. "If you want to ask me a few questions, I might be able to answer them," Sergio said.

I almost jumped out of my chair. I knew what this meant: Go fish. This is your chance.

"Tell me about Uruguay," I said.

"What do you want to know?" he replied without hesitation.

"I know about Miguel's trips there," I said. "I'm just missing the name of the bank he's using now."

It was a long shot, but not a bad one. As far as I could tell, the whole country was one giant bank.

"That's because he just transferred his money out of the Comercial to the Banco Internacional de Comercio." Sergio said. "It suits his needs better and provides better service."

Bingo.

"And what's the balance in the account?" I asked. Why not? I was on a winning streak.

"No way," Sergio replied. "You're on your own now."

This time, I sensed, he meant it. I jotted down the names of the banks and waited, just in case he might say something else useful by accident.

"Listen, Lupe, I don't know how much you've found out, but you'd better be careful." I heard genuine concern in his voice. "You're walking on very thin ice."

"I am?" I asked. "What do you mean by that?"

"I don't know what you're up to, but I give you my word that I'll keep your confidence," Sergio said. "If I can't help you, that's the least I can do. But watch yourself."

"You've said that—"

"I read in the paper about that investigator, how he was found stuffed in his trunk in Coral Gables. When I saw where he was discovered I figured that he worked for your agency, and it won't be long before other people make the same connection."

"But what—"

"I'm not the only one who reads the papers, Lupe."

He hung up.

I put down the receiver and stared at my notes. They were starting to make sense.

Twenty-four

After aerobics the next evening, I sipped a *batido de mango*—a mango shake—on the patio of a cafeteria on Eighth Street in Little Havana. I was still wearing my workout clothes, which I flattered myself enough to believe attracted the attention of the septuagenarian security guard and the male patrons.

My companion, of course, was having a far greater impact on testosterone levels in the immediate vicinity. I heard brakes squeal behind me and saw Suzanne cast an indulgent smile toward the street. I was sure she was on the Florida Highway Safety Department's enemies list.

We had just finished dissecting that evening's class—mostly speculating about which class member the instructor was currently dating—when I shifted the conversation to business.

"Suzanne, do you have any clients from Uruguay?" I asked.

She thought for a moment. "Two," she replied. "Why do you ask?"

"I'm still working the case you helped me with when you met with Pepe Salazar." I had chosen my words carefully; Suzanne was a businesswoman, and "meeting" was an appropriate word to describe what she did.

"I've got a lead that I need to pursue," I added. "It has to do with Uruguayan banks. I thought you might know someone who has expertise in banking there."

Suzanne frowned and I sensed a ripple of sympathetic concern from the males around us.

"Let me think," she said. "One of my clients is in cattle, which won't help you unless you want steaks. But I think the other one might be in finance. As a matter of fact, I'm pretty sure he is. I haven't seen Federico in a while, though. I'd have to check if he's still in town."

"If it doesn't create a problem for you, I need to know something as soon as possible," I said. "I have some pamphlets from the Uruguayan consulate, and I consulted with the attorney on the case. It hasn't been enough. I need firsthand knowledge from someone who's intimate with the system there."

"Well, if I find Federico, what do you want me to ask him?"

"How foreigners are treated in Uruguay when they open a bank account," I said. "I know the letter of the laws, but I need more actual information. Maybe you could hint that it's you who wants the account—say, to avoid taxes, or something like that. From what I understand, that's a reason that would make sense. You don't have to commit yourself, just do a little fishing. I'd be happy to pay whatever fee you want to charge me."

Suzanne opened her gym bag and found her ledger-sized address book. She flipped through pages packed with names and numbers until she found what she wanted.

"I'm going to use the pay phone on the street," she said. "I don't like to use the cellular phone for business anymore. I only use it when I have no alternative—I hear the airwaves are too easy to tap into."

"You heard right," I said. "That's smart."

Like everyone else on the patio, I sat and watched her talk animatedly on the phone for a few minutes. By the time she returned, I had bought her a fresh shake.

"You're in luck," she said. "I'm going to meet him late tonight. He said he was thrilled to hear from me." She rolled her eyes.

I looked at her gleaming baby blues, her long perfect platinum hair, the thin sheen of post-exercise perspiration glistening over her flawless features. "I'll bet he was," I said.

"Well, I told him I missed him," Suzanne said. Her childlike earnestness was instantly replaced by shrewd calculation. "That never fails to flatter them."

"I'll have to keep that in mind," I said.

"He has a business dinner tonight. We're meeting after that," Suzanne added. "Now, tell me again in detail what you need. I want to make sure I get everything right."

"Thank you so much for going out of your way like this. I don't know why I'm still surprised by you—you always come through," I said, genuinely amazed. "You have the best contacts in town."

"I'm the best at what I do," she said. She started to list her attributes on her slender fingers: "I'm smart, I'm nice, I'm funny, I speak fluent Spanish. In fact that's what I've been wanting to talk to you about."

I glanced at my watch. Tommy had invited me to his apartment for a late dinner, and I didn't want to keep him waiting. Things had been a little cool between us the past week or so. I suspected he wanted to spend the evening solidifying Cuban-American relations, and I wasn't entirely unwilling.

"What do you mean?" I asked, motioning to the waiter for our check.

"Well, first of all—I understand you haven't wanted to talk about your investigator, the one who was killed." She looked into my eyes. "But I heard about it. You know, Lupe, word gets around. I just wanted to say that I'm very sorry."

"Thanks," I said. I gave some cash to the waiter and zipped up my gym bag. "I suppose when this case is finished, I'll have time to really . . . I don't know, break down, probably."

"You poor dear." Suzanne's expression shifted. I couldn't tell what she was thinking. "But life goes on, you know. It's inevitable."

"I know." I said.

Then Suzanne did something very strange. She gripped either side of the table and leaned forward, lowering her voice to a whisper.

"Don't think it's crazy or horrible of me to say this at such a time, Lupe," she said. "But I want to work for you."

I started laughing. It obviously wasn't the reaction she had been looking for.

"I'm serious," she said. Her voice sounded hurt, and her lip pursed into a pout that must have completely destroyed the wills of countless men.

"Suzanne, you make at least three times as much money as I do," I said, purposely omitting the fact that she earned the money lying on her back. "And what happened to getting into the fashion business?"

She waved her hand dismissively. "I could always do that, maybe later in life," she said. "Look, I'm not saying I want to pull out of my business completely, at least not right away. But I'd like to get on your staff and work my way up to full-time investigations. I'm good, you know. You said it yourself."

"But, Suzanne, I—"

"What? I'm good enough to pump for information, but not good enough to put on the payroll? Is that what you think about me?"

"You know it's not like that," I said. "But look at what happened to Mike. Miami is a dangerous place, and it's getting worse. I've been wondering lately if I even want to stay in this business."

I was lying, of course; I had to stay in the business. It was my life. But I simply couldn't allow Suzanne to get hurt. She didn't like it, and I didn't ask for it, but I felt protective of her. It had taken me years to hone my own survival skills; it wasn't something one could learn in a day.

"My business gets tough, too," she said, raising her eyebrows theatrically. "And I probably know more about the dangerous people in this town than you do, so that excuse doesn't work. Don't try to mother me. You haven't given me one good reason why I can't work for you."

I picked up my gym bag and rested it in my lap. An involuntary sigh escaped from my lips. "I suppose you're right," I said. "This is all so sudden."

"I know it is, and I understand if you don't want to decide right now," she said. "It's just that I've been thinking a lot about my future. I think it's time to go straight."

Straight was the last word I would have used to describe private investigations. "I just can't believe you really want to make the change," I said. "All these years I've been harping on you to quit the life—well, why now?"

I really didn't need to ask. Suzanne's eavesdropping on Pepe Salazar and Ramon Hidalgo had given her a taste of the business, gotten her excited, and made her crave more. It was probably useless to try to convince her that my job typically entailed nothing but frustration and tedium.

"I think I'll like it," she said. "It's kind of sexy."

I rubbed my eyes. Now I had heard it all. "All right, Suzanne, I'll think about it. But that's all."

"I knew you would," she said with a sweet smile. "I always get my way eventually."

The drive to Tommy's apartment on Brickell Avenue took only a few minutes. He had told the security guard to expect me, so I was waved through with barely a glance. I took the elevator up to the twenty-fifth floor, and as soon as the door opened to the small hallway—there were only two apartments per floor—I smelled the delicious aroma of *arroz con pollo*. Tommy had a great sense of humor. I wouldn't have put it past him to plant a diamond in one of the chicken legs.

Tommy welcomed me at the door in a starched white *guayabera* and blue jeans. He handed me a daiquiri and headed for the kitchen.

I heard a clatter as he took the lid off the pot cooking on the stove. "Delicious," he said. "I thought you'd appreciate the joke, You've been getting too serious on me lately."

"I need a bath before we eat," I said. "I just got out of aerobics a little while ago."

"Fine, fine," Tommy said. He smiled at me. "You look good. I've been worried about this Delgado guy. I was starting to think he was having an effect on you."

"What do you mean?" I asked, feeling defensive.

"Nothing," Tommy said. "Like I said—you've been serious."

"Have you heard anything about the grand jury?"

Tommy twirled a kitchen spoon. "I think it's going to happen. I don't know when, but soon."

I sighed. "Damned Aurora."

"Don't think about it," Tommy said. "This chicken has some time still. Want some company in the bath?"

I thought about it for a second. "Sure," I said.

I couldn't say it, but it would be nice to forget about Luis for a while. Even though I knew it would be temporary amnesia.

I skipped breakfast the next morning, still full from the *arroz con pollo* from the night before. I had been in the office for about an hour, putting the various de la Torre files into some semblance of order, when I heard a delighted squeal coming from the reception area. A second later I heard Leonardo join in, making some weird noises of his own.

I should have guessed. I stepped out the door in time to see Suzanne hugging Leonardo. They were crazy about each other and went into a strange hyper state whenever they came into contact. Sometimes I yearned for the good old days, when I had been surrounded by normal people. But then, when I thought about it, I wasn't sure such a time had ever existed for me.

"Suzanne, it's great to see you," I said when she had disentangled from Leonardo. "But what are you doing here so early in the day?"

Suzanne beamed at me. "I wanted to check out my new office, and I'm going to need to get used to regular business hours."

Leonardo couldn't believe what he was hearing. "Your new office? You're going to be working out of here?" He gave me a worried look. "That's terrific, but we don't have any extra room," he said. "Lupe, does this mean that I'm going to have to give up the gym?"

It was eerie, this glimpse of what it would be like to have them both around all the time. "Will you both please just calm down?" I snapped.

All of a sudden I understood why Leonardo had been so concerned—he didn't know that Suzanne was thinking of changing careers. My cousin was actually willing to believe that I would allow Suzanne to take her clients to our office. I saw a light in his eyes—an indication that he was thinking *God help us all.* Maybe he visualized himself doing background checks on Suzanne's future clients.

I started to give Leonardo a dirty look, but I gave up. He was hopeless. "Do you want some *café con leche?*" I asked Suzanne.

Oh, good, coffee, wow," Suzanne gushed. "I mean, I was so excited last night that I didn't even go to bed. I mean, I didn't go to sleep."

Leonardo looked as though he were eager to join our slumber party, which would be more than I could take. "Could you get back to the de la Torre tags?" I asked. "I could use a complete list of those as soon as possible."

"Sure," Leonardo said dryly, obviously feeling left out.

I steered Suzanne into my office, wishing I looked so good after eight hours' sleep, much less after a sleepless evening. "So, was it a good night?" I asked her.

"I found out everything you wanted to know," she said, taking a seat. "In fact, Federico left only about an hour ago. I took a quick shower and came right over. I didn't want you to wait a minute longer, since this information is so important to the case."

I suddenly realized that Suzanne was auditioning for me. I didn't have the heart to mention that our usual methods of investigation seldom included sleeping with someone and utilizing pillow talk.

"First of all, I wasn't completely right when I said that Federico was a banker," she began.

"You said he was in finance," I reminded her. "That could mean a lot of things."

"Oh, it's all the same—" She stopped herself. "Oh, I get it! Details, right? If I'm going to be an investigator, I need to pay attention to details—everything people say and do."

"Sort of," I said, squirming.

"Well, he's a *retired* banker," Suzanne said. "His family had a bank in Montevideo, but they sold out to another bank in a merger. He didn't want it to happen, but his brothers and cousins outvoted him. I wrote down the names of both banks, just in case you might need them."

I took the paper she handed me, checking the names in case they matched the banks Sergio Santiago had listed. One of them did: the Banco Comercial.

"I told Federico I was thinking about opening an account out of the country—and that I was going to call up a Swiss bank later in the week," she said. "He fell right into the trap. He said, 'Suzanne, you don't even think about it. You must open your account in Uruguay. They will treat you better than those cold Swiss people.'"

Her imitation of Federico's accent and wheezy voice was hilarious; I let my guard down and laughed. "Sounds like you handled it pretty well," I said.

Her face brightened. "He told me Uruguay wants to be a major banking center like Switzerland and the Cayman Islands. So they drafted secrecy laws that go even further than those other countries. It was a very ambitious plan, and they imagined they were going to attract all kinds of international business."

This confirmed what I had read, and also Tommy's analysis. I jotted down a note, which seemed to excite Suzanne.

"Federico said there was a lot of interest in Uruguayan banking—and some success, but not as much as the country would have liked," Suzanne continued. "It's just too far away from the rest of the world, and it doesn't have the sophisticated communications and infrastructure to really pose a threat to the established banking havens. But the laws are still in place, and they still attract a respectable number of foreign depositors."

"So how do you open an account there?" I asked, pen in hand.

"Federico did everything but fly me to his old bank," Suzanne said with a giggle. "All you need is a passport to open one. Once the account is established, the client's name is never mentioned again. Number codes are used instead."

"How?" I asked.

"Different clients use different methods." Suzanne took a little stack of crumpled notes out of her pocket. "There's something called a Telex trade, where the client and the bank set up a complicated number code. All the numbers have to add up to the same number before the transaction can be completed. They do stuff like adding the day's date with other numbers they agree on in advance."

I thought about it. It sounded like an impenetrable system.

"Some banks require two signatories, some only one." Suzanne fished a pair of reading glasses out of her shirt pocket and put them on. They made her look like a professor in some college kid's dirty fantasy. "Some have a password, others take fax orders. It varies. The banks are really helpful to their clients, but they're impossible for law enforcement to deal with. They simply don't give out information about their clients—to anyone."

"Ever?" I asked.

Suzanne smiled; I had asked the right question. "Well, it is possible that a bank employee could be bribed. It's happened, but it doesn't happen often."

"This is truly excellent," I said. "This is precisely the sort of information I was looking for."

Suzanne finished her coffee and stretched, triumphant. "You don't even have to pay me this time," she said. "Consider it a job interview. But now I'm positive you have to hire me."

"Suzanne, I don't know," I hedged. "There's so much that goes into this kind of work. You can't even know the extent of it until you're really involved."

"My point exactly. So let me get started. Show me the ropes." She leaned over my desk. "You told me you didn't know anything until your mentor, Esteban, showed you how the business works. Someone trained you—just like you're going to train me."

"Sure, Esteban taught me just about everything I know," I said. I tried not to speculate on who had trained Suzanne for her current profession. "It's just that—"

"What? That you don't want to bother?" Suzanne put her hands on her hips. "Come on, Lupe. I'm a quick learner. And you can claim credit for saving my soul."

"I'm not sure I—"

"You always wanted to make a respectable woman out of me. Admit it!" Before I could reply, Suzanne said, "I have a college degree. I'm smart and a hard worker. Start me off slowly. You don't even have to pay me much until I start working full-time."

I had hoped she would have changed her mind since last night, but beneath that mane of hair was a smart, stubborn brain. She was serious and determined. I had prayed more than once that she would get out of hooking before anything harmful happened to her, but I never once imagined that I would have to make it happen myself.

"Suzanne, you have to give me more time to think about your proposal," I said. "This is too big for me to consider right now. I haven't even had breakfast."

Suzanne backed away from my desk, her smile fading just a little. "That's fine, Lupe. But don't take too long. I really want this, and I'm not going to give up."

A knock at my door rescued me from having to formulate a response. Nestor, wearing his favorite dark sunglasses, poked his head inside. His jaw dropped like a cartoon character's when he saw Suzanne.

"I'm sorry," he stammered. "I didn't mean to interrupt anything important."

"It's all right, really," I said. "Come in. Nestor, this is Suzanne."

"Oh, you're Nestor!" Suzanne chimed. "Lupe has told me so many nice things about you."

I couldn't remember ever mentioning Nestor's name to Suzanne, but he looked so happy I decided to let it pass. His eyes clouded over, and I could tell he was trying to decide if she was *the* Suzanne that I had told him about. He broke into a goofy grin and shook her hand.

"That's very nice," he said, still smiling.

"Well, I have to get some sleep," Suzanne said to me. "But I'll see you later. Nestor, Lupe's going to hire me as an investigator. That means we're going to be working together!"

Suzanne left and closed the door behind her while Nestor stood catatonic until I motioned toward the sofa. He took off his glasses, his eyes wide open and expectant.

"Don't ask," I said. "Please. Don't ask."

"I have to warn you, Lupe." Nestor said gravely. "If she works here, I'll never do field work again. The day she starts here I'm only going to be willing to work in the office."

"I don't want to talk about it."

"Who's going to train her?" Nestor asked, trying to look innocent.

"Are you offering your services?"

Nestor held his hand over his heart. "Well, someone has to do the dirty work."

"That's so generous of you," I said. "I'll keep your name at the top of the list."

"*Gracias,*" Nestor said. He threw his legs over the side of the sofa. "Any news from Marisol?" he asked.

"Keeping tabs on every beautiful woman you know?"

Nestor shrugged. "I'm a thorough professional."

I let that one pass. "She's been on the job four days," I said. "I get tired just reading her reports on Miguel's activities. I'm twenty-eight, this guy's twice my age, and I don't know how he does it. He has meetings over breakfast, lunch, and dinner—bank meetings, city and county meetings. He's a dynamo."

"Anything unusual?" Nestor asked. His eyes were starting to grow heavy.

"Maybe," I said. "I have a stack of names from Leonardo running tags, and rolls and rolls of film. It's time consuming. What about you?"

Nestor took a manila envelope out of his jacket and tossed it onto my desk—without sitting up. "As a matter of fact, yes," he said. "That's a present for you. You may now feel free to increase my hourly rate."

I opened the envelope and found a copy of a document confirming a wire transfer for $100,000 to a numbered account at the Banco Internacional de Comercio in Montevideo. I turned it over a couple of times in my hand, almost unable to believe what I was seeing.

"How?" I asked.

Nestor folded his arms behind his head. "Veronica, of course. She mentioned that Miguel had received something from Uruguay." He enunciated slowly, enjoying my rapt attention. "She noticed it because she's a stamp collector. I sat through a lecture on the different international stamps that have passed through the bank over the years."

"But how did you get this copy? Is Veronica going to get in trouble over this?" The document was, in fact, priceless to me. But, legally speaking, my possession of it was dubious.

"She doesn't know anything about it. I got the letter out of the mail room when I picked her up for lunch yesterday." Nestor pulled a toothpick out of his shirt pocket and stuck it nervously between his teeth. "Look, Lupe, she has no idea."

"You returned the letter, didn't you?" I asked.

"Of course," Nestor replied. "I took the letter to lunch, and while we were at the restaurant I told her I had to use the men's room. Instead, I sneaked into the office there and made a photocopy. I was all prepared—I had the knife, the glue, all my letter-opening equipment. No one will ever suspect a thing."

"Now we have an account number," I said, copying the numerals onto my note pad. "We still don't know how to access the account, though."

"Well, why would we want to do that?" Nestor looked even more nervous.

"To see how much money is in there," I replied.

"The transfer is for a hundred grand," He said. "Not exactly small change. Veronica said that Miguel's been getting mail from Uruguay the whole five years she's been working there. Not every day, but often enough to notice. She hasn't dared ask him for the stamps, for her collection, but she went on and on about how much she wants them. It's a strange hobby, when you think about it."

"No stranger than this job," I said. "God, I wish Sergio Santiago would help us."

"Another thing," Nestor added, "Veronica said all the envelopes from Uruguay look pretty much like this one—long, skinny, extra-thick security paper."

"That means they could all be wire transfer confirmations," I said. "I wonder how many wire transfers there've been, and for what amounts. I mean, are they all for $100,000? Is this one typical? Knowing would help us get a handle on what the de la Torres are worth—we need that kind of solid number to determine Luis's share. You know, Sergio told me I was onto something with Uruguay. He also told me I'd better be careful."

Nestor twirled the toothpick from one side of his mouth to the other. "You don't say."

We sat in tense silence for a couple of minutes. Nestor pretended to be occupied with a small stain on his sea-blue linen shirt. Finally he spoke: "You mentioned another idea. What is it?"

"Tell me what you think of this, hypothetically," I replied. "Sergio is really, really hard up for money. He has to work two jobs to pay off his late lover's debts. At the same time, we're hard up for the information and access he could give us. What do you say we promise him a percentage of recovery in exchange for his help?"

I hadn't even really thought through the idea properly before it escaped my lips. Once I had said it, though, it seemed to have a certain simple perfection. Nestor just looked at me as though I had gone completely insane.

"What are you saying?" He sat up. "Our job, as I understand it, is to provide Luis Delgado with information regarding Miguel de la Torre's finances, so he can proceed as he sees fit with regard to his family's stolen money. Our goal is to arrive at this net worth using proper, *legal* methods. We're looking for information, and information only. When you say 'recovery,' you're talking about something entirely different."

"I have a theory about Uruguay," I said. "I think Miguel has hidden lots of money there, for a couple of reasons. I've tried out several scenarios, and this is the one most consistent with what we know about the case. First, he's hidden money for the same reason everyone else stashes money outside the country—he hates the U.S. tax man. But second and more important, he's heavily involved in anti-Castro factions. It's all in the investigators' logs. Most of his everyday activities have to do with Cuba. I think his plans involve post-Fidel Cuba, and he's stockpiling money to get ready for whatever he has in mind. I talked to him a few days ago, Nestor. The man is obsessed with Cuban reconstruction.

"It's the only thing that makes sense. Look, he and Teresa have no heirs, so he doesn't have to worry about leaving an inheritance. He can spend his money freely—but he doesn't. Why? Maybe because he has other plans for it. He has no children. Maybe he wants to leave a legacy after he's gone. If he can't do it through blood, then why not through history?"

Nestor narrowed his eyes, thinking. "Fine. Suppose you're right. That's his choice. He's the one running a risk of getting caught. I'm no supporter of the IRS, you know, or Fidel Castro."

"I don't care what he does with his money, either," I said. "All I'm concerned with is the money he owes Luis Delgado." As soon as the words left my mouth I realized how defensive they sounded.

"You're holding out on me, Lupe. I don't like this at all." Nestor pointed at me. "If you're thinking about interfering with Miguel de la Torre's money—and I know you well enough by now to know how your mind works—you're asking for more trouble than I want to be involved in. As I see it, we only have Delgado's claim that Miguel and his wife tried to have him killed over that money—and we're still not sure what happened to Mike. We have no solid proof that Delgado is telling the truth. Maybe he hates Miguel and Teresa and made up this whole story to get back at them. He could have bought or stolen the diamond he showed you."

"I don't think you believe that," I replied, taken aback at Nestor's acumen. He was right, he did know me well.

"Maybe not, but you're talking about messing with Miguel de la Torre's cash—I'm sure of it now that I see your reaction. Did you ever see a mother in the wild defend her young? That's what's going to happen if you lay a finger on that man's wealth."

"I've told you already to feel free to quit the case anytime," I snapped. "And I meant it. You're doing a great job, but the case can go on without you. You can take a bonus and go on your way."

I was overreacting, to say the least, and I knew it. But it was too late to go back.

Nestor shook his head with an air of sadness. "You have one thing in your favor," he said. "The de la Torres probably still think that Delgado is dead. We don't know what's going on with Pepe Salazar, but for now we haven't dug so deep a hole that we can't climb out of it."

I didn't reply for a moment. I was thinking hard about everything Nestor had said. I felt threatened by his insight into me and the way I thought. It was making me irrational, but I couldn't help it.

"You know the saying 'Follow the money'?" I asked, needing to focus anew on a less sensitive part of the investigation. "Well, the money's leading me right to Uruguay."

"*Ay, Dios mio.* Now I'm really worried." Nestor looked into my eyes. "Have you spoken to anyone else about, about . . . about whatever it is you're thinking of doing?"

"No," I replied. I had hoped the situation wouldn't come to this, but now I knew what I had to do. I couldn't have Nestor second-guessing or anticipating my every move. "No, and I'm probably not going to, at least for now. But I've made a decision: You're off the case, as of this moment, Nestor."

I could tell by his pained expression how much this conversation was disturbing him. It disturbed me, too. This wasn't like me, and it wasn't the way we typically operated at Solano. We were always a team, and all or business was conducted out in the open, with no secrets. Well, that policy was going to undergo a temporary adjustment—for both our sakes.

"We've never talked like this, Lupe," Nestor said.

"I'm sorry," I replied. "I adore you, Nestor, and I love working with you. But this case has reached the point at which I have to go alone. It's as simple as that."

"This is a Cuba thing, isn't it?" Nestor asked bitterly. "It's not just about investigating a case, not just about Miguel and Teresa de la Torre. I don't have Cuba flowing through my veins, Lupe, so maybe I can be objective. When it comes to Cuba, you lose all perspective and reason."

No truer words had ever passed Nestor's lips. No non-Cuban exile can understand the mixed-up ball of tension that lives in our hearts: family honor and history, *patria*, the heritage of our country, and the burning need to see it brought to life again. I believed in all these things, and I had sided with Luis's family's justice against what I perceived as the de la Torres' callous, dishonorable reaction to him.

"Lupe, I'm worried about you. Promise me you won't do anything stupid." Nestor stood up and put on his sunglasses, seeming both hurt and annoyed. "And also promise me that you'll call if you need anything."

I got up and kissed him on the cheek. I prayed this wouldn't permanently damage our relationship.

"I promise," I said to him.

Of course, I hadn't specified which promise I intended to keep.

Twenty-five

Luis and I sat together on the seawall, our legs dangling over the side. We looked out over the sparkling expanse of Key Biscayne. Every few minutes a large wave would smash against the wall below us, spraying us with cool salty water. For a long time we didn't talk. Instead, we absorbed the air, the bright tumbling waters, and the mindless squawk of the birds feeding off the surface. The shrine behind us was bustling that day; a wedding was taking place inside.

"I asked you to meet me today for a specific reason," I said, staring ahead. "We've done a lot of work on your case. You'll be getting the official reports in a few days. But I've come up with an idea that's not going to be contained in those reports."

Luis lit a tiny, dark cigar, shielding the match from the wind with his jacket. "I'm always interested in what you have to say," he replied. He blew a cloud of smoke away from me. I noticed that the cigar was a brand that cost considerably more than Marlboros. He was starting to treat himself better—or perhaps he was now allowing me to see that he was.

In a clear and deliberate voice, I summarized all that I had found out about Miguel de la Torre. Then I told him my suspicion that Miguel had hidden money in Uruguay for investment in post-Castro Cuba.

"And you have proof of this?" Luis asked in an even voice. By then his cigar had burned down to nearly nothing. Old habits apparently died hard. He pressed it against the sea wall to extinguish it.

"No, but it all fits together," I said. "The last bit of information came in today. Like everything else, Luis, this is completely confidential. You're still aware of that, aren't you?"

I realized I was sounding condescending; Luis blanched for an instant and grimaced into a sudden breeze. "Of course," he said.

"About an hour ago I contacted a friend who works as an IRS investigator," I said. "I asked whether the de la Torres have declared any foreign accounts in their taxes during the last seven years. The answer was no."

Luis mulled this over. His suit jacket flapped in the light wind. "Then they are breaking the law," he said. "So can we go to the State Attorney's office? I know how taxes are in the United States. They can be thrown in jail for this."

I ignored the chilling, malicious edge to his tone. "I thought of that," I said. "But then you would lose any chance of ever recovering your family's money. The government would take over, and they'd never recognize your claim without documentation. It's a tricky situation. You can claim part of the money in Uruguay is rightfully yours—in accordance with the de la Torre and Delgado families' agreement, half of what the diamonds earned belongs to you—but that money is there against U.S. tax laws."

Luis spat over the wall. "Then we have lost," he said. "All of this was for nothing. I knew nothing might come of your investigation, but I allowed myself to hope. Now all this time and money has been wasted."

I grabbed his elbow. "But that's not necessarily true," I said. "There might be another option." Luis's eyes lit up. "That's what I wanted to talk to you about."

Luis glanced at my hand on his arm, seeming to respond to my touch. I pulled my hand away.

"The first step is to determine how much money is in the Montevideo account," I said. "We need Sergio Santiago for that. We got lucky, because we intercepted Miguel's mail, but it only takes us so far."

"For a minute there I thought you were going to suggest we blackmail them." Luis laughed out loud, then smiled with admiration. "How did you do that?" he asked. "You actually got to read the bastard's mail?"

"It doesn't matter how," I said, realizing I may have made a mistake by letting too much information slip out. I had carefully thought through what needed to be done since speaking with Nestor, but I wanted to keep some of the details to myself. "But we need Sergio. I know he's having serious financial problems right now. . . . If you authorize it, we can offer to pay him a lump sum of money to help us. At first I tried to appeal to his sense of revenge, but that wasn't enough."

"Curious, isn't it?" Luis said vaguely. "I had thought everyone could be motivated by revenge."

"I ran a credit check on Sergio," I said. "It'll take him years to dig out of the hole he's in, even working two jobs. In addition, I have a suspicion that he might be sick."

Luis stiffened. "AIDS?"

"I think so."

Luis shook his head sadly. I wanted to be able to read his expression, but I couldn't. I realized how effective he was at masking the true depths of his emotions.

"Offer him whatever it takes," Luis finally said. "We should be generous. I like him, and I sympathize with him. He shouldn't have to die destitute, like his boyfriend."

"All right," I said. A part of me couldn't believe we were going ahead with this.

"What is your plan after that?" Luis asked.

"We'll determine how much money Miguel has stashed in Uruguay, then compare that to his and Teresa's net worth in the States," I said. "We have a ballpark estimate of their wealth in American banks—half a million dollars—but that number is far too low to be their actual worth. The only answer that deserves consideration is Uruguay."

"The diamonds alone were worth two million dollars," Luis said. "Minus the four that were left with my father, of course."

"So, do you object to skirting the law to recover what's rightfully yours?" I asked.

There. I'd said it. In my seven-year career, I had always stayed within the law unless it was absolutely necessary to stray. It had happened twice: once when I went to Cuba illegally; another when I broke into a jewelry store to solve a case. Now I was in unknown territory. And, frankly, who was I kidding? "Skirting" was a criminal's euphemism for breaking the law.

Luis produced another cigar from his suit jacket and lit it. "What exactly do you mean?" he asked.

I looked into his eyes. I started to search within myself for the reasons I was doing this, but I felt it was already too late.

"I've thought about it," I said. "I've looked at it from every angle, and I've tried to figure out the right thing to do. But there's no other way. We're going to have to steal your money back from them."

Luis gave me an eager, amazed look. "Steal it? he asked. "Steal what's mine?"

"This is the reality, Luis. In all probability the bulk of the money owed to you is currently outside the United States." I caught myself sounding like Tommy when he lectured me, so I softened my tone. "The IRS can't get the money for you, and neither can the State Attorney. The most you would get is a reward from the IRS for turning them in for tax evasion—which might never happen, because the money there is so well-protected that Miguel might be able to wiggle out of the charges. Do you see what I'm saying, Luis? All of our possible legal routes lead to dead ends."

Luis stared into the glorious colors of the shifting sky. Sailboats were heading into the channel markers, aiming for shore. Pelicans perched atop the markers, waiting to swoop down on the fish pushed up by the late-afternoon currents. The wedding at the chapel had ended, and people were getting into their cars and pulling out of the lot behind us.

"I think I can get the code from Sergio to access Miguel's account," I said. "With the code and the balance, we can get at the money. There's nothing Miguel could do about it, because it's not even legal for him to have the account without reporting it to the IRS."

I lifted my feet up to avoid being splashed by backwash from the boats. Luis let his feet hang, his pants and shoes getting damp.

"I've done many things in my life, Lupe," he said quietly. "But I've never stolen anything from anybody. Not even in Cuba, when I had to fight just to stay alive."

"Don't think I'm comfortable with stealing, Luis," I said. "I've found a way for you to take what belongs to you. It's the only way I can come up with for now. But if you want, we can just drop the entire idea and walk away. Maybe that would be best for everyone."

Part of me wished he would take me up on this offer; we could forget the idea had ever crossed my mind. I had been searching my conscience all afternoon. Why did I want to do this? Maybe I was trying to prove myself, to play in the big leagues and bring down the most powerful bad guys. Surely Miguel and Teresa had something to do with Mike's death, and I wanted revenge for that. I also realized that my initial motive for taking the case was still strong inside me—to do something right, to bring honor to an unfair situation. But did the ends justify the means? Was I trading my own honor for someone else's vindication? And, while I was being introspective, I had to wonder what had become of my own definition of honor. I hoped it hadn't become a convenient, disposable notion that I used as it pleased me. I had seen too many others fall into that trap.

But I had forgotten to place Luis Delgado into the equation.

Luis shifted toward me. For an instant I worried that he was going to slip and fall off the seawall. I caught my breath sharply and started to reach for him. Before I could, Luis put his arm around me and pulled me to him with surprising strength.

His face drew close to mine and our lips met. He held my face in one hand and kissed me with gentle passion, which I returned without thinking. I faintly smelled tobacco on his cheek as I moved closer.

Then I caught myself. I pulled away, and it was over as quickly as it had begun. I had thought about this moment. I had thought I would be full of excuses, regrets, and reasons why this could never happen again. Instead I sat there, saying nothing.

"I can't walk away," Luis said in a breathy voice. "I have too much invested in this. Those people tried to have me killed. You and I both know they killed Mike Moore. They have dishonored my family. If I quit now, I might as well kill myself. I will have lost my reason for living. I'm in this for my life and soul, for the honor of my mother and my father and all they sacrificed for me."

I raised my hand to my mouth to hide my expression. My life was collapsing into something new and foreign to me. It was a world full of shapes and forms I couldn't recognize.

"And I have finally found someone who understands this," Luis added, "and who understands me."

It took me a moment to realize that he was talking about me. "Luis, don't," I said, turning away from him. I couldn't look at his face as he declared these feelings for me. I knew that if I looked into his eyes it would be in search of a lie or the truth, rather than in an act of acceptance.

"Do whatever you have to do," he said. "My life is in your hands now. Through you I can find my salvation. And maybe, soon, I can offer those same things to you."

I felt his hand on my shoulder, kneading the knotted muscles there. All the boats had come home to shore; all the birds had flown home. Miami would soon sleep in the unrest of a humid night. I wondered how long it would be before I slept well again.

Twenty-six

"Lourdes, do you want to have breakfast?" I was calling my sister on her portable phone. Dawn was just breaking.

"Are you all right?" she asked in a low voice. "What's wrong?"

I swear, all I had to do was breathe into a phone and Lourdes would intuit my state of mind in an instant. She would have made a great shrink—it must have been a gift from Heaven.

"I'm fine," I lied. "Why are you whispering? I can barely hear you."

"I'm in church," she said, her voice even fainter. "We're on the second rosary. I'm not supposed to talk on the cellular phone any-more. Mother Superior got on my case about it last week—she said it was frivolous. Can you imagine?"

"Well, can you speak up a bit? It's going to be hard to have a proper conversation if—"

I heard some rustling around. "What's going on, Lupe?"

"You sound better," I said. "Where did you go?"

"I'm under the pew." I heard more rustling. "We need to clean up more around here. You should see the dust. All right, where do you want to meet?"

"Versailles," I answered. "As soon as you can."

"I'm not supposed to leave. Praying the rosary is sacrosanct." When she paused, I could hear the singsong voices of the other nuns low in the background. "But you sound desperate, little sister."

"I am."

"Look, I just figured out how to leave without getting spotted. I'll crawl out of here—hopefully the others will be concentrating so hard on prayers that they won't notice. Wish me luck."

I jumped into the Mercedes and headed toward Eighth Street; I arrived just as Lourdes pulled up in her Toyota Camry. Papi had wanted to give her a Mercedes as well—so that all three of his daugh-ters would drive the same make of safe, reliable car. But Lourdes wouldn't accept the gift, saying something about the spirit and practice of her vow of poverty. Catholics are masters at rule-bending—our loose adherence to the ban on contraception comes to mind—but driving around in a Mercedes wearing a habit and wimple was a bit too much, even for Lourdes.

My sister and I kissed and hugged in the parking lot, then went into the restaurant arm in arm. I suppressed a smile as I noticed the dust bunnies clinging to her blue habit.

It was barely six-thirty in the morning, but the place was full. A table was cleared and set, though, the moment we arrived. There are advantages to dining with a holy woman.

We ordered a traditional Cuban-American hybrid breakfast: a bucket of scrambled eggs with burned bacon, Cuban bread slathered with butter, tumblers of orange juice, and *café con leche* so strong it could have been used to awaken coma patients. It was only when the feast was nearly finished that Lourdes started in on me.

"So?" she asked expectantly.

"I'm working a difficult case, and it's causing me all kinds of trouble," I began.

"You've had difficult cases before," she replied. "What makes this one so different from the rest?"

"I've broken a serious rule," I said. "And don't look at me like that. I know what you're thinking—that I break rules all the time, that it isn't a big deal for me. Just because you're a nun doesn't mean you have the right to act holier than thou."

Actually, she *did* have the right, but I was unstoppable. Lourdes listened in silence to my tirade, and as soon as I was done I felt terrible. I saw a hurt look cross her face.

"What's this rule you broke?" Lourdes asked in a calm, compassionate voice. "I'm sure it's not as bad as you think it is."

"I've gotten involved with a client," I said miserably. "I let my feelings get away from me."

Lourdes tittered. "Ah!" she said. "The world-famous self-control of Lupe Solano has faltered!"

This wasn't the reaction I had anticipated. "So you're not disappointed with me?" I asked.

"Lupe, honey, I thought you were going to tell me something serious. Like maybe that you had sex with a hemophiliac bisexual heroin addict." She sighed with relief. "That's all I could think about while I was driving over here. Trust me, after the scenarios I imagined, this little problem is small potatoes."

I could see her point, particularly because part of her duties as a nun involved caring for AIDS patients. Since we were on the subject of sex, I decided to ease her fears.

"I haven't slept with him," I said. "We've only kissed once. But emotionally, I . . . have feelings for him."

Lourdes frowned, more curious than disapproving. "Why?" she asked. "What is it about this particular guy that made you break your own rules?"

"First of all, he's Cuban. You know that I've never been involved with a Cuban man before." I rattled the ice in my water glass. "I have to admit it, he fascinates me. Lourdes, he's the kind of man I would have been dating in Cuba if Papi and Mami had stayed there, if Fidel Castro hadn't taken over."

Lourdes stared at me with an expectant expression, knowing I hadn't exactly answered her question. When she saw I wasn't going to offer further illumination, she said, "Does he know how you feel? And does he feel the same way about you?"

I couldn't tell my sister much more because I didn't know much more myself. "I haven't told him how I feel," I said. I didn't really want to get into it; in a sense, I was sorry I had started this conversation at all. "I know he feels strongly about me."

"How will this affect the case?" she asked. "You said he was a client."

Leave it to Lourdes to get to the salient point. I was reminded why I had called her. "We're right in the middle of the case," I said. "I don't want my feelings for him to interfere with my decision making. I have to maintain total impartiality, or else I'm not going to help either of us."

"Sounds like that's going to be hard to do," Lourdes said. "Why don't you refer the case to someone else?"

"I can't. I'm too involved with it." How in the world could I tell her the truth—that I was going to break the law for this man? Or that I wasn't even sure what my true motivations were?

"You can't, or you won't?

I didn't answer her. The truth was too painful for me to contemplate, much less say out loud—even to my sister. I motioned to our

waitress, who was dressed in Versailles's signature emerald-green uniform. I barely glanced at the bill, fumbled around in my purse for my
wallet, and dropped some cash on the table. Lourdes watched me,
not bothering to hide her worried expression. As efficient as our service had been, it hadn't warranted a 100-percent tip.

We walked out to the parking lot together. "Thanks for breakfast," Lourdes said, "and for the indigestion that'll come later—when
I'm thinking about what you told me in there."

I started flicking away the most prominent of the dozens of dust
balls on her clothes. I liked it better when she dressed in her usual
gear from Banana Republic or Gap; she was far too intimidating in
her habit. Besides, people kept staring at us. It wasn't too often you
saw a young, sexy nun.

"Well, I hope Mother Superior doesn't get on your case about
leaving during the rosary," I said. "I'll see you soon at home, all
right?"

Lourdes nodded sullenly as she walked over to her car. After she
had unlocked the door, she called out to me.

"By the way, Lupe," she yelled across the parking lot, "Aida
called me yesterday to say she's still worried about Papi and the
Cuban stuff."

"What do you mean?" I asked, shutting off my car alarm.

"He had the AT&T technician program the phones at the house
to play the Cuban national anthem whenever someone's on hold.
Talk to her, will you? Calm her down for me."

Ay.

At seven-thirty I called Sergio Santiago at his house; I knew First
Miami didn't open until nine. This wasn't going to be the kind of
conversation he would want to have at work.

"Sergio? *Buenos días.* It's Lupe."

Sergio sighed into the phone, sounding angry. "I told you
I'm not going to help you," he said. "You're on your own, remember?"

I felt for him, but I also needed his help. "Fifty thousand dollars,
cash," I said. I let the words hang between us for a moment.

"For what?" Sergio spat out, his resentment almost palpable.
"What am I selling my soul for?"

I kept my tone even and neutral. "The balance and the access codes for the account in Montevideo."

"You must have looked into my financial situation," Sergio said, now with a hint of sadness. "You're offering me the exact amount of money I need to get out from under all my debts."

"I can have the money to you by late this afternoon," I said. "I'll have it sent to your house by courier."

I had already planned this conversation, deciding to keep things simple. I didn't want Sergio to have to think about it too much. For my part in all this, I wanted to be the one to shoulder the weight of the ethical dilemmas—it was only fitting.

"If anything goes wrong, anything at all, I don't know you," he said. "I'll save my own skin and leave you hanging out to dry."

I heard a click as he hung up.

Twenty-seven

I walked back into my office after watching the courier leave my parking lot en route to Sergio's home. The courier departed with a white plastic box labeled DOCUMENTS: NO MONETARY VALUE, though in fact it contained fifty thousand dollars in cash. I hated the idea of sending cash with a messenger like that, but I couldn't afford to be seen in public with Sergio anymore.

I was mentally exhausted, having spent the past several hours meticulously going over my plan. My back ached from tension, and it all came down to one fact: I was about to break the law. I wasn't sure I could say that what I had done was for moral reasons, even if I were to apply my considerable skill at rationalization, and it wasn't a comforting feeling.

Once inside, I dialed Suzanne's number. I didn't want to mislead her about a job offer, but I needed her—I still considered her the best resource person in Miami.

"Lupe!" she said. "I knew you'd call today."

"I need to meet with you as soon as possible," I said. "Can that be arranged?"

"Of course," she purred. My heart plunged when I heard the enthusiasm in her voice.

Less than an hour later she knocked on my office door. When I let her in, I saw that her eyes were wide with anticipation. I hadn't had time to consider her request—and I wouldn't, not for a while. Suzanne looked as though she expected me to pull out a Bible and swear her into some shadowy secret society of investigators.

"*Querida*, look, I know you think I asked you to come here to discuss your working for me," I began apologetically. "The truth of the matter is that I haven't thought it through yet. I'm sorry to disappoint you."

"I *am* disappointed." The light in her eyes faded. "But you're not saying no, are you?"

"That's right," I hedged.

"All right." This seemed to placate her. "Well, then why *did* you ask me here?"

"I need a false passport," I said. "I have to take a trip out of the country, and I don't want my actions traced back to me."

"Cool," Suzanne enthused.

"Whatever. The thing is, it has to be a really good fake. I knew a guy, but now he's doing time in Raiford."

Suzanne pondered this. "Sure, I know someone," she said. "How soon do you need it?"

"As soon as possible. I've got the photos, and I wrote down all the phony information on this paper. Are you sure this guy is good?"

"I know his work," Suzanne replied. "He helped a guy I knew a few years ago who was about to be run in by the Feds. But I haven't seen him in a while. I'd better give him a call before I promise you anything."

Suzanne hunted through her bag for that priceless address book. She punched in some numbers using her cellular phone. She didn't use my desk phone, I knew, because she assumed the guy on the other end would have caller I.D. and would then be able to tell where the call had come from. She had told me in the past about her special cellular setup: Her calls registered "anonymous."

After a few seconds she frowned. "Bad news," she said. "His phone's disconnected. This isn't good. I know where he lives, so I can drop by his house. But a guy like this wouldn't let his phone get turned off."

I had mentally committed to following my plan step by step. Any obstacle scared me because it meant that I might reconsider and lose my nerve.

"I'll have to think of someone else," I said.

"He lives right off Brickell, close to me," Suzanne said. "If you want, we can drive by right now and see what's happening. I can't think of anyone else to recommend. This is touchy stuff, you know. You need a proven professional."

"Good idea," I said, grabbing my purse. "Let's do it."

Suzanne seemed wary, but to her credit she wasn't asking me any questions. I wanted to move, to make something happen, and most of all not to think. We got in Suzanne's Porsche and maneuvered through the traffic to Brickell.

Suzanne pointed out his window, and we could see that it was dark inside. I got out and checked the mailbox. Tape and shreds of paper were attached to it, as if someone had hastily removed a nameplate. There were thousands of fliers and items of junk mail spilling out.

I spotted a bald man walking a Schnauzer outside, and waved to him. He seemed wary, but I told him I was a real-estate agent and flashed a phony business card from the assortment in my wallet.

"I'm sorry to disturb you," I said. "But do you know if this town house is currently vacant?"

The man tugged on the leash as his hyper dog tried to run into the street. "My wife and I moved in three months ago," he said. "The place has been empty all that time."

"Excellent," I improvised. "We heard that the previous tenant had an illegal sublet going on. My company is trying to move the unit."

The man looked at me quizzically and muttered something about the place being sold six weeks before. So much for my bullshit skills. I gave him a friendly wave and rushed back to the Porsche.

We screeched out into traffic, but Suzanne pulled over and stopped the car after we had driven only a block. From her expression I saw that she was obviously ready to stage some kind of confrontation. It was the last thing I needed.

"Lupe, why do you need a false passport?" she asked.

I didn't have the energy to lie. "It has to do with the information you got for me about Uruguay. You probably already suspected that."

"Of course," she said, pleased with herself.

We had parked on a quiet street, and I could see lights on in most of the town houses around us. It made me think of quiet, uneventful lives, the kind I yearned for at that moment.

"You don't want to know more than that," I said. "Believe me."

"Don't give me that." Suzanne grabbed my arm, surprising me. "I want you to tell me. I want to help you. I want you to let me work with you! And we're not going anywhere until you come clean with me."

To illustrate her point, Suzanne flipped the switch on her door and locked us both inside.

"Don't be childish," I said. "Do you really think you're going to give up everything to become a private investigator? You'd get bored and quit within six weeks."

"This case has to do with Miguel de la Torre," Suzanne announced.

I tried to keep a poker face. "What are you talking about?"

"You didn't mean for me to know that," she said, "but you slipped and said the name to Leonardo when I was in your office last week. You see—I told you I could be observant."

"And I'm sloppy," I said, disgusted with myself for such a stupid lapse. It was a bad sign, but the floodgates were already open, so after swearing her to secrecy, I told Suzanne the rest of Luis's story—and then about my plan to extract the money owed to Luis from Miguel's bank account. I expected Suzanne to get excited; after all, this was real cloak-and-dagger stuff. But she just listened, intent and serious.

When I was finished she started the car, put it in gear, and eased out into the traffic. We were heading back to my office so I could pick up my Mercedes, but she was taking a roundabout route. I waited for her to speak, ready to counter her illusions about joining my firm.

"It's me that's going to Uruguay, then," she said when we had stopped for a light. "I speak fluent Spanish, and I have a Costa Rican passport that's good for two more years. It looks like you can't get a false passport, Lupe, so you aren't going anywhere."

I had thought I was incapable of surprise, but I'd been dead wrong. I waited a moment, trying to digest what she had said. "How in the world did you get a Costa Rican passport?" I asked.

"Oh, it's nothing." She glanced in the mirror and changed lanes. "A couple of years ago I got involved with this guy I really liked. I did something for him that required me to get a fake passport. It wasn't drugs, Lupe. It was illegal, but not immoral. Kind of like this situation."

Illegal but not immoral, I thought. She was a better rationalizer than I was, and I thought I was in contention for a world championship.

"I can't let you do it," I told her. "This isn't your problem, and it's too big a risk. Forget it."

"Don't be dumb, Lupe. Think about it." Suzanne sighed with exasperation. "I have the Costa Rican passport, and I have no connection whatsoever to the case. That's double insurance—nothing could be traced back to you. Also, I'm smart and you trust me."

"But—"

"You won't put me on the payroll until later, when everything's died down," she said. "You know I could get away with this far better than you ever could."

She was bargaining with me, that was clear—and the payoff was a job at Solano. I shook my head, trying to deny the fact that she was absolutely right. She could do the job, and she could be trusted.

Most of all, I was desperate. I had known all along that documents or witnesses might eventually reveal that I had gone to Uruguay. My connection to Luis was a matter of legal record, which meant that a run of bad luck could land me in jail. Suzanne, on the other hand, could fly in and out of South America with minimal complications. If she was successful, there would be no connection between her and what had happened. After all, who would suspect a Miami hooker of stealing from Miguel de la Torre's secret bank account?

Suzanne didn't realize she had swayed me, so she kept on bulldozing me with her argument. "Think about it—we'll be beating the bastard at his own game," she said. "You're doing this because it's a chance to do something right for once, even if you have to break a few laws, and I want to be part of it."

Simply by practicing her profession, Suzanne broke the law on a daily basis, but this wasn't the time for pointing out the obvious. And I didn't want to discuss with her my reasons for breaking the law. She knew I wasn't going to push Mother Teresa aside in a race to Heaven, but I did want her to retain some faith in the goodness of my character.

"Suzanne—"

"Come *on*, Lupe. I really want to do this."

"Let's go to my office," I said.

The Porsche's tires squealed as Suzanne hit the accelerator and headed back to the Grove. I couldn't believe I was actually considering letting her go to Uruguay in my place, but it was the only plan that really made sense. I looked at her profile as she drove, and it was as if I were seeing a completely different person.

Suzanne noticed me staring and turned to me with a big smile. "Now, Lupe, don't overanalyze this," she said. "You'll see. After I work for you for a few months, you'll wonder how you ever got along without me!"

She was positively on a high, and I found myself laughing with her. As we pulled into the parking lot I saw that the security lights were on, which meant that Leonardo had left for the night. I switched off the alarm system and held the door for Suzanne. She practically bounded into the place.

Leonardo had left an envelope on the middle of my desk, where I was sure to see it. It was official confirmation that the courier had handed over the cash—and, per my agreement with Sergio, it contained the access code and information about Miguel's account at the Banco Internacional de Comercio.

Suzanne studied the pertinent portions of the Delgado file while I telephoned American Airlines to book her on the next flight to Uruguay, using the alias she had put on her forged passport. I flinched when the reservations agent told me the cost of the fare: nearly two thousand dollars for flight 999 from Miami to Montevideo. Suzanne didn't qualify for the fourteen-day advance-purchase discount, nor was she going to get any frequent-flyer miles since she was traveling under an assumed name. The itinerary was a nightmare: an 11:30 A.M. departure from Miami, than a 12:24 arrival the next day in Montevideo, with a two-hour stopover in São Paolo.

I kept working, making hotel reservations under Suzanne's assumed name. When it was over, our mood turned more serious. I still felt as I had all day, that I had to keep moving and acting or my confidence would vanish.

I took out the paper that Sergio had sent me. It had been carefully typed, at my request, at a commercial secretarial office so that it couldn't be traced if the whole plan fell apart. I had the transfer instructions and access codes, in addition to the balance. The account contained twenty million dollars and change. That sounded about right.

I ran through all the steps for transferring the money, which Suzanne grasped easily on the first go-around. I kept reminding her that she would be on her own once she was in Montevideo. Her expression grew more and more sly as we talked; if nothing else, I realized, I would be making her happy.

We stayed late in my office, thinking up contingency plans for anything that might go wrong. Just before she left, I opened the wall safe and counted out four thousand dollars in cash for her—half for the airline tickets, the other half for the hotel and other incidentals. I had learned from Miguel's example. By paying for everything in cash, we would leave no paper trail. I tried not to worry about Luis's ever-shrinking proceeds from the diamond sale. This truly would be a case of spending money to make money.

I watched Suzanne store the cash and the envelope containing the instructions in her black fanny pack. Then I put the Beretta in my jacket pocket, turned off the office lights, set the alarm, and escorted Suzanne out to her car.

We parted there. I watched her drive away, and said a prayer to Mary Magdalene—the patron saint of fallen women everywhere.

Twenty-eight

I circled around the lower concourse outside customs at the airport, waiting for Suzanne to appear. I was chewing sunflower seeds because otherwise, I knew, I would destroy my fingernails.

American Airlines flight 924 from Montevideo was scheduled to be right on time, due in at the ungodly hour of 5:23 in the morning. I had stayed up all night watching TV to the point at which I thought Mr. Ed was talking to me from the set. Now I was alternating between hyperalertness and total exhaustion.

Suzanne had been gone three days. To occupy as well as to punish myself, I had written up old cases and helped Leonardo send out bills. In centuries past I might have gone in for self-flagellation, but I was unwilling to confess my transgressions on TV talk shows, the '90s version of donning the hair shirt. I had slept perhaps six or seven hours during the entire three days, and I was starting to show it—the circles under my eyes made me look like a demented raccoon.

Half an hour later she appeared, looking tired but triumphant. It wasn't hard to spot her, a tall, voluptuous blonde in black pants and a T-shirt—the same outfit she'd left in, albeit with a new black sweater tied around her shoulders. She looked around but didn't spot me pulling toward her in the Mercedes.

Even at that hour, the airport was bustling. I wedged in between two limousines and honked the horn. Then I remembered that Suzanne is nearsighted; she probably wasn't wearing her contact lenses. I got out, hopped on the hood, and started yelling her name. I scared the hell out of an old couple next to me, but it worked. Suzanne sprinted toward the car and enveloped me in a big hug before getting in.

"This sure beats the broken-down diesel taxi I had to take in Montevideo," she said by way of greeting. "You wouldn't believe the smell from that thing. Or the noise."

She had risked one phone call to me while she was in South America, so I already knew bits and pieces of what had occurred. But I couldn't stand the suspense. "Never mind that," I ordered. "Tell me what happened. All of it."

Dawn was breaking as I left the airport road and headed east on I-95 toward downtown. "The flight down took forever," she said, leaning back in the seat. "I slept some, but I was really wired. The worst part was knowing I had to fly back in two days. God!"

I allowed her to ramble on about how uncomfortable she had been on the flight. She had earned the right to complain: Two twelve-hour plane trips within three days was inhuman.

"Did you know there's a river that separates Montevideo from Buenos Aires?" she asked. I groaned. It looked like I had to endure a dawn geography lesson.

"The taxi driver gave me a tour as we drove in from Carrasco Airport," she added. "The road is called the Rambla. It's only a twenty-minute drive, but it was interesting. There was this fort—the Cerro de Montevideo. It was built to defend the city from Portuguese invaders from Brazil."

I drove on until I realized she was waiting for a response. "Is that right?" I asked.

She hunted around in her bag and pulled out a postcard of the fort, which she stuck into my face. I couldn't see to drive for a moment, but the traffic was so erratic that it probably didn't matter much. "See?" she asked. "You know, the Rambla's kind of like Miami Beach—big apartment buildings, lots of traffic. The American Embassy's there, too. I made a note of it, in case I had to go there for help."

"Good idea," I said.

She went on with her travelogue, oblivious to the fact that I was barely listening. I wanted to get to the meat of her story, but I was too tired to make demands. Even after twelve hours on a plane, Suzanne had twice as much energy as I did.

"It's so sad, Lupe, what the taxi driver told me," she said. "He kept talking about South American steaks—I didn't have the heart to tell him I'm a vegetarian. But he said that no one knows that Uruguayan steaks are the best in the world. Isn't that sad? If someone has to eat meat, then shouldn't they know where to get the best?"

I concentrated on driving toward Suzanne's Brickell apartment. "What happened next?" I asked, trying not to sound irritated.

"Well, the Victoria Plaza Hotel is really nice, Lupe," she said. "I should have known you'd book me into the only five-star hotel in the city. The porter told me it's been completely renovated."

She flashed another postcard in front of my eyes. "After that flight, the hot bath was incredible," she added. "I washed most of my clothes in the sink, but I had my pants sent to the cleaners. Is that okay?"

I laughed. "A dry-cleaning bill is the least of the expenses on this case. Of course it's all right."

"Well, it was still daylight when I got there," she said, looking relieved. "So I went walking around the *Ciudad Vieja*—the old town. I wanted to orient myself. They have all these buildings and old plazas—nothing like Miami. The main square is the Plaza Independencia—where there's this huge statue of José Gervasio Artigas. He's the national hero."

She put another postcard in front of me. I saw the statue of a man mounted on a horse, along with a bunch of cute guys. "Who are they?" I asked.

"The *Cuerpo de Blandegas*," she replied. "Also there was this area called *El Mercado del Puerto,* full of restaurants and shops. You know, one of these days we're going to have to go there together! For a vacation!"

Suzanne had gone completely native. I half-expected her to start singing the Uruguayan national anthem. I signaled a right turn off I-95 at the Key Biscayne exit and slowed down when I reached a red light at the bottom of the ramp.

"Tell me about the meeting at the bank," I commanded.

Suzanne was stuck in tourist-board mode. "Well, the banking center is about ten blocks from the hotel," she said pensively. "All the banks are pretty much bunched together, at the intersection of Veinte y cinco de Mayo and Missiones. Here, look."

I gripped the wheel and looked at another postcard.

"There's a bank there called the Banco de la Republica—it's made entirely of marble."

I braced myself for the next postcard, but none was forthcoming. It was strangely disappointing.

"What's the matter?" Suzanne asked.

"Nothing," I said. "Go on."

"Our target bank, the Primer Banco de Uruguay, is situated directly opposite the Banco Internacional de Comercio, Miguel's bank," she said. "I met this guy called Señor San Pedro. He was really nice, even though he was kind of weird-looking."

"What do you mean?" I asked.

"He was all one color: gray," Suzanne said. "I mean it: gray hair, gray eyes, gray skin, a gray suit. Lupe, he was even wearing a gray pearl tie pin."

"That's truly weird," I said.

"You're telling me." Suzanne laughed. "Anyway, he looked over my documents, made a copy of my Costa Rican passport, and had me fill out a form. I gave him all the phony information you and I agreed on, but really, it wasn't an in-depth form. I've had to answer tougher questions to get a department-store credit card."

"You mean he took your P.O. box in San José, Costa Rica, as a permanent address?" I marveled. No wonder Uruguayan banking was attractive to foreigners.

"I did what you told me to," Suzanne continued. "I asked him all kinds of questions about the secrecy laws there. He said he'd personally take care of my account. I wasn't surprised—the guy couldn't keep his eyes off my chest."

That was just what I wanted to hear. I had hoped we'd get a bank official who would be transfixed by Suzanne's hair, eyes, breasts— anything that might distract him from prying into her reasons for traveling to Montevideo.

"I told him I was opening the account with a thousand dollars," she said, "but that I would transfer a larger sum from another bank in the country in a day or so."

By this time we had arrived at Suzanne's building. I parked beside the ramp leading to her front door. "How did he react?" I asked.

"He didn't even raise an eyebrow," Suzanne said. "I think this kind of stuff goes on all the time there. I sort of hinted around to him that I was about to break up with a man who had a lot of money. You know, like I was getting a golden kiss good-bye."

"Did you ask him about domestic bank transfer secrecy laws?" I asked. This was critical.

"Of course," Suzanne said. "He said everything is confidential. The bank always protects the client's identity at any price. In return, they collect three percent of funds deposited."

"Three percent!" I yelled. "My God, that's robbery! They aren't bankers, they're loan sharks."

Suzanne frowned. "Well, Lupe, they go to a lot of trouble to protect their clients. Don't you think they're entitled to collect a good percentage?"

I had forgotten that Suzanne had become a lover of all things Uruguayan. "Never mind," I said. "Go on."

"I agreed to the fees, and we got down to business," Suzanne said. "We worked out the access code and wiring instructions, and I handed over the cash. Then he asked me to go to lunch with him."

Big surprise. "That's all there was to it?" I asked.

"That was it, except for the cozy lunch with Señor San Pedro." Suzanne took out a white business-sized envelope from her purse and handed it to me. "Don't lose that," she warned me. "That's the only copy."

I unsealed it and took out a single sheet of paper. Skimming it, I was startled to see how little paperwork was involved in opening an account at the Primer Banco de Uruguay. Suzanne's name appeared nowhere on the document, only the number of the account, a receipt for the thousand bucks, an access code, and the wiring instructions. A notation indicated that the customer could contact the bank twenty-four hours a day.

"You didn't have to go to lunch with that guy, you know," I said, folding the paper and putting it back in the envelope.

"I know, but I wanted to make sure he helped us any way he could," Suzanne said. "Besides, I was fascinated by his grayness. Even his wedding band was gray—I noticed it because he took it off before we left the bank."

This lunch disturbed me. So much for Señor San Pedro not being able to describe Suzanne. I'm sure he got an eyeful. I didn't bring it up, though. There was nothing to be done.

"Where did he take you to eat?" I asked. "Somewhere nice, I hope."

"We went to a really fancy place in *El Mercado del Puerto*," she said. "I have a postcard of it somewhere."

"Did he ask you any questions?" I asked. "You know, what your business intentions were, or anything like that?"

"No, he just tried to talk me into spending a week in Montevideo." Suzanne giggled. "He said he could show me sights that tourists never get to see."

"I guess he didn't mean Señora San Pedro," I said.

We both laughed. It was almost seven o'clock, and people were starting to emerge from Suzanne's building, headed for their jobs. I leaned over and kissed her on the cheek.

"You did a great job, Suzanne," I said. "I couldn't have done better myself."

Suzanne actually blushed. "I have to get some sleep," she said.

"I'll call you later."

She grabbed her bag and reached for the door. Before she got out, though, she stopped.

"I guess we did it," she said. It seemed that for the first time, she had seriously considered the ramifications of her actions. Our actions.

"I guess we did," I replied with real affection. Suzanne was probably the only person outside of my family whom I could have trusted to carry out the assignment. I had earned her undying loyalty after I saved her from her stalker boyfriend, but there was more to it than that. She was a straight arrow, the kind bred in the Upper Midwest. I thought she was probably a dying phenomenon.

"It's over," she added, getting out of the car. "Stop punishing yourself."

I looked up and smiled as I reached for my cellular telephone and started dialing a number I knew from memory. My self-punishment, I realized, was only beginning.

I felt wide awake after talking to Suzanne, so I headed for the office, eager to try accessing the Uruguayan account to make sure everything was in order. I had just put the coffee pot on the stove when the phone rang.

"Lupe, it's Charlie," said a familiar voice. "Remember that day we ran into each other at the Justice building?"

I felt my stomach lurch. It was never good news when Charlie jumped into a conversation without flattering me.

"Hi, how are you?" I asked pointedly. "And yes, of course I remember."

"Remember how I asked you the name of the guy whose record you were looking up?"

I leaned against Leonardo's desk. "Yes. I remember I told you it was some scumbag."

"That's right," Charlie said, "but you never told me the guy's name."

"Why are you asking me all these questions, Charlie?"

"We just got his prints back to formally ID him," Charlie said. "I knew him, of course. I put him away years ago. Now, Lupe, tell me the truth—was your guy's name José Salazar?"

I sat down slowly in Leonardo's chair, which was a mistake. I felt fatigue seep through my body—evidently all-nighters would soon be a part of my fondly remembered youth. "What is this?" I asked. "Charlie, it's too early for—"

"Also known as Pepe Salazar?" Charlie asked. "Hispanic male, thirty-eight years old, five-ten, two hundred pounds, lots of gold jewelry? Does that fit the description?"

I wasn't about to answer without getting information in return. "Keep talking, Charlie."

"Hey, I'm just tipping you off because I know about your investigator," Charlie said defensively. "Aurora's convinced you're concealing evidence. Once she hears about the M.O. on this one, she's going to assume there's a connection to Mike Moore. She's definitely going to pull you in. I just wanted to give you time—you know, warn you about this morning's catch. I want you to be prepared."

I rubbed my eyes. "Charlie, you're driving me insane," I whined. Exhaustion was dulling my mind. "What connection? I don't understand a word you're saying."

"Look, Lupe, I don't know for sure if you were checking on Pepe Salazar, it's just that the coincidence struck me. I don't want to get involved, and if I hadn't run into you at the Justice building I wouldn't have thought of it."

I heard Charlie fumbling around with a lighter, trying to ignite a cigarette while holding the receiver to his ear.

"I'm at the Medical Examiner's office," he explained. "I'm the A.S.A. on duty. Pepe Salazar's lying dead on the table in the next room, waiting to get cut up."

"Pepe Salazar's dead?" I asked.

"*Now* you're listening." Charlie took a deep drag. "He was fished out of the Miami River around dawn this morning. Thought you might want to know. Looks like I was right."

A stab of pain ran through my stomach. "Do you have any idea how he died?" I asked.

"The preliminary report is that he was strangled with some kind of wire," Tommy said. He exhaled deeply. "Probably piano wire.

Then he was dumped in the river. There's your connection. See, it's the same way your guy Moore died, so it looks like the cases might be tied together. After the autopsy I'll be able to tell you more."

"My God." I whispered, searching my brain for any connection that could lead back to me. I shivered, though the room was warm.

"I can't really talk now," Charlie said, which meant that he was finished with his cigarette. "I just wanted to give you the latest, so you'll have the jump on Aurora."

"Wait, wait," I pleaded.

Charlie ignored me. "I can only do so much for you," Charlie said. "But Aurora is after your ass like you wouldn't believe. I'll do what I can, but I think you'd better prepare yourself for war."

Charlie hung up. Piano wire, the same as Mike Moore.

No one would mourn Pepe Salazar, I was willing to bet, but it was small consolation. I heard the coffee pot gurgling and poured myself a cup topped with frothy hot milk. I drained half the cup in a gulp, burning the hell out of my mouth. It looked like it was going to be that kind of day.

In my office I stood at the window, watching the parrots going through their early morning routine. After a while I realized they were moving strangely, almost as though they were in slow motion. I got out the binoculars and peered closer. The birds were definitely acting goofy, jumping from one branch to the other and missing as often as they made it. A talk with Leonardo was definitely in order. I was all in favor of the entrepreneurial spirit, but I was chilled by the idea of Aurora Santangelo finding out there was a marijuana garden in the yard behind Solano Investigations.

I sat down at my desk and dialed the phone. A very sleepy voice answered, "This had better be important, Lupe."

"It is, Tommy," I said. "The cops fished Pepe Salazar out of the Miami River this morning."

"He wasn't snorkeling, was he?" Tommy asked. Awake or asleep, nothing fazed him. "Was he trapping undersized lobsters?"

"No, and he wasn't practicing for the Olympics, either—unless there's a new competition in swimming with a piano wire tied tight around the athlete's neck."

"Charming," Tommy said.

"And, by the way, I got word that Aurora Santangelo will probably use this to gun for me. She's going to make the cause-of-death connection between Mike and Pepe Salazar—and assume that I was involved. I don't know if she can do it, but I don't doubt she'll move Heaven and earth trying. Do you have anything new on her?"

"Actually, yes." Tommy cleared his throat. "I have a grand jury subpoena for you. Bright and early Friday at eight o'clock. It shouldn't be much of a problem for you, since you've apparently turned into a morning person."

We hung up. Today was Wednesday. That gave me two days.

I was still staring at the calendar, wishing for some sort of miracle, when I punched in the dozen numbers on the sheet Suzanne had given me to access the Uruguayan account. The system worked like a dream, confirming a deposit of $1,000 two days before. It was incredible; the sheet detailed how instructions could be given any time in any of nine languages, the last being Urdu.

I put down the phone. *Two days.*

Twenty-nine

I was hot, dirty, scratched up, and sore. And why shouldn't I have been; after all, I had just spent the last hour crawling on my hands and knees, searching the area where we had found Mike Moore. In addition, I had parked my car in Cocoplum Circle and had jogged to the vicinity of the de la Torres' home—a distance of around two miles. I wasn't in marathon condition, by any means, but I didn't have much choice since I didn't want to call attention to myself. Triplet specters were haunting me—Miguel and Teresa de la Torre, and Aurora Santangelo.

I had contacted Marisol and confirmed that the de la Torres weren't going to be at home. She told me they were attending a fund-raiser for a local politician in Gables Estates. Every so often I called her on the cellular phone to make sure they hadn't left early.

I had thought about it and I was convinced that the key to the identity of Mike and Pepe Salazar's killer was in Mike's missing camera. There was no doubt in my mind that the same person had committed both crimes. Pepe's appearing in the river had eliminated him as a suspect—unless Pepe's killer had used the method to throw the authorities off the trail. I didn't believe it.

It takes cold blood to get physically close to someone and extinguish their life; and these crimes bore the marks of a single, dangerous individual. A couple of possibilities crossed my mind. The one that seemed most likely was that Pepe had pushed Teresa too far with his tape, which implicated her in a murder-for-hire. If that were the case, he should have known better. Teresa had hired one killer, so why couldn't she hire another? She could have hired this second killer for personal security, which would explain how his path had crossed Mike's.

Two things could have happened to the camera. Mike's murderer could have taken it with him, intending to dispose of it later. If that reasoning were correct, my chances of ever finding it were nil. The second possibility was that Mike had hidden it because he had sensed he was in danger, knowing that whoever was lurking on the de la Torres' property could be identified by the pictures he took. I knew the police had combed the area as part of their investigation, but their search had been pretty much restricted to a perimeter immediately around Mike's car. Unlike the police, I knew the object of Mike's surveillance—which also gave me a much wider area to search.

I had finished my third sweep of the area when I thought back to the conversation I'd had with Joe Ryan when we were looking for Mike. Joe had told me that Mike had conducted a rolling surveillance much of the time, but that he had also occasionally hidden his car and shimmied up a tree for a vantage point. The biggest ones there were beautiful ancient olive trees, among the few in the area that had survived Hurricane Andrew. Since Mike's car had been parked on an out-of-the-way embankment, the only theory that made any sense was that he had been hidden in a tree and attacked while he was making his way back to his car. The question was, Why?

I looked from one end of the street to the other, seeking a tree with good visibility and lots of branches and leaves, as well as one that was strong enough to support a man's weight. Only two trees seemed capable of this double duty: one to the right of the de la Torres' house, and another on a diagonal line across the street.

I didn't think anyone had spotted me yet, but I couldn't be sure. It was time to make a move before I found myself hauled off to jail for loitering. I was a good fifteen years past my prime tree-climbing condition, so I thought for a moment which tree would be my candidate. A couple of years before, I'd climbed a mango tree in a hurry, but I had been in fear for my life then. I wasn't sure I could climb both of these trees, especially in shorts and a T-shirt.

The tree to the right of the property offered the best hiding place but a less-than-perfect view of the house. The tree across the street had a clear view of the property, but from what I could see, its possible perches looked uncomfortable and precarious.

What would Mike do? I asked myself. The answer was clear: He was a professional, and he would have sacrificed comfort in order to do a better job.

I walked under the tree and looked up, trying to see which branch might be capable of supporting Mike's two-hundred-pound weight. Then I said a fond good-bye to my smooth knees and elbows, knowing it would be a while before they recovered.

A couple of bicyclists passed by, not noticing me. When they were gone I hoisted myself up to the lowest branch. I thanked whatever saint watches over tree climbers, because I was able to make it up to the first branch without hurting myself. It would be comparatively easy going after that, I thought.

Maybe not. The higher I went, the more I saw that the tree was showing signs of rot. It groaned under my weight, and I seriously doubted whether it would have been able to support Mike. I gingerly lowered myself to the bottom branch and dropped down to the grass below. Then I allowed myself to curse my luck.

I crossed the street to plan my assault on the second tree, the one positioned near the de la Torres' easement. I circled around, trying to find a branch low enough to grab on to. Nothing. The only possible choice was a branch eight or ten feet off the ground—almost twice my height. I could have cried in frustration. Instead I examined the tree like a surgeon examining a patient's anatomy. There was one knothole, too high for me—but a taller person might have been able to swing a leg up and reach it. Mike was tall enough and athletic enough to have done it. I plopped down at the base of the tree and thought.

There was no way I was giving up. Which meant there was only one thing left for me to do.

I jogged back to Cocoplum Circle—huffing, puffing, and sweating—and found the Mercedes where I'd left it. I got in and drove with one hand while I dialed Marisol with the other.

"What's up, Lupe?" she asked. "You sound terrible."

"Never mind. Are they still there?"

"Yeah," she said. "This thing doesn't look like it's going to end any time soon."

"That's what I wanted to hear. Thanks."

When I hung up I had reached the de la Torres' street. I parked directly under the tree, careful to make sure my tags weren't pointing toward anyone's living-room window. The twilight was darkening, which would help me remain somewhat inconspicuous.

"Inconspicuous," I muttered to myself. "Listen to you."

What the hell. I took off my running shoes, not wanting to invoke Osvaldo's wrath by damaging the car's paint, then stood on the hood of the Mercedes. Stretching, I was able to reach the lowest branch and pull myself up.

I scrambled up two more branches to the densest part of the tree, then sat down on the thickest, sturdiest branch, gasping for air. Where I sat, it was almost pitch black from lack of sunlight and the density of the foliage. However, the tree afforded a near-perfect view of the de la Torres' home.

I began by groping around close to the trunk and found nothing. Then I inched away from the trunk onto a branch, which elevated me even further. I kept reminding myself to allow for Mike's height and weight—it would be easier for me to move around than it had been for him. I felt around the leaves on the nearest branch and discovered silver-foil gum wrappers molded together to the size and shape of a Ping-Pong ball. My heart began to pound. Mike had been a big gum chewer—they had to be his. Buoyed by my discovery, I felt braver. I stood up in the tree, holding on to the trunk for balance and feeling around in the dark.

I still hadn't found anything when I heard a noise below me. I clutched tightly to the tree trunk.

"Need any help?"

I looked down. There was a police cruiser parked next to the

Mercedes, with two officers standing next to it. One of them shined a flashlight in my face.

"No, thanks, officer," I said.

They stood there looking up, in no hurry to leave. I knew they were waiting for me to explain why I was crouched in the upper branches of an olive tree on a dark street. I was waiting for an explanation, too. I had been so single-minded that I had broken a basic rule: Always have a cover story prepared in case you're caught.

"I'm looking for my pet. My bird. My parrot," I improvised. Shit, I thought. If they believed that one, they should have their badges taken away.

"Your what?" one of them asked.

"My pet parrot," I called down. "I saw it fly into this tree. It's very excitable."

I saw them glance at each other, probably wondering what law I might be breaking. They looked at the Mercedes, then back up at me. Except for looking like a lunatic, I wasn't breaking any laws—the tree was on public property. If acting crazy in Miami was against the law, they couldn't have built enough jails for all the offenders.

The taller of the two walked over to the tree trunk and looked up. "Uh, can you manage on your own?" he asked. He pointed the light through the branches straight into my face, blinding me for a moment.

"Yes, thanks," I said. "If I keep calling for him he'll come back. This has happened before."

Just then the cellular phone in my fanny pack started to ring. I froze. The policemen looked at me expectantly.

I took out the phone and answered it.

"Lupe." Marisol's excited voice emerged through the static. "They just left, and they're headed for Coral Gables. You have seven to ten minutes—tops."

"Oh, hey, how are you?" I said. I tried to keep my voice light and casual.

"Lupe—didn't you hear me?" Marisol yelled. "Get out of there! I'm on their trail, and they're heading home."

"Okay, fine. See you." I shut off the phone and looked down at the cops. "That's my friend," I explained lamely. "She's waiting for me. I really have to go meet up with her."

I made a show of looking at my watch. I could sense that the officers suspected something was wrong, and I hoped they would just assume I was a little nuts. The three of us looked at one another, suspended in time. I had calculated that about a minute had passed since Marisol had called me, and reached for a branch so that I could climb down. I didn't want to imagine what would happen if the de la Torres arrived home to see me and the police gathered around a tree on their street.

"I guess he'll be all right for the night," I offered. "I'll look again tomorrow."

"What the hell—there's still a little daylight left," the younger of the two said hopefully. "We'll help you look for another minute or two."

I could have strangled him—not the most saintly thought, but strangulation happened to be on my mind.

The other officer took out a search light and pointed it into the upper branches. "What does it look like? What color is it?" he asked, methodically moving the beam back and forth.

I thought back to the parrots who lived in the avocado tree behind my office—the ones who had been sampling Leonardo's illicit gardening experiments.

"Green," I said, wishing my powers of observation were just a bit sharper so I could be fairly accurate. "Green, about a foot long, with an orange crown on his head."

I hoped neither of them was a member of the Audubon Society. I had probably just described a species of bird that didn't exist.

They shined their lights up again, then stopped, apparently tired of the search. "Just be careful up there," one of them said. "I hope you find your parrot."

They opened the cruiser doors. The officer on the passenger side pointed up at the tree. "I think there's a nest up there," he said. "Up in that corner. You should check there—birds like nests."

Other than demonstrating a real gift for stating the obvious, the officer had helped me. When I looked to where he had pointed, I saw a bundle of twigs that I hadn't noticed before. As soon as they drove away, I began inching my way to the spot. I had another minute or two, by my reckoning, before the de la Torres would arrive.

I felt around the mass of dried sticks, hoping there weren't any snakes or spiders inside. I was dripping so much sweat that it was hard to hold on to the branch. I let out a relieved sigh when my fingers touched cold metal. I wasn't sure what I had found—it was too dark, and now the sweat was dripping into my eyes—so I summoned all my courage and hoped the object wasn't a trap. I said a prayer for Mike as I carefully extracted the camera. I let out a deep breath and hung it from my neck.

I skinned myself coming down, but I didn't care. I grabbed my shoes from the Mercedes's hood, jumped into the car, and gunned the motor. I peeled out, grass and mud flying everywhere. A pair of headlights appeared in my rearview mirror, but I turned the corner before I could tell if it had been Miguel and Teresa.

I thought about going home to change—I was soaked with sweat and unbelievably filthy. But this was no time for vanity. I raced over to Eckerd's one-hour photo developing. On the way I called back Marisol and thanked her—after explaining why I had sounded like such an idiot on the phone.

The girl at the counter informed me that it would be more like two hours before the film in the camera could be developed. I swore and pointed at the "Speedy One-Hour Service" sign, but that earned me only a haughty once-over of my grubby outfit and skinned elbows. I guess I didn't look like a priority customer.

It was 8:30. I decided to go home for a quick shower, then get to the office to use the time constructively. I would have gone crazy standing around waiting. All I could think about was that finding Mike's camera was going to lead me to his killer. I prayed I was right.

By the time I reached my office I was a bundle of nerves. I had to wait an hour before I could return to Eckerd's. It was probably delusional of me to assume that I was going to get anything done until then, I thought.

I turned off the alarm and switched on the lights. I heard the parrots outside, but it was too dark for me to see them. I was disappointed—I was curious to know how inaccurate my description to the cops was.

I took out the Delgado file and started browsing. It became quickly obvious that I had neglected Marisol's reports. Leonardo had arranged her surveillance data into orderly lists of tag number ID's, and photos with dates and times clearly marked.

It was all waiting for me to make some sense of it. There was so much information that I knew Leonardo hadn't had time to review it; he'd simply compiled it and left it for me. The stack of license-plate printouts alone was almost an inch thick.

I had to start somewhere, so I took out the pictures. Again I saw the grainy snapshot in which there was a man I thought I recognized. I pulled out the tag numbers and found the listings for the date and place depicted in the photo. Marisol had made a notation that the picture had been taken in the parking lot of Casa Juancho. I ran my finger down the list of car owners corresponding to Miguel's lunch party.

My blood froze. Now I was certain that Leonardo hadn't reviewed these listings. If he had, he'd have noticed the name Ignacio Solano, with a home address in Cocoplum. I silently cursed Leonardo for neglecting his work and not bringing this to me earlier—but then I was equally at fault for not supervising him. Marisol had done her job. She had taken the photos and labeled them before handing them over to my cousin. It had been up to him to run the tags and compile anything that jumped out at him. Certainly seeing Papi's name—my father, his uncle—would have made him react.

I looked at the notation for the date on Marisol's report—it had been three days earlier. The report had sat on my desk for three days! I was disgusted. This was incompetence, and I was ultimately responsible.

Papi. I felt physically ill. I looked at the report again, thinking irrationally that maybe I'd misread it.

Of course I hadn't. I thought back to our conversation on the terrace at home. Papi hadn't said anything about knowing Miguel well enough to be socializing with him. And Miguel himself had known my father but had said nothing of their meeting. But then, why should he have? He met lots of people; it could have slipped his mind. Maybe I was reading too much into their meeting.

It wasn't so strange that Papi and Miguel should know each other—they were of the same generation, and they were both successful Cuban businessmen in Miami. But why had neither of them said anything about a lunch? That was the problem.

I gathered my purse and headed for Eckerd's, deciding to wait out the last half-hour at the Cubanteria. I had barely eaten all day, and I wanted to be fortified for what Mike's camera would reveal. As I drove I thought about how best to approach Papi about Miguel—or if I even should.

My impatience got the better of me. I stopped at Eckerd's first, on the chance that the clerk had been overly pessimistic. I was told that, if anything, it was going to take longer than she had thought.

It was that kind of day. I crossed the parking lot to the Cubanteria, hoping Gregorio was still cooking at that hour.

Gregorio spotted me coming in the door; he came out of the kitchen and called out my name in a loud voice that made all the other patrons look up.

"It's been so long!" he bellowed. "What can I make for you?"

I smelled hot food and suddenly I was starving. "Anything, Gregorio," I said. "As long as it's hot and Cuban."

He rubbed his hands together with glee. "You wait here," he said. "I know just the thing."

Before he left for the kitchen, Gregorio grabbed a blue plastic tumbler from under the counter and sat it in front of me. He opened a cabinet behind him and produced a bottle of wine. It was Sangre de Toro, a humble Chilean table wine, which you wouldn't know from the reverence and ceremony with which Gregorio poured it. The combination of the light-blue cup and blood-red wine wasn't particularly appealing, but I took a deep drink anyway.

The Cubanteria didn't have a liquor license, but Gregorio didn't care. He had told me before that he was under the protection of the gods.

"You enjoy," he said with a wink.

Fifteen minutes later, Gregorio returned with a steaming plate of *arroz con pollo*. I tried not to react as he fussed with the table setting. I was officially sleeping, living, and eating the Delgado case. As I took the first bite I wondered how the dish would have compared to the one cooked by Teresa de la Torre almost forty years before.

Business was slow that night, so Gregorio sat on the stool next to me after he refilled my glass. "Lupe, I sense trouble from you," he said gravely, wiping his hands on a rag. "Are you having problems?"

I didn't put much stock into Gregorio's esoteric religion, but the man had an unfailing sixth sense. Of course, tonight's insight hadn't taken much work. I was checking my watch every thirty seconds, eating alone in a cafeteria at ten o'clock, and gulping cheap wine from a plastic cup. I surely didn't look like the embodiment of peace of mind.

"I am, Gregorio," I said. The old man nodded somberly.

I tore off a piece of Cuban bread and mopped up the last bits of *arroz con pollo*. This dinner hadn't featured diamonds sewn inside the chicken parts, but it had been delicious. I checked my watch again and put a ten-dollar bill on the table, vastly overpaying.

Sliding off the stool, I was surprised to notice that I wasn't exactly steady on my feet. The wine had affected more than I thought it would. Oh, well. Maybe I'd be better able to deal with the photographs.

Gregorio walked me outside. He looked up at the stars and shook his head. "I feel a bad air around you, Lupe," he said. "I sense troubles. You be careful, very careful, *mi amor.*"

He turned and walked back into the Cubanteria, muttering to himself. He looked small, bent over, and lonely—precisely how I felt.

Instinctively I reached down the neck of my T-shirt until I touched the religious medals Lourdes had insisted I attach to my brassiere strap for protection. I found the safety pin and, hanging from it, three medals of the Virgin.

The clerk at Eckerd's frowned the instant she saw me, apparently not in a forgiving mood from my previous complaining visits. She shoved the envelope across the counter and, in an acidic voice, told me about two-for-one specials, free film, and all the other goodies I was eligible for.

The envelope felt hot in my hand, as though it were smoldering. I surprised the clerk by turning down all her discounts and paying full price. I walked out holding the pictures tightly.

When I had reached the privacy of the Mercedes, I opened the envelope. I took one look and ran out of the car, barely making it to a garbage can before I vomited all the wine and *arroz con pollo*.

It was only fitting, I supposed, that some of it splashed onto Luis Delgado's photographed face.

Thirty

I stayed in bed late into the next morning. This was so unusual for me that Aida and Osvaldo took turns checking on me to make sure I was alive. I kept them at bay by mumbling about a stomach virus, a false-hood that I embellished with mention of a bad fish the night before. At about noon I got up. They were checking on me so often that my evasions were becoming embarrassingly dramatic.

I was disgusted with myself. I don't know what made me more heartsick—the knowledge that Luis was a killer, or the fact that I had let him con me. I had gotten emotionally involved, and I had thrown my objectivity to the wind. I would have fired any investigator who had acted as I had.

Hunger finally drove me from my bedroom. In the kitchen I looked out the picture window at the beautiful early afternoon. As far as my mood went, there might as well have been a category-five hur-ricane raging outside. I had to make a plan, which was impossible for me on an empty stomach.

I was finishing my second *café con leche* when the phone rang.

"Leonardo said you weren't at work and to try you at home," Marisol said, her words coming in a torrent. "I'm calling you from the lobby of First Miami, Lupe. Miguel de la Torre was just carried out of his office on a stretcher."

The coffee rose in my throat. "What do you mean?" I shouted.

"I followed him from his house to the bank this morning, as usual," Marisol said. "I parked in the lot to keep an eye on his car, then about a half an hour ago an ambulance pulled up."

"Did you go inside?" I asked. "You're sure it was him?"

"I went in and stood around the lobby, like I was a customer," Marisol said. "Five minutes ago the emergency technicians came out with Miguel on a stretcher. I asked the security guard what had hap-pened, and he said that Miguel had had a stroke."

"My God," I said.

"I heard the rescue guys saying they were taking him to Doctor's

Hospital," Marisol continued. "They were pissed off because Jackson is closer, but Teresa intervened and made sure he was taken to Doctor's instead."

"Do you know how he's doing?" I demanded. "I mean, is he going to live?"

"I'm calling from my car, and I'm following the ambulance," she said. "We're headed north, so it looks like Teresa got her way. I don't know how he's doing, but I saw him on the stretcher and his color looked terrible. He was white as a ghost."

"Where are you now?" I asked. I started putting on my shoes.

"*Mierda!* I lost them!" Marisol fumbled with the phone. "Sorry, Lupe, I couldn't keep up with them. But they turned west on Bird Road, so they're definitely taking him to Doctor's. What do you want me to do?"

"Hang around the ER and find out about his condition, if you can," I said. "The press will probably be there soon. Miguel de la Torre collapsing is big news."

"I'll find out what I can," Marisol said.

I thanked her and hung up. I quickly finished my breakfast and headed out the door before Aida could ask me why I was in such a hurry. I drove straight to my office, realizing that I had better figure out what to do.

I found Leonardo at his desk, placidly slurping a ghastly blue potion. As soon as he saw me he stood up. "Lupe, are you all right?" he asked. "You look terrible."

"No, I'm not all right," I barked. "I'm tired, I'm in a bad mood, and everything's screwed up. And before you ask—I don't want a damned shake."

Leonardo's face dropped. I felt as if I had just beaten up on a kitten. I didn't have the heart to unload on him about not following up on Marisol's report. It was a conversation we needed to have—but later. "I'm sorry," I said, but my voice was still hard. "I'll be in my office. I'm not taking calls."

I locked myself in my office. Everything looked the same, but everything had changed. I looked outside for the parrot family, but they weren't around. Maybe they had figured out that I was trouble and had left town before things turned ugly.

There was no point avoiding the call I had to make. I felt like an actor, going through the motions fitting the pieces to a puzzle that I'd already solved in my head.

I sent a 911 emergency call to Nestor's beeper. He called a minute later. "I need you to call Veronica," I said. "Ask her if Miguel de la Torre received a letter from Uruguay this morning."

"I assume this means I'm back on the case," Nestor replied in a cold voice.

I had completely forgotten about firing him. "I'm sorry about what I said to you. Please, forgive me," I said. It wasn't an act. I should never have shut Nestor out of the case. He was capable of taking care of himself, and also I could have benefited from his advice.

Nestor said nothing.

"The last time I saw you, you made me promise to come to you if I needed help," I reminded him. "Well, this is for real. I need this information, and I need it now." I was groveling like a dog, but compared to the depths I had sunk to it was nothing.

"I can try," Nestor said. "What's happened, Lupe? You sound upset."

"Just call her, Nestor. Please. I'll be right here in my office, waiting to hear from you."

Nestor slammed down the phone with such force that I winced. He was right to be angry with me. I'd fired him from the case for no good reason. Then he picked up the phone days later only to hear me asking for a favor. I'd have to find a way to make it up to him.

The phone rang fifteen minutes later. It was Nestor. "Sorry it took me a while," he said. "Veronica was on her lunch break."

I gritted my teeth. "Well, did he get a letter from Uruguay? One like the others?"

"He sure did."

I looked down and saw that my hand was shaking. "Thank you, Nestor," I said. "I really appreciate your helping me."

"No problem," he said. "Call if you need anything else. And take care of yourself, Lupe. I really mean it."

He hung up, leaving me motionless as I tried to collect myself. It felt as though every little piece of information were another nail in my coffin.

I picked up the phone again and pressed Tommy's number on my speed dial. Sonia answered and said that Tommy would be in court all day, maybe until six or seven o'clock. I left a message for him to call me the second he stepped in the door.

I walked over to the window and looked out at the avocado tree. I had just begun to contemplate building a tree house out there and living in it—maybe no one would find me—when the phone jarred me back to reality.

Leonardo came on the intercom. "Lupe, I know you don't want to be interrupted," he said, "but I really think this is a call that you're going to want to take."

"Who is it?" I asked. Leonardo knew not to interrupt me at times such as this—unless it was literally a matter of life and death. There had to be blood on the floor for him to violate a "no calls" order.

"Teresa de la Torre," he said.

I made it to my desk in three strides—no small feat for someone my height. I waited a few seconds before picking up the receiver, trying to calm myself down. I wanted to be able to speak in a steady voice.

"Señora de la Torre?" I answered. "This is Guadalupe Solano speaking. Can I help you?"

"*Buenas tardes,*" she said. "We've met before—at Hector Ramos's funeral, then a few weeks ago at the Cuban-American Friendship Ball at the Intercontinental Hotel. Perhaps you remember?"

"Of course," I said. "How are you?" I suspected that Teresa wasn't used to reminding people where they had met her. It probably was always the other way around. So it was surreal to hear her ask me if I remembered her. But if I had done my job, she would think that the funeral and the ball had been our only connections.

Her voice was low and whispery. "I'm all right," she said. "But my husband, Miguel, isn't. I'm telephoning you from Doctor's Hospital in Coral Gables."

"Is anything wrong?" I asked. Of course something was wrong. She wouldn't be visiting a hospital for the cafeteria food.

"A few hours ago, Miguel had a very severe stroke," she said. "He's in intensive care at the moment, where the doctors are evaluating his condition."

Teresa stifled a sob, and there was a long silence on the line. "I remembered you told me you were a private investigator," she said, struggling to keep her voice even. "That is correct?"

Ay, Dios. "Yes, that's true." I wondered if she were playing games. Of course I was an investigator—hadn't she called me at work?

"Miguel and I need your assistance," she informed me. "I would like to speak to you about the services you offer."

"Services?" I repeated in a zombie voice. The woman must have thought I was an idiot.

"I realize all I know about private investigators comes from television and the movies," she said, "but part of your work is searching for information, correct?"

"Um. Yes. We investigate."

"The matter that I need help with is rather delicate," she said. "I wouldn't want to discuss it over the telephone, but I would like you to start working on it as soon as possible."

"Of course," I said. "When would it be convenient to meet?"

Teresa hesitated for only an instant. "Are you free this afternoon?" she asked.

I looked at my watch. "You said you were at Doctor's Hospital," I said. "Would you like to meet there, or someplace else?"

"I'll be here all night, probably. At least until my husband is out of danger. So it would have to be here, but please, Lupe—may I call you that?"

"Please, do," I said. Actually the only person who had regularly called me Guadalupe had been Mami. I couldn't have dealt with Teresa calling me by that name.

"Don't be offended, but we have to meet someplace private," she said. "There are news people here, and I wouldn't want them to see me meeting with you—since you're a detective. Please don't take this the wrong way."

"Not at all. You're only being cautious," I said.

This couldn't possibly get more surreal, I thought. In any case, I didn't really want to be seen with her, either—given the likelihood that this case was going to blow up in my face sometime very soon.

It wasn't exactly standard procedure, talking to a mark about prospective employment. I debated placing an emergency beeper call to Tommy; I was on thin ground ethically even talking to her, much less pretending to consider working for her. At that point, though, my ethics had gone the way of my first boyfriend—I knew they both had existed once, but it seemed so long ago it was hard to imagine when.

"I would be very grateful if you could come to the hospital," Teresa said, sounding relieved.

We agreed to meet in thirty minutes at a secluded spot near the staff parking lot. I recalled that there were some benches along the canal, which would give us privacy and a place to sit.

I beeped Tommy with a 911 code. I hoped he was wearing his pager, though I knew that they were prohibited in most Dade County courtrooms.

I waited until the last possible moment before leaving, hoping Tommy would call. He didn't, so I had to set out without the benefit of his counsel. I drove even faster than my usual heart-stopping speed.

When I pulled into the parking lot I spotted Teresa crossing the street, heading for our meeting place. I watched her walk: determined, straight-backed, proud. I reached into my shirt, patted my medals for good luck, and got out of my car. We acknowledged each other from afar with nods and headed toward the benches.

"Señora de la Torre." I offered her my hand with formality.

She would have none of that; instead, she kissed me on the cheek. "Thank you for coming on such short notice," she said, gesturing toward the paint-chipped, splintery bench. She made me feel as though I had been invited to sit on a golden throne.

"How is Señor de la Torre?" I asked.

She averted her eyes. "No change," she said quietly. "But he's holding his own. Thank you for asking."

"What can I help you with?"

Teresa looked straight into my eyes. "Before I talk to you, I have to be sure my words will be kept in strict confidence," she said.

It was evasion time. I wasn't going to lie to this woman. I was already meeting with her under false pretenses, and I was rationalizing to myself that this was part of the ongoing Delgado investigation—even if I wasn't sure who I was investigating anymore.

"I'm not sure I'll be able to help," I said, "without your telling me what you need assistance with."

Teresa studied me. I met her stare, realizing that she was measuring me for trust. I matched her face against all the photos and background checks that were stored in my office. She was three months shy of her sixtieth birthday, but she didn't show it. Even in the harsh sun her skin was smooth and flawless. Her black hair was in an impeccable chin-length style; her apricot-colored shirtwaist dress was cinched with an understated brown alligator belt. Her hands were perfectly manicured and polished in dark red. She was one of the most imposing people to whom I'd ever been in close proximity.

She smiled and broke off the staring contest. "I'll tell you why I called," she said conversationally. "It must have come as quite a surprise."

"Well, yes, it did," I said. I *had* been surprised. And terrified, apprehensive, suspicious, stunned. Take your pick.

"I called you because you're Cuban," she said. "You will understand situations that have to do with our people."

This was no great surprise. One way or another, it always came down to Cuba.

"I also called because of Miguel's association with your father." I must have looked surprised, because she added, "Your father understands the importance of removing Castro—as well as what happens afterward. I also recall working with your mother on charity efforts. She was a saint. You must have inherited her decency and sense of honor."

I could do nothing but sit there and listen. This woman had plotted to kill Luis, she had stolen from her oldest friends—and now she was appealing to me through my late mother's virtue and goodness. It was like some Fellini movie that I hadn't known was ever filmed.

Suddenly Teresa's kindly visage disappeared and in its place emerged a cold and willful look. "I want you to find a man for us," she said.

"Find someone? Here in Miami?" I asked. I knew the answer before I had even spoken the question.

"A Cuban man, a rafter," she replied. "He lives here in Miami, and he's very dangerous. He has stolen a large amount of money from Miguel and me."

Her eyes were as hard as the diamond on her finger. "He stole from you?" I asked. "How?"

"It's a long story," Teresa said. "It goes back to 1959, the year Miguel and I left Cuba. It's not necessary for you to know all the details. I just want you to find this man, and quickly."

I decided to play dumb. This might be my only chance to get information from her. "If someone stole from you, why don't you go to the police?" I asked. "I'm sure they could find him faster and easier than I could if he broke the law."

"No police." Teresa wagged her finger at me. "We want to keep this quiet. My husband's health is delicate."

She was used to giving orders and, apparently, having people accept her lame excuses. I pretended to consider what she had said.

"Well, in order to find this man, I'll need some information about him. I need his name, obviously. A birthdate would help, as well as his last known address."

Teresa reached into her pocket and handed me a white index card. On it was information and the name Luis Delgado. I glanced at it briefly, impressed by her preparation. Contacting me hadn't been a spontaneous decision.

We sat in silence on the weathered bench. Nothing in my experience as an investigator had prepared me for this. Any of it.

"How do I contact you when I have something to report?" I asked.

"Call me on my cellular phone." Teresa jotted down the number on the information sheet, next to Luis's name. "And you'll tell me how much I owe you for this service?"

"We'll talk about that when things have progressed."

She seemed to accept this reply. "There's something else," she added. "I want you to be very careful. Without going into my personal affairs, I have reason to believe that this individual hired an investigator to watch my husband and myself. There was an unfortunate incident. Perhaps I *should* give you some money now—"

"Say no more," I said. I couldn't stand to hear another word. "I'll tell you when I have some information. Don't worry about the money until then." Taking money from her would have been a final step into the abyss.

"I hope Señor de la Torre recovers quickly," I added.

I stood up, although protocol dictated that, as the older of us, she should end the meeting. With an agility that belied her years, Teresa sprang up and kissed my cheek.

I looked into her eyes, my mind working to comprehend what had just passed between us. I was past trying to understand my own motives for coming to meet her. All I knew was that I seemed to have acquired a new client, whom I had been hired to investigate by my previous client. I couldn't begin to speculate about the legal implications. I doubted that the Department of Professional Regulations—the regulatory agency that governs private investigators in Florida—had guidelines for a situation such as this. But I could worry about the legal implications later.

"Find him, Lupe," Teresa ordered me. "Find him fast."

Thirty-one

I waited for Sergio Santiago in the parking lot of the Publix supermarket a block away from First Miami. There was ten thousand dollars in cash in my pocket, tucked into a plain manila envelope. I was finished with caution. I wanted answers, and I wanted them yesterday.

In less than twenty-four hours, unless Tommy pulled off a miracle, I would face a Dade County grand jury, which would be the first step in my public immolation at the hands of Aurora Santangelo. I figured she had been eating raw meat for the past week, fortifying herself and drooling with anticipation at the thought of making me a guest of the Dade County Women's Jail. The truly scary part was that she didn't even know how much ammunition was out there against me.

As soon as I had left the hospital and I was sure I was out of Teresa's view, I pulled over to a grassy area under a frangipani tree and got to work. I needed to know what had happened in Miguel de la Torre's office earlier that day—and there was only one person who could possibly tell me.

I had called First Miami on the cellular phone from my car, praying that Sergio hadn't left for the day. After making my way through a maze of automated options, I finally got a real person on the line, who had put me through to Sergio.

I breathed a sigh of relief when I heard his voice, and I told him it was I. His reaction upon hearing my voice certainly had been different—his tone turned from professionally courteous to openly suspicious.

"Why are you calling me?" he said. "I don't want to talk to you—ever again."

"Wait! Wait!" I begged. "Don't hang up. Please, I have to talk to you. Just one more time."

"Get your ears checked—you need to work on your listening skills," Sergio said. "I'm through with you."

"I'll give you ten grand if you meet me in an hour," I offered. I held my breath. What the hell—it was Luis's money.

"What do you want now?" he snarled.

I exhaled. "The confirmation slip from Internacional de Commercio that Miguel received today."

Silence. I half-expected him to ask me how I knew, but he didn't. Like me, he was beyond surprise and, perhaps, pride. "There's a supermarket a block north of the bank. In the parking lot. One hour. Ten thousand cash."

He slammed down the phone. I was getting that reaction a lot lately.

I pressed the clear button on the phone and replaced it in its cradle. The phone glistened with sweat from my palms.

At the office I sprinted past Leonardo without an explanation, opened the safe, and took out the money. I had guessed that Sergio had used the fifty thousand to clear his debts and that he would be receptive to the breathing room another ten grand would allow him. Peace of mind was always a powerful motivator, not to mention a necessity.

Outside the market, I glanced every few seconds at the direction from which Sergio would be coming. The hour became an hour and a half, and I started to feel nauseous with anxiety.

I was almost ready to give up when I saw him heading toward me. He looked terrible, pale and haunted, thinner than before. He nodded in acknowledgment and gestured toward a corner of the lot away from the street.

When he had reached the back corner, Sergio stopped walking. I reached into my pocket and took out the envelope. "Here it is," I said.

He folded the envelope and put it in his jacket. He was too much of a gentleman to look inside or count it, or else there were limits to how low he would allow himself to be seen sinking.

"Sorry I was late," he said contritely. "I had to wait until I was alone in the office to get what you wanted. It's been crazy there since Miguel went into the hospital. You heard about it?"

I nodded.

"Of course you know," he said bitterly. "That's your business—knowing everything about everybody."

I didn't comment. He had no idea how wrong I could be about some people.

Sergio reached into his shirt pocket for a small folded envelope, which he gave to me.

"By the way, Lupe, you were wrong," he added. "It wasn't just one confirmation slip that Miguel received—there were two. No charge for the second one. They both came in one envelope."

Then he turned and walked away silently. I watched him all the way, until he turned the corner. He didn't look back once.

I opened the envelope and took out the two pieces of paper. It confirmed that ten million dollars had been withdrawn from the numbered account. Then there had been a second withdrawal, leaving a balance of only $250,000.

That was all that was left—a quarter of a million dollars—far less than we had planned. I felt as if I had been kicked in the stomach.

It didn't really matter. The paper in my hand confirmed that Luis Delgado was a liar, a murderer, and a damned thief. The only thing that surprised me was the fact that I *was* surprised. He had talked about honor. He had said that he had never stolen.

The question now was: Where was the money Luis had stolen? I got back into the Mercedes and drove to my office. I was pretty sure where the money wouldn't be, but I wanted to see for myself.

When I got there, I saw that Leonardo's car was gone. I was relieved, even though I knew he had probably left early because he was angry with me. I didn't want him, or anyone else, to see me in my current state of mind.

I locked the front door and headed to the kitchen, where I served myself a glass of champagne from the splits we kept in the refrigerator for special occasions. I played the messages on my machine, hoping to hear that my grand jury appearance the next morning had been canceled. Instead I heard Tommy's voice telling me—no, commanding me—to call him right away to review my testimony. He also complained bitterly that he hadn't been able to reach me all afternoon in response to my emergency page. Tommy, who had ice water in his veins, sounded genuinely worried.

After I had finished a glass and poured a second, I walked over to my safe. I punched in the combination and stepped back, careful not to get hit by the swinging door. Inside I found the envelope containing the access codes for the Uruguayan bank account Suzanne had opened. I activated the fax/phone in my office, punched in the necessary numbers, and gave the instructions I wanted carried out. Then I sat back to wait.

I had just finished the entire split when the information came back. I had to give Señor San Pedro credit for running a tight ship. The information was so clear and detailed that a sixth-grader could have followed it. In addition to the initial thousand dollars with which Suzanne had opened the account, another deposit of ten million dollars had also been made later the same day. So far, so good. That was the plan—that half the money in the de la Torres' account belonged to the Delgados. It should have stopped there.

But of course it hadn't. A second deposit had been made, for ten million dollars. The stolen money had been wire-transferred after the required twenty-four-hour waiting period, and then sent to a bank in the Cayman Islands. All of the transactions had been concluded by late last night. The timing was exquisite—not a minute had been wasted, eliminating the possibility of glitches.

How in the hell had he done it? As soon as I finished asking myself that, I answered my own question. I cursed myself for having telephoned him the moment Suzanne had returned from Montevideo and had given me the details of her trip, including the instructions for wire transfers. I questioned my motives for having done so: Was it because as my client he was entitled to have the information, or was it pride that my carefully concocted scheme had worked so well? I suspected the latter—no wonder pride was one of the seven deadly sins.

I told myself to calm down. I had to think this through. I closed my eyes and reconstructed the scene in which I had telephoned Luis to tell him the results of Suzanne's trip. Suddenly I realized I had not given him all the details—I had mentioned to him only how the wire transfers were made, not the numbers themselves. I told myself to think clearly. This was vital. I had to know with certainty what I had revealed. Maybe I had not screwed up completely. Well, if I hadn't, how had he come up with the information he needed to all but clean out the account? Knowing that I had only half-screwed up instead of completely doing so did not make me feel a whole lot less terrible, but it was better than nothing. I caught myself rationalizing again.

I walked over to the windowsill and watched the parrots. I was twelve hours away from facing the grand jury.

I picked up the phone and called Suzanne, then Luis.

Thirty-two

Investigations have a lot in common with other important aspects of life—love, war, and sex, for instance. In all of these, timing and preparation are essential for success.

I carefully plotted out all of the key elements for my meeting with Luis Delgado. My plan relied heavily on the domino effect—all the pieces had to be in place, and every aspect had to fall neatly onto the next.

I had called Luis and had arranged to meet him at the seawall behind the Ermita de la Caridad—our usual place. When I had done everything I needed to do, I actually had nervous energy left over. I worked out on two of Leonardo's machines—the treadmill and the StairMaster—one of the rare times I submitted myself to his torture devices. When I was finished I had worked off the champagne, and I felt sharp and ready.

At 9:30 I gathered everything, rechecked it, turned off the lights, activated the alarm, and got into the Mercedes. I arrived at the sanctuary fifteen minutes early to get a sense of the place. It was a clear night, warm, with a full moon casting shadows all around.

I quietly watched the waves breaking onto the wall, felt the spray hit my body, listened for Luis. Punctually at ten I saw headlights approach the parking lot, heard the soft sound of a slowing car and finally silence as it parked. A car door opened and closed, then I heard the crunch of feet on pebbles coming toward me. The wind carried the smell of his cigar to me before I actually saw him.

Luis stood next to me, looking out over the water. "It seems so long ago that I was on the raft crossing over," he said. "So much has happened in these three years."

He sat down next to me, his leg grazing mine. I tried not to pull away. "It certainly has," I agreed.

I knew the sight of him was a memory that I would carry with me forever. Luis was dressed in khaki pants and an open-neck light-colored shirt. His clothes were bright and clean; his pants had a sharp crease. On his feet were Top Siders with no socks. He puffed on his cigar, exuding calm confidence.

"Lupe," he said, and put his arm around me. I delicately removed it from my shoulder; I couldn't allow him to be so close.

Luis shrugged. "We have come so far together," he said. "You have helped me so much."

I ignored what he said. "Tell me what happened to the de la Torres' money," I ordered.

"The money?"

"The money in the bank in Uruguay." I glanced at my watch. I was still angry at myself for having given him the information about the bank account in Montevideo, but I had to control myself and focus on learning as much as I could from him. I tried to remember some relaxation exercises.

"Don't worry. It's in a safe place," he said patiently. "I transferred it out of the account you set up to another in the Cayman Islands."

"But that wasn't our arrangement."

"No, not really," he agreed. "But, you see, Lupe, I thought a lot about what Miguel and Teresa had done to my family—to me, in particular—and I decided that they didn't really deserve to keep the rest. Transferring the money internationally was very easy."

"How?" I asked, praying to all the saints that the answer would exonerate me. In spite of the depths to which I had sunk, the good girl in me didn't want total responsibility for this debacle.

Luis broke into an arrogant grin. "You're not the only one who can contact Sergio Santiago," he said. "He was open to a little enticement."

"So you stole their money," I said, relief flowing from every pore in my body. I was so grateful that I had not been totally responsible for enabling Luis to steal the money that I wasn't even angry at Sergio's double-cross. "Even though that was sinking to their level. You were doing to them what they did to you, right?"

"I think of it as justice being done," Luis said. "I took back what belonged to my family. I left two hundred fifty thousand dollars, which I calculated—based on what Tony had told us—would be the value of the four diamonds my father took from the de la Torres without telling them. I paid that debt back. Then I took the rest—to make sure they suffered just like the Delgados."

"And what about Mike Moore?" I asked. "He was helping you, he was working for you. Why did you have to kill him?"

I was keeping my voice calm and level, making sure that I was speaking clearly and sensibly. It was vital for me to keep my emotions in check.

"You know about the investigator?" Luis asked. He puffed on his cigar and looked at me curiously. I could see that he felt off-balance, not sure what I might do. Which was good.

"Yes, Luis, I know."

"I didn't mean to harm him," Luis said. "But he saw me when I was spying on Miguel and Teresa. I used to do that a lot, you know. I wanted to know everything about them."

"So you hid outside their house?"

"Know your enemy," he said flatly. "Your investigator surprised me. I had expected the girl who worked the night shift—I knew where she liked to hide, and I was always able to avoid her. But your man spotted me, and I simply couldn't let him live after he had seen me there. It would have compromised everything. He would have reported to you that he had seen me, and you would have questioned me. I could not allow you to become suspicious of me, at least not more than you already were."

In the dim light I saw the tip of Luis's cigar turn flame red. It was strangely beautiful.

"And what about Pepe Salazar?" I asked.

"That *hijo de puta*," Luis spat. "He was waiting for me last night at my rooming house when I got home from work. I don't know how he found me, but he had decided to blackmail me. He said I had to pay him off or else he would go to the de la Torres and tell them I was still alive."

"And what did you do?" I asked. We were talking about murder, but Luis was able to match my conversational tone with his own cold factual manner.

"I followed him after he left," Luis said. "And I strangled him. He deserved it. He was drunk, fat, and out of shape. I knew Miguel and Teresa were going to realize I was still alive—that wasn't the problem. I simply couldn't allow this stupid bastard to continue appearing in my life."

There in the moonlight, listening to him recount this series of horrors, I still felt his charm. He was sick, he was diabolical, I reminded myself.

"What are you going to do with the money?" I asked. "What do you need twenty million dollars for, anyway? You haven't seemed like the kind of man who wants to live like a king."

"You're right, Lupe. I'm not going to change much." He smiled imperceptibly, as if pleased with his own good sense. "I just wanted to strip Miguel and Teresa naked. I wanted to take everything away from them and see if they could start over again."

The strength of his malice was starting to get to me, no matter how hard I tried to keep the conversation moving ahead. I must have betrayed myself, because Luis shifted closer to me.

"I do have honor," he said insistently. "I left them a quarter of a million—so I paid them for the four stones my father took in Havana. There's honor—I repaid my family's debt."

That was the second time he explained about the $250,000. It meant a lot to him to pay it back.

"I see," I said, trying to smile. Honor. How many ways could the concept be sullied and abused?

"I want to share it with you," he said, taking my hand, his voice ringing with sincerity. "In the beginning I wanted the money for my parents' memory, but things changed as I got to know you more. I wanted to approach you as an equal, not as a *balsero* car mechanic. You're a good woman, Lupe. Look, see how much I trust you."

He reached into his pocket and handed me a slip of paper. "What's this?" I asked, trying to register everything he had just said.

"The account and the codes for the money in the Cayman Islands," Luis said. "It's for you. You'll never have to work again. You see—it's all for you."

I sat there in stunned silence, the paper feeling as though it weighed a hundred pounds—even though I didn't need it. Before coming to see Luis, I had enlisted Suzanne to see how strict Uruguayan secrecy laws really were. After she arrived at my office, I had coached her, then allowed her to make a call to Señor San Pedro's personal line.

Suzanne had told Señor San Pedro, her new best friend, that her sugar daddy had become jealous and suspected her of past infidelities. In tears, Suzanne explained that her bank account had been cleaned out and that the sugar daddy had hidden the money in the Caymans. She threw out a broad hint that she had mentioned Señor San Pedro himself in conversation, which might have sparked the jealousy.

I had sat at my desk, watching Suzanne work. After more tears, and after she implied that her sugar daddy had turned violent over all this, Señor San Pedro had caved in. He put her on hold and, within minutes, returned to the phone with the Cayman Island account number and access codes.

I looked at my watch again. Almost time.

My heart started to pound. I felt blood rushing inside me and heat spreading up through my chest. The only thing I knew was that I couldn't sit there any longer holding Luis Delgado's hand. In one smooth motion I pulled away from him and pushed him off the seawall into the black waves pulsing below.

I saw his head bob up in the water; the last image I had of him was his look of total disbelief. He could save himself, I thought. After all, hadn't he left Cuba on a raft? Hadn't he wished to go windsurfing? I wasn't at all worried about his survival.

I sprinted through the parking lot to the Mercedes. I was

so nervous that I fumbled with the keys and dropped them. I picked them up and struggled with the lock. My hands shook out of control.

I had just started the motor when I saw two cars filled with shadows of people heading down the long driveway toward the seawall. I ducked down, looking over the dashboard to confirm that it was Teresa de la Torre who was arriving.

She was out for blood and revenge over what had happened to her husband. I had heard it in her voice when I had called her earlier to say that I had located Luis. I knew what I was doing when I had told her where he could be found at 10:30 P.M. that night—no earlier, no later. I knew Teresa would find a way to make Luis pay and that I would be an accomplice in whatever his fate might be.

He had it coming. For all his talk of honor, it was clear that he had been after only the money. I had underestimated the power money exerted over the lives of those who had always done without it. In Cuba, money meant survival, and I had forgotten that fact. Miguel and Teresa had money, and they lived well. Luis, Maria del Carmen, and their son, Luisito, had lost everything and lived in poverty and fear. I suspected that Luis himself, as he grew up in Cuba, didn't fully understand the power that money had over him. He had used honor as an issue to make his motivations more palatable to me, and perhaps to himself. And maybe he had been vindictive enough to wish upon the de la Torres the deprivation his family had endured.

I had been too blinded by him to see it. He had hooked me with talk of honor and duty, not to mention my guilt as a Cuban-American when I heard what my countryman had endured. He knew just which of my buttons to push. He had manipulated me into helping him, but he had wanted only three things all along: the cash, the revenge, and the girl—me. And now he was trying to consolidate numbers one and three. Pretty calculating and efficient of him—if it worked, that is.

I almost regretted that I couldn't witness what was going to transpire between him and Teresa. It would undoubtedly be a scene worth watching.

————

After Teresa and her posse passed by, I drove out, tires screeching, and headed for a house in Little Havana. I had a friend there—not a friend, actually, an associate—who would be waiting for me. I took a roundabout route to make sure I wasn't being followed, then arrived at a nondescript one-story house badly in need of a paint job.

I knocked three times—as we'd agreed—and the door opened. The living room was furnished with a single dilapidated sofa and two rickety chairs upholstered in flowered velveteen. I wasn't there to judge the decor, though. I was more interested in the guest bedroom.

That room was equipped with the latest state-of-the-art electronic equipment. The man who led me in there and sat heavily on an uncomfortable-looking stool was a technician nicknamed "Spliceman" for his virtuosity with magnetic tape. I had known him for years; he used to head the Dade County police electronic surveillance lab. He had been fired for conducting personal business on county time—much to the chagrin of the State Attorney's office. They had known that his expertise would never again be duplicated in local law enforcement—not at a county employee's salary, anyway. To Spliceman, a tape deck was like a violin in the hands of an orchestra's soloist. Spliceman could edit a tape and make it sound as though it had never been touched.

"Lupe, Lupe," Spliceman mumbled by way of greeting. "How's it going? Long time."

I hadn't seen him in a while, and unlike fine wine he hadn't improved with age. He resembled nothing more than a bald, out-of-shape, rather dissolute ferret.

"Thanks for helping me out," I said, kissing the top of his head.

He was so surprised by this show of affection that he broke his usual norm of behavior and actually made eye contact.

"What can I do you for?" he asked shyly. "You said this was an emergency."

"Turn around first," I commanded him. I took off my shirt and pulled off the adhesive tape that had been holding the wires to my upper body. "Shit! That hurts."

It felt as though I had peeled off several inches of skin—I guessed I had gone overboard earlier that night when I had wired myself up. I had worn a wire before, but it had never been this important.

I put my shirt back on, told Spliceman he could look again, and gave him the cassette. He put it into one of his machines, and a moment later we were listening to my conversation with Luis at the seawall. It sounded perfect, and we could hear every detail of what was said.

"I need you to erase every mention of money and bank accounts," I said. In addition to myself, I realized I had to protect Papi. I had no idea of the extent of his involvement with Miguel.

"No problem," Spliceman said. "You want to wait for it? It'll take two hours. Maybe three."

I looked at my watch: 11:30. "Is there someplace where I can lie down and take a nap?" I asked.

"There's a bed in the next room," Spliceman said. "I'll wake you up when I'm done."

I left him there with the overhead light shining on his hairless head. My last thought before drifting off to sleep was wondering if I should tell Spliceman not to tie his sparse remaining hair into a ponytail.

The bed was lumpy but clean. It felt as though I had just closed my eyes when someone shook me on the shoulder.

"All done," he said, standing in silhouette from the hall light. "No banks, no accounts, no reference to any of it."

"You got it all?" I asked, groggy.

"It's history. Come, listen."

I followed Spliceman into his lab, where we listened to the tape together. The man was a genius, I thought as he twice played back my conversation with Luis. He gave me a pair of copies, plus the original, unaltered version. One never knew. I dug in my purse for the money to pay him—with a little extra, since it was a rush job.

Outside, I looked up and down the street to make sure I didn't see anything out of the ordinary. Satisfied, I got in the Mercedes and drove home to Cocoplum. I felt clear and alert as I maneuvered through the Miami streets.

Dawn would be coming soon. At home I showered and picked out an appropriate outfit for my appearance before the Dade County grand jury. It was too early for even Aida to be up, so I made myself a huge meal of eggs, bacon, toast, and bread, which I took out to the terrace and ate while I waited for the sun to come up. At six o'clock I called Tommy.

"It's me," I said, interrupting him before he could complain that I hadn't called him earlier. "Can I come over? I have a tape I think you'll want to listen to."

Thirty-three

"Lupe, you don't have to answer if you don't want to."

Charlie Miliken peered at me over his sunglasses. Those baby-blue eyes could drive me to distraction, especially now that he had such a nice tan from two days of lounging in the sun.

"Okay, I won't," I said.

"Come on," he insisted. "What really happened outside that grand jury room last week?"

"What do you mean?" I mumbled.

We were lying on side-to-side chaise longues under a thatched umbrella on the beach behind the Ritz-Carlton hotel in Naples, on the west coast of Florida. We were deeply immersed in our main occupation during this vacation: doing nothing.

After two days we had established a pattern: wake up late, have breakfast from room service, then head down to the beach until lunchtime on the terrace. We'd have an afternoon nap, then a swim, then we'd walk on the beach until cocktails and dinner. Our most crucial decision of the day involved what movie on the Pay-TV to order up to the room. It had been perfect, and now Charlie wanted to start asking me questions.

The best aspect of the vacation was that it was being paid for out of the pile of crisp hundred-dollar bills from my safe—Luis Delgado's money. I had given Sergio Santiago an extra five thousand, after we talked and he confessed that he had been diagnosed with AIDS. If I couldn't restore Sergio's health, at least I could buy him some peace of mind. Even if he had sold me out and gone behind my back with Luis by selling information to him as well as to me.

Charlie didn't know any of this, of course. He knew only that I had called him the morning after my grand jury nonappearance and invited him to run away to a place where we didn't know anyone and where no one knew us.

"C'mon, Lupe, I've been good so far. Now talk." Charlie propped himself up on one elbow, staring at me until I was forced to open my eyes.

"I reported to the grand jury room, as ordered," I said. "But then Tommy talked to Aurora for a while and the case was dismissed."

I tried closing my eyes again, but I knew Charlie wasn't going to let me get away with such a skeletal explanation.

"What a candid account," Charlie scoffed. "Come on, I want the scoop. Whatever happened between her and Tommy McDonald, Aurora was so upset she used all her vacation and sick time to leave town for a while. She was crushed, Lupe. She had been bragging about how she was going to be there for your strip search when they booked you into jail."

"I don't know what Tommy told her. All I know is that I never had to testify." I reached for the bottle of sunscreen. Charlie groaned next to me.

"Okay, it's fine if you don't want to tell me about it," he said. "But I would like to know what happened sometime before I die."

I wasn't about to tell this secret, even to someone I trusted as much as Charlie. I still felt guilty about hiding the original tape from Tommy—but I figured the less he knew, the better.

Besides, I still had plans for the money. I knew that before he had talked to Aurora, Tommy had contacted Detective Anderson and told him he had Luis Delgado—his own client—confessing on tape. Detective Anderson was offered the opportunity to be credited for solving two cases without doing any additional work. Tommy offered to trade the tape and Mike Moore's photographs in exchange for getting me off the hook with the grand jury. He had given Detective Anderson an hour to pull off the deal—because I was due to face Aurora at eight.

It turned out that Detective Anderson wasn't particularly fond of Aurora, either. Aurora had been dating one of the detective's friends, a policeman who had decided to break up with her. Aurora hadn't reacted well and had abused her position as an Assistant State Attorney to have her ex-boyfriend transferred to Princeton—a tiny town north of Homestead—where his new job involved overseeing school crossings.

So Detective Anderson had a means of achieving two objectives he held dear: getting credit for solving two murders, and obtaining revenge against Aurora. He got busy, and sure enough, by the time Tommy and I arrived outside the grand jury room, Aurora was waiting for us—pale, shaking, and with a look of frightening fury in her eyes. After taking one look at us, Tommy and I knew Detective Anderson had succeeded in calling her off.

"Lupe, would you kindly stay here," Tommy had said. "I'd like a word with Ms. Santangelo."

"Of course," I answered courteously.

I tried not to look at them, but I was too curious. Aurora went into classic hysterical mode, gesturing wildly and pointing at both me and Tommy. Tommy played the stoic statesman, keeping his posture calm and composed and his voice low.

After a few minutes, Tommy returned to me. He took my elbow and guided me to the escalator.

"We're leaving?" I asked. "Just like that?"

Tommy nodded and smiled. I couldn't resist a parting glance at Aurora. She was still standing in the same spot, her fists clenched, a look on her face as though she had learned that Santa Claus was a sham.

I smiled, remembering it all. I had been sweating the grand jury appearance, to say the least. I sure as hell didn't want to lie—in fact, I had been sure I couldn't lie under oath, even to protect my own ass.

I looked over at Charlie, who was snoring gently. Just then, under the umbrella, with the sun shining, the waves breaking on the shore, the ocean breeze gently blowing, I felt a small degree of peace. I was sorry to have to return to Miami the next day, but it was unavoidable.

I thought about it for a minute and realized I was probably readier to return home than I was willing to admit to myself. After all, a two-day vacation notwithstanding, the Luis Delgado case still hadn't concluded for me.

I was on the terrace of the Cocoplum house, having a *mojito* and watching a particularly colorful sunset. Soon the conch fritters would arrive, I thought, but then Papi came out wearing a worried expression.

"*Qué pasa*, Papi?" I asked. Papi seldom looked worried about anything. He usually left the fretting to my sisters and me—especially Fatima.

"Oh, Lupe," Papi said, looking sadly out over the water. "It's my friend, Miguel de la Torre."

My heart sank. Eventually I knew I would have to find out the nature of Papi's relationship with Miguel. "What about him?"

"He's very sick," Papi said. "You probably read in the news that he had a stroke three days ago. I just found out he's never going to walk or talk again."

I nodded. "It's been in the papers, yes. I remember meeting him at Hector's funeral." I paused, trying to decide whether to press on. Papi was in an emotional mood. This was probably as good an opening as I was going to get.

"One time I asked if you knew Miguel, and you said yes," I began, choosing my words carefully. "But I didn't get the impression you were so close. It seemed like a business friendship, maybe. But you seem very upset, Papi."

Papi sat down heavily in the chair across from me. For the first time in recent memory, he truly looked his age.

"Well, Lupe, *querida*," he said, "perhaps I wasn't as honest as I could have been about Miguel."

"Why, Papi? Why didn't you tell me the truth?"

I was soon reminded where I got my virtuosity for dodging questions and hedging replies. Papi's eyes twinkled as he said, "Well, I didn't lie to you, either. I just didn't tell you the extent of our friendship. We share the same dream, you see—to go home to Cuba. That's what we've been planning all these years, and now Miguel will never see his dream come true."

"But you will," I reminded him. "You'll go back to Cuba, and you'll see it free again. You know you will."

I tried not to betray myself with my voice, and it wasn't easy, sitting there, discussing with Papi what had happened to his friend Miguel. Even the knowledge that, in a sense, he and Teresa had brought their downfall upon themselves did little to assuage my guilt over having been the catalyst. As I had been doing for the past few days with increasing fervor, I cursed myself for having taken the case. I knew this feeling would haunt me for years and that I would probably never fully come to terms with my sense of responsibility for Miguel de la Torre's condition. I prayed that at best I would one day at least come to terms with my role.

"First your mother, and now Miguel," Papi said. "I'll take your mother's ashes back home and bury them there—just like I promised her."

Papi pounded the table to reinforce his point, but leaned back when Osvaldo arrived with a fresh pitcher of *mojitos,* along with a sizzling platter of conch fritters and Aida's spicy sauce.

I let Papi pour a glass and take a drink before pressing him. "What were you and Miguel planning?" I asked.

"The overthrow of Fidel Castro, and then the reconstruction of the Cuban economy," he said plainly. He drained his glass and poured another.

"Those are ambitious plans, Papi," I said, holding out my glass for a refill. "Wouldn't it take a lot of money?"

Papi shrugged. "There was a fund for this," he said. "There was money set aside."

"How much money, Papi?" I asked. "And where is it?"

"*Ay,* Lupe, so many questions." Papi smiled. "You don't have to know the details, really. The fewer details you have, the better."

I knew how he felt.

"Only Miguel knew where the money was, anyway," Papi added remorsefully. "And only he knew how to get at it. So it's gone forever."

"Why, was it kept out of the country?" I asked.

Papi looked at me sharply. "What are all these questions about, Lupe? Do you know something about this?"

"It's the only answer that makes sense," I said. I had learned to evade from the master. "Miguel would have had to keep the money out of the United States. He probably wouldn't have wanted to report it to the IRS, and anyway, it's illegal to back the overthrow of a foreign country. I'm right, aren't I?"

By now we each needed another refill. Papi shook the last few drops from the pitcher into our glasses.

"The money's gone," Papi said. "Only Miguel knew how to get

it, and he's practically a vegetable. All those millions, all the planning, all our hopes—gone."

Papi seemed on the verge of tears. I couldn't bear to watch, especially since I knew where the money was and how to access it.

I knew only one thing for certain—I wasn't giving it to Papi so he could go off with some half-assed scheme of gun running and starting a revolution. For now the money would sit in the Caymans, gathering interest, waiting to be put to good use. I already had some ideas, in keeping with the spirit of the goal for which it was intended. And I had taken the precaution of transferring it from Luis's account into a new numbered account, with the wiring codes and access instructions safely locked in my office safe. I had paid a high price learning to move money around, I figured, so I might as well put that knowledge to work.

I was angry for myself for not listening to Osvaldo, Fatima, and Aida when they had warned me that Papi was associating with men obsessed with Castro's ouster. I had always known Papi's consuming passion for Cuba, but I hadn't guessed how powerful it had become.

"Why didn't Miguel entrust anyone else with the information?" I asked. "Wasn't it dangerous to leave only one person with access to the money?"

"Miguel had reasons not to trust anyone with details of the Cuba Fund, which is what we called it," Papi explained. "The most important was that he was afraid of Castro's spies. He worried that a traitor would infiltrate the group and report back to Havana about our plan and the money."

"Wasn't it hard to keep the plan a secret?" I asked. "After all, there were several men involved." I assumed that to be true, given what I had learned from carefully studying the surveillance photos and logs from the investigation.

"We all took an oath of secrecy," Papi replied, not questioning how I knew what I did. "But, still, you never know if someone is for sale or being blackmailed. Most of our members have relatives still in Cuba. Castro might figure this out and use it as leverage to make someone inform."

Papi was shaking his head sadly when Osvaldo arrived with fresh *mojitos*. His timing couldn't have been better; this was the most talkative Papi had been in years.

"Remember Juan Pablo Roque?" Papi asked suddenly.

I took a drink and searched my memory. The name seemed familiar. "Oh, I know," I said. "The traitor. The man who flew with *Hermanos al Rescate* but had infiltrated the group to spy for Castro."

"That's right. The one who betrayed his brothers—may he rot in hell." It was very uncharacteristic of Papi to swear.

So Miguel did have valid reasons for thinking that someone might infiltrate the Cuba Fund, I thought. He hadn't been merely paranoid. Still, I had other questions.

"But Papi, almost all the exile groups in Miami plot and plan to get rid of Castro. It wouldn't be possible to infiltrate all of them—there are hundreds of known organizations. Why would yours be any different?"

Papi smiled slowly, then talked to me as if I were a child. "Lupe, because of the money that our group collected. All the de la Torres' funds after personal expenses were funneled into the account."

"All of them?" I asked slowly.

Papi nodded. "This is why Miguel was the leader of the Fund. He had no children, and he was fervently patriotic. He put everything he had into the account."

"He was able to hide all that money?" I asked, knowing the answer.

Papi laughed softly. "Once Miguel told me that if someone tried to calculate how much money he and Teresa had, what their net worth was, they would be surprised to see how little they would find."

How well I knew it. I was starting to see a clearer picture now. Luis never had a legitimate chance to recover half of the de la Torres' money. Even if they had wanted to honor the agreement, they couldn't have. Luis certainly would have questioned their net worth as they would have presented it to him, thinking it was impossibly low.

No wonder Luis had been such a threat to Miguel and Teresa—not just personally, but for the Cuba Fund. If they had taken him in as the son of their old family friends, they might have risked exposing their plan to him. For all they knew, he might have been a spy sent by Castro to infiltrate their lives and send back information about the Fund. For them to honor their agreement, they would have had to tell the truth about their financial arrangements—which was an impossibility. No wonder they had turned to Pepe Salazar. They had felt they had no choice. Luis, even if his intentions had been honest, had never stood a chance.

Papi waved his hand in a typically equanimous gesture. "Miguel would often say to me and other businessmen that the less we knew, the better, in case we were ever questioned about it. It made sense, Lupe, if you think about it. And that's the way Miguel was, really. People didn't question his judgment."

"What about Teresa?" I asked him. "Wouldn't Miguel trust his own wife with that information?"

Papi shifted nervously. "Well, Lupe, *querida*, I am not privy to the nature of Miguel's relationship with his wife. But I can tell you that one time at a meeting, one of the old-timers—it was Hector Ramos, now that I think about it—asked Miguel that same question." Papi chuckled. "Miguel said that Teresa knew of the Fund but that she knew none of the details. He said that women didn't understand such things."

"He certainly paid a high price for his chauvinism, didn't he?" I asked. I couldn't resist.

If I lived to be a hundred, I realized, I would never completely understand all that had happened with the Delgado case. So many secrets had been kept, at such a high cost.

Papi and I remained on the terrace, watching the pelicans swoop down from their perches on the channel markers onto hapless fish that had swum too close to the surface. Aida fried up another batch of conch fritters, and Osvaldo refilled our glasses from the new pitcher of *mojitos*.

Papi and I had spent a long time in silence, each of us contemplating secrets that only we knew, when Osvaldo came out and announced that Tommy was on the phone for me. I stood up, feeling wobbly from all the *mojitos*, and went inside to take the call. I didn't want to navigate the stairs, so I went into Papi's study and closed the door.

"Hello, Tommy. What's up?"

"I hear you've been hitting the *mojitos* again," Tommy said, sounding amused. Osvaldo and Aida, I thought. There were no secrets in our household—at least not as long as those two were around.

"I'll reform my ways tomorrow, all right?" I said. "For now, I'm sitting outside with Papi. We're watching the sunset and talking about Miguel de la Torre."

"I see," Tommy said. "Speaking of that illustrious Cuban family, I have something to tell you. Are you sitting down?"

I plopped down into Papi's cushioned leather desk chair. "All right," I said, "hit me with it."

"I received a call from Teresa de la Torre about half an hour ago," Tommy said. I nearly dropped the receiver.

"What did she want?"

"She wants me to defend her," Tommy replied. "There's an inquiry looking into the death of Luis Delgado."

I had no reply. I had assumed that Luis had swum away that night and had been hiding out somewhere. Once the business with the tape had been concluded and Aurora had been forced to drop the charges, I had tried to block out the events that night at the seawall. I hadn't wanted to consider what had happened to Luis after I had left him at Teresa's mercy. I had pushed him into Biscayne Bay, but I was sure he had made it to safety.

Pushing him into the water had been my means of exorcising him from my life. He had arrived from the waters of the Florida Straits, and I had left him bobbing in the sea. I wasn't proud of leaving him to Teresa's vengeance, but I had done what I felt I had to at the time, without the luxury of many choices. I had realized that he might escape from Teresa, but I didn't fear that he would come after me. I had been wrong about him before, true, but I felt sure I would never see him again. I thought I was untouchable in his eyes. He had courted me in his own way, and honored me in the highest way he knew, by telling me where the money was. Even though I had put that money out of his reach, I had felt that he would leave me alone.

There had been no need to worry. I tried to ignore the surprising sensation of relief that had started to spread through me.

"Tell me the whole story," I said. I suddenly felt very sober. "Start at the beginning."

"Well, Teresa reminded me how we met at the Cuban-American Friendship Ball a couple of weeks ago," Tommy said. "Miguel told her that night that if she ever got into trouble, she should call me. He said I was the best defense attorney in the county."

I listened quietly. Tommy often liked to start things off by puffing out his chest a bit.

"After she was done flattering me, we got down to business," he continued. "She said that the body of a drowned *balsero* had been found floating off Elliot Key, and that the police had reason to believe that she knew him and might have knowledge of what had happened to him. Apparently the cops had done a background search on him and had found out that she and Miguel had sponsored Luis when he came from Guantanamo. Teresa told me she had become nervous with all the questions and had gotten all flustered. She doesn't know how much they know, or don't know. She told the investigating officer she wanted a lawyer, and got on the phone to me right away."

"Did Teresa give you any details about Luis's death?" I asked. I held my breath. Drowned. I felt a burning deep in my chest, somewhere inside where I had placed all my guilt and confusion.

"Lupe, you know better than to ask me a question like that."

"Are you taking the case?" I asked. "After all, you have a conflict of interest. You were Luis Delgado's lawyer."

"No, I'm not taking the case," Tommy said. "Not because of Luis, but because of you."

"What do you mean?"

"I wanted to sit down, calmly and rationally, and have you tell me what happened in the Delgado case. Now is as good a time as any." Tommy's tone had turned serious. "Tell me the truth, Lupe. Is there anything you need to tell me—anything you think I should know about what happened between you and Luis Delgado?"

I took my time before answering. I had lied, cheated, and stolen for Luis Delgado. I had compromised my morals and ethics; I was undoubtedly instrumental in causing his death; I had falsified evidence; and, worst of all, utterly destroyed my hard rule about becoming emotionally involved with a client.

"No," I replied. So much for honor, I thought. It would be a while before I understood again precisely what the word meant.

With a single push, I had concluded the lengthy chain of events that ended the long and previously distinguished Delgado family line. Luis Delgado, Sr., had kept four diamonds long ago without telling Miguel de la Torre—an act of desperation. Luisito, the son, had used those diamonds to bring destruction to his father's friend and to himself. Maria del Carmen would have been devastated to know how her son's life had ended. Perhaps she, too, had a role in the tragedy. She had told her son about the deal with the de la Torres, and she had instilled in him the notion that in Miami there was a fortune that was rightfully his. Luis's parents, along with the de la Torres and finally Luis himself, paved the way for his destruction.

Not that I had forgotten my role in any of it for an instant. Nor would I ever.

I went back onto the terrace to finish my *mojito*. Then to have another, and another. Until I could no longer see Luis Delgado's face in the gentle nighttime waves.